*Passion, plea...*
*desire...*

# THE CONNELLYS:
# SETH, RAFE &
# MAGGIE

A trio of compelling and exciting
stories brought to you by three of your
favourite authors

We're proud to present

### MILLS & BOON®

# SPOTLIGHT

*a chance to buy collections of bestselling novels by favourite authors every month – they're back by popular demand!*

July 2007

## Men to Marry

*The Groom's Stand-In* by Gina Wilkins
*Good Husband Material* by Susan Mallery

## The Connellys: Seth, Rafe & Maggie

*Featuring*

*Cinderella's Convenient Husband*
by Katherine Garbera

*Expecting...and in Danger* by Eileen Wilks

*Cherokee Marriage Dare* by Sheri WhiteFeather

August 2007

## In His Bed

*Featuring*

*In Blackhawk's Bed* by Barbara McCauley
*In Bed with Boone* by Linda Winstead Jones

## The Royal Dumonts
## by Leanne Banks

*Featuring*

*Royal Dad, His Majesty, MD* and *Princess in His Bed*

# THE CONNELLYS: SETH, RAFE & MAGGIE

Cinderella's Convenient Husband
**KATHERINE GARBERA**

Expecting...and in Danger
**EILEEN WILKS**

Cherokee Marriage Dare
**SHERI WHITEFEATHER**

MILLS & BOON®

*MILLS & BOON and MILLS & BOON with the Rose Device
are registered trademarks of the publisher.*

*This collection is first published in Great Britain 2007
Harlequin Mills & Boon Limited,
Eton House, 18-24 Paradise Road, Richmond, Surrey TW9 1SR*

THE CONNELLYS: SETH, RAFE & MAGGIE
© Harlequin Books S.A. 2007

The publisher acknowledges the copyright holders of the
individual works, which have already been published in the UK
in single, separate volumes, as follows:

*Cinderella's Convenient Husband* © Harlequin Books S.A. 2002
*Expecting...and in Danger* © Harlequin Books S.A. 2002
*Cherokee Marriage Dare* © Harlequin Books S.A. 2002

*ISBN: 978 0 263 85680 4*

*064-0707*

*Printed and bound in Spain
by Litografía Rosés S.A., Barcelona*

# Cinderella's Convenient Husband

## KATHERINE GARBERA

## *KATHERINE GARBERA*

loves a happy ending, so writing romance came naturally to her. She is a native Floridian who was recently transplanted to the Chicago area. 'Living in a place where there are seasons is strange,' says Katherine. Her stories are known for their lush character detail and sensuality. She is happily married to the man she met in Fantasyland and has two children. She is an active member of Romance Writers of America, Novelists Inc and The Authors' Guild. Visit her home page on the internet at www. katherinegarbera.com.

For Maureen Walters, who is encouraging
while at the same time realistic.
Thanks for your support.

# One

"What can I get for you?" asked the blond waitress.

Seth Connelly looked straight into eyes he'd never forgotten. They were the deep purple of crushed African violets. Lynn McCoy had been a troublemaking brat for the first five years of their acquaintance then she'd blossomed into a beautiful young woman. One who tempted him to forget that her older brother was closer to him than his own.

"Hello, Lynn," he said. Somehow when he'd thought of those he might see in Sagebrush, Montana, he'd forgotten about Lynn and that one awkward kiss they'd shared the night of her sixteenth birthday.

He'd never returned to the ranch again, aware that he'd crossed a line that shouldn't have been crossed.

Aware that he'd taken a step that would alienate him from Matt. Aware that it was time to stop running and return home to Chicago.

But his birth mother's betrayal had made Chicago into a tense place, and he'd hit the road hoping to find some semblance of the man he'd become. Because as he'd fallen once again for Angie Donahue's lies and manipulation, he'd realized that he didn't know himself anymore.

He hoped Lynn didn't remember the embrace—it was so long ago. But life had taught him that if she did, more than likely it haunted her. That one brief brush of lips still plagued his dreams on restless nights, because she had tasted innocent and he never had been.

Her eyes widened in recognition and she smiled at him. There was weariness on her face, and an instinctual part of him recognized that expression for what it was. She was running from something as well.

*Not your business, old man.*

"Hi, Seth. What brings you to our little corner of the world?"

He was a successful lawyer from a wealthy family so he knew all about people who complained when they had plenty, and he wouldn't be one of those. He couldn't tell her that he'd come here searching for something that he'd found in his youth. Something he couldn't really explain to anyone. It had been a feeling, really, maybe something more but not definable.

"I'm hoping for a cup of coffee and a steak."

"You've come to the right place. But I should tell you it's probably not as fancy as you'd get in Chicago."

"That's okay. The atmosphere's better here."

"Really? I'd have thought all those sophisticated people would win hands down."

"Nothing beats the mountains in Montana." Even though night had fallen, the view from the diner was one he'd never forgotten.

"You can say that again."

Their eyes met and held in a moment of pure appreciation for what nature had so splendidly given this area of the country.

"What kind of dressing do you want on your salad?"

He told her and she walked away. The quiet conversation that buzzed around him reminded him why he liked Sagebrush. Here in this small town he wasn't the illegitimate son of a Mafia princess and Chicago's most revered citizen. Here he was that wild boy who'd had his ear pierced and wore a leather jacket even in the heat of summer. Here he was a man without a family—and Seth needed that.

Here he was a friend of the McCoys and treated as such. That warm feeling was why he'd returned in late fall when winter beckoned around the corner.

Lynn brought his coffee and salad and then hurried away to take care of the rest of her tables. Another waiter brought his steak, which was perfectly cooked.

The meal was one of the best he'd had in a long

time, simple food prepared for taste instead of presentation. Seth knew he'd made the right decision. The tension that had been dogging him receded. It didn't disappear completely but ebbed enough for him to relax his shoulders.

Lynn looked tired, he thought.

And not unlike his half-sister Tara had looked when she'd been trying to have her missing husband Michael declared legally dead. What kind of problems hung on her shoulders? Why wasn't Matt here to relieve that burden for her? He knew that Matt McCoy and he shared more than friendship but also an overwhelming urge to protect those dear to them.

What was Matt thinking to let his sister work in a diner when there wasn't any reason for it? The McCoy spread was the biggest and most profitable in the area. Seth knew this not only from his youth but also from his yearly treks to meet Matt for vacations. They always discussed the ranch. But never Lynn.

She stopped by to refill his coffee cup. "Can you join me for a minute?"

"Just real quick."

"You're a hard worker, Lynn."

"Thank you," she said tentatively.

"Why the hesitation?"

"The last time you complimented me I found myself soaking wet on a cold evening."

"Hey, you're safe for now. I've grown into a boring old lawyer," he said.

"Not boring or old. Lawyer?"

"Okay, get it out of your system," he said, knowing few people could resist the urge to lob a few lawyer jokes when they actually met one.

"What?" she asked, all innocence. She looked breathtakingly lovely in the dim light of the diner.

"You've got to have a joke about lawyers."

"Not me. Besides, I have nothing but respect for you," she said.

"Yeah, right. If memory serves, the last prank you played on me involved stealing my clothes and leaving me naked at the swimming hole."

"I left your hat, didn't I?"

It had been uncomfortable to be outsmarted by a girl a few years younger than he was. Because at home no one got the jump on Seth Connelly. He still felt a little embarrassed when he recalled the number of times she'd gotten the better of him. "I think we're square."

"Yeah, I think so. Are you here to see Matt?"

"Yes."

"He's not home."

"I thought his tour ended last month."

"It did but he was on an assignment that he felt needed him and reupped."

Damn. He wasn't going to be able to stay at the McCoy Ranch if Matt wasn't there. He'd counted on the wide-open spaces, the cattle lowing in the distance and the fragrance of jasmine to lull him to sleep.

"I'm surprised you didn't call first."

"I didn't know I was coming until I got here."

She nodded. "I've got to get back to work. You take care, Seth Connelly."

She walked away and this time he watched and wanted. She was exactly as he remembered from that late-summer night. Sweet and funny but tempered with the experiences life had used to test her. And he knew that it was probably for the best that Matt wasn't here and Seth would be moving on...again.

Lynn McCoy let the smile drop from her face the minute she entered the kitchen. She'd been worried that maybe Matt had sent him. But it seemed he was only looking for Matt, not trying to find out what kind of trouble she was in. Trouble was about the only thing she had right now.

And it looked as if another helping was on the way. Childhood crushes were supposed to end well before thirty. Lynn knew this in her rational mind but her heart beat a little bit faster as she thought about Seth Connelly. He hardly resembled the rough loner who'd first visited her family's ranch the summer she was eleven.

Now he had the kind of quiet self-assurance he'd lacked as a youth. Though his gray eyes were stormy like the north Atlantic, his body language said there was nothing he couldn't handle.

He'd looked surprised to see her at the diner. She knew he had to be. After all, the prosperous McCoy ranch had never failed to support the generations.

What had brought him to Montana in October?

There wasn't much in the way of tourism in Sagebrush. Besides, she knew he was involved in his family's business and wondered if he was having family problems again.

Part of what had initially drawn her to Seth had been that he was so alone. Though she knew she could never really trust him, her brother considered Seth closer than a blood relation.

Her first impulse had been to settle into the booth with him and spend the evening catching up on the past, but she knew that she fell in love too easily and she'd learned that lesson the hard way. She felt almost proud of the way she resisted that urge.

She waved good-night to the cook and left before she gave in and returned to the corner booth where Seth sat. Keep walking, Lynn. The night air bit into her clothes and she shivered in her leather coat. It had been her grandfather's and would keep her warm once she buttoned it.

The employee parking area was well lit, and Lynn approached her truck with no trepidation. But the stenciling on the side gave her pause. The McCoy Ranch—Home Of The Best Beef In Montana.

For how much longer? She had barely one hundred head left because that was all she could work on her own and still make ends meet. Tears burned the back of her eyes at her own stupidity. Trusting too easily had been her biggest weakness. Though she'd never be able to look at the world with a truly cynical eye, a part of her had been forever changed when Ronnie had taken her money and left her.

The highway ran behind the fence and she listened to the cars flying past. She'd never understood the obsession everyone had with getting out of Sagebrush. She'd loved her hometown and had never ventured farther than the airport in Billings to pick up friends.

Suddenly her entire world was in danger of falling apart and she was at the end of the line. She'd tried everything she could. She'd sold all the horses except for Thor, her gelding, leased part of the grazing pasture, boarded horses for the folks in town and taken this job. But there still was more debt than she could cover.

What was she going to do? Her plan, which had seemed so brilliant in the middle of the night, seemed a little weak today. She'd worked double shifts at the diner, and as she waited on tables, her mind had puzzled over the options.

There seemed damn few. Then the past had to walk in the front door like the precursor to a bad storm and look at her as if she was...what? A woman. It had been a long time since any man had looked at her like that. Ronnie had taken more with him than she'd realized. He'd taken part of her femininity with him, leaving her vulnerable and unsure in the one area she'd always been confident.

"Lynn?" Seth's voice brushed over her like a warm wind, but she knew better than to believe what it promised. A man's silky voice at night had never brought her anything but pain.

Damn. Instead of a clean getaway, now she was going to have to face him again. She pivoted toward him. He was cast half in shadows by the lamplight. His features were sharp and bold and for a minute he looked more comfortable than she'd ever seen him.

That disturbed her, but she shook it off. She needed to get home and get a good night's sleep so she'd be prepared for her meeting tomorrow.

"Yes, Seth?"

"Why are you working here?"

"I like the change of pace."

She'd never been able to look anyone in the eye while she lied to him. And it had gotten her into hot water more than once.

"You look tired," he said.

She felt the fatigue as if for the first time. She glanced up and met his gaze. He compelled her to tell him the truth and she did. Just a little bit, a sop for her conscience. "I am."

"Why are you really working here?"

"I don't know. The people, I guess."

"Really?"

"Yes, it's too quiet at the ranch." That was the truth. With the hands gone and the big old house to herself, she needed some conversation to distract her.

"If you ever need anything, Lynn, let me know. I owe your family." She'd never seen him so earnest before. She'd seen him tough and ready to take on three older boys in a fight. She'd seen him eager to learn how to rope and brand cattle. She'd seen him with his dreams in his eyes as he'd looked at the night sky and told Matt about the solar system.

"You don't owe us anything. You worked those summers you spent here." And he'd given her brother someone to imitate. Someone to bond with and look up to. Especially after Daddy had died. She thought maybe the McCoys owed Seth more than he'd ever know.

A red tinge colored his neck. "Well, I tried to do my part."

She realized then that Seth wasn't all that comfortable with praise, and it made him seem a little more human. "I've got to go."

"Will you give Matt this note when he comes home?" he asked, holding out a sheet of legal paper that had been folded neatly into thirds. Matt's name was printed in large block letters. There was nothing timid about Seth, she thought.

"Sure," she said, trying to convince herself that whatever she'd felt for Seth Connelly had died a long time ago. But somehow her hormones didn't get that message. Her skin tingled when their fingers brushed. Her breath seemed harder to come by and her heart beat a bit faster. Chills spread up her arm. Her nipples tightened and her breasts felt heavy. For some reason her feet seemed planted to the ground.

She recognized the symptoms. *Lust*. Not now, she thought. Not again. The last time she'd followed her impulses around Seth she'd ended up brokenhearted. She'd learned too much and come too far from that sixteen-year-old girl to behave that way again. Or at least as a thirty year old she'd like to hope she did.

"I'll stick it in the next letter I mail him," she said.

"Thank you."

She tugged her hand out from under his. "You're welcome."

She didn't like the way he made her feel. Didn't like that for the first time since Ronnie had taken her money and her heart, she was interested in a man. Especially didn't like that the man was Seth.

Resolutely, she marched toward her truck and unlocked the door.

"Uh, Lynn?" When she turned to look at him, his eyes held the maturity of age and she knew that whatever she remembered of him she'd always liked him. Which was dangerous to her. Because he looked as if he needed a shoulder to cry on.

"Yes?"

He rubbed the bridge of his nose and then stepped closer to her. "It occurs to me that I owe you an apology."

Oh, God. "I can't imagine why."

He moved another step closer. So close she could smell the coffee he'd drunk with dinner. "For that kiss I stole when you were sixteen."

She didn't want to have this conversation with Seth now. *Never* sounded like a good time to chat about it.

"You didn't steal it."

"I felt like I did after I walked away without a word."

"Hey, I'm a mature woman now. I barely remember an embrace that long ago."

"Really?"

No, but she'd rather give away the ranch than admit it. She shrugged.

"It haunts me," he said simply. He started to walk away, his shoulders set and his stride bold.

His words cut through the protective layers she'd wrapped around herself. "Seth?"

He stopped, glancing over his shoulder at her. A light snow began to fall and it dusted his head and black trench coat.

"I…"

He nodded. She wasn't sure he understood what she'd been trying to say.

"Me too," she said finally and opened the door to her truck. She climbed in quickly and drove away, watching Seth standing there in the lightly falling snow.

For the first time in months she didn't dream about the ranch or the diner. Instead, a pair of silver eyes plagued her dreams.

# TWO

It was well after midnight when Seth gave up trying to find a motel and turned down the familiar road that led to the McCoy ranch. He consoled himself with the thought that he could sleep in the bunkhouse with the ranch hands but he knew Lynn's bed was where he really wanted to spend the night. A light flickered over the porch as the house came into view. A sole pickup was parked next to the kitchen entrance.

He pulled his Jag to a stop and went to the bunkhouse. It was deserted and locked up tight. Questions formed quicker than he could answer them. But he was tired and would seek those answers in the morning.

It was cold outside and he doubted he'd survive the

night if he slept in the car. His options were limited. He'd have to disturb Lynn.

Only fair, his raging hormones agreed, since she'd been disturbing him all evening.

In the old days a spare key had been kept under the potted planter on the front porch. He was glad to see at least that hadn't changed. He unlocked the door, replacing the key before he entered quietly. That was the one good thing to be said for a misspent youth; he knew how to move so silently that no one could hear him.

He turned left off the entryway toward the living room. As he made his way to the couch, he slammed into an ottoman that hadn't been there in his memory and cursed under his breath. His shins ached and he heard footsteps upstairs.

''Matt, is that you?'' Lynn's voice was sleepy and husky.

Awareness tingled down his spine and stirred the flesh between his legs. He walked to the foyer and flipped on the hallway light. ''No, it's Seth.''

She descended the stairs before taking time to get a robe. The silk long johns she wore did little to mask her body, instead it seemed to frame it in a way meant to tease a man. But her clothes, imprinted with cartoon characters, clearly weren't articles of seduction. She should have looked sweet and innocent instead of seductive. ''Seth, what are you doing in my house?''

''There's no place to stay in town.''

She stopped a few feet from him. He hadn't realized earlier how much taller than she he was. She barely cleared his breastbone. His libido supplied him with the image of the two of them naked in a bed where she'd fit very comfortably into his arms.

She's my best friend's little sister, he reminded himself.

"Where are you headed?" she asked.

Straight to hell, he thought. He cleared his throat. "This is my destination."

"Oh."

"I thought I'd bunk with the men," he said so that she wouldn't suspect that he wanted her.

"No, you can't. You'd better stay up here." She wouldn't look him in the eye, and he knew it was because she was planning on making up some story about where the cowpokes were who used to live there.

"I've been to the bunkhouse, Lynn. What happened?"

"Oh, we don't have such a great need for overnight staff anymore." Her hair fell to the middle of her back in tousled waves and the light reflected in it. He'd always loved her hair. Even as a tomboy teenager she'd had miles of hair. After she turned sixteen it had played into more than one of his fantasies while he'd slept under this roof.

"Why not?" he asked, trying to focus on anything but her body.

She sighed. "It's the middle of the night and you must be tired."

Seth knew the gentlemanly thing to do would be to get in his car and drive back down the highway until he found a place to stay, but he was tired.

"Can I stay here tonight? I'll head back to Chicago in the morning." He'd been turned out of better places and for less reason than Lynn had.

She touched his arm, and though he knew it was impossible, he seemed to feel her heat through the layers of his jacket and shirt. "Of course you can. I didn't mean you should leave."

"Thank you. I'll grab my overnight bag and bunk down here," he said. She'd tilted her head back to look him in the eye now that they were standing so close, and he realized she had a long, graceful neck. Her skin looked as pale as the moonbeams, and he wondered if it would taste as sweet as it looked.

"Do you really want to sleep on the sofa?"

"No. But I don't want to disturb you."

"You won't. I didn't even hear you enter the house."

"I can be very quiet."

"And then really noisy. What happened?"

"The ottoman."

She chuckled. "Are you okay? I've hit that thing a time or two myself."

The piece was old and heavy, made of solid oak with a pretty, embroidered covering that he knew Mrs. McCoy had made during her first year of marriage. It was a tradition in the McCoy family that the newlyweds made a piece of furniture for their new life together.

"Go get your bag. You can sleep in Matt's room. I'll change the sheets for you."

"Thanks, Lynn."

"No problem, Seth."

The way she said his name made him wonder if she wasn't remembering what it had been like to kiss him. And though he knew that would be a big mistake, it was all he could think of as he retrieved his overnight bag from the car. Think of her as your own sister, he cautioned himself. He tried to imagine one of his half sisters in those long johns waiting upstairs for him. But as he entered the house and climbed the stairs, he knew it wasn't Alexandra, Tara or Maggie up there.

Even an image of Matt's glowering face couldn't keep his blood from flowing heavier or his loins from tightening. The only one who could do that was he. And the one thing Seth had always been able to do was keep his cool and his control. Why, then, did it feel as if he was barely hanging on?

Lynn turned off the shower at nine the next morning. She'd been up since dawn feeding Thor and the other horses that she boarded for the townsfolk. She'd slept better last night than she'd expected to. The security of knowing she wasn't alone on the ranch should have been enough to ensure she didn't spend the night twisting and turning in her bed. But Seth's icy gaze and warm touch had haunted her dreams.

She'd hurried out of bed and refused to dwell on those thoughts. Seth was nothing more to her than an old family friend, and she didn't have too many of them left. Most had died or moved on, leaving her alone for almost five years. Longer than she'd ever expected. Perhaps that loneliness was why she was so willing to latch on to Seth.

She had an appointment at the bank this morning and needed to get dressed. Her closet was a fashion nightmare, dominated by faded jeans and western shirts. In the back, in a plastic dry-cleaning bag, was her one suit, some designer label that she'd bought to wear to her mother's funeral.

She dressed in it quickly but with care. If she had a chance of persuading Mr. Cochran at the bank to extend the loan, she needed to exude success. But how did success look? Seth would know, she thought.

It was too bad she couldn't tell him the truth, because she could use his advice. He knew about making money. Heck, he came from one of the wealthiest families in Chicago. But he'd tell Matt and she wasn't going to ask her big brother to bail her out of another mess.

She twisted her long hair into a chignon and applied the light makeup that she wore to church. The suit was cut with classic lines that flattered her lean frame. For a minute she glimpsed who she might have been if her family had lived in a city instead of this small rural town.

She didn't hear any signs of life from Matt's room as she walked down the stairs. Maybe she could sneak out before Seth woke. He'd be gone when she returned and she wouldn't have to see him again.

The smell of coffee warned her that her luck was running par. She entered the kitchen and poured herself a cup of coffee. At the breakfast table Seth had set up a laptop computer attached to her phone jack.

He made a few keystrokes on the computer and then turned to smile at her. For a minute she forgot why she thought she couldn't trust him.

"Good morning." His voice was low and husky, masculine in the early morning. She wasn't used to a man's voice and it startled her. Seth had obviously taken a shower before coming downstairs and was dressed again in casual elegance.

"Morning," she said, gulping her coffee and scalding her tongue. She hated it when she did that. Damn, if she was this rattled on her home turf, how was she going to handle the bank?

"Sleep well?" he asked, eyeing her. She wondered if she'd smudged her lipstick on her teeth. Surreptitiously she rubbed her tongue over her front teeth.

"Yes." She sat down across from him.

"Good, because I have some questions."

"About?" Not now, she thought.

"The ranch, Lynn. What the hell happened?"

She knew he'd ask. Anyone with eyes would wonder the same thing. But her answers were hard to come by. She was a proud woman—always had been—and telling this smart, handsome man that she'd fallen for a con was not in the game plan.

"Times are tough. NAFTA didn't do ranchers a favor."

"Most of the ranches aren't this bad."

She glanced over his shoulder at the wallpaper that had once been a bright spring floral print but had faded with time. She had a moment's fear that she was glimpsing the future. That someday she'd be as old and faded as the wallpaper and have seen just as little of life.

Carefully she considered her words. "True, but most of them aren't run by one person."

"The McCoy ranch never has been in the past."

"Well, it is now."

"Lynn, unless you want me to place an emergency call to your brother, you better start talking."

"Why?" she demanded. Seth had been away for a long time, and though she knew he had fond memories of the summers he'd spent here, they couldn't be reason enough for him to probe into ranch matters.

"What?" he asked.

"You heard me. Why do you care what's happened?"

He sighed and rubbed the bridge of his nose with his thumb and forefinger. He looked stressed. She wondered if this questioning wasn't his way of hiding from whatever had driven him from Chicago. No matter what he'd said the night before she didn't believe he just felt like visiting her brother on an impulse.

"This ranch is important to me." Seth's sincerity had never been more apparent.

"Then why haven't you been back for fourteen years?"

"It's not my ancestral home."

"I'm doing my best to save it."

"What do you think Matt will say when he sees this place?"

"It won't look like this when he comes home."

"Really?"

"Yes, I have big plans."

"Tell me what's going on."

"I can't."

"Why not?"

"Because you won't understand."

"Trust me, Lynn. I'm on your side."

"The last time I trusted you, you kissed me and walked away."

"Is that what this is all about?"

"Of course not. I'm just saying your track record isn't the best."

"And yours is?"

"I didn't walk away."

"You didn't come after me either."

"I don't want to have this conversation. I'm due at the bank at ten and I don't want to be late."

"Just tell me what's going on. Is it money? Maybe I can help."

"Why are you here, Seth?"

He was silent.

"That's right," she said with a nod. "You have your own secrets and I have mine. Let's keep them that way."

"Your family meant a lot to me."

"I know. But it's better this way. Besides, you're leaving today."

"I could still help you."

"No, you can't. But I'll make a note that you tried."

Lynn walked away from him wishing she felt a little more confident. Wishing for a miracle she knew she had faint hope of getting. Wishing that Seth wasn't leaving today.


"Lynn, wait. I'll drive you into town."

She'd gathered her purse and a sheaf of documents. This was a Lynn he'd never seen before. He'd be lying if he said she didn't attract him. She wasn't the rough-and-ready ranch girl that he didn't know how to handle. For the moment she was a city woman, like every other woman in his life.

She glanced over her shoulder at him, her eyes hidden by a pair of dark glasses. Mystery surrounded her, and Seth wanted to investigate the changes. Would the real Lynn McCoy please stand up?

"I'd rather take myself."

Of course you would, Ms. Independent. She reminded him of his stepmother and sisters. They'd take any challenge but they'd do it in their own unique ways. And he knew he had to respect Lynn's way of doing things even if it wasn't his own.

Reality intruded. She'd said she was going to the bank. More than likely that meant she needed money and the only way she was going to get it was to look as if she didn't need it. The Jag was a showy car, pricey and elegant; it spoke volumes for whoever drove it without him having to say a word. It had netted him invitations to the nicest residences in Chicago, even though he knew many of those old-money folks looked down on him because of his dubious parentage.

"The banker will be more likely to listen to whatever you have to say if you arrive in the Jag."

"Okay, but I drive." The haughty look she'd conjured up made him want to kiss her. She seemed untouchable in her upswept hairdo and her fancy suit. He wanted to rumple her up and find the girl who'd let him sleep in her home last night. To find the girl with hair hanging down her back wearing silky long johns.

Though Lynn's suit made her look more like the other women he knew, he realized that he wanted her to be different. The thought floored him. Maybe he had an ulterior motive for wanting to help?

But he knew more than lust motivated him. There was a soft spot in his soul for the McCoys.

"No one drives my Jag." He spoke from the gut.

The car was as important to him as his laptop or his Swiss timepiece. He wasn't going to chance it.

"Now where's the trust?" she asked softly. Her words cut right through the superficiality of what he'd been thinking.

He did feel a bit like a child on Christmas morning who'd been asked to share his new toy. "Who's talking about trust? This car is a finely tuned machine and you're used to driving that tank over there."

"Is it the car you're worried about or your tough-guy image?"

He remained unfazed. "Whatever the reason, the result is the same. I'm driving."

Deliberately he walked to the passenger side of the car to open the door for her. "What a gentleman you are, Seth Connelly. Too bad I know the real you."

Though he knew Lynn had meant her remarks as something else entirely, she'd struck a nerve. "I think the door's unlocked."

She didn't know the real Seth—no one did. And he'd made it his life's mission to make sure that the situation stayed that way. He didn't like Lynn's innuendo that he was less than civilized. But maybe there was a kernel of truth in her words. Underneath his civilized veneer beat the heart of a warrior, not a Prince Charming.

He'd never been anyone's white knight but he was the guy they'd turned to in a fight, knowing he'd never lose. That had been true at twelve when he'd come to the Connellys and it was true now in the courtroom where he won every battle he took up.

Whether Lynn liked it or not, he was in her corner. The debt he owed the McCoy family was too big for him to not step up to the plate now.

Five years of military school and six years of college had ensured that he could converse within any circle and not embarrass his family. Lessons from his stepmom, Emma Connelly, on deportment and manners had made sure he was every inch the gentleman.

"Are you going to check the door?" she asked.

Seth realized he'd been standing next to the car. He should just turn around, lock the door and drive her to town. He should pretend that her words hadn't ripped away a scab he'd never known was there. He should not lean down so that her face was only inches from his and her sweet breath brushed across his cheek.

"I don't think anyone knows the real Seth."

She cupped his jaw in her hand and Seth was humbled by the touch even as it started a series of fires throughout his body and brought the hardness to his loins that had made sleep uncomfortable all night.

"I do."

"Then who is he, Lynn?"

"He's a man who's strong and loyal. A man willing to go to any lengths for those he cares for, even putting up with the tantrums of his best friend's younger sister."

"You weren't throwing a tantrum. You were right. I don't like to share my things."

"That's because you've never been sure they were really yours." Her insight was a smooth balm over his aching wounds, and he stood before he did something stupid like kiss her.

He closed the door firmly and went to the house to make sure it was secured. As he walked back to the car, he tried to tell himself he'd resisted Lynn because she was Matt's sister. Tried to tell himself it was because she was in trouble and needed his help. But deep inside he knew the real reason—she saw too much of who he really was.

# Three

____

Lynn held her breath until Seth drove off of her property, leaving behind the visual reminder of her mistake. She'd trusted her heart to a smooth-talking man from New York City who'd promised to give her the world and share her life. And then convinced her to mortgage the ranch and put the money into a short-term, high-yield fund.

The only thing Ronnie had forgotten to mention was that he'd be the only one getting rich from her money. He disappeared with her cash exactly eighteen months ago.

Seth pulled the Jag to a stop on the shoulder of the road. Her first thought was they'd run out of gas. But she soon realized that Seth had given in only to get his own way.

''We're not going any farther until you tell me what's going on.''

Tears burned the back of her eyes. He'd driven far enough that she couldn't walk back to the ranch and still make her appointment at the bank. Time was running out. She heard the beating of the countdown clock in her mind and she could scarcely breathe as she stared at the long, empty road ahead of her.

She felt cornered and betrayed by someone who'd lulled her into feeling safe. The sensation was much the same as the one she'd experienced when she'd realized Ronnie was never coming back. She knew of only one way out of this situation. Actually, two—fighting or telling the truth.

Seth Connelly might wear the trappings of civilization, might have spent the last twenty years with a silver spoon in his mouth, but underneath the exterior beat the heart of a street warrior who'd seen the seamier side of life. She knew he'd come from the mean streets of one of Chicago's most dangerous neighborhoods before his mom left him with the Connellys.

Military school had honed that rebellious boy into a controlled man who knew how to manipulate circumstances for his own good. And though she knew in her heart that he wasn't acting out of malice, her pride chafed at having been fooled once again by a man.

Truth was really the only option she had left. But she had to ensure some provisos before telling him anything. Matt mustn't be put into jeopardy because she'd listened to her heart instead of her head.

"I want you to promise me you won't call Matt or interfere."

Rubbing his jaw, Seth shook his head. "I can't make any promises until I hear the circumstances." For the first time, she understood how different their personalities were.

She would have agreed to the stipulation without thinking the entire situation through. But Seth was cautious. Maybe he could offer her some other ideas than the one she'd come up with—selling off part of her ranch.

She took a deep breath and looked out the window at the barren landscape. Montana was preparing for winter. The deep freeze within which she'd surrounded herself began to thaw just a little as she talked about the situation for the first time with someone other than a loan officer.

"The ranch is being foreclosed on in nine days."

Resting one arm behind her on the seat and the other on the dash, he leaned toward Lynn. She felt his presence everywhere; it was totally nonthreatening, yet at the same time arousing. He smelled crisp and clean with a faint spicy aroma. He moved the hand to her shoulder, urging her to look at him.

He's your brother's best friend, she reminded herself.

She met his gaze. It was hot and heavy, filled with questions and something more. Her skin tingled, and she forgot that he'd maneuvered her to this place where she was acting on his will. Forgot that he was her brother's friend and he'd owe his loyalty to Matt. Forgot that the last time she'd thrown caution to the wind for a man she'd ended up in this situation.

Snap out of it, girl. She leaned away from him, pressing her back against the cold glass of the window. Everything would be easier if he wasn't attracted to her. When she mixed with men, things ended in disaster.

"How did that happen?" he asked, his tone so matter-of-fact that she thought he might be a researcher following clues to a new discovery.

I don't know, she thought. You come close to me, and my mind shuts down. Then she realized he'd meant the foreclosure.

"There was this guy, Ronnie. He gave a seminar on investing and I took his advice. The deal went south, and I was left with a mortgaged ranch."

"Things are never that simple. I need more details."

No way, she thought. She wasn't going to tell Seth Connelly that she'd fallen for blue eyes, blond hair and an all-American smile. That she'd mortgaged her property so that Ronnie would stay with her instead of moving on to Los Angeles and the promise of bigger investors. That she'd given her soul to a man without one.

"You mortgaged the land to get the capital to invest?"

She nodded.

"Where did he invest your money?"

"Supposedly on Wall Street."

"Supposedly?"

"It seems I fell victim to a con man."

He cursed.

"I know it sounds unbelievable but it didn't at the time."

"It never does. What have you told Matt?"

"Nothing. His job is very risky. I don't want him thinking about me and the ranch instead of his assignment. I can't bury another member of my family, Seth."

"I know," he said, caressing her jaw.

Silence fell and they both stared at each other.

"What's the plan?" Seth asked.

"I've been working double shifts at the diner and have been boarding horses for the folks who live in town. I've got about five thousand I can give the bank today. I'm hoping that will be enough to buy me some time."

"What are you going to do with the time?"

"Find a buyer for the outer land. I hate to give up even an acre of the property, but I can't lose the house."

The thought of anyone other than the McCoys owning the land seemed like sacrilege to him. But at the same time her dilemma was his way out of what he owed her family. It was ironic that he'd visited the ranch as a boy with no money and he'd returned a wealthy man. The solution seemed obvious to Seth.

"I'll pay off your loan and you can pay me back."

She smiled at him, and it was the saddest expression he'd ever seen. If he'd had a heart, he thought it would have broken. Her deep violet eyes were wide and watery as she tried to keep from crying.

"Seth, that's so sweet. But I...no."

Lynn shouldn't look like this, he thought. She should be riding her horse across the same land she'd ridden as a child. Never should anyone else own an acre of land that had been the McCoys since pioneers had first settled in the West.

"Lynn, be reasonable." If she took the money, he could leave and not be tormented by images of the two of them making love in her bed. Or, he thought, leaning closer to her in the front of his car, if he put the seat back, she'd fit nicely in his lap.

She's your best friend's little sister, he reminded himself. But his body didn't care about that.

"Reason has nothing to do with this. I can't take your money. If Matt were here, he'd do the same thing."

Seth struggled to remember that he wanted her to take the money so he could go. Returning to Chicago wasn't what he wanted right now, but it seemed safer than staying in Montana and tempting himself with a woman he knew was off limits.

"Matt would pay the loan off himself or take my money."

She considered the idea for all of a second. "It's not Matt's debt to pay nor yours. Don't suggest it again."

"The next time a woman tells me how hardheaded men are, I'm going to direct her to you." Her jaw clenched and she didn't look as if she was going to cry anymore. Slug him maybe, but not break down.

"I'm not stubborn just—"

"Proud," he said. He couldn't blame her. If he were in her shoes, he'd do whatever he had to—on his own. He wasn't a team player and he knew it. He was more the alpha wolf leading his pack, and now he wanted to protect one of his own. Because whether Lynn knew it or not, she was definitely his.

Where had that come from? He didn't know, but it made an odd sort of sense. Taking care of Lynn the way her family had taken care of him in those summers long ago would fill something in him that had been empty too long.

"I believe in paying my own way," she said. "I made this mess and I'll be the one to clean it up."

She was so close he could smell the sweetness of her perfume and the underlying scent of woman. He closed his eyes. It's about money, man. Keep your mind there.

"How about if I make you a loan and you can make payments to me?"

"Seth, be serious. You're never going to take my family's land."

She was right. He'd deed the land back to her as

soon as the paperwork was finalized. But he was in a position to give a gift that huge if he wanted to. And he wanted to. He thought it might be more of a need because he was so hard right now, if they didn't compromise on the bank soon he was going to try putting his seat back and pulling her across his thighs. And that was something he shouldn't do.

He'd tried one time to bridge the gap between them and he'd ended up leaving Montana and hurting Lynn in the process. He wouldn't hurt her again.

"What do you suggest?"

She closed her eyes and bowed her head, looking defeated. That was the one way he'd never wanted to see this proud woman. She should be standing tall.

"Going to the bank and talking to Cochran. Which, by the way, we should be doing now."

"I'm not driving anywhere until we find a solution that has at least a fifty-fifty shot of working."

He'd never met a woman who didn't look out for herself first, to the exclusion of anyone else. Lynn was totally different from his mother. A woman who'd used his birth to milk his father's family for more than money. But there was a part of him that believed she'd do the thing that would keep her in comfort.

"I guess this is stalemate."

"I'm not going to stop at anything short of complete surrender."

"Why?" she asked, glancing up at him.

"This place was my saving grace, Lynn, and I won't let anyone, even you, throw it away."

"I can't take money from my brother's best friend."

"Who can you take money from?"

"Matt."

"It seems we're back to the beginning."

"Let's go into town and let me meet with Cochran. He might agree to my plan. Or perhaps he'll agree to take the land and leave me the house."

"I don't want your land in anyone's hands other than yours."

"I'm always going to remember how noble you were about this, Seth."

"I've never been noble but I do know right from wrong, and what you're proposing doesn't feel right."

"It's the only way."

He didn't say another word, just turned forward and started the car. He drove into town, his mind swimming with possibilities. He'd let Lynn try to work her deal with the bank, and if that didn't work, he'd arrange for one of the banks that he used in Chicago to buy the loan. He knew there was a way to manipulate the banks and the system for it to seem as if Lynn were still making payments to the institution, when in reality she'd be making payments to him.

Part of him chafed at the thought of deceiving this woman to whom pride meant so much, but another part realized that there were times when the situation called for desperate measures. As the thought entered his head, he wondered if his mother had ever justified using him by just the same thought.

*  *  *

Lynn left the bank with a heavy heart and anger pulsing through her veins. She'd never met a person she couldn't out-stubborn until this morning. Cochran wanted her land—but he wanted all of it and he wanted her out of the house in less than ten days.

Seth leaned casually against the hood of his car. Give him a cigarette and a leather jacket and he'd look the same as he had fourteen years ago. Her heart pounded a little faster at the sight of him, but she knew that nothing could come of it. Men were bad news for her.

"What did he say?" Seth asked, straightening as she approached.

She tried to utter the words, but her throat closed and she had to wrinkle her nose to keep the tears from falling. Instead, she just shook her head.

"Take my money," he said to her.

Never in her life had her pride stung more than at that moment. She wanted her ranch, but taking money from Seth Connelly was something she simply couldn't do. "I can't."

Anger crossed Seth's face, but she sensed it wasn't directed at her. "I'm going to talk to this man. Give me your notes."

"I don't think it will help. He's a barracuda."

"I'm a lawyer, sweetheart. We're known for being sharks."

"I don't want to think of you swimming in the same water as that man."

"Wait in the car. I'll be right back."

"Seth—"

"Let me do this, Lynn. I owe your family a debt, and it's the only option you've left me."

"Okay." She handed over the folder that held all of the paperwork on the ranch's mortgage. She was careful not to let their fingers brush, remembering the sensation that had rocked her the last time. But more than anything, she wished she could lean against him. Rest against his tall, strong body and let her troubles recede if only for a few minutes. But Seth was a weakness she couldn't afford.

He opened the Jag's door for her and she watched him walk back into the bank. It was a cold, blustery day and the mountains in the distance seemed to look down on the little town of Sagebrush with wise eyes. She felt their stare and knew that the mountains weren't really censoring her for giving her trust blindly. But realizing that her friends and neighbors would know how foolish she'd been didn't make her feel confident that they wouldn't look on her the same way.

She tried to weigh her options objectively. If Matt were here, would he take Seth's money? She doubted it. Matt preferred relationships that were equal, and if he'd taken money from Seth, their friendship would be forever changed.

Should she call her brother? She knew he couldn't come home. He might offer to send some money, but she doubted he had the funds available to appease the bank and Mr. Cochran.

She couldn't sell the land in time to save the house, she knew. There simply wasn't enough time. She glanced down the town's main road. The diner she'd been working at seemed gloomy in the muted light of day. Her future didn't hold the shining promise it had during the summer when she'd been riding a mountain trail on the back of Thor, her gelded bay. Instead, she saw that choices—foolish choices—had led her to a point where she was going to have to give up all she owned.

His shoulders straight, his stride purposeful, Seth walked out of the bank like a man with too much confidence. A force unto himself, she thought. She watched him move and realized the feelings she'd felt for him at sixteen still throbbed within her. There was something about the aloof aura he projected that made her want to open her arms and pull him into her embrace. To show him in a very physical way—just a hug—that he wasn't alone in the world.

He opened the door and slid behind the wheel. Silently he passed her folder back to her, and Lynn set it in her lap and stared at him. He quirked one eyebrow at her.

"What happened?" she asked.

"You were right about Cochran."

Damn. She'd felt a twinge of hope when she'd seen Seth returning, but now she knew it had been irrational. Cochran wanted the McCoy land, and he wasn't going to be easily swayed from taking it.

"Thanks for trying, Seth."

"Hey, don't give up yet, sad eyes. I didn't say that I wasn't successful."

Her heart pounded so loudly that she couldn't hear for a minute. "Did you get him to agree to take payments from me?"

"Not exactly."

"What exactly is the deal you made?"

"It's kind of complex. I'm not sure the front seat of the car is the right place to talk about it."

"I can't wait. I need to know if my ranch is going to be mine next week or if I'm going to have to start living over the diner."

"Whatever happens with the ranch, I promise you, you will never live over the diner."

His words touched her as little else had in the last eighteen months she'd been totally on her own with the huge debt hanging over her head. "Thank you."

"Don't thank me yet. You might not like the solution."

"I'm not letting you pay it off."

"Cochran won't accept the money from me. Or let me buy the loan from him."

"I told you he was a barracuda."

"He made a tasty meal," Seth said.

"How did you get around him?"

"I presented the one solution even he couldn't refute."

Lynn waited for him to continue. Seth was one of the smartest and most successful men she knew. His solution was probably something she'd never considered because she'd never dealt in finance.

''I told him that we were getting married and that I'd be back in three days' time as your husband to pay off the loan.''

Lynn blinked at him. ''What did you say?''

''Marry me, Lynn?''

# Four

**T**he words had come out of nowhere. Marriage wasn't something he'd been looking for. He preferred the quiet solitude of his empty condo to large family gatherings. But the more he thought about marriage, the more strongly he was compelled to convince her to agree.

Besides, Cochran was being stubborn about the money. He wanted the McCoy land for his own and would stop at nothing to get it. But then he'd never tangled with Seth Connelly before.

"You can't be serious," she said. For the first time since he'd exited the bank, she didn't look as if she was going to cry.

"Why not?" He was a little offended that she

thought he was joking. He'd never proposed marriage to a woman before and frankly, he'd expected a different reaction.

Conversely, he was also relieved. She was his best friend's little sister. Which for some reason had never made her seem off limits even though it should have.

"We've never been friends," she said. They'd had what could only be called an adversarial relationship.

"We did just fine on that one summer night." He still remembered the setting sun and warm breeze. The feel of her slender, budding body in his arms and the taste of her strawberry-pink lips under his. The irrational urge to swear he'd protect her for the rest of his life.

"We were teenagers then, and even that didn't really work out. Marriage is a big step. I don't see us together for the rest of our lives. Besides I've heard tales about you from Matt."

He doubted she'd heard anything too strong. Matt was very protective of Lynn, which made Seth's position all the more precarious. He honestly believed the only solution was marriage, but he also knew he lusted after her and wanted to claim her for his own. Something that Matt wouldn't approve of.

"The front seat of my car isn't the place for this kind of conversation. Let's go back to the ranch and sort out the details."

"Sounds good to me."

Seth put the car in gear and backed out onto Main Street. He drove carefully down the thoroughfare, watching for pedestrians and being mindful of the speed limit. On the interstate he rode with the wind, but in the city he'd learned caution. You only had to see a victim of a hit-and-run at the hospital once to take your foot off the gas.

"It seems strange for you to be driving the speed limit down this road. You always flew like a bat out of hell."

"I've learned that speed isn't everything."

"I haven't," she said quietly.

"You've never been on the run. Only impulsive," he said, driving out of town toward the McCoy spread.

"I've let life direct me instead of directing my life."

"That sounds deep. Obviously you've been thinking about that for a long time."

"There's not been much to do lately except think."

"Well, don't dwell too much on your troubles. I'll help you sort them out."

"Seth, I'm not Cinderella waiting for her prince to come and rescue her from a life of manual labor."

"I know." Life would be so much easier if she were. But he knew that he wouldn't want her to pretend to be something she wasn't. Hadn't he been living an illusion for most of his adult life? The price was too steep to be paid by Lynn.

"I want to rescue myself."

"Even heroes sometimes need a hand."

"A hand—not a shove out of the way so that someone else can shoulder the burden."

"I've said it before, but damn you're stubborn." He turned into the McCoy driveway and pulled to a stop next to Lynn's truck. He made a mental note to call the town mechanic and have her truck tuned up after he convinced her to go to Vegas and marry him.

"Let's get inside and warm up. It's chilly today." Seth opened his door and went around to open Lynn's, but she was already getting out of the car.

"I'm not going to be impulsive about this," she warned.

"I've got all the time in the world. You're the one with the minutes ticking by."

She hurried away without saying anything, leaving him to regret his truthful words. But Seth had never been able to stomach even a polite lie. He'd spent too long being surrounded by the details of his birth.

He followed her into the kitchen. "I didn't intend for my words to hurt you."

"They didn't." She paused. "Look, I know you're right but the last time I trusted a man I ended up in this situation."

"I'm not any man."

"No, you're Matt's best friend."

"I'd like to think I'm your friend too, Lynn."

"Friendship is all we have?"

"Friendship and mutual love of this land."

"Why are you doing this?"

"Because you belong riding your horse not slinging hash in a diner."

"That's not much of a reason."

"Maybe I've always wanted to be a part of your family."

She sank into a kitchen chair and rested her head on her hands. She shouldn't look like this. He knew that God would never forgive him if he walked away from her and her troubles. To say nothing of how his best friend would react.

"Trust me on this, Lynn."

"I'm trying."

"What would reassure you?"

"I don't know. Would it be a real marriage?"

Yes, his libido screamed. But he knew that this was one time when he had to be ruled by his head and not his penis. Though he hated deceit of any kind, he knew that he couldn't stay married to his best friend's little sister. He was only doing this to help her out. No matter how much his body might clamor for something more, he was only going to be her husband on paper.

"Is there any other kind?" he asked.

"Sure, there are those business-deal ones."

"We'll have to see how it works out."

She stared at him, her eyes wide, her lower lip trembling. Damn, he'd learn to love cold showers if she didn't want to sleep with him. Hell, he'd marry her, fix this place and go back to Chicago before he forced himself on her. If and when Lynn came to him, it would be because she wanted to be in his arms.

Her words shook him to the core. ''Will you marry me?''

''Yes.''

Lynn wasn't sure she'd made the right choice. Every time she'd followed her impulsive nature, she'd ended up in trouble. And Seth wasn't a man she was immune to.

She'd wanted him longer than she'd admit to anyone. There was a part of her that was still sixteen and kissing him for the first time. She wondered how much he'd changed. Life had made her a different woman and Seth couldn't be the same man he'd been then.

Though he'd only been eighteen, there had always been a part of Seth that was mature. She wondered if maybe he didn't need her as much as she needed him. Perhaps, she thought, he needed someone to show him how to lighten up and enjoy life. That could be what she contributed to him.

Seth had promised her a real marriage, and though she wasn't ready for intimacy with him, they really had no choice. They had to marry—and quickly. But Seth had always struck her as a man who thought through every decision to the tiniest detail. Did he have another motive for marrying her?

''I'm not even sure what you have to do to get married,'' she said.

"Well, I don't know about other brides, but all you have to do is sit back and let me take care of the details."

"I'm not used to being passive, Seth."

"Try it this once."

"Okay."

Once he decided on a course of action, Seth moved at the speed of light. Lynn was still trying to come to grips with the fact that she didn't have to worry about losing the ranch.

"How does Vegas sound for a wedding?"

"Tacky."

He looked offended. "Hey, I'm a Connelly. We don't do anything less than classy."

"In Vegas?"

"Yes."

"Then I guess we'll get married in Nevada. When do we leave?"

"That depends on you. How long will it take you to pack?"

"Is this just an overnight trip?"

"The banks will be closed until Monday, so we'll stay through the weekend."

Though they'd decided to marry to save the ranch, they hadn't talked about emotions. Could she spend her life with a man who didn't love her? And why hadn't she thought about love earlier?

"Seth, I need to ask you something."

"Go ahead," he said.

Her heart was beating frantically. She looked at the

man who'd given her so much and knew no matter what happened, she'd do whatever she had to. Because she owed Seth.

"I don't know how to say this, so I'm just going to blurt it out. How do you feel about love?"

"I'm sorry?"

"I mean, we haven't talked about what our marriage will be like and I know we don't know each other well enough to be in love, but someday do you think I'm the kind of woman you could love?"

"I'm not going to delude you, Lynn. I think I could care deeply for you. As deeply as I do for my family in Chicago. But love? I've seen the dirtier side of that emotion and I'll never be that weak."

"Love's not a weakness."

"It is in Chicago, baby."

"But we're in Montana."

"For now."

She hadn't thought they'd live anyplace other than the ranch. "Does this mean we'd have to live in Chicago?"

"My job is there. We'll have to work out those details. Go get packed while I book a flight."

As she climbed up the stairs to her room, the house she'd lived in her entire life suddenly looked different. She knew it was because she was seeing it with new eyes. Before she got too hopeful, she reined herself in and tuned in to the part of her that worried that marrying Seth might be the biggest mistake she'd ever made.

"What are we going to do in Vegas for a few days?" she asked. "I'm not that big on gambling."

"I don't think we'll have a problem entertaining ourselves."

The warm look he gave her made her flush. She'd had a few torrid fantasies about Seth when they'd both been teens. Spending the day with him, seeing the man he'd matured into convinced her that Seth had grown into a man she could fall for easily. But her heart wasn't as trustworthy as she'd once believed, and life had a way of reminding you of those things.

It didn't stop the images of Seth making love to her in a showy Vegas hotel room. His muscled body moving over hers. She looked away, sure he could read the desire in her eyes.

She turned away before she did something she regretted. Something impulsive, like letting him see how easily she could fall in love with him. Something like smiling at him and dreaming of a lifetime of love when he had something else in mind.

She packed a duffel bag she used for overnight camping trips to the mountains. When she realized there was no suitable dress in her closet for a wedding, she suddenly worried that she wasn't good enough for Seth.

Not that he'd ever treated her as if she wasn't. But the women he knew no doubt had designer luggage and closets full of appropriate clothing for any occasion. She had jeans and a battered bag. She looked at herself in the mirror and almost changed her mind. She wasn't good at pretending to be something she wasn't.

She grabbed her bag and hurried back down the stairs. Seth was on the living-room couch, talking on his cellular phone and making notes on a legal pad. He looked up when she walked in and smiled at her. It was a reassuring expression that should have stilled the butterflies in her stomach but didn't.

"Can I get married in this suit?" she asked to change the subject.

He quietly ended his phone conversations. "No. We'll fly to Vegas tonight and get married there tomorrow. I'll arrange for a couple of wedding dresses to be sent to our suite for you to try on."

"Thank you. I've never been married before and I would like to wear a white dress."

"No problem, this is my first wedding too. But I think we should plan on it being our last."

"Yeah?"

"Yeah, I know we haven't had a chance to hammer out the details, but we can make this work. I'm not a quitter and neither are you."

"You're right."

"Are you sure about this, Lynn? I don't mind making a gift of the money."

She'd given her word and she wouldn't change her mind now. "Marriage is fine with me."

"I don't want to pressure you."

For the first time since Ronnie had left with her money, she found something funny. "You're not."

"This is your last chance to back out."

Maybe he'd changed his mind. "If you don't want to marry me, Seth, just say so."

"I want you more than any woman I've ever met."

His words brought sunshine to a soul that was weary and battered from its encounters with the opposite sex. She felt like a flower that had lain dormant for too long, and knew she owed Seth more than she could ever repay. They'd make a good marriage, she promised herself. She would do whatever necessary to ensure it.

The first flight to Vegas wasn't until eight that night. By the time they'd finished packing, arranged for a neighbor to watch the animals and driven to the airport, they barely had thirty minutes to spare.

Lynn shared her concerns as they took their seats in the plane. "I've never flown before."

"Are you scared?"

"A little. I mean I'm one of the people who stays behind and guards the homestead."

"Not this time," he said.

"I'm not sure I'm ready to leave."

It struck him that Lynn wasn't the type of woman he was used to. She hated change. She liked to stay in her safe routine, found something reassuring about it.

"I saw this special on *48 Hours* about engine failure in airplanes."

"What did it say?"

"That there was a defect the airlines didn't want you to know about."

"Lynn, relax. I fly all the time and haven't been in a single crash."

"There's always a first time."

"Okay, Ms. Sunshine, enough of those thoughts." He hailed a passing flight attendant and asked for two glasses of champagne.

She returned quickly with them and he handed one to Lynn. As she watched him warily, he had the strangest urge to tease her, to find a way to put her at ease—even though laughter created the strongest bonds he'd ever experienced. The last thing he needed was a stronger bond with her.

He raised his glass. "To the future of the McCoy Ranch."

Lynn tipped her glass to his and took a sip of her drink.

"Your turn."

"To arriving alive."

He narrowed his eyes at her and she gave him a mock kiss. Damn, he wanted it to be real. Needed it to be real. How was he going to keep this platonic, when he'd all but promised her that they'd have a real relationship? An adult relationship—one that would start before they returned to Montana.

Don't be sweet, he told Lynn in his thoughts. Keep

on being Matt's little sister and not the funny, attractive woman whom I want more than my next breath.

She broke into his thoughts. "Okay, a real toast. Ready?"

He nodded, not trusting his voice.

"To our life together."

She clinked her glass to his once again, but he couldn't drink. Her sincerity burned straight to the heart of the lie he'd given her for reassurance and now he had to live with the consequences. Had to find a way to make her see that the hurt he knew he'd have to deliver down the road would be for the best in the end.

Ah, hell. Just once couldn't life deal him a hand that was fairly easy to play? He knew that their life together would be relatively short. It affected him more than she'd ever know to realize that for once he wanted to hold on to someone, even though he'd learned it was better to let go.

They finished their champagne. Seth knew if he didn't put some barriers in place and fast, he was a goner. He'd lose Lynn, the McCoy Ranch and his best friend in one fell swoop. Because there was no way Lynn McCoy would ever be happy being a Connelly.

The only plan that had even a slight chance of working was an annulment. And it required only one thing—celibacy. He reminded himself as Lynn reached across his lap to retrieve her magazine and her breast brushed against his leg. Damn, he wanted to feel more of her. The cabin was dark and no one would have to know, he thought. But he'd know. And he was being noble.

Once the plane took off, Seth pulled out his laptop to work. He needed to focus on something other than the woman beside him. Even though he was on a leave of absence from his job, weird things had been happening in his family. His oldest brother was going to be King, his mom was connected to the mob and he'd left Chi-town to keep the Connellys safe. And he couldn't stay completely out of touch. Lynn read a magazine and then curled up in her seat. Seth powered down his computer, got a blanket from the flight attendant and draped it over her.

That small action should have been brotherly. And it was, he reassured himself. He'd preserved the wall around him by working and showing her that he couldn't—wouldn't—be able to be on for her 24/7.

She stirred in her sleep and shifted toward him, ending up with her head on his shoulder and her arm around his waist. In that instant, he'd gone from being an island to being a peninsula. In the scheme of things it wasn't a big change, but simply being connected to something shook Seth to the core.

# Five

Vegas always felt like a second home to Seth. He'd always been fascinated by the world of bookies, con men and showgirls. His childhood had been kind of surreal—only son of a poor, single mom, then the son of a wealthy family. On his mom's side of the family he had a few cousins who worked here.

They were simple men who'd accepted the fact that they existed in the gray area of life. Something that Seth had always thought he'd be able to do if his father hadn't taken him in. The gray area wasn't bad. It was almost legal and didn't involve the innocent.

Unlike his current predicament. Lynn didn't look as if she'd come home. In her faded jeans and boots she looked fresh and…ah, hell, innocent. Dammit. He wasn't sure marrying her was the right thing to do. But once he'd settled on a course of action he didn't turn back.

His plan that had seemed so simple and easy in Montana was now more complex. The more time he spent in Lynn's company, the more he realized that keeping his hands off her was going to be nearly impossible. She drew him with her sharp wit and soft smiles. By turns she was a prickly, stubborn woman and then a sweet lady.

The cab pulled to a stop in front of one of the Merv Griffin hotel/casinos. Night had fallen and the Strip was resplendent with lights and tourists. Lynn stood on the sidewalk as he tipped the cabdriver.

"Wow! I've never seen so much…"

Sin? he thought, but didn't say it. He didn't want to point out the differences between them if she didn't see them. He knew Vegas suited him like a one-of-a-kind leather jacket, and the feel of it was soft and smooth.

"What?" he asked, taking her by the elbow to lead her into the hotel. She could easily have walked inside without him guiding her but he wanted to touch her, even if it was through layers of clothing. In fact, he wanted nothing so much as to strip away the layers of cloth and caress the woman underneath.

"I'm trying to find the right word."

She was smart. She'd figure it out sooner or later and he didn't believe in lying.

"Sin, lights, tourists."

She laughed. It was a sweet sound and he stopped to smile down at her. "You sound so cynical."

"Maybe I am."

"No, you're not." She touched his cheek, and met his gaze full on. In her eyes was the promise of something he'd never experienced before. Something he'd never seen in anyone's eyes as they looked at him.

He was struck by the twin urges to protect and ravage this woman. This petite blonde who was his opposite in every way. He took her hand and held it firmly in his own, leading her into the hotel. The sensual scent of flowers and an essence that was only Lynn surrounded him. His groin hardened as they approached the concierge desk.

The better part of him—his rational mind—told him he should contact Matt and get as far away from Lynn as possible. He should take the first flight back to Chicago.

But his body was making a stronger argument than his mind, and for the first time in his life Seth was taking what he wanted. He wasn't being shaped at military school into someone worthy of the Connelly name. He was just Seth. And Lynn accepted him as such, which was as much a turn-on as her sexy body and long blond hair.

"I was going to say opulent."

"Merv does know how to do a hotel the right way."

"I feel so out of place."

"You're not," he said.

"It's just that I know I come from a run-down ranch in Montana and these people look like they were born here."

"Vegas is all illusion, Lynn. Don't forget that."

"What do you mean?"

"What you see isn't what you really get. What you see is a mirage."

"I see you," she said softly.

Her words cut to his soul, and for a minute the reality of what he was doing struck him. He was marrying her to repay a debt and he knew she wouldn't want that. But he wasn't turning back. Couldn't let her go at this late time.

"And I see you. Just remember that what we are here is an illusion."

"You look like you belong here," she said.

He nodded. "I know."

As they moved forward in the line, Seth wanted to put his arm around her to keep her close by his side but didn't. He wasn't a needy man. He was solitary by nature and experience and he was savvy enough to know trouble when it looked at him. Even if it was only through Lynn's violet eyes.

Those eyes took in everything around them, assessing, deciding. "It's different but I think I like it."

"What do you like the most?"

"I haven't experienced everything you promised yet."

Her words went through him like a gambler through his winnings. She wanted him. He wondered how quickly they could get married tonight, because he needed her in his bed. He needed to make her his in an elemental way.

"Want to get married now?" he asked, his voice guttural.

Her eyes widened. He thought he saw maybe a hint of fear in them but she smiled slowly. "You promised me a white dress."

There was hope in her voice and he knew that she had to feel a little vulnerable without her family. It struck him that Lynn and he weren't all that different. They were both essentially alone in this world. "I always keep my promises."

"I know you do, Seth."

"Not everyone does," he said without thinking. His father hadn't said a word when it was revealed that his mother had once again tried to betray the Connellys; but Seth had seen the coldness in Grant's eyes and knew once again he'd let them down.

"Then they don't know the real Seth Connelly."

"Sometimes I don't think that I do."

She leaned up and kissed him on the cheek. "He's an honorable man who lives by his own code."

"Next, please," called the concierge.

Seth walked over to check in, aware of Lynn's gaze on him the entire time. Her words echoed in his mind and he felt a twinge of doubt at their union. There was no way he could live up to her expectations of him. But a part of him wanted to.

The next afternoon Lynn knew she'd made a big mistake as soon as she held the first wedding dress. Seth had gone to the other room to make some business phone calls, so she was alone in the luxurious bedroom. The carpet was plush under her feet, the champagne was expensive to the taste and the music was refined and elegant in the background.

She knew then that she was in real danger of buying into the whole reality. How could she remember that Seth thought this was all an illusion, while she held a dress that dreams were made of? She couldn't pretend he was nothing more to her than a business partner in the ranch when he looked at her as he had in the lobby.

Or when he showed her his vulnerability. Seth had never been an easy boy to know. When the rest of her brother's friends were open and obvious, Seth was guarded. He'd always enthralled her.

Her heart beat a little faster when he knocked on the door.

''How's it coming? Have you picked a dress yet?''

Tears burned the back of her eyes. As a little girl she'd dreamed of doing this with her mother. The pain still felt sharp. Her mother was gone, her brother was deep undercover and she was with a man who warned her that he didn't believe in love.

She knew without a doubt that she did. And she knew, as she stared at herself in the mirror, that she could fall in love with Seth Connelly with very little trouble.

The world tipped on its axis.

"Lynn, are you okay?"

There was a caring in his words. She didn't know if it was concern for his best friend's sister or for the woman he'd asked to marry him. And were those two people different for him?

Though he'd been subtle, she knew he desired her. But did he want the woman as well as the body? That question mocked her as she let the dress fall to the padded chaise. She couldn't marry him unless he wanted to marry her for herself.

Not because Matt wasn't here to rescue her. Not because Seth needed something to take his mind off whatever had sent him from Chicago. Not because lust ran rampant through their bodies.

"No, I'm not," she said, opening the door.

Seth had shed his jacket and tie while he'd been on the phone. His dark hair was ruffled as if he'd speared his fingers through it, and his collar was open, revealing his dark skin. He looked tired and weary and she wanted to open her arms to him. To offer him a place to rest from the crazy world.

"How'd your phone call go?"

"As well as expected," he said.

"Can I help?"

"You are."

"I don't see how."

"You're giving me a chance to prove I'm more than what my parents made me."

"Seth, what demons are you running from?"

"Not the kind you'd ever want to know."

She wanted to touch him but sensed his control hung by a thin thread. Insight was late coming but she realized that Seth needed her as much as she'd needed his rescue and his money. He needed her to help him through whatever family problems had once again sent him to Montana.

"What's wrong with the dresses?" he asked.

"Nothing. They're beautiful."

He nodded and waited for her to continue. But somehow she couldn't bring herself to say out loud that she wasn't right for the dresses. Or that she wasn't right for this suite. Because then he'd know what she really meant—she wasn't right for him.

"Those dresses are too much."

"I asked my sister Tara to pick them out. She made a few calls from Chicago. So I'm sure they're just right."

"Maybe for a Connelly."

"Which you will soon be."

"I'm trying not to buy into the illusion."

"What illusion? We really are getting married."

"I don't want to become your wife because you need a distraction."

"Hell, that's not why I'm marrying you."

"Then why are you?"

Silence. The dead quiet in the room seeped through her layers of clothing, chilling her to her soul. There was no reason why he was marrying her. No reason at all except that he knew Matt would want the ranch when he got out of the service.

"Because I needed rescuing," she said.

"Partly. There's something about you, Lynn. There has always has been something that entrances me."

"In your youth it made you want to play pranks on me."

"Only to keep alive the premise that you were still a kid and I was a man."

"I'm not sure you were a man at eighteen."

"Funny, I've felt like one since I was eight."

His words struck a chord and she realized that he did want from her something other than a bedmate. Trying to put it into words wasn't working for him, but his gray eyes were sincere.

She closed the distance between them. Wrapping her arms around his waist, she rested her head against his chest. His arms stayed by his sides and she wondered if she'd misread him.

She felt him sigh, and then tentatively his arms enclosed her. She never wanted to leave this spot, she realized. His heart beat steadily under her ear, his warmth surrounded her, and for this one moment she felt as if he cared.

The cool sophistication Seth had learned to imitate from his brothers and stepmom disappeared. He finally had Lynn where he'd fantasized about having her. Though he knew he shouldn't let this embrace go beyond a brief hug, instinct took over.

He lifted her face toward his. Those luscious lips of hers, free of makeup, tempted him more than any of the glamorous women he knew in Chicago. Her skin felt like silk to his fingers, softer than anyone he'd ever touched.

He wanted to linger but was afraid she'd bolt. And he needed to know how she tasted more than he needed his next breath.

The iron control he'd exerted since he'd first entered military school was the only thing that allowed him to slowly lower his head. His gut urged him to crush his mouth to hers. To plunder it for the sweetness that only she could provide, and drink until his thirst was quenched. Suddenly it felt like years since he'd had a woman in his arms.

Lynn's violet eyes were wide open, watching every move he made. Her gaze was welcoming but distant. As if she feared this embrace as much as she wanted it.

Later he knew he'd regret this, but he closed the small gap between them. Her lips were full and warm, pliant under his own, and there was no awkwardness to the embrace. He slid his tongue across the seam of her mouth and she sighed.

Her mouth opened and he felt her invitation to come deeper. She tasted of something elemental. Something he'd never tasted in an embrace before. Something that was Lynn.

Her tongue reciprocated, tasting his mouth and setting his hormones ablaze. In a rush he hardened uncomfortably against the inseam of his trousers.

He slid his hands down her back, settling them on her backside. She adjusted her body to cradle his erection. Ah, yes, he thought, here was what he needed. What they both needed to distract them from the vulnerability that they both felt.

Though Seth wouldn't admit it to a living soul, he needed comfort from Lynn now. He needed her to marry him because for the first time he looked at the future and it was cold and empty.

He groaned at the rightness of it. He tore his mouth from hers. Her eyes were wide and questioning. Lynn had never felt more fragile to him. Her slender shoulders under his hands made him feel big and manly, a stark contrast to the ethereal woman in his arms.

Her lips were full and welcoming, her tongue shy but knowing. Almost like Lynn herself. Tentative were her touches and he wondered if she was afraid of him or herself.

Leaning back against the wall, he pulled her even closer. He lifted her thigh so that he could press his arousal more fully against the center of her body. She moaned a deep throaty sound that almost made him lose control.

Her fingers tunneled through his hair and she pulled his mouth to hers. She kissed like someone who was on the verge of orgasm, and he didn't want her to ever stop. With his hands on her hips, he urged her to move against him. Quicker until her breath caught.

Her nails dug into his biceps and he knew she hung on the precipice. He moved his hips, rubbing against her with more strength than before, and she opened her mouth on a gasp.

The sound was fire to his body that was already hotter than the sun. "Like that?"

"Oh, Seth, why does this feel so good?" she asked.

She slid her hands under his clothing. Her fingers were long and cool against his back and he wanted her touch somewhere else. Her words barely registered. He could think only of her touching him where he needed her most.

"More, baby?"

"Yes…"

He did it again and she arched against him at the end of his thrust. Damn, the clothing was in the way. He reached between them to free himself, and as his hand rubbed across the center of her desire, she shuddered in his arms. He held her trembling body.

Her face was flushed, her eyes tightly closed and Seth had never seen anyone look lovelier. Her climax had brought him to the edge, but he was still hungry for Lynn. Hungry for her body clenching around his. The next time orgasm put that look on her face, he vowed to be hilt deep inside her.

Hopefully the next time wouldn't be that long from now. He lifted her in his arms and carried her to the king-size bed that dominated the room. Other than a small wedge of sunlight that peeked out from between the black-out drapes, the rest of the room was in shadows.

Seth felt the comfort of that dim room in the same way that Vegas had welcomed him. He was at home in the shadows. Always had been. Even in the big Connelly house, he spent a majority of the time hiding.

He wondered if he was hiding from more than Lynn in this darkened room. He settled her in the center of the bed and reached for her shirt. A knock on the door of the suite stopped him. That was probably the lady Tara had arranged to show Lynn veils.

Lynn sat up on the bed. Even in the shadows he knew she'd changed her mind. She was saved by the bell and he was damned by it.

"Second thoughts?" he asked. His body throbbed in time to his racing pulse. She was so close he could smell her sweetness, and he didn't know if the veil lady would be enough to keep him from having her.

He should have taken her where they'd been standing. But Lynn deserved a bed when they made love, not a hurried coupling against the wall.

"And third and fourths," she said.

"Not tonight, eh?"

"I know it sounds silly. But we're getting married tonight and I want our wedding night to be special."

"What if we're not compatible?" he asked.

"Please, if we were any more compatible, this room would have gone up in flames."

"I almost did," he said.

''I did. Thank you.''

He knew that she probably wanted to escape. She'd been so vulnerable a few minutes ago, and the fact that she wanted to wait made him realize she probably still didn't trust him. He didn't blame her.

But he wanted to hold her for a few minutes. Hold her for just a short while here in the shadows where no one could see him. Hold her now while it was safe to do so, because he'd only just realized that she had the power to burst through his outer walls and see straight to his heart. In the shadows maybe she wouldn't realize the control he'd been powerless to stop from giving her.

# Six

Seth left the suite once the lady from the bridal shop arrived. Lynn didn't know where he was going but she didn't try to stop him. They both needed some fresh air. Especially Seth.

If that knock hadn't sounded on the door when it had, she would have made love with him. She still wished she had, but she knew that what she would have seen as a meeting of the souls, Seth would have viewed as physical gratification. After her last adult relationship, she needed it to mean more to him.

She didn't think that mere hours would make that big a difference, but she was determined to make the most of that time to show him they had more than a past filled with mischief and a present filled with hot sex.

All of the dresses were lovely and showy. The kind of gowns that only a woman who was confident of herself and her femininity could wear. Lynn freely acknowledged that Ronnie had wounded something very feminine in her when he left, but she didn't think she could have worn those dresses in any circumstances. They weren't her.

She'd pretended to be someone she wasn't with Ronnie and that had backfired. The only way she'd survive a lifetime with Seth was to be honest about who she was.

"Do you have anything a little…plainer?"

The saleswoman looked her over with a practiced eye. "I have a new Vera Wang that might work. I'll have it sent right up."

"Thanks. These are all so pretty but they're not me."

"I think you're right."

The saleswoman left, and while she was gone, Lynn tried on veils, choosing a simple one that flattered her slim features and long hair.

After the assistant returned with two dresses, Lynn tried the first one on and fell in love. Even the ladies from the boutique smiled knowingly when she fastened the back of the dress. It was simple yet feminine and made Lynn feel as if she was a fairy-tale princess for the first time in her life.

The ladies left, taking the extra dresses with them, and Lynn knew she should change out of her wedding gown but couldn't. Though night was falling on Vegas, only a small lamp illuminated the suite's main room. Lights spread out under the window for as far as she could see. And she saw something else—her reflection in the floor-to-ceiling glass.

She spun around and then moved closer to study that woman. Was that really Lynn McCoy?

Seth entered the suite without knocking. She pivoted to face him, not wanting him to see her gawking at herself. His shirt was open at the collar and his suit jacket flung over his shoulder. Though he looked at ease, there was nothing casual about him. An intensity burned in his eyes that made her tingle in the most delicious way.

He paused just inside the doorway. The look on his face was unreadable. She hoped it was okay that she'd picked out a dress on her own and not one that his sister had selected.

Silence grew and she started to forget that in this dress she looked like a fairy princess. She started to feel like the dusty cowgirl who'd come in from the range. She started to remember that Seth wasn't her Prince Charming though he'd saved her ranch. He didn't want her.

"It's bad luck for you to see my dress. You should have knocked."

He closed the door and crossed the suite. "Honey, I've had Lady Luck on my side most of my life and have yet to feel lucky."

"I never have."

He moved closer to her and she could see that he

wasn't unaffected by her dress. His erection strained against his zipper. His reaction to her caused a definitely equal reaction in her body. Heat pooled in her center, and her nipples beaded up against the satin of her dress. The design made it impossible for her to wear a bra and right now she was glad of it.

"Maybe it's time things changed for both of us," he said, brushing his finger along her cheek.

Though he was not a soft man, there was a gentle side to Seth that she doubted he even realized he had. But he touched her so carefully sometimes that he made her feel as though she was the most important thing in his world.

"I hope they can." In fact, she'd placed her future on that sentiment.

"Turn around so I can get the full effect of the dress."

"Don't you want to wait and be surprised at the wedding?"

"Turn," he ordered.

She pivoted and knew he saw her bare back. In the reflection of the window she watched him reach out as if to touch her and then pull back. He didn't trust something. Her?

"Seth?"

"Yes," he said, his voice husky. She finished turning and saw that his eyes were shuttered and his hands jammed deep in his pockets.

"I let you dodge the subject in the car but I think we need to hammer out those details now."

"It's late, Lynn. I just spent the last two hours in the bar, reminding myself that you're Matt's sister. But I have to tell you all I can see when I close my eyes is the way you looked when you came in my arms earlier."

She flushed. "I…"

"Honey, I know this situation isn't one you can control and you don't like that. Hell, I don't like it. But I can't talk to you right now when all I can think about is that bed in the other room and how lovely you'd look lying on it."

In her heart she'd believed he cared for her, even if it was only the warmth of his friendship with her brother spilling over. But she realized as he stood next to her radiating sexual energy that it was only lust.

"If we have sex, can we talk after?" she asked.

Taking a step back, she was ready to bolt, but he caught her hand, stopping her escape. She needed to get out of this dress, because she'd bought into the illusion even though he'd warned her not to. Her eyes burned. She had to escape and quick.

"Dammit, Lynn. When you and I do go to bed together, it's going to be more than sex."

Carefully she slid her hand out of his grasp. "I wish I could believe that."

Let her go, he told himself.

Women were more trouble than they were worth. He'd learned that lesson more than once since he'd been born. He was the cynic here, he thought.

Lynn was the one with the faith in love and happy-ever-after. If she was running away, then they were in more trouble than he'd thought. Maybe he should end this now. The money was being wired to him and he'd be able to pick up the cashier's check when they checked out. The McCoy ranch would soon be safely in the hands of the McCoys again. A few calls to some colleagues of his had netted an expert in ranch management who was on his way to Montana to take over the day-to-day tasks so that Lynn could enjoy the ranch.

Yet he couldn't let her go. Or was it *wouldn't?* He admitted to himself that he liked the way she made him feel. As if he was her hero instead of the mischief-maker who'd brought disgrace to his family. The sensation was heady and he never wanted it to end.

But he knew that Lynn needed more. And he wasn't certain he had that much left to give. He needed to remember that or else he'd find himself alone again. And without a refuge to run to.

He needed the McCoys—not just his friendship with Matt but this new thing he had with Lynn. He knew it was more than the hard-on in his pants.

His hormones urged him to go after her, but his heart that had learned to be wary told him to stay where he was. Lynn McCoy had way too much stubbornness and pride but not enough ego. No man would want only sex from her.

She represented the girl next door to him. She was his secret fantasy because he'd always been surrounded by showgirls and sophisticated women. He actually craved someone all-American. Even if he'd never met her brother, he'd still treat Lynn with respect. She normally exuded a kind of self-assurance that demanded it.

"Honey, stop."

She paused on the edge of the shadows in the bedroom. Her white dress glowed in the soft lamplight and her back was so stiff and straight she'd have passed inspection at the military school he'd attended as an adolescent.

"Don't call me honey in that soft voice, Seth. I know you don't mean it but it sounds like you care, and I'm trying real hard right now not to buy into the illusion."

Damn. He'd hurt her. He could tell that from her voice and the way she wouldn't look at him. Lynn always faced her opponent in battle yet now she was retreating.

"I do care." She'd be surprised to know how much.

"Only until I try to get to know the real you. Then you push me away."

"The real me. I'm not even sure who that man is anymore."

"Give me a break. He's a successful lawyer from a wealthy family. What's not to know?"

If only that were the whole story. He didn't want to sound like a sad sack whining because his mother didn't love him. But Angie's betrayal had left a gap deep inside him that made him question certain cornerstones he'd always taken for granted. "Something like being betrayed by your biological mother might make a man question who he believes he is.''

She turned to face him. Moisture made her eyes glassy but she was concerned now. Concerned about him. Part of him realized he'd known she would be; for all her toughness, there was something very soft about her. He realized that was part of her appeal. Once he'd set on the course of saving the ranch, it was safe for him to acknowledge the attraction he'd felt for her for a long time. And unless he'd lost all of his perception where women were concerned, she felt the same.

''Want to talk about it?'' she asked.

The compassion almost undid him. Survival depended on one thing, he reminded himself. Being able to stand alone. And confiding in Lynn wouldn't enable him to do that.

''Not really,'' he said, coming closer to her. He could smell her floral perfume. It swept over him in a wave, reminding him of how long ago spring was and leaving him feeling alone and cold in its wake.

She held her hand up to stop him. ''I can't deal with this right now. Getting married without any family around me is taking all the control I have.''

''What do you want from me?'' he demanded. He was rock hard with an erection that showed no signs of waning. Emotionally he'd had more than he could take for one day. And she wasn't through with him yet.

''Understanding.''

''You've got it.''

''Compassion?''

He nodded.

"Affection?"

He understood where she was coming from. Marrying someone for reasons other than love went against the grain, against the fairy tale that all young girls grow up believing in. "You are the only woman I've asked to marry me. That should tell you something."

"It does but I need more. I'm looking to you to provide some reassurance."

He'd never shirked from the truth and didn't hedge now. "I care for you. I always have."

"It's more than affection for my family because we took you in when you needed a safe harbor?"

"Yes. I wouldn't marry you if I didn't want you. My desire for you has nothing to do with that."

"What does it involve?"

"Raging lust and very little thought."

She gave him a half smile that said she understood. He closed the gap between them, held her in his arms. Though he wanted to ravage her body, to pull that fantasy bridal gown from her body, more than that he needed to comfort her. To give her some reassurance with his body that he could never offer in words.

But there was no time. "We're getting married in two hours, then having dinner with some cousins of mine."

"I don't think I'm up to a meeting with your family."

"You'll like these guys, I promise."

"And you always keep your promises, right?"

He nodded.

"Then promise me this marriage isn't a mistake."

He brushed his lips against her cheek and stepped back because he couldn't keep holding her and still get them downstairs in time to be married.

"I promise this marriage won't be a mistake."

"I'm going to hold you to it," she said and walked into the other room to finish getting ready.

Seth took the tuxedo bag from the hall closet where he'd asked the bellman to deliver it earlier and went to the shower. He tried not to admit the importance of what he'd just promised, because he knew he had no way to make that promise real unless he let Lynn inside his soul—and there was no way he'd ever be that vulnerable.

They were married in a small wedding chapel on the sixth floor of the hotel. The ceremony was discreet and subtly sophisticated with none of the garishness one would expect of a Vegas wedding. It still didn't feel right to Lynn. Her only family in the world was far away, unreachable, and she sensed he wouldn't approve of her marrying Seth.

Matt was the only one who knew that they'd kissed that long-ago night. In those days he would've been thrilled to have Seth as a brother-in-law, but Seth's rogue ways were too much for Lynn, and Matt had warned her to stay away from the Chicago bad boy.

If only Matt could see Seth now. Seth had done his best to make the ceremony as low-key and comfortable for her as he could. He wasn't the young hood he'd been in the past; he wasn't even the calmly confident lawyer she'd glimpsed at the bank yesterday.

He was a mature man taking care of his own. Lynn was touched beyond words.

When the photographer posed them for pictures, she broke down. Her parents were long gone, her brother's life was separate from hers and her future was tied to a man who'd warned her not to buy into the illusion.

The only illusion that she was even close to falling for was Seth. Since the officiant had pronounced them man and wife, her heart beat quicker. She knew she was dangerously close to believing that Seth was her forever man.

He never had been. Since the first time they'd met, he'd been on the run. Why would he change now? Why would he stay in Montana when she was the only thing holding him there?

Seth dismissed the photographer and witnesses from the room. Pulling a snowy-white handkerchief from his pocket, he dried her eyes. "What's wrong?"

She took a deep breath and tried to find the words to tell him what she was feeling. But they wouldn't come. There were some things she couldn't say to Seth—actually quite a few—and telling him that she was falling in love with him was one of them.

"I don't know," she said, hedging.

"Changed your mind already?" His demeanor was stiff and unsure, almost as if he'd expected her to back out of their agreement. Thinking about his mother and what she knew of his past, she didn't blame him for thinking the worst of her.

She wouldn't do that to him. Seth was important

to her. More important than he'd ever know and not just because he'd saved her ranch from the bank.

"No," she said. "It's just this isn't what I expected." Lynn knew her words misled him, because Seth had exceeded her expectations.

"I know."

If only he really did know. But her days of hitching her wagon to a distant star were over. She was standing on her own this time. But why did he have to look so appealing, so strong, and his shoulders so damn able to carry her burdens?

"Weddings have always kind of creeped me out," he said.

"Why?"

"I don't know. Maybe because my parents were never married."

She inhaled and closed her eyes. She didn't want him to think he'd made a mistake this soon. She had to stop reacting like an emotional invalid. Though in essence she knew she was.

"How did you feel about that?"

"When I was little and lived with my mom, it seemed as if no one had a normal family. We all ran together on the streets. The next generation of punks."

"No one would ever have called you a punk, Seth."

"You're wrong. My father did the first time he saw me."

"Mine didn't."

"Hey, I'd had a semester of military school. I'd lost some of my edge."

"I don't think you lost it. You may have smoothed it out a bit but it was still there when we met."

He nodded. "I know this isn't your dream wedding, but if you keep crying I'm going to have a hard time convincing everyone that you wanted to marry me."

"Oh, Seth," she said with a weak smile.

"Are you okay now?"

"Yes."

"Good. I'll call the photographer back in.... Are you sure it isn't the thought of meeting my cousins?"

"No."

"I know they can be a little intimidating. In fact, they've used it to their advantage over the years."

"Are you trying to tell me something about them?"

"I don't want to mislead you, Lynn. My father's side of the family is upstanding and well respected. My mom's family— Let's just say they aren't."

"That doesn't bother me."

"I'm glad because I'm more at home with these guys than with the Connellys in Chicago sometimes."

"Why is that?"

"I've never really thought about it."

"Maybe if you did, you'd stop running."

He cradled her close to his chest and she could hear his heart beat under her ear. It was reassuring.

"You okay now?" he asked.

She took a deep breath. "I will be."

He tilted her face up toward his. His eyes compelling her to meet his gaze. She wondered if he'd kiss her, because more than anything in the world she wanted his lips on hers.

"I promise you that fate wants us to be together."

His words rocked her, made her feel secure in a way she'd never felt before. He set her away from him and walked to let the photographer back in.

Seth had made her feel special in a way no man had before. He valued her opinion and listened to her when she talked. The only other man to ever do that had been her brother and that was solely because she was the only one on the ranch for him to talk to.

Seth returned and they were posed once again in front of the altar. The photographer had them smile at the camera and then asked them to face each other. Lynn looked up into Seth's eyes and knew she'd made the right decision. Despite the fact that Seth wasn't from her hometown, he was solid and dependable and she needed both.

# Seven

Nearly an hour later, Lynn still hadn't recovered her equilibrium. Seth's cousins Paul and Michael were two brothers who seemed ill at ease in her presence. But were genuinely fond of Seth. The brothers were at least five years older than her new husband.

"Congratulations on your marriage," Paul said.

"You're getting a great guy," Michael said.

They embraced Seth in turn, and when they all were seated, Seth ordered a bottle of champagne. Paul and Michael treated her with respect and called her ma'am. And though Seth said they were related to him, she could see little resemblance. Aside from the fact that you had a feeling these two didn't lose many fights and neither did Seth.

Paul was the more outgoing of the two and kept her entertained with stories of the showgirls he knew. Lynn had a moment's realization that there was an entire world of which she knew nothing about.

It also made her realize that Seth's life in Chicago was probably as different from Montana and her daily routine as showgirls and slot machines. Doubt assailed her. Had she taken the easy way out of her problems instead of making a logical decision?

A waitress came and took their order and Lynn was surprised when Paul ordered in French. Ruefully she reminded herself not to make snap judgments. A quick glance at Seth showed he knew that Paul had surprised her.

After the waitress had left, conversation flowed around the table. Lynn tried to keep track of it but had a hard time focusing. So much had happened in the last thirty-six hours. This was the first time she'd sat down, and suddenly she was overwhelmed.

Michael got a page before they'd ordered dessert and made a quick call on his cell phone, after which both brothers soon excused themselves.

Lynn was disappointed to see them go for two reasons. Firstly because Seth seemed so relaxed around them, as if he forgot his troubles for just a little while—something he hadn't been able to do in her presence. And secondly, the brothers were a barrier between her and her new husband. The man who warned her not to buy into the illusion and then said things like "Fate wants us to be together."

"Paul and Michael are an interesting pair. Are you close to them?" she asked.

"I fly out here twice a year to see them. We roamed the streets together as youths."

"What does that mean?"

"Skipping school."

"What was that like?"

"It was incredibly scary when I was eight. But then by the time I turned nine it wasn't so bad."

She couldn't imagine any mother leaving her child alone for that amount of time, especially at so young an age. "Didn't your mother object?"

"No. She was busy."

"Working?"

"I guess you could call it that. She does whatever my uncle tells her to. They told her I'd be okay with Paul and Michael and she believed them."

"Were you?"

"Yes. The three of us always got along."

She sipped her cappuccino and tried not to let Seth seep past any further barriers. But it was hard. The more she learned about him the harder it was to resist him physically and emotionally. There was a maternal part of her that wanted to cradle him in her arms and comfort the small boy who'd been cast out alone. But then there was the elemental woman who wanted to cradle him in a totally different way. He confused her.

Closing her eyes, she tried to come up with something to say that wouldn't make him more appealing.

That wouldn't reveal more of the man who didn't seem to fit his world-weary image.

"I have a silly question," she said.

"Go ahead."

"Why are Paul's and Michael's shoulders so big? I'd think it was genetic but yours aren't that large. I've seen wrestlers who'd look puny next to them." Paul and Michael both had dark hair and a muscular build.

"Should I be offended?"

She blushed. "I didn't mean you looked small."

"Lynn, you're going to give me a complex."

"I doubt it."

"I don't," he said, meeting her gaze. His eyes promised darkly sensual things.

"Tell me about your cousins."

"Most of it is muscle and the rest is a shoulder holster."

"I can't believe your cousins are in law enforcement."

"More like enforcement."

"I don't understand."

"They work for a loan shark. And when people don't pay up, they track them down."

"Not exactly a tame line of work."

"No, it isn't."

He stared at the seats vacated by his cousins as if seeing someone who wasn't there. "Sometimes I wonder if I wouldn't have been happier leading that kind of life."

"I can't imagine you being satisfied working for someone else."

"I do every time I enter a courtroom."

"Yes, but you do it on your own terms."

"So do they."

"But your code of honor would be tarnished, Seth."

"Do you really think I have a code of honor?"

"I wouldn't be in Vegas with you if you didn't."

"Thank you."

Though she'd been warned she felt reality and illusion meld as the jazz trio played "Our Love Is Here To Stay" while Seth paid the bill. She looked at Seth, feeling the world tip on its axis, and saw not the boy she'd had a crush on, not the man who'd walked into her diner a couple of days earlier, but the man she'd married and who'd come to mean more to her than she'd ever imagined he would.

Lifting Lynn into his arms as the elevator doors closed softly behind them wasn't something his mind ordered but something his gut did. There was an emotion in her dark violet eyes that made him want to be the Prince Charming he saw mirrored there. Even if he knew it was only an illusion.

Seth knew he was going to pay for this night for a long time. He'd originally fooled himself into marrying Lynn by pretending he could make her his in name only. As he shifted her in his arms to carry her across the threshold of their suite, he knew he couldn't.

"Why are you carrying me?" she asked, her breath fanning his neck and starting a chain reaction that ended in his groin.

"For luck?" Maybe if he said it out loud his body would believe it. But he knew good fortune was the last reason why he was holding her in his arms. Raging lust beat it hands down.

He'd already crossed boundaries that he shouldn't have. He'd already taken steps that would drive Matt from his life. He'd already condemned himself, he thought. And the boy who'd been raised to believe that the law was something to be skated around asked himself, why not go all the way?

But for all her spunkiness, there was something innocent about Lynn McCoy, and he wasn't about to destroy it. He didn't want to do whatever that stockbroker on his way to Los Angeles had done to her. He somehow wanted to be better than he really was for her.

The fire that she'd lit in his body hadn't been extinguished by anything as mundane as dinner and conversation. Her insight and keen understanding had in fact fanned the flames. For the first time he felt like he knew who the real Seth Connelly was, and that scared him because it felt as though he'd only found the knowledge with Lynn.

She wouldn't stay.

Women never did.

Especially once he started needing them.

He knew then that he could never need Lynn. Already she affected him more strongly than anyone else he'd dated before. This insanity had to end, he thought, before it destroyed them both. But he was just a man. And temptation was stronger tonight.

"I've always dreamed of being carried by a strong, handsome man." She looked up at him with stars in her eyes. With her slender fingers she caressed his neck and jaw. Involuntarily he clenched it.

He'd never been touched by a woman except for sex. Lynn's touch now was a caress that was foreign to him and he resented that.

He didn't want to feel, but she made his emotions churn like never before. First he was her brother's best friend, then hers, then he was the man who could rescue the ranch. But the man he could never be was her husband.

There was nothing he wouldn't give to be just that man right now. He shifted her again, realizing how fragile she was in his arms. Realizing the precious gift she'd given him when she'd agreed to marry him. Realizing that despite his physical strength, at this moment the real power was in her hands.

Those strong, slender hands that touched him so softly. Like he was a man who'd never seen the seamier side of life. Like he was a man who'd fulfill her dreams. Like he was a man who could be a hero—her hero.

Damn. She tempted him. She lay so trustingly in

his arms, watching him with that intent gaze that reminded him that she'd been on an emotional roller coaster since the moment they'd met. Her breast was less than an inch from his fingers and though he knew he shouldn't, he caressed her on the sly, the way he would have palmed treasure from a store in his youthful shoplifting days.

She wrapped her arms around his neck. "If you say so. Are you sure this is all just for luck?"

He knew there was more than luck involved with him carrying her. But no one liked to look too closely at their own weaknesses. He was no different.

"What else could there be?" he asked carefully. He'd tried to bank his desire for her and stop touching the full globe of her breast. But knew that he'd done a poor job of it.

Probably because he wasn't paying as close attention to that detail as he should. But when he closed his eyes, all he saw was the way she'd shuddered with her climax in his arms.

"I don't know. But it might have something to do with the way you're touching me," she said.

He hesitated outside their suite door, feeling her nipple bead under his fingers that had wandered farther than they should have. He'd give up his fancy car, his career as a lawyer and the Connelly name to have her naked in his arms. He should be getting out the key card, carrying her over the threshold and taking a very cold shower. Instead he looked into her eyes and saw desire mirrored there. Saw need and hunger and couldn't quite stop so soon.

"How am I touching you?" he asked, brushing a butterfly kiss against her hairline.

"I'm not sure," she said, though her fingers in his hair belied her words, as did her lips against his neck and the teasing brush of her teeth against his skin.

He shuddered. They had to get out of the hallway. He had to get her out of his arms before he did something he'd regret even longer than he regretted the fact that he'd never really be a Connelly, even if his father had invited him into the fold.

"What does it feel like?" he asked against her ear. She shivered and squirmed in his arms. He wished he could see her responses.

"A fantasy. Something I can't touch in the light of day."

That was who he was. The shadow master. A man at home in the dark but not the bright light of day. "Then let's have this night."

"Can we?" she asked.

"You have to ask for what you want." He should stop flirting with her but couldn't help it. The heat of her body seared his skin and he knew he'd never be the same.

"I thought nothing was real here."

"Nothing is, except you and me." Since when had he ever been able to protect someone he cared for?

When had he ever been able to protect himself from someone he cared for? He knew then that he had to proceed carefully with Lynn. Despite the lust raging through his body he had to force his mind to take charge before it was too late.

"Then why am I trembling?" she asked.

He had no idea why. He shuddered because his control was razor thin and the only thing keeping him from stepping over the edge was the thought of losing the only family he'd ever felt a part of. "Because this is real."

"Is it?" she asked, pulling his head toward hers. He knew that the fantasy they'd woven around themselves couldn't last, wouldn't even withstand the faint light of dawn. But there was no power on earth that could keep him from tasting her again, from sating a thirst he'd never realized he had until he'd met her again.

He lowered his head, knowing this had to be the last time he gave in to temptation. But maybe just for tonight, he thought, he could forget reason and illusion. Forget Connelly and McCoy. Forget everything but this tempting woman in his arms.

The wine she'd consumed with dinner had to be to blame for the feelings coursing through her now. There was no reasonable explanation why she couldn't decipher between fact and fiction, but at this moment the line was blurred. She knew only that Seth looked real.

He felt real, too, strong and solid under her hands. His mouth against hers was more exciting than any she'd experienced before. She knew better than to trust her instincts where men were concerned. But she was a new bride and entitled to a wedding night.

Seth's mouth brushed against hers lightly. Just a breath of a touch. She forgot for a moment why Seth wasn't her forever man, because since he'd come back to Montana he seemed different. He'd certainly learned more about how to kiss a woman.

She longed for a deeper contact. Longed for his body pressed to hers. Longed for something she wasn't sure she should ask him for.

She parted her lips and skimmed her tongue over his bottom lip. He groaned deep in his throat—the sound primordial—sending shivers of awareness down her spine. She needed him.

He reciprocated, running his tongue around her mouth then dipping inside for a more intimate taste. He thrust deeply, claiming her for his own, not raising his head until she'd forgotten where they were.

He lifted her into his arms and swept her over the threshold. The room was dimly lit and the night seemed shrouded in fantasy. Never had she craved the chimera more.

''Don't wake me up if this is a dream,'' she said, not realizing she'd spoken until Seth set her on her feet in the bedroom.

Cupping her jaw in his large hands, he said, ''I won't.''

The words sounded like a promise. But she knew better than to believe a man's word when he held her in his arms. Seth's words sounded true, but in her heart she knew they weren't.

Seth walked to the windows and pulled back the draperies. Their twentieth-floor room was filled with the lights of the city. They illuminated Seth's profile. He seemed tough and alone as he stood there staring down at the street and lights.

He didn't move, just stood there. "Seth?"

"I don't want to force anything on you, Lynn."

She walked to him. His spicy masculine scent assailed her. "You aren't."

"I need you tonight," he said, the words raw as if torn from someplace deep inside him.

"I need you, too," she said, and knew those words for the truth they were.

He started to say something else, but she covered his mouth with her palm. "Enough talk. I'm ready for some action."

His eyes widened above her hand. He carefully bit the fleshy part of her palm, which still covered his mouth. The touch sent the forerunners of desire through her body, making her realize how much she wanted him.

She knew she wasn't the most attractive woman in the world, but when he touched her like that, his eyes dancing over her with a heat that could burn, feminine awareness flooded her and she knew that she was meant to be with him.

She pushed his tuxedo jacket off his shoulders. It hit the floor with a swish. He raised one eyebrow but she only smiled seductively at him and removed his bow tie. The studs on the front of his shirt were next, and when she reached his waistband she didn't hesitate.

She slid her hand down the placket of his pants, feeling the zipper beneath her fingers and the masculine hardness underneath.

He sucked in a breath and held it. She fondled him through the cloth of his trousers. Never had touching a man excited her so much. Languidly, she popped the snap at his waistband and slowly slid the zipper down.

"You're killing me," he said between his teeth.

"I know," she replied with a small grin.

She removed the remaining studs from his tuxedo shirt and stood back. A small wedge of masculine chest was visible between the parted edges, revealing tanned skin and a light dusting of hair. His opened pants defined his erection. She shivered, realizing that this sexy, virile man was hers for the night.

"Come here, vixen, and finish what you started," he said.

She returned to him and he pulled her close, bending to take her mouth in a kiss so deep and carnal, her mouth melted into his, and it was impossible to tell where one of them began and the other ended.

A hollow longing pulsed through her—the need to be filled with him, the compulsion to be connected to him in every way imaginable.

He caressed her back, releasing the side zipper of

her dress as he went. He lifted his head. "I've been wanting to do this since I first saw you in this."

Tugging on each sleeve, he pulled the dress away from her body and let it pool at her feet. She should have felt awkward, standing in front of him in heels, thigh-high hose and white lace panties, but the warmth in his eyes kept those feelings at bay.

He ripped his shirt off, flung it to the floor and pulled her to him. His chest was warm and solid against her. The hair stimulated her nipples. He kissed her again, his body moving against hers in need.

He pushed her back on the bed but didn't follow her. Instead he stood above her, watching her body in the shadows. She felt exposed. Her nipples were hard and her panties damp. She wanted him so badly that the separation made her feel vulnerable.

"Scoot back," he said.

She did as he asked.

"Stretch your arms out to each side."

"What are you going to give me if I do it?" she asked, to even the odds.

"Pleasure beyond your dreams."

She positioned her arms as he'd asked. He knelt on the bed over her, one tuxedo-clad leg on either side of her nylon-covered ones. Resting on his haunches, he touched her from crown to panties and back again, first with his gaze, then with the lightest brush of his fingertips. It was just a teasing caress that was gone before she realized it was there, all the way down her body to the waistband of her underpants.

Then his mouth took over. The wet heat engulfed her and had her writhing on the bed. She was consumed by him. Surrounded by him. Taken to another plane where only the two of them existed.

He dropped love bites on her neck and then he reached her breast. He paused and she glanced down at him. Her nipple was a firm berry right next to his mouth. His mouth was so close she could feel each exhalation over her aroused flesh, but still he made no move to take her into his mouth.

"Seth?"

"Waiting heightens the pleasure," he said. He was right, but she felt as if she was going to explode.

She lifted her arms and clasped his head in her hands. His hair was rich and luxuriant. Arching her body, she brushed her nipple against his mouth. He resisted at first but then with a moan, opened his lips and sucked lightly.

His touch assuaged the immediate hunger she felt, but then an even stronger one built in its place. He suckled her so strongly, as if he was finding a sustenance that only she could give him. She slid her hands down his back, burrowing her fingers under his pants and briefs, to caress his backside.

He treated her other breast to the same caress, then leaned back and blew softly on each. Her nipples tightened painfully.

"Seth, I need you."

"Soon," he promised. He continued his journey down her body, his tongue tickling her belly button and his teeth nipping at her stomach. He traced the edge of her panties with his lips and then pulled them down her body with his teeth.

When he reached her feet he watched her again. Lynn's hands moved restlessly on the bedcover and her body writhed, needing to be filled by him.

Seth stood and pushed his pants and briefs off in one motion. He grabbed a condom from the nightstand and quickly sheathed himself. He climbed onto the bed from the bottom and slid carefully up her body. His heat enfolded her before his limbs did. He held her so closely that she felt protected by him.

Then his mouth took hers and she felt ravaged, plundered, as if all her secrets were revealed to him. She wanted—no, needed—to back away from him, but he left her nowhere to turn except his arms.

He touched her with passion that demanded she respond to him. And she did, arching off the bed into the touch of his fingers as they stroked her most feminine place. "You're so beautiful when you blossom. Do it for me again now that I can feel it."

He found the bud that was the center of her desire and pressed in a circular motion with his thumb. He inserted first one finger into her body then a second. Returning to her breast, he suckled with powerful motions, and she was powerless to resist the tide that rose in her and swept through her.

His mouth and hands worked in harmony and brought her out of herself. Her entire body tightened and she cried out as pinpoints of light danced beneath her eyes. Then she clung to Seth, urging him up and over her. Needing him to meld with her. Needing him to fill her. Needing him to be vulnerable in the same way she was.

He raised himself slightly from her. She held his shoulders and realized that sweat covered his back. He'd paid a price for his restraint. Slowly he entered her, an aching inch at a time. His eyes met hers and once he was fully seated, he leaned down, his pectorals resting against her breasts, his mouth against her neck and his hands entwined with hers. He rocked slowly, building the fire in her again with each thrust of his hips.

He pulled all the way out with each thrust and then slid home. His mouth left her neck and he thrust his tongue deep into her mouth. The rocking motions of his body, the thrusting of his hips and tongue swiftly built her to the pinnacle again.

She arched frantically against him, searching for the release only he could give.

"Come on. Together this time," he said.

His hands left hers and he grasped her hips, holding them still for his thrusts. They went so deep she felt as if he'd touched her soul. When she again climbed to the stars, she knew that he had too, as pinpoints of light flashed behind her eyes and his groan of completion filled her ears.

# Eight

Seth woke to the bright sun spilling in the windows and the phone ringing in his ears. The pillow next to him was empty, and he heard the shower in the distance. He grabbed the phone and answered it.

"Connelly," he said.

"It's Dad. I got your message, what's up?"

His father had a tone of voice that always made him feel as if he was being called on the carpet and without fail sent him back to those first weeks when he'd arrived at the Connelly household. "I got married last night."

His father sighed. "To whom?"

"Lynn McCoy."

"Are you sure about this, son?"

Seth thought about it carefully. Grant rarely called him son. He never knew how to take his Dad.

"Her ranch was in danger of foreclosure. I couldn't let that happen. The McCoys are like family to me."

"I understand."

"How's everything back home? I'd like to stay in Montana for a few more weeks but I can fly back to Chicago if you need me to."

"No need for that. Enjoy your new bride."

"It's not that kind of marriage, Dad."

"I didn't realize there were different kinds."

"There are. How's Charlotte Masters doing?"

"Rafe has Charlotte living with him to protect her and her baby. He told us that he's the baby's father."

His brother was going to be a father. Somehow that news made Seth long for things he knew he'd never have. "Dad, I'm sorry for my family's part in this mess."

"It's no more your fault than it is mine," Grant said.

Seth wondered if his father ever regretted having a son with Angie Donahue; if he ever regretted the affair that had brought Seth to life. Those thoughts were a big part of the reason why Seth had left Chicago. And only after he knew the answers would he feel comfortable returning.

He said his goodbyes and hung up the phone only to realize that the suite was very quiet. Rolling over, he saw Lynn standing in the doorway leading to the bathroom. She wore the thick terry robe provided by the hotel.

He smiled at her but she didn't smile back.

"Uh, that was my dad."

"I heard."

"How long were you standing there?"

"Long enough to be reminded that this is an illusion," she said, turning away and closing the bathroom door behind her.

"Dammit, Lynn. I didn't lie to you."

She didn't answer. He got out of bed and went to the bathroom door and tried the handle. It was locked.

"Come out and let's talk about this."

"As soon as I'm dressed."

"You're covered in that robe."

"Not enough."

"What's that supposed to mean?"

"Whatever you take it to mean, Seth. I just don't want to encourage intimacy between us."

"There already is intimacy between us."

"No there isn't. That was lust, Seth. Plain old-fashioned lust."

"Don't say it as if it were gone."

"Believe me it is."

He stalked to the bed and pulled on his pants. He wished the door wasn't between them.

"What happened this morning?" he asked quietly through the door.

"I heard you say it's 'not that kind of marriage.' What kind of marriage is it?"

"It's a business arrangement."

"Where we sleep with each other? Because that makes me feel cheap."

"No, it's not that at all. Lynn, come out so I can see you."

"No," she said. He heard the sound of tears in her voice and cursed himself for the bastard he was.

He'd known better than to give in to the temptation that was Lynn but had anyway and now he'd pay the price. And so would she. "The last thing I wanted was to hurt you."

"You warned me when we got here."

"That wasn't just an illusion last night."

"But it was. I'm tired of Las Vegas, Seth. Can we go home?"

"Yes," he said. He'd give her anything to make up for the hurt he'd unwittingly caused.

Lynn had never thought a few hours could feel so long. But by the time they landed in Montana she was more than ready to interact with other people, even if it was only the skycap who collected their bags. She tipped him while Seth went to get the car.

She shivered as she stepped outside. A cool breeze blew, making her wish she had a heavier jacket on. A light dusting of snow was falling and Lynn tilted her head back to watch it. Around her, people hurried and a cool breeze blew, but she only watched the snow, knowing soon the land would be covered in a pristine white that made it look innocent.

But despite what she'd always believed, she knew that innocence once lost could never be reclaimed. Her anger at Seth was superficial. She was really angry with herself. Watching the snow, she knew that she'd tried to keep him from realizing how much of herself she'd revealed.

But there'd been something in his eyes on the plane that made her realize he knew how vulnerable she was right now. And so he was treading lightly.

The Jaguar coasted to a stop in front of her and the trunk popped open before Seth got out of the car. She started to lift her bag but Seth glared at her. "Get in the car, Lynn."

She realized she may have gone too far earlier and wished there was some way she could go back in time and stay in the shower longer. If she hadn't overheard Seth's conversation, she'd still believe her hasty marriage could last.

But time travel wasn't an option. Besides, Lynn was a big girl. This wasn't the first time she'd taken a gamble on a man and come up empty.

"I'll admit that I haven't always been at my best with you," Seth said as he climbed into the car and put it in gear. "But I've always treated you with respect."

"Yes, you have."

He nodded and concentrated on his driving. She realized she'd offended his honor. This man was so complex, she thought. She knew that if she pushed hard enough she'd find a man who could love; knew that if she was willing to take the risk, Seth Connelly could be her dream man. But she wasn't sure she was tough enough to reach his heart without being hurt in return. One thing was for certain: she owed him an apology, but wasn't sure where to start.

"Hungry?" he asked after twenty minutes had passed. She stared at his profile. She could maintain her anger or get over it. And when she thought of the future, she didn't want to imagine her and Seth fighting.

"A little."

"I think there's a fast-food joint up ahead. Feel like cardboard burgers and cold fries?"

"That's fine.... Seth?"

"Yes," he said without looking at her.

"I overreacted this morning."

He pulled the car onto the shoulder and put it in park. "No, you didn't."

"Yes. I shouldn't have been eavesdropping and I certainly shouldn't have jumped to conclusions where you're concerned. You're a family friend who's done me a tremendous favor."

"I'd like to think I'm more than a family friend."

"Are you sure? Because earlier when you spoke to your father it didn't seem that way."

"Things with my family are complicated."

"Does it have to do with why you came to Montana in the first place?" she asked. She tried to turn the conversation away from her, because, knowing that she meant nothing to Seth, she'd be mortified if he realized how much he meant to her.

He nodded.

"Tell me. Is there anything I can do to help?"

"I doubt it," he said.

She recoiled, knowing she'd been tricked again. Knotting her hands on her lap, she promised herself this was the last time. How many times was she going to play the fool before she wised up? "My mistake."

His hand covered both of hers on her lap. "I didn't mean it that way. Damn, I'm no good when it comes to talking, but believe me when I tell you that it isn't you."

"Then what is it, Seth?"

"My mother has betrayed the Connellys once again. She's part of the Kelly crime family and she set my family up. This time involving me in her scheme."

"I'm sorry," she said. Her heart ached. The last thing Seth should have done was take on her burden of the ranch and now this marriage. He had enough problems of his own. Over the years she'd heard little about Seth's family, knowing only that he was the illegitimate child of a wealthy man. But she didn't realize the implication of being a child of that union.

He rubbed her hands in an affectionate gesture. "Thanks. But it taught me something that I should have already learned."

She waited. But he didn't speak. She glanced up at him. "What did you learn?"

"That I'm not meant for love."

"Don't be silly."

"I'm not. I believed my mother's lies when she came to see me, and good people were put into danger—even a pregnant woman. How am I supposed to handle the fact that I wanted so desperately to believe my mother wanted a relationship with me that I overlooked certain half-truths she told?"

"She's your mother. Of course you want to believe the best in her."

"Women lie," he said.

Her heart stopped for a minute. His words revealed something she didn't even realize he was hiding. It wasn't just his mother he didn't trust, or her, but all womankind for the betrayal that had started in his youth.

"What about your sisters?"

"They do it, too."

"I haven't lied to you, Seth."

He shook his head. She knew he couldn't trust her. She'd hurt him; he'd hurt her. Together the only thing they'd done right was their lovemaking, and even that had turned into a mistake.

She shook her head. "Let's go get that food you promised me."

"I don't want to leave this unsettled between us."

"One of us is going to have to trust the other for our relationship to change."

"I do trust you."

"To leave you someday," she said.

He didn't respond, only put the car back in gear and pulled back onto the desolate highway. In her heart she knew what she had to do if she wanted Seth Connelly in her life. She had to teach him that love wasn't a minus, but the biggest plus you could have on your side.

They arrived at the ranch just before lunchtime. There were three pickups in the yard; voices spilled from the windows of the bunkhouse and a new herd of cattle roamed the pasture. One lone cowboy wandered in from the range and headed for the bunkhouse.

"Where did all these people come from?" she asked.

"I hired them. Isn't it nice to see the ranch full of life again?" Seth asked as he helped Lynn from the car.

She shouldered her own bag and led the way to the house. Using her key, she opened the front door and was met by the scent of simmering stew. The hardwood floor under their feet had been polished and a new runner led the way to the stairs.

"But what's going on?" Lynn asked.

"I made some arrangements to start the ranch back down the path to its former success, which included hiring a new housekeeper/cook. I've also hired back as many hands as I could and ordered more cattle. The few you saw when we drove up are just the first shipment.''

She dropped her bag on the floor and stood in the sunlight that spilled through the glass pane next to the front door, hands on her hips. "Thank you for making these arrangements. But it'll be a while before we can afford these kinds of changes. I mean, the little I had saved up to pay the bank will only cover two hands' wages for a month."

Seth hung his coat in the closet and then helped Lynn out of her coat. She looked the way he always pictured her in boots, a western shirt and faded jeans that clung to her long legs like a second skin. He knew that after this morning she wouldn't let him back into her bed, but he longed to be there even though he knew that he'd made a tactical error in sleeping with her. His body didn't care about that, and he adjusted his stance to give his erection some room.

"You married a rich man."

She took the coat from him and hung it herself. "That doesn't have anything to do with the McCoy Ranch. I still intend to pay back the money I owe you."

"We're married now. There is no yours and mine, only ours."

"If we were really married, I'd be the first to agree to that. But we aren't."

"I have a piece of paper in my pocket that says differently."

"But you told your family it wasn't that kind of marriage."

"Are you going to remember that forever?"

"You said it this morning. I'm not going to fool myself again, Seth. You wanted a business arrangement and that's what we've got."

"Be reasonable. The ranch is too big for you to handle. I only want to help."

"I was getting by."

"And working yourself to death. I'm only helping you out until you get back on your feet. Give the changes I've made a chance. If you don't like them, I'll put everything back to the way it was."

"Are there more changes than cattle and ranch hands?" she asked.

She started walking through the house, pausing in the living room to take in the changes. Finally she reached the kitchen where the wallpaper had been replaced and a new countertop installed. The floor had been buffed and refinished. The room resembled the one from Seth's memory and he was pleased with the work that had been done.

Coming up behind her, he said, "I had some craftsmen come out and repair the house as well."

She pivoted to face him. "We were barely gone a day and a half."

He shrugged. He'd thought the changes would make her happy. In fact, he'd almost forgotten he'd made the calls before they'd left for Vegas. With fire in her eyes and her hair hanging down her back, she enticed him, but he knew better than to come close this time. He'd hurt her this morning and he had a feeling it would take a lot for her to trust him again.

"I get results," he said with a shrug.

"I didn't count on this. There's no way I can pay you back for everything you've done."

He crossed to her. "I'm not looking for repayment."

"This is what I was trying to avoid. Things are worse now than when we left for Vegas."

"Do you really believe that?" he asked, because this was the first time he'd reacted from the gut and he'd hoped she'd be pleased.

"I don't know what I think anymore. This is too much. I wasn't expecting all these changes. I'm not sure I belong here."

"This is the only place you do belong."

"What about you?"

"I haven't found that place where I belong but when I find it I'll do whatever is necessary to keep it."

"It would be easier for me to accept all the work on the ranch if I thought you were going to stay here."

"I can't," he said, knowing that if he remained he'd forget that Lynn couldn't be his forever and eventually she'd lie to him and he'd have to move on.

She shook her head. "I know. I guess I'm just cranky. I need some air."

Seth watched her walk away, wishing things could

be different but knowing they couldn't. If he was ever going to have a night's rest again, he needed to make sure that Lynn was safe and secure. He never wanted her to have to worry about losing the ranch again. And if it took every penny he had in the bank, then he'd use them.

# Nine

Lynn walked out of the house as fast as she could. That Seth thought nothing had changed between them made her want to scream. But she didn't do the part of the enraged woman really well, so instead she settled for leaving before she said something she'd regret.

The changes in the ranch were alarming. But the barn was soothingly familiar with scents and sounds she'd smelled and heard since childhood. The barn was dim, scant sunlight filtering through the open door.

"Can I help you, ma'am?" said one of the new ranch hands.

"No, thank you."

"Name's Bill if you need anything," he said, and went back to the tack he'd been repairing.

She hadn't noticed him in the shadows, but the evidence of his presence was there in the room. She skirted by him, grabbing her tack and leaving quickly. She saddled Thor and mounted him.

Riding out of the barn, she felt her control slipping. She wished that Seth was really her husband so that she could talk to him about these changes. So that she could find a way to make him understand that she needed to be a part of the ranch, the way it was a part of her.

The hustle and bustle of the ranch around her told her she wasn't necessary to the daily chores, and that made her sad. Since Matt had left and her parents died, she'd been the lifeblood of this place, but suddenly she wasn't anymore.

Three ranch hands looked at her as she rode past them, each tipping their hats to her. Did they know she was their boss?

Was she, really? Or did Seth have something else in mind? She clicked to Thor as soon as they were past the last gate and he took off. Only when the wind was rushing through her hair and the sun beating on her neck did she let the tears flow freely down her face.

Thor stopped under a copse of trees near a small pond. It was her thinking place. She and Matt would sneak out here when they were children to talk and swim. It was, she realized as she dismounted, the place where she'd shared her first kiss with Seth.

She walked quietly around the tree, swamped by images of the past. She remembered the way things used to be but could never be again. Remembered Seth as a boy and now more intensely as a man. Her man, she'd thought. But maybe not.

The sound of a galloping horse got her attention, and she watched a rider approach from the same direction she'd come from. The man was tall with dark hair and no hat. She knew instinctively that it was Seth. Part of her—the girl who'd given her money to a con man—rejoiced at the fact that he'd followed her. But a more sensible part—the girl who'd been left with a bankrupted ranch—knew that he had to have a reason.

He slowed the horse to a stop in front of her and sat there watching her for a few minutes. The silence was uncomfortable but she didn't want to break it.

"Can I join you?"

She shrugged.

"I brought offerings with me."

He dismounted and began removing containers and a blanket from his saddlebags. He'd brought lunch, she realized.

She helped him settle the blanket on the ground under the tree, and they opened the containers of food. She set a place for them with the picnic dinnerware and cutlery he'd brought. Coming from Seth, this wasn't a ham sandwich and Coke picnic, but a wine, cheese, fruit and crackers meal.

He poured them both a glass of wine and then leaned back against the trunk of the oak that provided shade for them. "Want to talk about it?"

"The ranch?"

He shook his head. "Whatever is bothering you."

"I don't know where to start."

He just sipped his wine and ate a piece of cheese, waiting for her to find the words to tell him her troubles. Waiting for her to bare her soul to him. Waiting, it seemed, to rescue her once again.

"I don't like change," she finally said.

"I can understand that. But change isn't a bad thing, you know."

"For me it is. Every change that has happened in my life has brought about some sort of worsening circumstances."

"Remember the luck I was talking to you about on our wedding night?"

She nodded.

"I think your fortune is changing, Lynn."

"I feel so…"

"Scared? Alone?"

"Silly," she said.

"You could never be silly."

"Thanks. And I mean for everything you've done."

"I should have asked you first before I instigated so many changes."

"I would have protested."

"Arguing with you is half the fun," he said.

He stared up at the branches of the tree. A cool breeze blew through the air, causing her to shiver a little. He lifted his arm in silent invitation for her to join him. She slid closer to him, snuggling into the warmth of his body.

"I've visited this place many times in my memory," he said.

"We had some fun out here during those summers you stayed with us," she said softly.

"We did, but that's not why I remember this place," he said.

"It's not?" She hoped he remembered their first kiss.

"You know it's not. Childish pranks pale in comparison to a lovely blond-haired beauty."

"Oh, Seth."

"I've never forgotten that evening. The stars shone so brightly, your hair was free, like it is today, and you came into my embrace with all the eagerness and passion with which you do everything."

He tilted her face up to his. "I don't want you thinking I'm a bad change."

Before she could respond, he lowered his head, blocking out the sun. All she could do was respond to this man who'd already claimed her body. She had a feeling that her heart was next.

Seth lingered over her mouth but pulled back before things went too far. Not physically but emotionally. The changes that Lynn had spoken of were external ones, but he knew their marriage and intimacy had been just as hard for her to adjust to. "I didn't come out here to make love to you."

"You didn't?" she asked, all sassy woman, confident of her appeal to the man she was with.

"I wanted to see why you were out here alone. To make sure you weren't hiding."

"I wasn't hiding. Just running from the truth, I guess."

He knew what that was like. Though he wouldn't admit it to a soul, he'd been running since he was twelve. And he knew it deep inside. "Maybe I've given you a reason to stop."

"Am I reason enough for you to stop running?" she asked.

"What?" He scooted away from her, not sure what she was trying to ask him.

"You've been using this ranch in Montana as a place to hide from your family for as long as I've known you. Has it helped?"

He thought about it. His first instinct was to bluster around and make sure she knew that he wasn't running from anything. Cowards ran. He didn't.

"I'm not running," he said firmly. He wasn't about to let Lynn draw him into an emotional discussion. She was the one with the adjustment problems, not him. He was well adjusted, at least most of the time.

"My mistake. It's just when someone shows up

unexpected with hardly a bag packed, it might seem like he left unexpectedly...maybe when he sensed trouble.''

''Are you calling me a chicken?'' He reacted with anger—the safer of the emotions funneling through his body like a winter runoff out of control.

''Never. A person might see it differently if they didn't know you as well as I do.''

''Well, sweetheart, you need an updated lesson.'' He wasn't sure why she thought she could beat him in a war of words. He was a lawyer, words were his lifeblood.

''Teach me.''

He'd like to teach her something. She seemed so smug in her summation of his life. As if she knew everything there was to know about him.

''I doubt you could be taught.''

She leaned across the blanket and cupped his jaw. That one touch was so soothing, so intimate in light of their conversation that he shivered under it. He wasn't going to let her manipulate him.

''Tell me,'' she said. She was his own personal Siren sent to call him to the rocks.

And like a man, he followed the sweet sound of her voice and found himself talking about stuff he never discussed. Not even with his half siblings. ''I told you about my mother. You don't know what it's like to have to take responsibility for a mess your parent has made. To know that you helped make the mess because you hoped maybe this time she was sincere when she said she needed to be near her child.''

She watched him with those big eyes, focusing so intently on him that the words seemed to flow from someplace deep inside where he'd always hidden them. ''Then my dad sent me to military school. And it was so different from the world I'd known.''

''Oh, Seth.''

''No pity. I don't want that.''

''I understand.''

''You can't possibly, because you think I took the easy way out and left Chicago. But I couldn't stay. I couldn't let my mother use me against the Connellys.''

''You wouldn't let yourself be used that way.''

''I don't know. My mother, even though I see her infrequently, is still a big influence.''

''How?'' she asked.

''I've never understood why she left me with my dad when I was twelve.''

Lynn crawled across the blanket and embraced him. She held him so close that Seth couldn't remember a time when she wasn't in his arms. Her scent— flowers and sunshine—surrounded him and made him feel safer than he'd ever felt. He'd never had security, but he'd created it for himself. And suddenly this woman, his wife, was showing him that what he'd created was only an illusion.

''Sometimes love means letting go,'' she said

softly. "Your mom probably saw a better future for you with the Connellys."

"I don't know. I think she tired of having to be responsible for another person."

"Could be. But I think it's time for you to let go of your mom and the past."

"I don't know if I can."

"Only you can decide. But remember that it took a lot for me to trust a man again."

"Me?"

"Yes, you. There's no one else I would have accepted help from."

"That's because I wouldn't take no for an answer."

"Details, details."

She led him to a safe middle ground, and he followed her willingly. But he didn't like the shift in power. Until this moment he'd been in control both of his life and their future. But something had shifted. And he was ready for it to shift back.

Leaning closer to her, he claimed her mouth again. He knew that one taste wasn't going to be enough to sate his thirst. And that scared him more than anything in his life ever had.

Having Lynn in his arms was more temptation than he could bear. Even knowing that he couldn't return to Chicago without her wasn't enough to keep him from kissing her. The touch of her lips was healing balm on his bare soul.

He didn't examine it too deeply. The blood rushing through his veins demanded he make love to her. Demanded he claim her as his woman. Demanded he take her now before she realized that he wasn't good enough to be her man.

The wind ruffled through the trees and a fish jumped in the lake. He absorbed all of these sounds with a feeling of timelessness. He wasn't Seth Connelly about to make love to Lynn McCoy Connelly. He was man about to claim his woman. Not for a moment, not for convenience—but for all time.

He wanted this moment to be a gentle merging of their bodies, a quiet affirmation of the bond their words had formed. But his soul cried out for immediate gratification.

His hands shook as he undid the buttons of her blouse. Today the sunlight bathed them. There were no shadows to hide in for either one of them. He stripped the clothing from her. With the light pouring onto the branches and dappling her skin, she was illuminated and he knew she was the most beautiful woman he'd ever seen.

The knowledge that she had so profound an effect on him humbled him and made him realize he must never let her have that knowledge.

The body he'd learned by touch he now learned by sight. She was exquisitely formed. Her breasts high and full, her stomach gently curving and the mound at the apex of her thighs covered with blond downy hair.

"I have to touch you," he said.

"Please…"

Starting at her neck, he claimed her for his own. As he swept his hands over her skin so much paler than his, she trembled under his touch. He bent and let his breath warm her skin, blowing gently on the curve of her neck, her breast, her stomach and her center. She shifted restlessly on the blanket.

"Do you want more?"

"Yes," she said.

"Then let me give you everything I am."

He started again at her neck, biting her flesh softly, then soothing her with a small lick. Her pulse accelerated and his own answered. Her skin was an addiction in itself: having had one taste, he couldn't get enough. He slid down, lingering over her full breasts, suckling them and teasing her until her hips left the blanket and her hands clutched the back of his head.

She urged him farther down her body and though his instincts screamed for him to hurry, to take the sweet nectar he'd drawn from her, his control was greater. As was the need to have tasted all of her. To have driven her beyond anything she'd ever experienced. To have made her his in a way that was so complete she'd never leave.

Her stomach and belly button were next and tasted as addicting as her breasts, but he was so close he could smell her arousal, and the need to taste her essence drew him lower. And then lower still until he was crouched between her spread legs.

He rested his cheek against her softness, heard the cry she tried to stifle and looked up at her. Her breasts heaved rapidly with each breath she took. Her hands moved restlessly from the blanket to her stomach and back again. Her hips undulated under him, and he lowered his head slowly.

"Lynn?" he asked, knowing that there was no turning back once he took her this way.

She grasped the back of his head and lifted herself to him. Nothing he'd ever been offered had he craved more.

"Touch me, Seth," she said.

He did. He parted her gently, laying bare the focus of her desire and then bent to lap at her with his tongue. She tasted like a woman—his woman.

She moaned deep in her throat, her hips moving more urgently now. He eased two fingers into her tight sheath and continued working his tongue against her. She gasped his name on each breath, and her hands had left his head, her fingernails digging into his skin with greater strength, until she thrust her hips high against him and cried out.

Her cries echoed in the wind, surrounding him. He didn't bother to remove his shirt or boots. He needed her flesh to surround his. He needed it now.

He freed his erection and thrust into her. He could feel her sheath still throbbing with her climax. Her arms surrounded his shoulders and her hips caught his frantic rhythm. He held her hips, slowing them down, knowing that the pleasure would be more extreme if they had to wait for it.

The small of his back tingled, sweat gathered on his chest and with each thrust her nipples teased him.

"Come on, Seth," she urged. "Faster."

"Not yet," he said between clenched teeth.

"Please…"

He slowed his thrust a margin more. She moaned and attempted to force him deeper. As a punishment he keep his next thrust shallow.

"What are you waiting for?"

"You."

"I don't want to go alone again."

He realized he didn't either. Lacing their fingers together, he glanced down into her eyes. He saw her soul staring back at him. He hoped his wasn't revealed to her.

"Now," he said and pulled completely out of her before driving heavily into her one last time. Buried hilt deep, he started to come. Her body tightened around him and she cried out again. Seth could only answer with her name.

Spent, he rolled onto his back and pulled her with him. They were still joined and he was reluctant to separate them. He pulled a corner of the blanket over them and they lay entwined until the cold and falling darkness drove them back to civilization.

# Ten

"**I** had no idea it would get dark so quickly," Seth said as he rolled the blanket and placed the last empty container in his saddlebags. Twilight spread across the land as the sun dipped behind the mountains. The darkness wasn't total but she knew it wouldn't be long before it was.

"You've never visited in fall before," she said.

He nodded. A breeze ruffled the tree branches and she shivered a little. Winter was definitely on its way.

"Let's go home and sit in front of a fire," Seth said.

"Sounds good."

It sounded better than he could know. She hoped that Seth would find her house his home. That together they'd restore the ranch to its former glory, working together to make it successful, sharing a life filled with love and hard work.

But a part of her doubted he'd stay, knew that he planned to return to Chicago and acknowledged that he needed to. He had to resolve things with his mother and his family. But would he leave her a whole man and return to his family and summer vacations with Matt? Or would he leave her temporarily and return to make his home with her?

That uncertainty dulled the sweet sensations lingering from his lovemaking and the quiet serenity she'd felt being cradled in his arms. Too much was unresolved in their lives. She hoped she wasn't putting her heart in jeopardy by believing in something that didn't exist.

"Good thing the trail back to the house is on flat land," she said, hoping none of her doubts showed on her face.

"I wouldn't let anything happen to you," he said, tugging her to him and holding her so tightly she couldn't breathe. Surrounded by his warmth and his scent, she rubbed her nose against the collar of his jacket and tasted his neck.

"I won't let anything happen to you either," she said. Hope blossomed in her heart, that maybe this time she'd chosen a man who'd stay with her. He dropped a lingering kiss on her mouth.

"We'll have to do this more often," he said, taking a step back. But he held her hand as he led her to her horse. There was a sense of rightness to this time they'd spent together here. The secret she carried in her heart blossomed fully and she realized she loved Seth. Way more than she'd loved Ronnie, who'd taken her money and run for the West Coast. Way more than the land she'd almost lost. It was scary and exciting, humbling and exulting at the same time.

But the girl who'd been left alone wanted to believe that this time she'd found the real thing. But part of Lynn feared she hadn't.

"Will we do it again before you return to Chicago?" she asked, needing some sort of confirmation.

"Hm-mm." He kissed her again and she didn't feel secure by that nonanswer. Seth had said it before: he was a lawyer and he made his living playing with words. Why not use one now?

And why didn't she just ask him? She was scared of the answer but knew that not knowing was worse than his leaving. So she took a deep breath and asked what was on her mind.

"Seth, are you still planning to leave?" she asked, looking up into eyes that were as dark as the land around them.

His fingers tightened on hers and she knew that he wasn't sure. Somehow that lack of security coming from Seth made her feel better.

"I'm not sure," he said.

"That's not the answer I'd like to hear."

"Baby, I know that. It's just…I don't know."

She nodded. It was something. Actually it was

more than a little thing. She knew that Seth was beginning to realize the truth of love. That was why he didn't know where the future would take him.

"Let's go," he said, boosting her into the saddle and mounting his own horse.

Seth moved with the surety of someone raised around horses, though he hadn't been. She knew it was the summers he'd spent here that had given him that confidence and knowledge. It reassured because if he'd retained his horseman's skills, surely he'd retained the other thing her family did very well—love.

Seth was quiet on the ride back. Twilight darkened around them, and shortly the house came into view. It was as if fourteen years had been erased. She remembered the summer Seth had kissed her. They'd done everything together that year: rode the herd, swam, and spent hours talking under the very tree where they'd just made love. She'd felt as if she'd found her true love. But she knew she'd been wrong before. Was she this time?

In the bunkhouse the hands were settling in for the evening meal. Lynn wasn't sure who'd be waiting for her in the house. The barn was empty when they entered, which relieved her.

"Does the housekeeper spend the night?" she asked.

"No, she drives in from town. Her hours are nine to five, but you can change them if you want to." Seth dismounted and started removing his horse's tack.

"Why would I do that?" she asked, doing the same herself.

He took her saddle from her, carrying it to the tack room. "She works for you."

"I don't want to be her boss. I want to work the land and take care of my stock."

"Baby, you don't have to do any of that anymore."

"What do I have to do?"

He scooped her up in his arms and carried her toward the house. "Just keep loving me."

His words echoed what was in her heart, but she had a feeling he was referring to something physical, while what she wanted to give him was more than her body. It was her heart and soul. And she was very afraid he already owned them.

His words echoed in his head and he knew that he had to distract her before she realized just how much of his soul she'd claimed. Her weight was insubstantial as he carried her through the yard and bounded up the stairs, but the weight of her trust and emotions weighed heavily on him. For the second time in his life he felt out of control and he didn't like it. He'd have given anything to know how to handle Lynn.

The world was spinning farther and farther away from his comfort zone. He was a mover and shaker in Chicago but here in Sagebrush he was a man at the mercy of one small woman. And he hoped she'd never know it. But there was a gleam in her eyes as

she watched him that let him know she had a glimmer
of realization.

He hadn't planned to make love to her again and
without protection. But knowing that he had sealed
his fate. He wasn't going to be able to divorce Lynn.
In retrospect, the thought of marrying her and leaving
her down the road hadn't been a good plan.

He shifted her weight to open the door. The
sconces in the hall had been left on, creating an inviting glow. He set Lynn on her feet and helped her
remove her jacket, hanging it with his in the hall
closet. She stood a few feet from him, illuminated in
the glow. She looked ethereal and he felt very human
and big and bulky in her world.

The house felt the same way it always had except
now it also felt like his home. Never in any of the
houses he'd dwelled had he ever really felt home.
Except here. He remembered his first night here only
days ago, when he'd been hesitant to enter, and now
he knew why. Somehow he must have sensed that he
wouldn't be able to leave Lynn or the McCoy Ranch
easily.

He hesitated, seeing the dark shadows of furniture
in the parlor. Lynn had a lifetime of memories to
surround herself in. Seth had always felt as if he was
running from the past. Lynn had a family that had
always supported her and taught her to believe in herself. Seth didn't know what support and love were
until he was twelve.

Lynn chuckled as she turned her gaze the same way.

"What are you laughing at?"

"You and Mama's footstool."

Seth smiled. Then he realized that he would have to make a piece of furniture for her. He didn't have any idea how to start. He wasn't even sure what to get for her.

"Are you making me something?" he asked. Maybe she wouldn't, considering the business aspect to their marriage.

"What?" she asked.

"Your family tradition—the furniture. Is there something you're making for me?" An awkward feeling spread through him. Maybe he should have kept his mouth shut.

"What do you think?" she asked, suddenly serious.

Damn. Now he felt naked in front of her. If he said yes, she'd know how important it was to him that she treat him as a real husband. And if he said no, he was afraid he'd hurt her feelings. "I don't know."

"Why not?"

Double damn. Now he knew he should just pick her up and carry her upstairs. When she was writhing under him in bed, she didn't ask questions that cut through his armor and pierced his heart. "I'm not sure you want me to stay."

When she closed the distance between them and

cupped his jaw in her hands, he felt soothed to his troubled soul. "Oh, Seth. Of course I do."

He stared into her eyes and saw the truth of her words revealed there. He held her tighter, feeling the fragility of her bones under his embrace. He was so much stronger than she was, but there were times when he knew he was the weaker one.

"Show me."

She nodded and took his wrist to lead him into the darkened parlor. He followed her willingly, realizing that the hold she had over him was stronger than the hold he had over his willpower. Suddenly the sweet seduction he'd been wallowing in changed in timbre and he knew he couldn't let Lynn take the lead.

"I'll show you," he said, sweeping her into his arms and carrying her up the stairs. He shouldered open the door to his bedroom. The room was bathed in moonlight through the open draperies on the windows. The full-size bed was neatly made, and his laptop glowed in the darkened room.

He laid her lightly on the bed and began unbuttoning his shirt.

"Stop, Seth."

"Why?"

"I want to do this my way."

He felt vulnerable to her because of their conversations. Letting this woman who meant so much to him make love to him was out of the question. He needed to wrest back control from her, to reaffirm his place as the leader in their relationship.

"I—"

She knelt on the bed and tugged him down beside her. "It will be painless, I promise."

She forced him to lean back and brushed his hands aside, opening his shirt and pushing it off his shoulders. She tugged it down but stopped before he could free his arms. He was trapped or at least he let her believe he was.

"Comfy?"

"Not really."

"You just need to trust me."

"If you didn't have that devil gleam in your eyes, I might be able to."

When she leaned down and nipped at his pectoral, the touch of her teeth on his flesh zapped him straight to his groin. He moaned and reached for her, only to find his hands shackled by his shirt.

"Like that?" she asked.

"Oh, yeah."

"Still not sure you want to be here?"

"Being here was never the issue."

"Control was," she said. "Surrender to me, Seth. I'll keep you safe."

In the end he had no real choice. She seduced him with quick nibbles of his flesh, with hands that searched out each of his pleasure points and lingered on them, with eyes that caressed with a caring that made him ache to possess her. And finally when he was ready to surrender anything she asked, she moved over him and took him deep in her body.

They moved together as if they were made for each other, and before long they shot to the stars—together. As they drifted slowly back to earth, Seth held her as closely as he could and knew that he'd glimpsed heaven with this woman. He prayed for the first time since he was twelve years old and standing in the opulent foyer of his father's mansion. And his prayer had the same desperation now as it did then.

*Please, God, let this be real and not a dream.*

Lynn woke shaken and alone and intensely vulnerable. The pillow next to hers was cold, telling her that Seth had been awake for a while. It was seven-thirty, past time for her to be up and doing the morning chores.

She dressed quickly and hurried downstairs to find coffee waiting, breakfast on the table and Mrs. Stuffings in charge of the kitchen and house. Lynn hurried outside to the barn, only to find that the men had taken over that space.

For the first time her home wasn't hers.

What was Matt going to say when he returned home? The ranch was as much his as it was hers. She'd done everything in her power to save it, but now the reality of her actions was that Seth had more or less taken control of it. She felt cut off from her own land.

Snap out of it, girl, she told herself. The land was still hers. Just her role on it had changed.

At loose ends and with nothing to do, she sought

out Seth and found him ensconced in her father's old den. Seth looked right sitting behind the oak desk, a piece her great-grandfather had made.

His laptop was plugged in, and a slim printer was spitting out papers. Seth talked into his cellular phone while typing something into the computer.

He looked up when she entered but motioned for her to give him a minute. She glanced around the room. The floor-to-ceiling bookcases held books that had taught generations of her family to read. As she skimmed her finger past the titles, she saw an old carpentry book that her mother had used to make the footstool in the living room.

She really needed to get to work on a piece for Seth. But what did he need? And would he be staying to use it? If she made him a new desk, he could use it wherever he went. She made a mental note to stop by the lumberyard that afternoon.

Her route around the room took her to the large bay windows that overlooked the pasture and barn. The ranch bustled with activity, and despite her earlier thoughts, she knew that she'd done the right thing by marrying Seth. As much as she didn't like the disruption of her routine, she knew this change was for the best.

Seth patted her on the butt and tugged her down onto his lap. He was still talking softly into the phone. She leaned into his warmth and for a minute felt the sense of rightness for which she'd been searching a lifetime. She knew that Seth was the man she was meant to spend her life with and wondered if she'd be strong enough to let him go when the time came.

Part of her knew that he could never make his life here in Montana. He was a lawyer, a big-city mover and shaker whose entire affluent family waited for him in Chicago. She was a small-town working-class girl who didn't want to leave the splendor that was Sagebrush. She needed the fresh air, snowcapped mountains and open spaces to survive.

When the quiet rumble of his voice stopped, she looked at him. He winked at her.

"Seth?"

"Almost done, honey," he said, still clutching the phone to his ear.

As much as she enjoyed sitting on his lap, she felt restless. Clearly Seth wasn't going to have time to go for a ride with her any time soon.

She glanced at the clock and realized she had about thirty minutes until her shift at the diner. She hadn't quit her job yet and she welcomed the distraction it provided. She scooted off his lap.

Seth covered the mouthpiece of his phone. "Where are you going?"

"To town. I'll be back later."

"We need to talk," he said.

She nodded and turned toward the door.

"Don't I get a goodbye kiss?"

"You seem rather busy."

"I always have time for you," he said.

She bent toward him, intending a swift kiss, but

when their lips met, Seth took over the embrace. Setting his phone on the desk, he cupped her face, tilting her head so that he could thrust his tongue into her mouth. The kiss was deep and carnal, and when he lifted his head, her breath wasn't steady.

He tugged her back into his lap. His erection nudged her hip and she knew that if she waited for him to conclude his call they'd be back in bed. Tempting though that was, she knew she needed to be more to Seth than a bed partner. She needed to be a contributing partner.

She took his face in her hands and kissed him with all the love that was welling in her heart. Kissed him as if it were the first time their lips met and as if it were the last time. As if all time had stopped around them and nothing but he and she existed in the world.

Then she dropped her hands, caressed his arousal that strained against his inseam and walked toward the door.

"Honey," he called, "give me ten minutes and I'll meet you upstairs."

Though she knew she shouldn't, Lynn nodded and went back upstairs to his bedroom. But ten minutes came and went and when it reached thirty, she grabbed her purse and headed for the diner. It seemed that Seth didn't need her as much as she needed him. And though she tried to pretend it was anger coursing through her, she knew it was also hurt. The kind of hurt that only love could heal.

And Seth had already told her he wasn't a man who'd ever love again.

# Eleven

Seth cursed the situation with his family. Both sides of it. The Connellys were riding a string of bad luck that had to end soon. And his mother's family seemed to be responsible for every bit of it. He was going to have to go back to Chicago soon. But Lynn's words echoed in his mind.

*You can't keep running from your problems.*

Thinking of Lynn soothed the savage part of his soul that was torn between two families. He hurried up the stairs, hoping she was still waiting for him. But it had been forty minutes since she'd left him alone and wanting her.

When he found his bedroom was empty, he optimistically checked the one that used to be hers, but it was empty as well. He hurried downstairs but couldn't find her anywhere.

"I think Mrs. Connelly took her truck and headed toward town," Mrs. Stuffings said. "This came for you a few minutes ago."

She handed him an envelope from the banker, Mr. Cochran. It held the deed to the McCoy Ranch. A feeling of rightness filled him. Despite the way he'd started out in life, he realized he'd become a good man. And a month ago he wouldn't have been able to acknowledge that.

Lynn had given him something irreplaceable and he was glad he'd been able to save her ranch for her. He went back into his office and wrote a brief note to make sure she understood the ranch was hers. Then knowing there were some words he could never say out loud, he wrote them instead on the note.

He went upstairs and put the envelope on her pillow. Then he grabbed his keys and went out to the Jag. He took a quiet pride in the way the ranch was starting to take shape. It was beginning to resemble the memories he had of it. He'd left a message for Matt, at the base where his outfit was stationed, updating him on the situation with Lynn. He expected to get a call about thirty seconds after Matt read it.

If Matt had suddenly married one of his sisters, Seth knew he'd call Matt and demand to know what the hell was going on. Seth realized he was going to have to have a better explanation for Matt than "I did it to save your ranch and repay your family." Matt wouldn't buy that. He'd know there was more to it than that.

Seth wasn't sure he was ready to admit there was more to his marriage than he'd revealed to Lynn.

Lynn's truck was parked behind the diner on Main Street. Maybe she was visiting friends, he thought. She'd seemed kind of restless earlier.

He hoped she didn't resent him but knew she probably did. Hell, he'd be ticked off if someone had taken over the way he had. But Seth knew he was a man of action. He didn't like to sit around when he saw a way to change things.

He pulled his car into the parking lot and realized he'd chosen the same spot he'd had on the first night he'd arrived in Sagebrush. How had she become so important to him in such a short span of time?

He couldn't believe how much had changed since then. Yet at the same time his relationship with Lynn had always been a part of him. There was a sense of rightness to it, as if fate had always meant for them to be together.

Frankly that frightened him. Almost as much as the soul-shattering lovemaking they'd shared the night before. He felt the same desperation he'd experienced every time he'd depended on his mother.

Though he believed in carving his own destiny, a part of him wondered how long Lynn would stay with him. Common sense said he'd be the one to leave. But he didn't know how long she'd stay with him.

His feelings for Lynn were stronger than any he'd

ever experienced with another woman. And though he'd always balked at fear and faced danger head-on, he knew love made him weak. These soft emotions she inspired in him made him weary.

He sat in the car staring into the diner. Lynn wasn't visiting with friends. She was working, he saw. She smiled at a couple in a booth as she poured them coffee.

He felt her slipping farther and farther from his grasp. The fragile hold he had on her was weak and he knew it. Bonds of the flesh weren't strong enough to hold a woman like Lynn. But showing her how he felt was a risk he couldn't take. There had to be some way to convince her that he was worthwhile without revealing how deeply he needed her in his life.

He climbed from his car and walked inside the diner. She glanced up as the door opened, her eyes weary as she watched him. It seemed his rotten luck with relationships was holding. He'd managed to put her on guard.

On the positive side she didn't seem that angry with him for standing her up earlier. But as she drew closer, he realized he was mistaken. Hot emotions glittered in her eyes, and he thanked God they were in a public place. Otherwise he had the feeling Lynn would have let him have it.

"Table for one?"

"I was looking for you," he said.

"You've found me."

"Yes, I did. And not for the first time."

"I wasn't running from you."

"I know. That's not your style."

"No, but it is yours."

That zing cut to the bone. It never paid to let anyone close. "Can we have a civil conversation?"

"Yes. I'm sorry. Not enough sleep last night."

"I'd gladly give up all my restful nights to spend every night with you."

"Would you?"

He nodded. "Can you sit down and talk to me?"

"Let me put this coffeepot down and get one of the other girls to cover for me."

He took a seat in the booth he'd been given his first night in the diner, though the anxiety in him now was so much more intense than it had been that first night. He had so much more to lose than he'd had before. Before, he'd been running from his own shame in his mother's actions. Because he'd desperately wanted her love and ignored what his gut had told him. Now, he realized, he was here because of his own.

Lynn slid onto the bench seat across from him. Resting her elbows on the table, she leaned in. "I've only got ten minutes so we'll have to talk quickly."

"You don't need to work here. Why don't you give them your notice? I'll take care of you."

She sighed. "I don't want you to solve all my problems. I've been working all my life and it's too late for me to stop now."

"Maybe you can find pleasure in being a wife. You used to work on the ranch and enjoy it."

"There's nothing for me to do there anymore."

"There will always be stuff for you to do."

"I can't sit around. I need to know that I'm contributing to society. You should understand that."

"I'm trying to."

"I appreciate all you've done for me. I feel like Cinderella after she's been swept away by Prince Charming. But the reality is, Cinderella wouldn't have been happy sitting in the castle the rest of her days and doing nothing. And neither am I. I have to know that I'm not just an ornament on your arm."

"Honey, you are more than that."

"Don't speak so quickly, Seth. I was in the house this afternoon when you made certain promises and then didn't deliver on them."

"Lynn—"

"I understand that business comes first but I can't just wait around until you have time for me."

"I know. I apologize. We can figure out something for you to do."

"Like what?"

"I don't know. Not working as a waitress."

She shook her head. There was a deep sadness in her eyes that spelled doom for his tender heart. A heart he'd hidden behind a shield of cynicism and weariness but one that she'd reached regardless.

"I don't think this marriage is going to work," she said.

"Yes, it can." Damn, did he sound desperate?

"What makes you so sure?" she asked.

Come on, guy. Bare your soul, he thought, realizing he couldn't he tell her a partial truth. It was, after all, the reason he'd originally married her.

"The debt I owe your family is too high for me to allow this marriage to dissolve."

"Are you saying you married me to repay my family?" she asked in a hoarse voice.

He knew he'd made a tactical error. He'd made them a time or two in the courtroom but this was only the second time he'd made one in real life. The first had resulted in the endangerment of an innocent young woman. This second one held consequences too harsh to examine.

"Yes, I did."

"Well, I guess it's safe to say I now understand why this marriage of convenience has been so important to you."

Lynn stared at the man she thought she knew and realized once again that she'd fallen for the illusion. In real life there was no Prince Charming on a white horse that was going to save the Cinderella from a cold, lonely life. Reality was that Prince Charming would use his money to make her life easier, and her heart would remain locked away—forever.

What had been blossoming in her heart as love had been nothing more than a game to him. She felt little and foolish. Every bit the small-town hick to his big-city sophistication.

She'd fallen for a guy who'd promised her the world once before. At least Seth hadn't paved the way with pretty lies. He'd done it with sincerity and integrity, but he'd done it all the same. When all was said and done, she'd be alone and heartbroken again.

This time she had no one to blame but herself. Even Seth had warned her not to be tricked by the smoke and mirrors. But her heart was easily duped. And it had led her once again to an intense vulnerability.

The power Seth had over her made her weak as she realized she didn't wield the same strength over him. Her hands trembled, and for a moment she couldn't breathe. She laced her fingers together and squeezed until the shaking passed.

"Lynn, are you okay?" he asked.

She closed her eyes and tried to pretend that he wanted more from her than— What exactly had he wanted from her? It wasn't her family's land or her money. He'd wanted to absolve himself from some lingering feelings of gratitude left over from a lifetime ago.

The backs of her eyes burned, but she refused to let her tears fall. She wasn't that weak. She would never let him see how deeply he'd hurt her.

She shook her head and glanced around the diner. Anywhere but at the man who'd made a place for himself in her life with a network of deceptions. "I'm fine."

"I didn't mean that—"

Staring down at her clenched fingers, she searched for words that wouldn't reveal how deeply he'd cut her. She searched for a way to deal with the emotions rocketing through her at superspeed. "I know exactly what you meant. I'm your penance."

"You are *not* my penance."

"Well, it sure as hell seems like I am. Either that or your punishment."

He shoved his hands through his hair and looked to her like a man caught. She knew that she'd come close to the truth but she'd never be able to discover it on her own. He had to trust her enough to tell her.

That, she realized, was something he'd never do. Seth had been betrayed by the women that he'd depended on too many times for him to ever really trust her. And without trust they had nothing.

"Why did you have to make it feel real?" she asked, finally looking at him.

His eyes seemed haunted as he rubbed the bridge of his nose. Her instincts urged her to soothe him. He'd been working nonstop since they returned from Vegas—was it only a day ago?

"It wasn't an intentional thing," he said. "I've tried to be as up front as I could."

But his words reminded her that there was more to Seth Connelly than met the eye. He played his cards close to his vest and from their time in Vegas she knew he played to win.

"You've never sounded more like a lawyer. Omission doesn't absolve you."

"I'm not trying to be absolved."

"Look me in the eye and tell me you weren't using me to assuage your guilt for the past."

He wouldn't. Instead he placed his large hand over her clenched ones. The hand that had caressed her body to heights she'd never experienced was now a touch she could not tolerate.

She unclenched her hands and slid them out from under his grasp. Glancing up, she saw that his gaze was shuttered. He'd revealed more emotion the first night he'd come into the diner when he was still a long-lost friend to her than he showed tonight after he'd become closer to her than her breath.

"I can't," he said at last. The words told her that there was no future in her relationship with Seth.

She started to slide out of the booth but he stopped her.

"Neither of us was looking for a love match," he said. "This is a situation that lets us both have what we want. You have the ranch, I have the knowledge that I've finally done something for the McCoy family that has worth."

"What about me?" she asked, knowing she had nothing left to lose.

"I don't follow," he said.

"I'm more than a means to an end," she said more loudly than she'd intended.

His gray eyes were diamond hard and she wished there was a way to get him to release the emotions he kept bottled inside. "I know you are."

"Then why did you use me?" she asked at last. She could understand his wanting to repay her family. Heck, she knew she'd never have a moment's peace until Seth was repaid for what he'd done for the ranch. But making her his wife in body if not in soul had crossed a line.

"I never did. You needed me and I came through for you. I solved your problems and restored your home."

She had needed him, but she hadn't realized she'd been so transparent. He'd given her back something uniquely feminine that she'd lost when Ronnie had taken her money and left her. "I didn't ask to be rescued."

"No, you didn't but you needed to be."

She couldn't admit to that. She may not have been wildly successful on her own but she hadn't been a total loser. "I was doing okay."

"I beg to differ. Anyway, you left me no choice."

"How did I do that?" she asked. Why didn't she just get up and walk away? There was no way they were going to ever come to an agreement. Not until her heart had time to mend. Maybe they could meet again in thirty years and she'd be able to forgive him for making her fall in love with him.

"I couldn't let you lose the ranch."

"Well, I appreciate that, Seth, I really do. But why did you have to make it personal?"

"Emotions have nothing to do with the ranch."

"Don't they have anything to do with us?"

"You know they do. I want you more than any woman I've ever dated."

"I'm not talking about lust."

"Neither am I."

"I wish I could believe you."

"Why can't you? You've trusted every two-bit con man that's come through town. Why can't you trust me?"

"I do trust you," she said.

"Sure you do, honey. You trust me to disappoint you like every other man in your life."

"Matt has never let me down," she said.

"Maybe not intentionally but he wasn't here when you needed his strength and advice."

"I don't blame Matt for this."

"I'm not saying you should. My point is I've never let you down."

Feeling vulnerable, she lashed out. "It's hard to trust a man who doesn't trust himself."

Lynn's words cut deep to a part of himself that he'd hidden away for a long time. He stopped trying to make peace with her. "You don't know what you're talking about."

"Maybe, but it seems to me that a person who

takes to the road when things get tough isn't someone who trusts himself to survive the situation.''

He grew very still. He wasn't sure where she was going with this conversation, he only knew that her words made him realize she saw through the trappings of wealth and education to the tough street hood who still lived underneath.

''Are you calling me a coward?'' he asked.

She shook her head then tilted it to one side, her eyes piercing his, and he knew she saw all the way to his soul with that gaze. ''I guess I am.''

''No man would still be standing if he said that to me.'' That was the tough little boy who'd learned to fight before he entered school. The rough kid who'd thought nothing of picking pockets or shoplifting. The wild teenager who'd stolen a car to prove he was a man and then had his father teach him there was nothing manly about bravado.

''I'm not insulting you. You are a brave and honorable man when it comes to work and strangers, but once it gets personal, you put up barriers, and if that doesn't work then you leave.''

He knew that she was trying to protect herself, the same way he was. Could they ever find a way to live together in this intense vulnerability they seemed to generate in each other? ''I haven't left you.''

''Telling me that emotions have nothing to do with our relationship is the same as running away. Until you trust yourself you'll never be able to love me.''

''Why do you want my love?'' he asked.

"Oh, Seth…"

He stared at her. Her big violet eyes were wide and glassy like spring pansies wet with rain. And he knew that he was the cloud that had rained on them. "I want your love because I love you."

For a minute a sense of relief washed over him. It was right that she loved him. But he knew that it wouldn't last.

He wished he could believe her. But love didn't work like that. He'd seen his father who professed to love his wife cheat on her. He'd seen his mother who professed to love him use and betray him. He'd seen other women whom he dated profess to love him only to leave him when they realized he was a working man with a working man's values.

Truth was a paramount value for him, and when he saw the hope glistening in those eyes he knew he had no choice.

"No, honey, you don't," he said as gently as he could.

The color left her face as she stared at him. "I thought trust was our problem, but now I know it isn't."

"Then what is?"

"Your lack of humanity. Because no man who's shared what we've shared—the joining of our souls and the deep conversations—no man whom I've let see my dreams could look at me and say I don't love him."

She stood up and yanked off her apron with vicious

movements that betrayed more than her anger. "I feel sorry for you because no matter how far you run you'll never find a home until you acknowledge that you love others and are yourself lovable."

He said nothing. He'd never be that weak. He'd seen love destroy stronger men than him. He'd seen what people did in the name of undying affection and he wasn't going to be victim to that.

She shook her head and walked out the door of the diner. He watched her leave with a certain sense of inevitability. He'd known she'd go someday. He'd hoped she'd stay longer but he wasn't surprised she'd left.

He realized the customers in the diner where staring at him, so he put on his tough-guy face and shrugged.

"Want some free advice, partner?" asked a gnarled cowboy seated across the aisle from him.

"Not particularly," Seth replied. "I've found advice to be worth what you pay for it."

"Well, son, this one's on me. Go after that girl and tell her whatever she needs to hear. Or one day you'll wake up and realize the mistake you made in letting her go and it will be too late."

Seth knew the man was right. "I... Thanks."

"No problem. I wish someone had said the same thing to me years ago. Then maybe I wouldn't have only horses to keep me company."

Seth liked the old cowboy. He wasn't looking for sympathy and there was something about his attitude that reminded Seth of himself. "You looking for work?"

"Most ranchers won't hire an old saddle bum like me."

"I'm not most ranchers. Stop by the McCoy Ranch and tell Buck, the ranch foreman, that Seth Connelly sent you."

"I'll think about it," he said and went back to eating his meal.

Seth walked outside. It was a crisp cool day. He shoved his hands deep into his pockets as he walked to his car. He got in but didn't start it.

He had two choices, and he had to be honest— pointing his car east and heading back to Chicago was the safest thing he could do. But he couldn't leave until Lynn told him to go.

He wasn't going to walk away from her or the home he'd found with her until he'd given their relationship one more try.

He told himself it was because she liked the silences he fell into so often. He told himself it was because she was sexy and flirty and could turn him on with the most innocent look from under her lashes. He told himself that it was because she listened to him talk about the past and didn't judge him.

But he refused to acknowledge the real reason even to himself. He only knew that a life without Lynn in it wasn't one he wanted to live. He only knew that Lynn and he had a bond that went deeper than time or location. He only knew that he'd never be able to walk like a man again if he didn't convince her to stay with him.

He started the car and pulled out of the parking lot, hoping he'd be able to make his peace with Lynn. But her words came back to him from that afternoon they'd made love under the tree.

*Sometimes love means letting go.*

He hoped he was strong enough to let go of her if necessary, but a part of him realized they were meant to be together. He only hoped he could convince her of that.

# Twelve

Lynn pulled her truck to a stop in front of the house she'd lived in her entire life. But she didn't get out. Her face was wet from crying and she didn't want to go inside and see the housekeeper. She wiped her face and watched a man walking around the house. She realized he was a housepainter and that he was restoring the finish that she'd never had the time to.

Seth was a man capable of such generosity that she knew he had to have a heart. If only he could trust himself to love.

But she knew that life had taught him hard lessons. That didn't excuse him for not being able to realize the gift they had been given, but it made his actions more understandable.

She was no stranger to heartbreak, but this time…oh, this time it felt as if she'd never recover. Slowly she exited her pickup and as she closed the door she saw the stenciling on her truck: McCoy Ranch—Home Of The Best Beef In Montana.

Seth had given that back to her. He'd given her the seed to make the future as glorious as the past had been. She went inside and heard the housekeeper in the kitchen. She didn't want to talk to a woman she hardly knew so she quickly went down the hall to the den.

The room wasn't hers anymore and she sensed Seth's presence as clearly as if he were in the room with her. She walked slowly to the desk where he'd been working this morning. She ran her fingers along the back of the executive-style desk chair where he'd sat.

Leaning forward, she rested her cheek against the back. The scent of his cologne lingered, and she had to close her eyes against a longing so deep that she knew she'd never really be free of it.

Never had she found a man who'd put up with her the way Seth had. He'd actually seemed to like her feistiness when most men could barely tolerate it. Never had she found a man who'd listen to her dreams and desires and then make them come true for her because he wanted her happiness. Never had she found a man she felt safe enough loving….

And she'd managed to drive him away.

Her encounter with Seth at the diner had made her

realize she needed to talk to her brother. She couldn't spend the rest of her life trying to protect those she loved by keeping things from them. Before she could change her mind, she found the card Matt had given her before he left, and dialed the number.

A stranger answered and she asked for her brother. Matt was unavailable but they'd have him call her. She felt better for her actions and knew she should have gone to him long ago for help. Being independent was fine, but asking for help when she was in over her head wasn't a bad thing.

She knew that was what Seth had taught her. Even if they didn't find a way to make their marriage real, she'd always be glad he'd shown her the value in having another person help you with your problems.

The thought of never seeing Seth again made her want to curl into the fetal position and never get up. Instead she decided to do something. She ran her hand along the scarred wooden arms of the chair. Suddenly she knew just the piece of furniture she'd make for Seth—not a desk but a new desk chair so that he'd be surrounded by the love he didn't believe she could have for him whenever he was working.

If he didn't come back to the ranch she'd send it to him in Chicago. The love she had for him was too strong to be broken by anger. She might even have to leave the ranch if he proved stubborn and didn't return to her.

But leaving the ranch no longer frightened her the way it used to. Living alone was what she feared. And if they weren't together, she knew that she and Seth would never find true happiness.

She decided to get changed before heading out back to the carpentry shed and starting on Seth's chair. As she entered her bedroom, she glimpsed herself in the mirror and realized that she wasn't a quitter. She'd never given up on anything.

Seth Connelly had better be prepared for the battle of his life if he returned to Chicago instead of to the ranch.

There was an envelope on her pillow and she recognized Seth's bold masculine handwriting on the outside. It was just her name.

She opened the large manila envelope and pulled out two papers. The first she recognized as the deed to the McCoy Ranch. The second was a folded piece of paper. Slowly she opened it up. Her heart was in her throat as she forced herself to see what he'd written.

It occurred to her that Seth didn't have to return to the ranch now. She knew that he'd accomplished what he'd set out to do: rescue her and her ranch.

Lynn,
Enclosed is the deed to the ranch. I hope that we will be able to make your ancestral lands into the home I've always been searching for.

Seth

They were simple words that could mean anything, but Lynn knew Seth well enough to look beneath the surface. He wasn't going back to Chicago, she realized. Unless she'd chased him away by telling him he lacked humanity.

If she had, she knew she'd go after him, because the man who'd written this note was a man who could love her for all time. A man who felt things that he could never say. A man who needed to have a home to come to when he was weary of battle.

She knew that his life with his families was a battle for him at times. A torn allegiance to the woman who had given him birth and the man who had fathered him. A torn allegiance to the people who'd taught him to survive and the people who'd given him a reason to. A torn allegiance between what he was given and what he craved—a real family.

She bit her lip and knew that the chair would have to wait. She had to find Seth now. She ran down the stairs and threw open the door—only to crash into Seth. Their heads knocked together and stars danced in front of her eyes.

He caught her close and she leaned into him, knowing she'd found in this man the love that had always eluded her. But how was she going to make him see that it was just the thing he needed?

Seth was afraid to let go of Lynn. She'd come through the door like a woman with a mission. She felt right in his arms. His head ached from where their heads had bumped but he didn't mind the pain.

It was proof that she was really in his arms. Never had the embrace of another person been more important to him. Never had he needed that human contact more than right now. Something new had sprung to life inside him on the drive to the McCoy Ranch, and the change wasn't finished yet.

All he knew was that he intended to make sure that she stayed with him. That she didn't give up on him yet. That she took the opportunity fate had given the both of them.

He'd broken all speed limits to get back here to her. And now that he was here he didn't know what to do. He knew the words she wanted from him, but the one time he'd muttered those words his mother had patted him on the head and left him in a stranger's home.

"Are you okay?" he asked. Her eyes were wide and vulnerable. A faint wetness lingered under her eyes, and the knowledge that he'd made her cry made him want to curse.

Despite the circumstances of his birth he'd always tried to rise above what he'd been born as. But looking at Lynn's wet eyes, he acknowledged he really was a bastard when he wanted to be. Hurting Lynn, the one woman he'd always wanted to protect, made him realize that he needed to change.

"You've got a hard head," she said lightly. But the attempt at levity cost her, and she had to look away from him. They'd both said too much earlier and not enough.

He wiped the wetness from under her eyes. She flushed a little and he knew she'd hoped that he wouldn't know he'd made her cry. "I'm sorry."

She nodded.

"I mean it, honey. You gave a precious gift and I rejected it."

She closed her eyes. Was it too late? he wondered. Had he killed the love she'd professed to have for him? Was there a way to keep her by his side without showing her how deeply he needed her there?

"You were right about me. I've never been able to trust that I was worthy of anyone's affection."

"But you are. I wish I could show you that."

"I did a lot of thinking after you left," he said, trying to find the words to tell her what was in his heart.

He noticed the paper clutched in her hand and realized she'd opened the deed and the note he'd left for her. He dropped his arms and stepped a few feet from her. It took all his control not to turn and get back into his car. Not to drive away as fast and far as he could. Not to leave her while she held the most vulnerable part of him in her hands.

"I see you opened my note." *God, please don't let me screw this up.*

The shrewd look in her eyes worried him. He wished she'd tell him again that she loved him. It would make everything so much easier. But then again, easy things weren't always worth having, he thought.

"You are a fraud, Seth Connelly."

"How do you figure that?" he asked, again worried he might say the wrong thing.

"You love me. You might not know it, but this piece of paper proves it."

Seth froze, feeling much the same as he did that first night in his father's home: afraid to move or breathe in case he broke something. He'd come so close to hurting Lynn, he'd already made her cry today. He knew that his rough edges wouldn't disappear overnight—hell, they might never go away—but he knew that for Lynn he was willing to try to soften them.

Despite his designer suits, fancy car and penthouse apartment, he was still at heart a street punk who wasn't good enough for this woman who had a generous heart.

He clenched his hands to his sides, still not sure what to do. The tingle in his gut that had started in his car when he'd realized that he couldn't live without Lynn now spread throughout his body. His ears buzzed.

Lynn closed the space between them and wrapped him in her arms, holding him so tightly he thought she'd never let go. He wanted her to never let go of him. She cradled his head in her hands and looked up at him.

"Tell me I'm wrong," she said.

He unclenched his hands and slid them up the back of the woman who'd come to mean more to him than life itself. Her breasts nestled against his chest. He hardened against her and knew that if he took her to bed, he'd be able to show her easily that she was right. But she wanted words.

"No, you're not wrong."

"Can you say the words?"

"The last time I said them I was wrong."

"When was that?"

"To my mom when she introduced me to my father."

"Seth, my love isn't like hers. Mine is a love that isn't going to end or change even if you can't ever say the words."

"Are you sure?"

"Yes, I am."

He knew he had to tell her the truth that was in his heart but couldn't here or now. The sun shone on them, making him feel more exposed than if he'd been in the dark.

"Where were you hurrying to?" he asked.

"To find you."

Her words made his heart beat faster and he knew that whatever the future held they'd be together. He scooped her up in his arms and carried her into the house.

"Where are you taking me?"

"To bed. I might not be able to tell you how I feel but I damn sure can show you."

Seth placed her on the center of the bed and lowered himself to her. He kissed her with the passion she'd come to crave from him, thrusting his tongue deep in her mouth until she forgot the individual tastes of each of them and they were only one.

He undressed her with ease and surety, and within a minute she was lying naked in front of him. He stood to disrobe, his eyes never leaving her body. She felt like the sexiest woman alive in that moment. The fire in his gaze started one that pulsed through her with the beating of her heart, pooling in the center of her body.

The cotton quilt on the bed felt soft under her naked hips and she stretched her arms out, beckoning him to her. He crouched at the foot of the bed and moved up slowly, caressing her from her feet to her legs, stopping at the mound of her femininity.

Instinctively she tried to close her legs.

''Don't,'' he murmured and settled himself between her legs.

He parted her tender flesh and lowered his head to taste her, dropping first soft, light kisses on her most sensitive flesh and then as her hips began to rise to meet him, using a stronger touch on her there.

He slid two fingers inside her and she clenched her body around them. Being filled by him was pleasure but she wanted more. She wanted his hardness to fill her. She needed him to be with her at this moment.

''Come to me,'' she said.

''Not yet. This time is for you.''

He lowered his head again, this time to suckle at

her breasts. She felt voluptuous as his hands and body brought her close to the edge of climax. His mouth left her nipples to slide once more back down to her center and this time when he touched the bud of her desire she went over the edge.

She shivered in his arms as he moved over her. His chest rubbing against her breasts and torso. His mouth nibbling on her neck. His hands clutching her buttocks and that hard, hot part of him seeking entrance to her body.

She opened herself to him, wrapping her legs around his waist as he slid inside her. He buried himself so deeply that she finally felt as if they'd become one.

He moved slowly, building her once again toward climax and this time as her nerve endings began to quake she called out his name.

"I love you," she said, gazing deep in his eyes.

He thrust into her with more and more urgency, his eyes never leaving hers, and he shouted his climax. She held him in her arms as they slowly drifted back into themselves.

His head rested on her breast, his breath tickling her nipple. She imagined they'd spend the rest of the day and night here in bed. Life, she realized, had a way of giving you exactly what you needed. Though a part of her would always want to hear the words from Seth, he did a wonderful job of showing her how he felt.

"Thank you," she said.

He rolled to his side, carrying her with him and settling her head onto his shoulder. "I should be thanking you."

"Why?"

"For all of this," he said, indicating the house around them.

"I wouldn't have my house to share with you if you hadn't stepped in."

"I might have given you back your ranch, but you've given me a gift that I never knew existed."

"What was that?" she asked.

"The knowledge that life is empty no matter how many possessions you own. Life is meaningless unless you have someone to say those three little words to you."

He leaned closer to her, held her so tightly to him that she couldn't breathe and whispered in her ear, "I love you, Lynn."

Tears burned the back of her eyes and she whispered back. "I love you, too."

They spent the afternoon making love and talking about their plans for the future and knew in their hearts that they'd been given a second chance to find happiness.

# Epilogue

Lake Shore Manor, the Connelly home in one of Chicago's finest neighborhoods, was an overwhelming sight to Lynn.

"I don't belong here," she whispered to Seth as they stood in the marble-floored foyer.

"Yes, you do," Seth replied, kissing her.

"Why are you so sure?" she asked.

"Because you are by my side and finally I feel like I belong here."

She smiled at him and Seth knew that he and Lynn had really completed each other.

"Come inside, Seth," said his father. "The family is waiting for you."

"Dad, this is Lynn, my wife." A quiet sense of

pride filled Seth as he said the words. He'd never wanted a spouse, but having committed his life to Lynn had filled him in places he'd never realized he'd been empty.

"Welcome to the family, Lynn," Grant Connelly said, embracing her. Watching his dad and Lynn chat, Seth realized that his father had welcomed him the same way when he'd arrived. His father's heart was a big one and had room for every one of his children and, as the family continued to grow, their spouses.

"It's good to be home," Seth said.

"I'm glad to hear you say that," his dad said.

"Emma, Seth's here."

Emma Connelly still looked regal and glamorous despite her sixty years. She embraced Seth, and for the first time he realized that he had a mother who loved him and she'd been here all along. He didn't know how to tell her that but there was a glimmer in her eye that told him she already knew.

The family was waiting for them in the formal living room. He introduced Lynn to his sister Tara, and the two of them got along very well. He knew they would.

His brother Drew, who was speaking on the phone despite the cacophony around him, walked forward to embrace Seth in a welcoming hug. He held out the phone. "Daniel's on the phone."

He took the phone from Drew, eager to speak to his eldest brother who'd claimed the throne in Altaria almost a year ago.

"Congratulations, Seth," Daniel said. "I can't wait to meet your new wife."

"Thanks, Daniel. I never thought I'd marry or settle down."

"It's amazing how the right woman can change your life."

"You can say that again. How are things in Altaria?"

"Life would be better without a Gregor Paulus—the man's driving me crazy. Is it possible to fire a royal retainer?"

"Are you asking me as a lawyer?"

"Nah, just venting to you as a brother," Daniel said. "Is Dad nearby?"

"Hold on."

Seth finally felt equal to the task of being a Connelly man. As if he'd found his home and his place within his family. He passed the phone to his father and rejoined Lynn.

She was chatting with his sister Maggie, who seemed upset. "You okay, Maggie?"

"I'm just worried about Lucas Starwind," she said.

"Why?"

"At Tom Reynolds's funeral he seemed so enraged. I don't know if he was angry with himself or the fact that Tom died while investigating our family's case. I just wish I could help him deal with all of that pain."

"Some things a man has to work out for himself."

"I know that."

"Don't do anything impulsive, Maggie. Let him be."

"I will," she said in an unconvincing tone. "I barely know him."

Seth gazed at his sister, wondering just how deep her concern for Starwind ran. He hoped she wasn't getting in over her head. He'd heard that the other man was a tough-as-nails P.I. who preferred to keep to himself.

Lynn slipped her arm around his waist and he let his worries for his sister melt away as she left them to get a drink from the wet bar.

"So this is your family," she said softly.

"Yes," he said. "My family. I guess I just didn't feel like I belonged until I had you."

"Really?"

He nodded. He bent close to kiss her, thanking fate for the twice-in-a-lifetime chance he'd been given with Lynn and his family. He knew that this time he wouldn't push it away, because the gift was too precious to turn aside.

\* \* \* \* \*

# Expecting...
# and in Danger

# EILEEN WILKS

## EILEEN WILKS

is a fifth-generation Texan. Her great-great-grand-mother came to Texas shortly after the end of the Civil War. But she's not a full-blooded Texan. Right after another war, her Texan father fell for a Yankee woman. This obviously mismatched pair proceeded to travel to nine cities in three counries in the first twenty years of their marriage. For the next twenty years they stayed put, back home in Texas again – and still together.

Eileen believes her professional career matches her nomadic upbringing, since she has tried everything from draughting to a brief stint as a farm-hand – raising two children and any number of cats and dogs along the way. Not until she started writing did she 'stay put', because that's when she knew she'd come home. Readers can write to her at PO Box 4612, Midland, TX 79704-4612, USA.

My thanks to all the other authors who participated in this continuity – what a great bunch! – with special hugs for Leanne and Sheri. I also want to thank Patricia Rosemoor for her help with streets, neighbourhoods and buildings in Chicago. Mills & Boon writers are some of the most generous people anywhere.

# One

The Windy City was living up to its name the second time someone tried to kill her.

At least Charlotte thought they'd tried to kill her. Sprawled across the hood of a parked car, with panic pounding in her chest, her hip throbbing, her calf burning and her coat flapping in the wind, she couldn't be sure. Maybe the driver simply hadn't seen her.

"You all right, lady?"

She stirred and looked up at the concerned face of a tall black man with a gold ring in his nose, another in his eyebrow, a leather jacket and a Cubs cap on his apparently bald head. Several others had stopped on the busy sidewalk to stare and exclaim. She caught snatches of conversation— "Crazy drivers!" and "Must have been drunk..." and "Where's a cop when you need one?"

Not here, thank goodness. The last thing she needed was to draw the attention of the police.

"I'm fine," she said to the concerned and the curious. "Thank you for asking." She pulled herself together mentally as she climbed off the car. Her knees weren't sure of themselves, but after sorting through her aches, she concluded she wasn't badly hurt. The car had missed her, after all. Thanks to the wind.

Charlotte had been crossing the street—with the light, of course. She always crossed with the light. She'd finished her bagel two blocks back and had been holding on to the sack, which was destined for the next trash can. A strong gust had grabbed it right out of her hand. She'd turned, meaning to chase it down so she could dispose of it properly...and saw the car.

It had been headed right for her in spite of the red light that should have protected her. It had even seemed to speed up in that split second between the instant she'd seen it and the next, when her body had taken over, hurling her out of its path.

But maybe that was paranoia speaking. Although it wasn't really paranoia, was it, if there truly were people out to get you?

"You sure you're okay?" the man in the Cubs cap and nose ring asked. A hefty woman advised her to call the police; another suggested she go to the hospital; someone else thought she should get a lawyer, though what she'd do with one, he didn't say. Charlotte took a moment to assure them again that she was fine, though she grimaced over the ruined panty hose—four-ninety-five a pair, dammit—and the trickle of blood running down her leg.

She put a hand protectively on her stomach. A little wiggle inside assured her that all was well, and she drew a deep, relieved breath.

Her backpack. Oh, Lord, she couldn't afford to lose that. Where—? Kneeling, she spotted it halfway under the car and dragged it out. Her arms felt like overcooked spaghetti.

"Hey, you want me to call someone to come get you?" It was the Cubs fan.

"Thank you, but that won't be necessary." Standing with the backpack slung over her shoulder was a good deal harder than it should have been. Her knees weren't in much better shape than her spaghetti arms.

Surely it had been a freak accident.

"Better sit down a minute. You're pale as a ghost. Bleeding, too."

Irritation threatened to swamp good manners. She hated being fussed over. "I'm always pale. I'll take care of the scrapes at work."

"You got far to go?"

"Just up the block, at Hole-in-the-Wall."

He cast a dubious glance that way, which she perfectly understood. The restaurant was aptly named, an eyesore in an area that had once been solidly blue collar, but was skidding rapidly downhill. The neighborhood was seedy, a little trashy, not quite a slum…everything she'd fought so hard to leave behind.

"You ain't up to working yet," he informed her with that particular male brand of arrogance that scraped on her pride like fingernails on a chalkboard.

"I appreciate your concern, but it isn't necessary." She started limping down the sidewalk, hoping he would get the hint and go about his own business.

It didn't work. He kept pace with her. "Don't trip over your ego, sister. I'm not hitting on you. Don't care for teeny, tiny blondes with big mouths." He shook his head. "You sure talk fancy for someone who works at the Hole."

Her unwanted escort had a pleasant tenor voice with surprising resonance. "Do you sing?"

He gave her a startled glance. "Why?"

She sighed. Most of the time she managed to keep her unruly tongue under control, but every now and then it flew free. "I wasn't hitting on you, either. I don't care for bossy males. Your voice reminded me of a tenor I heard sing 'Ness'un Dorma.'"

"You listen to opera, but you work at Hole-in-the-Wall?"

"You recognize an aria from *Turandot,* but you poke holes in your body?"

"Smart-mouthed, too," he observed. "Why you working at the Hole?"

"For my sins." Which was all too literally true. But she was going to get things straightened out soon, she promised herself for the fortieth time. Somehow.

They'd arrived at the steps that led down to the kitchen. She thanked her escort as politely as she could manage, hobbled down and pushed the door open.

The kitchen was a long, narrow, crowded room. The cook, a stringy old man with limited notions of personal hygiene, gave her a sour look. "Better get moving. Zeno's in a bad mood."

"How can you tell?"

He snorted. "You go right ahead and smart off to him today like you been doin'. You'll see." He went back to flipping hamburger patties.

Charlotte hobbled to the cubbyhole where employees could leave their things. Dammit, she really did need to mind her tongue. She needed this job, and the Hole—for all its obvious drawbacks—did have three things in its favor. First, it was within walking distance of the cupboard-size apartment she'd found. Second, Zeno was allergic to cigarette smoke, so the entire place was smoke-free. Third, he was sloppy about paperwork and regulations—a definite drawback in terms of health and safety regulations, but a plus for her personally. He hadn't called any of the bogus references she'd listed on her application, and he didn't question her social security card—a good thing, since the number wasn't hers.

A man who was running a bookie operation out of his restaurant really ought to be more scrupulous about following the rules in his legitimate business, she thought as she slung her backpack under the table. She pulled off her coat, giving the shabby, shapeless brown material a look of distaste as she hung it on a hook. Best not to think about the beautiful new cream-colored wool coat hanging in the closet in her apartment—her old apartment.

The rent was paid up until the first. They won't have

sold her things yet, she told herself. Maybe she would still
be able to get them back.

"You're late," a deep voice growled from the doorway.
"Shift starts at five, not whenever you get around to showing up."

She jumped, scowled and looked at the doorway. Zeno
stood there glowering at her. He was a man who could
glower well. The paunch, thick eyebrows and bristly jowls
gave him a head start in the mean-and-nasty sweepstakes.

*Watch what you say,* she reminded herself, and reached
for the dusty first aid box on the top shelf. "A car nearly
ran me down at the light."

"Late's late. It happens again, you're out of here."

"I would have been a lot later if the car had hit me."
She gave the cap on the peroxide bottle an angry twist.
"And yes, I'm all right, thank you so much for asking."

"If you're all right, you can get your butt out there and
take orders."

"As soon as I've wiped the blood off. I'm pretty sure
it's a health code violation for me to bleed on the customers." *Stop that,* she told herself. Zeno was not the kind of
tyrant who admired those who stood up to him. He preferred quivering timidity. She pressed her lips together and
began to clean the long scrape on her calf.

"Maybe I didn't explain when I hired you. I hate attitude. What I like is 'yes, sir, no, sir, right away, sir.' Got
that, you stupid— What the hell do you want?" He turned
on the waitress who'd come up behind him, a doe-eyed
young woman named Nikki—"with two *k*'s and an *i*,"
she'd told Charlotte when they were introduced. Like Charlotte, she was blond. All of Zeno's waitresses were blond.
Nikki was the kind the jokes were made for, though.

"Mr. Jones wants to talk to you," Nikki said nervously.
"Table twelve."

"Why the hell didn't you say so? And *you,* Madame
Attitude—" he jabbed a thick finger in her direction
"—you've got five minutes to get out on the floor, or
you're fired."

She tried to make herself say "yes, sir," but the words wouldn't come out. She'd said them to her former boss a thousand times, said them easily, naturally. Because he was a man who deserved her respect. Her throat closed up. Grant Connelly wouldn't care about her respect. Not now. Not after what she'd done.

She managed to nod stiffly. Zeno gave her one last glare and stomped off. Charlotte threw the bloody swab in the trash.

"What happened to you, anyway?" Nikki asked, her eyes big.

"I had a little accident on the way here. Stand in the doorway so no one comes in, would you?" She had no doubt Zeno had meant what he said about firing her if she wasn't on the floor in five minutes. Her panty hose would have to come off right here. Charlotte grimaced, but accepted necessity.

Nikki obligingly stood in the center of the narrow doorway while Charlotte took off her shoes, then reached up under her skirt to pull down the ruined panty hose. Her legs were going to freeze on the walk back to her overpriced cupboard when her shift was over...but cold legs were the least of her problems.

"Zeno's sure on a tear. You'd better put your apron on."

"It's pink." She pitched the panty hose in the trash, fumbled her shoes on and grabbed her order book. "I don't do pink."

"We're supposed to wear the aprons."

"I know." Nikki wasn't a bad sort—a bit dim, and with all the backbone of cotton candy, but nice enough. Charlotte found a smile for her. "Come on, let's get on the floor before I'm fired." She moved out into the kitchen, Nikki trailing behind.

"I guess you're worried that the baby will show if you tie the apron around your waist, huh?"

She froze. "I don't... What are you talking about?"

"Oh, c'mon. I mean, you're not showing much, but there's that little bulge, isn't there? And when Serena sneaks a smoke in the kitchen, you turn green. My sister Adrienne was the same way when she was carrying my nephew.''

Charlotte got her breath back, but couldn't make herself turn around. ''Zeno's allergic to cigarette smoke, and I'm pretty sure *he* isn't pregnant.''

Nikki giggled. ''If he was, he'd be having triplets, wouldn't he? How far along are you?''

Sighing, Charlotte turned around. Her cover had been blown by a pink apron. ''Five months. Please, if Zeno finds out, he'll—''

''As if I would! Tell Zeno? What kind of person do you think I am?''

''Sorry. I can't help worrying. I need this job.''

''Then we'd better get moving.'' Nikki gave her a gentle shove and they headed for the stairs at the back of the kitchen. The restaurant's seating was on ground level, the kitchen in the basement. She'd be going up and down those steps a hundred times tonight.

''I guess it's scary when you're on your own,'' Nikki said. ''Did the father walk out on you?''

Was flying to the other side of the country the same as walking out? Maybe not, since he didn't know about the baby. All at once Charlotte was dead tired. Everything was wrong, and she couldn't seem to make any of it come right again.

Not everything, she reminded herself. At least she knew Brad was safe. Probably. As long as no one knew where he was. ''We shouldn't talk about this here,'' she said. ''Maybe you won't say anything, but if someone over-heard…''

''Like that Serena.'' She nodded, making her platinum curls bob. ''She'd split on you in a second. Good thing she never looks past her mirror.''

Charlotte pushed open the swinging door. ''True. Which station do I have tonight?''

''Four. Serena's on two, I've got one, and—hey, what's wrong?''

"Nothing." She hoped. "The tall guy with the shaved head and Cubs cap in my station. The one talking on a cell phone. Have you seen him in here before?"

Nikki cocked her head. "Don't think so. Why?"

*Idiot.* Why had she told him where she worked? "He said he didn't like teensy blondes," she muttered.

"Who, that guy? He's kinda cute." She cocked her head and smiled. "Maybe he likes tall blondes."

Had it been coincidence that he'd been there when the car nearly ran her down? He'd seemed nice, in a rude sort of way. But he'd insisted on walking with her, and now here he was.... Panic flared. She didn't know what to do, whether she should run or stay. Charlotte took a deep breath.

She had her backpack. If she had to—if he seemed too interested, or acted funny—she could be out the back door in a flash. "Want to swap stations? You could find out if he likes tall blondes better than dinky ones like me."

For the next half hour she tried to keep busy. But her nerves were jumping, and each minute jerked into the next in a painfully slow way. Her admirer—if that's what he was—didn't make any effort to talk to her. So why was he here? He wasn't a regular, and he hadn't spoken to Zeno, so he wasn't here to bet on the horses, or whatever.

Finally she couldn't stand it anymore. After delivering a French dip, a pastrami on rye and two hamburgers to the third table in her station, she went up to Mr. Cubs Cap.

"Okay," she said, trying to ignore the way her heart was pounding. "I want to know why you followed me here."

"Didn't." He pounded on the bottom of his ketchup bottle. "Your ego's showing again, sister. I was here, I was hungry, I decided to eat. Hey, you think you could get me some more ketchup? This one's about dry."

Automatically she took the bottle he held out. "I don't believe you."

"And I don't care. You going to get me some ketchup or not?"

A hand landed heavily on her shoulder. "Never mind, Dix. I'll take it from here."

In her dreams Charlotte had sometimes plummeted in an out-of-control elevator. That was what this felt like now—the stomach-dropping second of disbelief sliding into greasy fear and guilt. And, God help her, mixing with the swift kick of desire.

Her eyes closed. "Rafe," she whispered.

"Got it in one." His voice was cordial—and achingly familiar. His grip on her shoulder was tight. "I guess that means you haven't forgotten me entirely, even if a few other things have slipped your mind."

Slowly she turned. His hand fell away.

His trench coat was long, black and leather. His jeans had probably come from a discount store, but the dark blue shirt would be the finest Egyptian cotton because Rafe liked the way it felt. He'd told her that once. His wavy brown hair was too long, as usual, wild and shaggy. It looked as if the wind had been playing with it.

Or a woman. That, too, would be as usual.

He doesn't belong here, she thought with a rising sense of panic. He wasn't supposed to be here, not in a place like this. He was too blasted *perfect* for a place like this.

The thought gave her courage. Maybe it was a fool's version, born of anger and untainted by common sense, but she'd take what she could get. She straightened her shoulders. "I suppose you want to talk to me, but it will have to wait until my shift is over."

"No," he said slowly. "I don't think it will." He took her hand and started for the door, dragging her with him.

"Rafe." She tried to pull her hand free. "Have you lost your mind? I can't go with you now."

"Sure you can." He didn't slow as he wove through the crowded tables.

People were staring. She set her feet firmly so he couldn't keep tugging her along like a reluctant puppy, and for a moment it worked. He gave her a hard look over his shoulder and a sharp jerk on the hand imprisoned in his.

She nearly toppled. It was either stumble after him or fall to the floor. He dragged her another few steps. "Dammit, you're going to get me fired!"

"Do you think I give a flying—"

"What the hell is going on here?" Zeno planted himself in front of Rafe, glower firmly in place.

Charlotte had never imagined she would see Zeno in the light of a savior. "This idiot is dragging me out the door!"

"I don't want any trouble here," Zeno said, sparing her a condemning glance, as if it were all her fault this madman was trying to abduct her. "Whatever your problem with her is, you'll have to settle things when she's not working."

"She won't be working for you anymore after tonight," Rafe informed him calmly.

"Yes, I will." She gave one more hard tug, but only succeeded in hurting her wrist.

Rafe went on as if she hadn't spoken. "She shouldn't be working here now, not in her condition."

"What condition?" Zeno demanded.

Don't tell him, Charlotte chanted mentally. Don't tell him, please...

Rafe's eyebrows lifted. "You didn't know that she's pregnant?"

"She's *what?*" Zeno rounded on her. "Why, you lying little bitch. Is that why you've been wearing those puke-ugly sweaters?" He grabbed the hem of her sweater, pulled it tight, and put his hand on the bulge of her stomach.

Rafe dropped her hand. And swung once, clean, short and sharp, his fist connecting with Zeno's jaw with a solid thunk. The older man's eyes opened wide in amazement just before he collapsed.

Rafe rubbed his fist. "No touching," he growled. Then he grabbed Charlotte's hand and towed her out of there.

# Two

"Have you lost your mind?" she shrieked as he dragged her out the door. "You just punched out my boss!"

"Something tells me he isn't your boss anymore."

It was fully dark now—as dark as this corner of the city ever got, at least. The air was cold, the night punctuated with horns and headlights. Neon draped its tawdry glitter over buildings, cars and faces. Those faces were fewer than before and their owners moved more slowly, the ones in groups laughing too loudly, those alone wary and watchful. Or simply empty. The women's skirts were shorter, their lips brighter red. And none of the night people crowding the sidewalk seemed inclined to take exception to the man in a black leather trench coat who bullied his way through them, or the way he dragged his unwilling victim along.

She tried again to reason with Rafe. "It's cold. My coat...my things...you have to let me get my things." Her backpack, especially. She couldn't lose it.

"My car's just up the block. The heater works."

"You can't just drag me off this way! It—it's illegal."

"Yeah?" He stopped and turned so abruptly she plowed into him.

She landed with her free hand bracing her against his chest, preventing her from falling up against him, body to body. The leather coat was cool and supple beneath her hand. His chest was hard. So were his eyes, and the sarcastic curl of his lips wasn't a smile. She remembered the feel of that mouth on her and hastily pulled back.

"If you think I'm doing something illegal, you should yell for a cop." The curl grew into a sneer when she remained silent. "That's what I thought. Come on."

How Rafe had managed to find a parking spot right where he needed one, she didn't know. It was typical of the man, though. Luck, skill, karma—whatever force you credited, Rafe had more of it than any one man should. He had everything, from wealth and good looks to a successful career and a loving family. He should have been spoiled, shallow, dull. He wasn't. He was fascinating. Unaffected, unconventional, outgoing, generous.

The man's sheer perfection was the most irritating thing about him.

The hubcaps were still on his car, she noted as he shifted his grip to her arm and unlocked the door. But the car itself was not what Rafe Connelly was supposed to drive. He ought to have a dangerous, low-slung sports car, not a dark blue domestic sedan.

That was the second most irritating thing about Rafe— he never did what you expected him to do.

"Get in," he ordered as he swung the door open.

She sighed and did it. There was no point in arguing. He'd already gotten her fired, so she had little left to lose. They might as well get this over with. It wasn't going to be pleasant. She knew that. But she'd made it through a lot of life's unpleasant moments. She'd get through this one, too.

His car might not be the sports car that fit her image of him, but it was new and expensive. And familiar. She passed a hand over the cool leather of the seat and tried not to think about the only other time she'd ridden in Rafe's car.

He slid behind the steering wheel, slammed his door and started the engine. Sound poured from the speakers—some kind of rock with screaming guitars, lots of bass and a pounding beat. Cold air poured from the vents. No doubt his car did have a great heater, but the engine wasn't warm yet. She shivered and hugged herself for warmth.

With a flick of his wrist, he cut the stereo off. Silence fell. He glanced at her, grimaced, flung his door open again in defiance of the traffic, got out and shrugged off his coat. He tossed it at her and climbed back in without saying a word.

Charlotte drew the coat over her like a blanket. The lining held the heat from his body, and the warmth released scents that drifted up to tease her. Leather and man and memories... How unpredictable he was. First he dragged her along willy-nilly, then he gave her the coat off his back.

His voice was quiet. "It's mine, isn't it?"

He wasn't talking about the coat. Charlotte closed her eyes, but that petty escape didn't help. He was here, he was asking, and she had to face both him and the facts. "Yes."

He smacked the steering wheel with his fist. Hard.

She jumped.

"Did it at any point occur to you that I'd want to know? That I had the *right* to know?"

"I was going to tell you. When—when I could."

"And when would that have been? When my son graduated from high school, were you going to send me an announcement? Maybe hit me up for college tuition?"

She looked down. Beneath the enveloping coat, her hands were clasped tightly together. "It might be a girl," she muttered.

"What?"

Her head came up. She scowled at him. "It might be your *daughter* who graduates, not your son."

"Girl, boy, what does it matter? The point is, you're carrying my child. So of course you ran off and took a job at a dive so you could live hand-to-mouth, stay on your feet for hours, then walk home late at night. In *this* neighborhood.''

Her mouth twisted in bitter humor. She'd grown up in neighborhoods like this one. "I can take care of myself.''

"And one helluva job you've done of it, too. Considering that the mob is gunning for you.''

She swallowed and didn't reply.

"Damn shame the way things worked out for you.'' He turned in his seat, leaning against the door so he could survey her. His hand tapped the back of the seat in a quick, restless rhythm. "Selling out my father should have netted you a nice chunk of change, but you've ended up on the bottom of the food chain, haven't you?'' He shook his head in mocking sympathy. "You should be more selective about your business partners in the future.''

"It wasn't like that,'' she said, low-voiced.

"No? You want to tell me what it was like, then?''

Her lips felt stiff, numb. She'd known this would be unpleasant, but she hadn't realized how bad it would be. She hadn't known he would assume she'd done it for money.

But why wouldn't he? It was absurd for her to believe he should have known better. Illogical. "I told the police. That's why there's a contract on my life.''

He sighed and his hand stopped its restless tapping. For a long moment he didn't say anything. He just looked at her.

She tilted her chin up and looked right back at him. And found herself caught, trapped in the fascinating topography of his face.

His eyes were so deep-set the lids hardly showed. In this light his eyes looked black, as dark as the thick slash of his eyebrows, which were much darker than the medium brown of his shaggy hair. His beard, too, grew in dark, and there was a rakish trace of stubble on his cheeks tonight. His nose was straight and perfect, with that fascinating little dip beneath that inevitably led her eyes to his mouth. Oh, that mouth…it was a mouth made for smiles and kisses, the upper lip a perfect match for the lower. But it was entirely too sensual for the aristocratic nose, too wide for his narrow face, too frivolous for those dark eyes.

Rafe was composed of too many unmatched pieces. His parts shouldn't have added up to such an enticing whole, and she resented mightily that they did.

One corner of that enticing mouth kicked up. "You'd stare down a cat, wouldn't you?" He ran a hand over his head, further messing his hair. "Dix said someone nearly ran you down this evening."

Dix? Oh. Her surly Good Samaritan. "The man in the Cubs cap. He called you. He's working for you."

"Dix is a friend, but yeah, he's been working for me." A muscle jumped in his jaw. "Helping me find you. I've been trying to do that for months."

She rolled her eyes. "Oh, yes. You tried so hard."

"I called. You never called back."

"How could I forget? A month after climbing out of my bed, you did get around to leaving a message on my answering machine."

"I was out of town. You knew I had to leave the next morning. And I left several messages, dammit, not just one!"

Eventually, yes. He'd called three times. It had been too little, too late. "If you'd really wanted to talk to me, you knew where I was—until last month, at least."

"Yeah." His voice was flat. "Right there in my father's office, pretending to be his loyal assistant while you sold him out to the Kellys."

"So I'm slime." She stared straight ahead, determined not to cry. "You'd decided I wasn't worth the trouble long before you found out what I'd done."

He shifted, looking away. "It wasn't like that."

Right. She didn't want to hear whatever version of "you're just not my type" he'd cooked up to explain himself. She knew very well how little they had in common, aside from some combustible hormones. She'd known it all along.

And still she'd made a fool of herself with him. Tension knotted her jaw and neck. She took a deep breath, trying to relax those muscles. It didn't help. "How did you find me?"

"You used your mother's social security number at that dive I just rescued you from."

"Rescue? Is that what you want to call it?" Temper warmed her. She shoved his coat down into her lap. "And how would you know what number I used?"

He shrugged. "Dix can find pretty much anything that's in any computer file, anywhere."

"He's a hacker, you mean." She shook her head. Rafe never made sense. Why would a computer systems analyst who specialized in corporate security have a hacker friend?

"One of the best. I asked him to check the social security records of the family members listed in your personnel file at Connelly Corporation. Earnings have been recently reported under your mother's number—pretty amazing, considering she passed away nine years ago."

If Rafe could track her that way, so could others. Suddenly she wasn't warm anymore. "Maybe I'd better not go back to my apartment." That made two apartments she'd had to abandon.

"Congratulations. That's the first sensible thing you've said tonight."

But where would she go? She had only her tip money in her pocket; the rest was in her backpack, back at Hole-in-the-Wall. She needed to go back and get it, but two hundred and thirteen dollars wouldn't go far.

God. She was practically a street person. She knew what she had to do, but she hated it. Hated it. "I don't like to ask," she said, her throat tight, "but could you loan me some money? I don't have enough to get another place to stay."

Rafe didn't think he'd ever been this angry. Or this scared. He didn't like either feeling, but he especially hated the cramped, cold feeling in his chest he got when he thought about how close she had come to being hit by that car earlier.

Hell, he thought, dragging a hand through his hair. At the moment, he didn't like much of anything—not her, not himself and for damned sure not what he had to do about their situation.

There was one small consolation. She wasn't going to like the next part, either. "No, I won't loan you any damned money." He put the car in gear and pulled away from the curb.

Her voice stopped just short of shrill. "What are you doing?"

"I used to think you were fairly bright. Figure it out."

Good thing he'd kept an eye on her as well as the traffic. He managed to snag her arm and jerk her back before she could get the door open. "Uh-uh. Jumping out of a moving vehicle is not allowed."

He let go of her arm, but continued to divide his attention between her and the road. She might try it again when they stopped for a light. "Put your seat belt on."

Already she was taking deep breaths, getting herself back under control. Dammit. He wished he didn't enjoy it so much when she ruffled up like an outraged hen then carefully smoothed each bristly feather back into place. Perverse of him, and showed a sad lack of judgment. The woman was a liar and a crook, or at least in the pay of crooks. She'd betrayed his father. He needed to remember that.

"Rafe, I have to get my backpack before it's stolen," she said in that reasonable tone that always made him want to unbutton something. Not that she had any buttons showing right now, but she used to wear a lot of prim, buttoned-to-the-throat silk blouses to work. No doubt she'd thought covering everything up would keep the men she worked with from turning into ravening beasts.

Foolish of her. But Rafe had figured out long ago that most women had no idea how little it took to turn a man's thoughts to sex. Her prim blouses had just made him notice the way the silk shined and shifted over those soft, round, gorgeous breasts…breasts whose shape and texture he knew now.

He shook his head and tried to banish the memory. "Forget your backpack. I'll buy you another one."

"I don't want you to buy me anything. I want *my* backpack."

He eased to a stop at the light. "Listen, Charlie, someone tried to kill you on the way to your job. You can't go back there."

"Don't call me Charlie."

Her rebuke was automatic, he felt sure. As automatic as the way the nickname had slipped out. How many times had he called her that in the past two years, since she took over as his father's executive assistant?

He'd called her Charlie when he'd come inside her, too.

"All right, *Charlotte,*" he said, hating the name and halfway hating her, too. "Put your seat belt on. It's not safe for the baby if you ride without one, and I'm not letting you make any escape attempts."

She scowled, scooped his coat out of her lap and twisted around to deposit it in the back seat. Either she was warm enough now, or she didn't want anything of his touching her. Or she didn't want anything slowing her down when she made her break for freedom. He tapped the steering wheel with one hand, ready to grab her with the other.

"Rafe, I agreed to talk with you. I did not agree to be abducted."

"Tough. You haven't done such a great job of protecting yourself and our baby, so I'm taking over."

"If you're thinking about—about the incident today, it may not mean anything. Heaven knows Chicago has plenty of bad drivers."

"I've always admired that tidy brain of yours. I wonder why you aren't using it. Maybe you don't think I can use my brain. Yeah, that's probably it. You think you can persuade me there's no connection between people trying to run over you, and people shooting at you.'' The light changed and he accelerated. ''That's too much of a stretch for me, I'm afraid.''

Her hands made small, frustrated fists in her lap. ''Take me back to Hole-in-the-Wall.''

''No.''

Her tongue darted out nervously to lick her lips. ''If you're thinking of taking me to the police, please don't. The other time—when I was shot at—that happened as I was leaving police headquarters. I think someone in the department tipped them off. I don't want to go in a safe house. I don't think I'd be safe.''

''Amazing. We agree about something. Now put your seat belt on, or I'll reach over and put it on you.'' For a supposedly sensible woman, she sure wasn't paying attention to sensible precautions. ''My apartment's in the Bucktown area. We'll probably run across any number of bad drivers on the way there.''

''Your *what?* No.'' She shook her head so hard her hair flew into her face. ''No, I am not going to your apartment.''

''You don't have any choice. God knows I don't have much choice, either.'' He took a deep breath. Might as well get it said. ''You're carrying my baby. We'll get married.''

''That's not funny.''

He gave a short bark of laughter. ''You think I'm joking? If so, the joke's on me.'' Humor faded, settling into grim determination. ''I hope you don't have your heart set on a big wedding, because we can't go that route. We'd be issuing an invitation to the hit man along with the guests. He's been remarkably unlucky so far, but we can't count on his bad luck continuing.''

She looked stunned—and not with joy, either. At least she wasn't trying to leap out of the moving car.

''No comment? Good. We'll get the blood tests tomorrow.''

''You don't want to marry me!'' she burst out. ''You don't want to get married at all.'' She rubbed the back of her neck as if her head might be hurting. ''If this is some kind of noble gesture, all right, then. You've made it. I hereby let you off the hook.''

"I want my child.''

She closed her eyes, sighed and leaned her head against the headrest. "I want you to be part of the baby's life. You don't have to marry me for that.''

"I don't want a weekend now and then. I want my *child.* I want it all—3:00 a.m. feedings and diaper rash, school dances and college entrance exams.'' He shook his head. "Weird, isn't it? I had no idea I'd feel this way, so I can't blame you for being surprised. But there it is. I want to be a full-time daddy, so we have to get married.''

The hand that had been rubbing her neck fell into her lap. "And if I refuse to marry you, what will you do? Will you try to take the baby away from me?''

He shot her an irritated glance. "You think I'm some kind of monster? The last thing I want is a custody battle. That's why I'm proposing. Look, you need me.''

"I don't need anyone. And you don't want me. I mean, you don't want to marry me.''

His eyebrows lifted. Did she think he didn't want her now? Wrong, but interesting. Maybe useful. "You're right about me not wanting to get married. I don't. But I wasn't raised to duck my responsibilities.'' Of course, his parents hadn't raised him to have unprotected sex, either. He still didn't understand how he could have been that careless.

He realized he was scowling and tried to lighten up. "If you're worried about the sex part, don't. We can make things work out there just fine.''

Her stony expression suggested just the opposite. "I don't suppose it's necessary for you to actually like a woman to go to bed with her. I'm a little pickier. I'm not marrying a man who despises me.''

He hadn't expected this to be easy. Charlie was nothing if not stubborn. "Whether you like it or not, you do need me right now. You're running from some pretty big bad guys, and you lack the resources to do it right. If I could find you at that dive, they can, too. It looks as if they already have.''

She chewed on her lip. It was a small enough sign of nerves, but welcome. He was getting to her. Good.

Rafe switched tactics slightly. Let her think she'd won a compromise from him. Women were crazy about compromises. ''Look, you don't have to say yes or no about marriage right away. Stay at my place, though. Let me protect you. Don't endanger my baby out of pride.''

Silence descended for long moments.

''All right,'' she said abruptly. ''I won't marry you, but I'll stay in your apartment for now.''

It was more than he'd expected from her this quickly. He frowned, chewing over her capitulation in his mind. Maybe she was a lot more scared than she'd admitted—but there was no point in asking her. You could put Charlie in a cage of tigers and she'd insist she was fine. Or else she had some plan in mind. Something devious.

It was probably a sign of depravity that he was looking forward to figuring out her scheme. And stopping her.

Rafe considered himself a simple man. Computers were the one place he enjoyed knots and puzzles. He worked hard because he liked his work, and, he admitted, because he had his share of Connelly ambition. He played hard, too, when he was in the mood, but he also relaxed just as completely. He got more complexity than he needed from his big, maddening, high-profile family. When it came to his personal life, he kept things simple.

So how had he ended up in such a messy relationship with such a complicated woman?

There were her breasts, of course. He stole a sideways glance at her. Truly excellent breasts—not especially large, but beautifully shaped. And Charlie was great fun to tease—she always rose to his bait, but not always in the way he expected. She gave as good as she got, too. But while great breasts and teasing might account for his initial interest, they didn't explain why he'd taken her to bed the second he'd had the chance. Not when he'd known—dammit, he'd *known*—that she was a regular porcupine of complications.

She fascinated him. She was so charmingly tidy yet mysterious, keeping her private self tucked out of sight. He supposed a woman like Charlie needed to keep her externals orderly in order to cope with her complicated interior.

Yet in spite of her reserve he'd thought he knew her. Not all of her, maybe, but enough to like her. To trust her. Hell, his father had trusted her, and Grant Connelly was rarely wrong about that sort of thing.

Why had she done it? Why had she betrayed his father's trust?

He knew damned little. Last Christmas his oldest brother, Daniel, had surprised everyone, including himself, by becoming the heir to the throne of Altaria, the tiny Mediterranean country their mother hailed from. Almost immediately, someone had tried to kill him. Grant Connelly had hired a pair of private detectives—Lucas Starwind and Tom Reynolds—to look into the matter, but neither they nor the police had made much headway. They knew the attempt had been carried out by a pro, and that it was related to Daniel's new royal status. And that was about all they knew.

In May the Connelly Corporation computers had suffered a major crash. No surprise there. Rafe had been urging his father to upgrade his system for the past two years. At the time, Rafe had been involved with a big project in Phoenix. There had been no way he could take on another job. Charlie had suggested a technician who was familiar with the system and programs used at the corporation, and the tech seemed to have fixed things easily.

He'd fixed things, all right.

There had been no reason to suspect a link between a computer crash and the assassination attempt on Daniel. Not until last month. A connection had turned up then—a dead man.

Someone had murdered Tom Reynolds, one of the private detectives investigating the Connelly troubles. His body had been found in the alley behind the office of the computer tech who had restored the Connelly Corporation's system after the crash. And shortly before he was killed, Reynolds had called Grant to suggest that the corporate computer system needed to be checked out.

The technician himself had disappeared.

Charlie was the link between the tech and Connelly Corporation, and the police had picked up her up for questioning. At first she'd refused to talk in spite of the fact that Grant Connelly didn't want charges pressed against her. Then, as she was leaving police headquarters, someone had nearly managed to put a bullet between her eyes.

She'd talked after that—and then she'd vanished. Rafe couldn't find out much about what she'd told the police. They were being disgustingly closemouthed on that subject. All he knew was that Angie Donahue, the mother of his half-brother Seth, had somehow persuaded Charlie to use that particular technician.

And Angie Donahue was connected to the Kelly crime family.

Now there was a price on Charlie's head.

It all added up to one big, deadly mess. Rafe had canceled his next job, finished up the last one and flown home as soon as he could. Ever since, he'd been trying to find out what the tech had done to the corporate computers— when he wasn't trying to find Charlie.

City lights streamed past the windows on one side. On the other side the vast darkness of Lake Michigan was blocked by hotels and office buildings, with an occasional empty space giving a glimpse of the lake, spotted here and there by the running lights of freighters.

He glanced at the woman beside him. She was staring out the windshield as if she'd forgotten he existed. She'd been silent a long time. Dammit, he just knew she was coming up with new complications for him to sort out. "Does it move sometimes?" he asked abruptly.

"What?" She turned toward him, her eyes blank, as if she'd been far away.

"The baby. Do you feel it moving sometimes?"

"Oh." Her hand pressed her stomach, the fingers spreading as if she already had a big belly to support instead of a little bulge. A smile slipped over her face, changing it, making her look softer than he'd ever seen her. "Yes. She or he is asleep right now, I think, but I've been feeling movement for about a month now. It feels..." She shook her head, her expression full of wonder. "I don't know how to say it."

"It's a good feeling, though? It doesn't hurt or anything?"

Her glance was almost shy. She nodded. "It's good."

"Will you tell me the next time you feel it move? I'd sort of like to feel it, too."

Her cheeks flushed and she tucked her chin down as if he'd asked for something intensely personal. "I guess so."

"Good." He thought a minute. Maybe agreeing to let him share the baby before it was born was an intimacy she hadn't planned on. So he added, "Thank you."

She nodded and fell silent again.

Oh, she was going to make things difficult, he knew. She probably couldn't help it—she was a difficult woman. But he had some complications of his own in mind for her.

Charlie didn't want to marry him, but she had to. For her sake, his sake, and most of all for the sake of the life she was carrying. So he'd persuade her. Rafe knew just how to go about that—the same way he'd gotten himself into this mess.

He'd seduce her.

# Three

Charlotte hadn't known what to expect of Rafe's apartment. She'd been pretty sure it wouldn't resemble his parents' home on Lake Shore Drive. Grant and Emma Connelly lived in a Georgian-style manor furnished in antiques and elegance, with landscaped grounds that included an ornamental pool and a boxwood maze. It was altogether gracious and tasteful, not to mention intimidatingly rich.

But Rafe wouldn't be interested in gracious or traditional. He was fond of the casual, the eclectic, the downright odd. So she hadn't been surprised when they'd arrived at a converted office building in an area that was as much commercial as residential. But still…

Whatever she'd unconsciously expected, she thought as she stood in the middle of Rafe's living space, *this* wasn't it. She rubbed the back of her head, where the threatened headache had settled, and turned in a slow circle, taking it all in.

Except for the kitchen, the entire downstairs was one big

room. The floor was wooden, the ceiling high, the colors
bold. Furniture and floor treatments rather than walls defined the spaces. A change from wood to tile marked the
dining area, which was anchored by an enormous painting
of a jester, complete with whimsical hat, tasseled costume
and airborne balls of many colors.

A sectional sofa in glowing apricot created an L-shaped
conversational area in front of a fireplace. The fireplace
itself was modern and white; the wall that held it had been
painted deep blue. That same wall also held bookshelves,
three windows, a stereo and a huge-screen TV. Facing the
TV were cushy chairs upholstered in green and yellow and
purple. A hammock swung gently in front of the single big
window on the right-hand wall. Next to it was an iron staircase flanked by a stunning wooden statue of a nude woman.

"You have a strange look on your face," he said. "If
you don't like the place, blame my sister Alexandra. She
picked out most of the furniture."

She stopped looking at Rafe's things and looked at Rafe.
He stood in the middle of all that color, looking dark and
dangerous and out of place in his beard stubble and shaggy
hair. In this light, the color of his eyes wasn't black, but
blue—dark blue, like a stormy sky. "There's a tie on your
chandelier," she said.

He glanced up, surprised. "So there is."

A bubble of laughter rose in spite of her aching head.
She turned away, fighting a smile. The room was classy,
expensive, extravagant—and extravagantly messy. Things
were everywhere they didn't belong. Books, magazines,
newspapers, clothing. A guitar. Two big, thoroughly dead
plants. Computer parts were strewn across the glass-topped
dining table, along with more papers, a pair of socks and
a tool chest. The leather coat he'd loaned her was tossed
across a low hassock. The wooden nude by the stairs wore
a plastic lei and a Cubs cap.

She found the clutter oddly endearing. Rafe had always
seemed like too much of a good thing—too sexy, too rich,

too confident. His bright, sloppy apartment made him more human. Something warmed and softened inside her.

He sighed. "It's a mess, isn't it?"

"Ah…" She hunted for something tactful to say, but came up empty and settled for honesty. "Yes."

"Messy doesn't bother me, but you like things tidy. I'll see what I can do tomorrow." He glanced around, frowning as if he wasn't at all sure what that might be. "It is clean. You don't have to worry about that. Doreen comes at least once a week when I'm in town, and the woman is a demon on dirt. She'll clean anything that doesn't get out of her way. Nearly vacuumed me once when I was taking a nap, but fortunately I woke up in time."

Oh, the smile was winning, damn him. She bent to straighten a leaning pile of newspapers. "Were you napping in the hammock?"

"It's a restful spot. You don't need to do that."

"I can't help myself. What's behind the red wall?"

"The kitchen. There's also a half bath down here. The full bath is upstairs, along with my bedroom and office."

"And the guest room? Where I'll be staying—is that upstairs or down?"

"Ah…" He rubbed the back of his neck. "There isn't exactly a guest room. I used that for my office."

Temper made her head pound. "If you think I'm going to climb into your bed—"

"You'll be there alone…if that's what you want."

She refused to dignify that bit of blatant provocation with a reply. Turning, she headed for the stairs.

The rooms upstairs were smaller than down, but still much larger than the living room of her old apartment. A glance through the first open door revealed a room that was mostly high-tech office, though piles of papers and odds and ends of workout equipment hid some of the computer paraphernalia.

A glance through the opposite doorway made her smile and step inside.

His bathroom was long and narrow, walled in cobalt-blue tile, with gleaming white fixtures and a large shower stall bricked in glass blocks. That long wash of blue ended at a square, step-up tub deep enough to drown in. "Oh, my." She went straight for the tub. "I think I'm in love."

Rafe stood in the doorway. "Who would have thought it? The efficient Ms. Masters is a closet sybarite."

"Just a bathtub sybarite." And Rafe had her dream bathroom. She sighed in pleasure and envy and glanced over her shoulder. "So why are the towels hung up instead of dumped on the floor?"

"Childhood trauma. My mother was fierce on the subject of damp towels left on the floor. You want to take a bath before we eat? It might help that headache you've been nursing."

Her eyebrows twitched in surprise. "How did you know I've got a headache?"

"I'm psychic. And you're rubbing your head again."

She blinked and dropped her hand self-consciously.

His grin flashed. "Come on. I'll get you something to change into." He vanished into the short hall, his voice reaching her easily. "I'll fix dinner while you soak. Steaks okay?"

"Don't go to any trouble." She followed, confused by his shifting moods and wondering about the condition of his kitchen, given what she'd seen of the rest of the place. "Sandwiches or takeout would be..." Speech and feet both drifted to a halt when she reached his bedroom.

At first all she saw was the bed—huge, unmade, with tousled sheets, scattered pillows, and the comforter dragging the floor at one corner. It looked much the way her bed had on one morning five months ago.

Had someone shared that bed with him recently?

He spoke, drawing her attention to his amused face. "Don't worry. The mere sight of a bed won't make me pounce on you."

"Why bother?" she muttered. "Been there, done that."

As soon as the words were out, she cursed her slippery tongue. "I didn't say that."

"Yes, you did. You're thinking of the last time we were in a bedroom together."

"No." Memories pressed at her, an insistent thrust of heat and haste and impulse. The flavor of his mouth. The feel of his hands, quick and demanding. And her own dizzy need rising to meet those demands. "Not at all."

"I am. I'm remembering the way you taste when your pulse is pounding here." He lifted a hand and touched his own throat beneath the jaw.

Her own hand lifted involuntarily, mirroring his gesture, and quickly dropped. Her pulse *was* pounding. Dammit. "I don't care to wander down memory lane tonight. I'd rather wash the grime off."

"Why do I like that cool, sarcastic mouth of yours so much?" He shook his head. "Hell if know."

His lips were smiling. His eyes weren't. They were dark, intent. Hot. Oh, she knew that expression, was as fascinated by it tonight as she had been five months ago. As fascinated as birds are said to be by the gaze of a snake. That's superstition, she told herself. And couldn't keep from falling back a step when he moved toward her.

His smile widened. "Your nightie," he said, and held out what she only then noticed he held—an old sweat suit. "I told you I wouldn't pounce, but if you get the urge, feel free to jump on me."

"In your dreams."

His mouth still curved in that infuriating, knowing smile. "Oh, you have been, Charlie. You have been."

Her mouth went dry. Something fluttered in her chest—something too much like yearning. She snatched the clothes from him and escaped with as much dignity as possible.

The air was warm and moist, the water warmer and soothing. Her hair smelled of almonds from Rafe's shampoo. Charlotte lathered her left leg, then drew the razor along her calf.

This bathroom might have been conjured out of one of her private fantasies. *Oh, admit it,* she thought. The entire apartment seemed to belong in one of her daydreams, not her real life.

Except for the mess. Her mouth curved. She'd never pictured her dream apartment with so many piles of misplaced objects. Or a hammock. But the expensive furnishings, the artful use of color and space, the curving iron staircase and fireplace and beautiful rugs—she'd dreamed of a place like this, possessions like these, for years.

Charlotte had a hunger for nice things. *A product of my deprived childhood,* she thought with bitter humor, dipping her leg beneath the water to rinse. It wasn't a quality she admired in herself, but she accepted it. Possessions would probably always matter a little too much to her.

She leaned against the back of the tub. Had he really dreamed of her?

It didn't matter. It couldn't matter, she told herself fiercely. She knew better than to confuse fantasy with reality. Maybe he *had* dreamed of her. They'd been incredibly good together in bed. But dreams weren't a guide for real life, and great sex wasn't a basis for a marriage.

In dreams, she thought, her eyes drifting closed, anything could happen.

Someone rolled over inside her.

Her hand went to her stomach. It amazed her every time, this motion created by another being right inside her body. Would she grow used to the sensation in the next four months? Would she be more grouchy than awed when the baby was bigger and woke her up at night, kicking?

She smiled. She didn't think so. Much to her surprise, she loved being pregnant. Oh, at first she'd been scared and nauseous, appalled that this could happen to her, that she could have been so irresponsible. But the first time the baby had moved…she rubbed her middle, smiling, her eyes still closed. Now she even liked the way her body was expanding, the solid shape the baby made inside her. After being alone in her body all her life, she couldn't stop marveling at being two instead of one.

Funny. She'd never dreamed about being pregnant, yet now that she was, she loved it. Her fantasies had usually revolved around success in some form. Stock options. A well-fed 401K. Beautiful things of all sorts, from handmade quilts to designer suits to a hopeless craving she'd suffered from for months for an antique rolltop desk.

Though there had been another dream.... No, that was too important a word for her foolishness. A silly fantasy, that was all it had been. It had seemed harmless. She'd worked at the Connelly Corporation for three years and as Grant's assistant for two, and Rafe had never asked her out. She'd been sure he never would, sure her longing would go safely unrequited...until the night five months ago when the Connellys had held a barbecue at their lakeside cottage.

She'd gone there to get Grant's signature on a contract. And Rafe, damn his observant eyes, had realized something was bothering her. Grabbing at the first excuse that had come to mind, she'd claimed to be ill. Big mistake. Grant had refused to hear of her driving back to work. He'd refused to hear of her driving at all.

Rafe had offered to take her home. And she, foolish dreamer that she'd been, hadn't protested nearly enough....

*One night in May*

"So what's wrong?" Rafe asked as they headed back to the city on Lake Shore Drive.

"Just a bug, I guess." Outside, the air was dreamy with dusk. To their left, the vast waters of Lake Michigan were turning gray and secretive in the fading light. There were secrets inside the car, too. They pressed on Charlotte, weighed her down, made her want to be anywhere but here, with this man.

She leaned her head against the headrest and tried to relax. The ride was smooth and quiet, the leather seats absurdly comfortable. But the tension vibrating inside her wouldn't let go. "I'd pictured you with a sporty little two-seater."

"If I get the urge to travel with my knees jammed up to my chest, I fly economy class. No need to buy a car that does that for me."

A smile tugged at her mouth. Rafe had a way of making her smile, making her angry, making her feel all sorts of things she didn't want to feel. "I'll bet you've never flown economy in your life."

"You'd lose." He signaled and slowed the car. "I don't think you're sick."

She sat up straight. "What a strange thing to say. Unless your ego is crowding out your brain, and you think I lured you away from the party to have my wicked way with you."

He chuckled. "Don't I wish. No, you did your best to get out of accepting a ride. You've got an annoyingly large independent streak, Charlie."

"My name is Charlotte," she corrected him automatically, looking down at her lap. Her fingers rested there calmly enough, but inside she was rattling like a poorly tuned engine. There was a giddy intimacy in riding in Rafe's car, alone with him as darkness eased up on the city. But this pull she felt was the last thing she needed right now. It distracted her. She needed to be thinking about how to find out what that tech had done so she could undo it, not about the way Rafe's forearms looked with his sleeves rolled up.

He glanced at her, his grin flashing. "Nervous about being alone with me?"

"Don't be silly."

"If Dad hadn't been there to bully you, you'd never have gotten in this car with me."

"Your father doesn't bully. He's been very good to me." And in return, she'd betrayed him. But what else could she have done? Oh, Brad, she thought, miserable in her love and guilt. Somehow she would make things right again. If she had to go to the office every weekend, she'd make things right.

*For everyone else,* a little voice inside whispered. She might be able to put things right for others, but her own dreams were forever spoiled. There never had been any chance of a future for her and Rafe, she reminded that whispery voice. They were too different. Besides, he liked to tease, he liked to flirt, but he'd had three years to fall for her, if he was going to.

Obviously he wasn't.

She kept her eyes closed, faking the sleep her unquiet mind wouldn't allow. Rafe either believed she'd dozed off or was willing to let the conversation drift to an end. Neither of them had spoken for perhaps fifteen minutes when he broke the silence. "Here we are."

She straightened, frowning as he pulled to a stop. "*Where* are we?"

"A couple blocks from a great Italian restaurant." He turned off the engine, got out and came around to her side. She remained where she was, flustered and angry. When he opened her door she said, "I'm not in the mood for a kidnapping."

"This isn't a kidnapping. I'm taking you to dinner."

"I don't recall being asked."

"If I'd asked, you'd have said no. Look, Charlie, you're not sick. You just said that because you didn't want to talk about whatever has you upset. Man problems, probably. But I'm not a bad listener. You might try not holding everything in, see if it helps."

Oh, yes, he was just the person for her to confide in. *You see, gangsters forced me to let them do something to the computers at your family's corporation....*

"No," she said firmly. "Thank you, but no. I'll be fine."

He nodded. "That's what I thought. You look like a woman in need of a good cry, but you aren't about to let your hair down and take advantage of my broad, manly shoulders, are you? So I decided to feed you instead. Tony makes great lasagna."

To her alarm, the quivering inside threatened to spill outside. She bit her lip to keep it steady. "I'm sure you know a lot about women, but I don't think you know much about the therapeutic effects of a good cry."

"I've got sisters." He heaved a huge sigh. "Lord, do I have sisters."

"Three sisters might make you seem like a poor, outnumbered male if you didn't also have five brothers."

"Seven brothers now."

Of course. She felt like a fool for forgetting. Rafe had grown up with five brothers, including a half brother, but last month the family had learned of two more Connelly men—twins, the product of a youthful affair of Grant's that had taken place before he married Emma.

A discovery like that might have torn another family apart. Not the Connellys. Oh, there had been some turmoil. She'd heard raised voices in Grant's office a couple of times, but that sort of thing happened from time to time anyway, and meant little. The Connellys were stubborn, strong-minded people, every one of them. Sometimes they were angry and loud. But the storms came and went, leaving the family still solid. United.

What would it be like to have such a family? So many, and so close. There would always be someone to listen, to help if you needed it.... The squeeze of something horribly close to self-pity made her voice sharper than she intended. "You prove my point. Testosterone seven, estrogen three. The testosterone count wins."

"Come on. You've met my sisters. Can you really believe any of us poor males ever wins?"

She chuckled in spite of herself.

"That's better." He reached in and took her hand. "Come on, Charlie. Eat. You'll feel better. If you're good, I'll even spring for tiramisu."

Charlotte lay in the cooling water, remembering the crowded little restaurant, the wobbly table covered by a cheap vinyl tablecloth and the incredible lasagna. They'd shared a bottle of wine while they talked, teased and argued. And she'd forgotten to worry. Or maybe she'd willfully shoved worry aside, seizing the chance to feel good with both hands, like a greedy child.

Rafe had taken her home. He'd insisted on walking her up to her apartment. At her door he'd kissed her...and all those dreams, all those foolish, impractical dreams had blazed to life along with her body.

She remembered the look in his eyes when he'd lifted his head. The way she'd felt when his hand sifted through her hair. His hand hadn't been entirely steady, and she'd let herself hope. For a moment hope had bloomed in her, bright and mute as sunrise.

Maybe he'd seen it in her eyes, because she remembered very clearly what he'd said. "I want to come in, Charlie. I want to be with you. But we need to be clear with each other." That gentle hand had cradled her head, his thumb spread to stroke her temple. "No expectations beyond what we can give each other tonight."

She'd let him in. Even as those silent hopes died, she'd let him in, wanting passion and memories, craving whatever temporary oblivion he might bring her.

Rafe had been a skilled lover, and a greedy one. And he'd left before sunrise. She'd pretended to sleep while he found his clothes in the dark. Even when he'd bent over her and his lips had brushed her cheek, she'd faked sleep, afraid that if she spoke, if she did anything to acknowledge his leaving, she would embarrass them both.

No expectations. He'd wanted to be with her, but once had been enough.

She sighed once and stood, reaching for one of the thick, oversize towels. He had at least left her a note. She'd burned it.

The blasted towel smelled like him. She made a face and rubbed herself dry briskly. None of that, she told her excitable hormones. Since the night when she'd tumbled into bed with him so easily, she'd done a much better job of shutting out foolish dreams. In fact, she hardly dreamed at all anymore.

# Four

**R**afe was using his favorite knife on a fresh shitake mushroom when he heard Charlie coming down the iron staircase. She'd spent an ungodly amount of time in the bathroom, but he'd expected that. He'd once asked his sister Maggie what women did in bathtubs that took so long. She'd given him one of those "I Am Woman" superior looks and told him he wouldn't understand.

Women and bathtubs. He shook his head and got the steaks out of the refrigerator, where they'd been marinating. The broiler was already hot. He was forking the steaks onto the broiler pan when she spoke.

"You're cooking!"

"I said I would."

"No, I mean *really* cooking. I smell herbs—oregano?—and you're cutting up vegetables."

"Vegetables for the salad, oregano and rosemary in the marinade for the steaks." He closed the oven door and glanced at her. Then paused, startled. "Your hair is curly."

Her hand lifted self-consciously to touch the damp curls. "I couldn't find a blow-dryer, so I towel-dried it."

"I don't have one." He couldn't stop staring. She looked so pretty with her face all warm and pink from her bath and her hair all messy with curls. His sweats pretty much swallowed her, of course. She'd rolled up the sleeves and the pant legs several times. "You always wear your hair all smoothed out." He shook his head. "It looks nice smooth, but I like it like this. Curly and a little wild."

"I like it smooth." She wandered around, inspecting his kitchen with a small, worried vee between her eyebrows. "I had no idea you knew how to cook. Your kitchen—" She waved one hand at the counter. "Everything's clean. Not just wiped-down clean, but put-away clean. The rest of your place is a mess, but the kitchen is neat. And you've got enough pots hanging in the pot rack to open a kitchen supply store."

Her consternation made him smile. "We're learning a lot about each other. I thought your hair was straight. You thought I couldn't cook." He shook his head sadly. "I had no idea you were sexist."

"Most men *don't* cook." When he lifted an eyebrow, she added with dignity, "That's an observation, not a sexist comment. And your family...you must have grown up with a cook."

"I remember one of them—Abraham. He gave me great advice when I was in college. Women are turned on by a man who cooks for them."

Her mouth made a small, disgusted moue. "I should have known." Moving to the chopping board, she picked up the knife, finished slicing the mushroom and reached for a carrot.

"You like to cook, too?" He moved closer, stopping behind her. His shampoo sure smelled different on her than it did on him. He bent to sniff.

Her hand stilled. "Sometimes. I do know how to use a knife."

"Threats. How exciting." He lifted a strand of that damp hair and let it curl across his palm in a soft question mark. "Want to slip into something leather and say that again?"

The muffled sound she made might have been a laugh, quickly stifled. "Anyone ever tell you you're easy?"

"I hear it all the time." He released the strand of hair he'd been toying with and let his fingertips trace the soft skin along the side of her neck. "Anyone ever tell you your skin feels like rose petals?"

"Rafe." Her shoulders stiffened. "Don't."

He didn't want to stop. He wanted to bend and nuzzle the warm place where her neck met her shoulder. To slide his hands up beneath the sweatshirt and find out if she was wearing a bra, or if she'd left herself deliciously bare. She had such beautiful breasts. He wanted to see them again, taste them.

He wanted it—wanted her—a little too much.

When he stepped back, his heart was pounding. He was as hard as if he'd been playing with her breasts instead of thinking about them. It was ridiculous, alarming, to be this aroused this quickly. He cleared his throat. "What's your preference? I like medium rare myself, and I'm warning you I have moral objections to well-done."

Her head moved back and forth in a single confused shake. "Well-done what?"

"It's a sin to ruin a good T-bone by cooking it into leather."

"Oh. The steaks." At last her hand completed the motion she'd started moments before, and she started slicing the carrot. "Medium, please."

There was a husky note in her voice. It was some consolation to know she'd been affected, too. But not a lot. He scowled as he went to the pantry, where he grabbed a bottle of rosé. "Are you allowed to have wine?"

"Best if I don't." Her voice was already back to normal. Oh, she was a cool one, Charlie was—except for that hair. The drier it got, the friskier it got. It looked like scrambled sunlight now, a messy red-gold riot skimming her shoulders.

This was why he'd never asked Charlie out, he thought. Why he'd teased and flirted and argued with her, and been careful to never see her outside his father's office. She stirred him, yes. That part was fine. But there was something else, something about her that set off all kinds of warning bells. She was too complicated, kept too much of herself hidden. A woman like that could get her hooks in a man so deep he'd never be free again.

It was a little late for him to worry about his freedom, wasn't it?

"So what do you want to drink?" he snapped. "I'm going to have wine."

Her glance was puzzled. "Fine. Milk would be great for me, if you have some. Or water."

"I've got milk." Rafe jabbed the corkscrew in. He'd slipped the noose around his neck himself when he took her to bed, and she'd been bothering him ever since. The blasted woman kept showing up in his thoughts when she had no business being there. And now—*now* she had the gall to say she didn't want to marry him. He gave the corkscrew a vicious twist.

"The salad's ready. What kind of dressing do you want?" she asked, moving to the refrigerator.

"There's fresh vinaigrette in a bottle in the door. What kind of ring do you want?"

She frowned. "Is that what soured your mood all of a sudden—thinking of wedding rings? Cheer up. I'm not marrying you."

He looked at the slight bulge of her belly beneath the sweats, the round breasts and the drying curls that were so different from the in-control image she liked to present to the world.

In bed, Charlie lost control. Soon, he promised himself,

he would begin uncovering some of those secrets she hoarded so zealously. "You may not plan to, but you will, Charlie. You will."

It was a strained meal. The food was delicious, and Charlotte ate more than she'd expected to. But the company lacked a certain something. Like the ability to carry on a conversation.

Usually Rafe's moods were easy to read. When he was angry, he exploded. When he wanted to charm, he charmed. Happy, gloomy, tired, funny—his thoughts might be a mystery, but whatever he felt was usually right out there for all to see. But usually he talked. Whatever his mood was tonight, it involved a lot of silence. The monosyllabic replies she received when she tried to start a conversation annoyed her into her own silence.

For a man who claimed he wanted to marry her, he certainly didn't seem interested in speaking to her.

She escaped to the kitchen as soon as possible, insisting that since he'd cooked she would handle the cleanup. He gave her an unsmiling glance, shrugged and told her to have fun. When she finished loading the dishwasher, he was nowhere in sight. She glanced at the stairs and caught the faint sound of the shower running.

She would stay down here, then.

Her headache was gone, but in its place was a jittery sort of exhaustion. She moved around the room picking up a few of the more obvious bits of debris and putting them where they belonged. Dealing with Rafe's things was easier than dealing with him—or her feelings. She hung his coat on a wooden hanger and bit her lip.

She wanted to go home.

With her eyes open, staring at the bright miscellany of his apartment, she could see *her* place, her things—the blue sofa she'd bought secondhand. The crystal lamp she'd bought new, for a ruinous price. Her own pocket-size kitchen, less than half the size of Rafe's, with her baking equipment and cookbook collection.

She was homesick. Oh, my. She shook her head. At twenty-six years old, after living on her own since she was seventeen, she was seriously homesick. How ridiculous. Absently she rubbed her chest, where the ache seemed the strongest, and drifted over to look at the big painting of a jester.

It made her smile. There was that huge, absurd hat, rakishly tilted. The balls that floated so improbably, kept airborne by will or magic. The jester's wicked eyes and cocky grin. He was very sure of himself, certain he could keep all those balls spinning.

"What's the Mona Lisa smile for?"

She turned. Rafe stood at the foot of the stairs, rubbing a towel over his hair. He was wearing silky blue pajama bottoms...and nothing else. Her heartbeat went silly. To compensate, she lifted one eyebrow and answered in her coolest voice. "Have you decided to speak, then?"

He didn't smile. "Sorry. I've been thinking."

"And it's so difficult to do two things at once. Like think and speak."

He brought the towel down across his chest as if chasing a stray drop of water. Her gaze was dragged right along with that towel. "I did irritate you, didn't I?"

"Yes." Was he doing that thing with the towel on purpose? She turned back to the painting. "I like this. Is it from a local gallery?"

"Not a gallery, but it is by a local artist. Maggie painted it for me when I got this place. She claims he reminds her of me."

Oh, that cocky, confident grin... "I'd say she knows you pretty well."

"We seldom know people as well as we'd like to think." His voice told her he'd moved closer. "Why did you do it, Charlie? Why did you sell out my father?"

Her stomach muscles jerked, drawing her spine straight. Her mind filled with the noisy buzz of excuses, explanations, apologies…guilt. She couldn't get a single word out of her dry mouth.

"How much did they pay you? Or was it blackmail—do they have some hold over you? Dammit, Charlie!" His hand closed around her arm, and he turned her to face him. "You owe me some kind of explanation!"

"Maybe I owe your father an explanation. He…" Her voice faltered. She hadn't seen Grant since she'd confessed to the police. She didn't want to see him, but at some point she would have to. Apologies mended nothing and explanations were kissing cousins to excuses, but he deserved at least that much from her. That, and a chance to tell her what he thought of her.

She straightened her shoulders. "But I don't owe you a thing."

"We can't start a marriage with this between us."

She knocked his hand away. "What marriage? Read my lips, Rafe— I am not marrying you."

His upper lip lifted in a snarl of temper. He grabbed her shoulders and crushed his mouth down on hers.

She jolted and tried to shove him away. Quick as a striking snake, he captured her hands and twisted them behind her, holding them easily with one hand while his other grabbed her jaw, trapping her face so she couldn't twist away from his mouth.

It was nothing like the first time he'd kissed her. Then he'd cupped her face in one hand, not captured it in a grip she couldn't break. Then his mouth had been sure and gentle, not hard and hot with demands she couldn't refuse. Her eyes went wide in shock. She couldn't move, couldn't even turn her head aside, could only stand there and let him take her mouth. Fear skittered through her system like fire chasing dried leaves.

But fear was supposed to be cold. This wasn't. The wild current flickering over her skin brought heat, a prickly flush that woke an ache deep inside. He wasn't hurting her. His mouth was eating at hers, and his hand had left her face to caress her throat, his thumb making slow circles over her racing pulse. Her inner thighs clenched. The muscles across her shoulders and back went loose, and her hands were suddenly limp in his grasp.

She'd been wrong. It was exactly like the first time he'd kissed her. Perfect.

Her mouth opened and she knew him, knew his taste and the wild beating of his heart. Her own heartbeat turned strange and unpredictable, a foreign drum sounding a rhythm she didn't understand. A mad confusion seized her, making her want to lick her way down his chest where she could take his heartbeat into her mouth. Making her want to hit him, hurt him, spurn him—or take him deep inside her, so far inside he could never get free again.

It was that confusion rather than any gram of common sense that had her twisting free.

He still held one of her hands. He'd turned loose of the other at some point. She hadn't even noticed. His eyes were dark and hot. "Charlie," he said, and reached for her again.

She flinched.

He froze. Then, moving very slowly, he put his hand on her cheek, just rested it there, his fingers curving up around her temple. "If you were thinking of sticking me with a knife, don't bother. The way you looked just now..." He drew in a shaky breath. "I'm sorry."

"I don't *like* not having a choice." Her voice shook. She hated it. Maybe she hated him, too—for the gentle way he touched her now as much as for the way he'd kissed her a moment ago. "You don't have any right to hold me and—and do those things. No right. You—you— I never know what you're going to do!"

"I didn't know I was going to do that, either." His thumb made a soothing circle on her cheek. "With you, I keep surprising myself."

His tenderness frightened her more than his force had. She tried to make herself move away from that soothing hand. And couldn't.

"What do you want, Charlie? Do you want me to say I'm sorry I hurt you?" His thumb dipped to her mouth, touching the upper lip. "I am."

She stiffened and stepped back. "You didn't hurt me. You made me furious, but you did not hurt me."

One corner of his mouth tucked down in mild frustration. "Whatever you say."

"You're making me furious now, too."

"I make you feel plenty of things, which is why you're angry. We'll have a lively marriage."

Her breath puffed out in exasperation. "Rafe. Be reasonable. Fifty years ago a pregnant single woman might have had to get married for the sake of the baby. That isn't necessary anymore."

"Maybe not necessary, but it's best. Be reasonable," he echoed her, lightly mocking. "I wouldn't make a bad husband. I've got money—and that matters, you know. Maybe more than it should, but the way this world is set up, money can make a big difference in the kind of start a kid gets. It makes a difference in the stress levels of the kid's parents, too. I know you like pretty things, and no one likes worrying about how they're going to pay the bills. I can take good care of you and the baby."

Her mouth tightened. "Thank you very much, but I don't need to be taken care of."

"Then there's family. I've got plenty of that, God knows. I'll admit they can be aggravating at times, but it's good for a kid to have family—aunts, uncles, cousins. Grandparents."

That went right to her gut. A large family was the one thing she couldn't give her child. "Your parents... I think Grant and Emma will accept the baby whether we get married or not."

He grimaced. "Of course they will. When I told them it was my baby you were carrying—"

"You told them? What...'' She wanted to know what

they'd said, how they'd reacted. She was afraid she wouldn't like the answer. "When did you tell them?"

"As soon as I got back. I told them I was going to marry you, too."

"I'm sure they loved hearing *that*. Especially your father."

"He didn't object. Look, Charlie, our baby will be a Connelly no matter what its last name is. But if we're not married, *you* won't be part of the family. How do you think our child will feel, knowing that his mother isn't one of the clan? A little different from the rest? Maybe not quite as good?"

She looked away. "Lots of children have divorced parents. They don't all feel like outsiders."

He must have known he was getting to her. He cupped her shoulders. "But we don't have to take the risk that our child will feel that way."

"Talk about risks! Marriage is a risk under the best circumstances. These are hardly the best."

"Everything in life is a risk. If we don't get married, we'll be guaranteeing that our child won't grow up with two parents in the same home." He squeezed her shoulders gently. "What can I say to convince you? Tell me what you want. If it's money—" He paused, grimaced. "We can handle things that way if you like. A settlement of some kind. I've got enough to be generous."

*Oh, thank you,* she thought, dizzy and numb from the sudden blow. *Thank you for reminding me what you really think about me. What else could I possibly want, but money?*

"So." His smile was a masterpiece—charm with a whiff of seduction from the lingering heat in his eyes. "What do you say?"

She gathered the ragged edges of her pride around her. "I'd say you're a fool to want to marry a woman who's more interested in what you own than what you are." His hands and the skin around his eyes tightened. Good. Her own blow had landed. She smiled at him, bright and brittle. "But that's your affair. I'll give your proposal some thought and get back to you once I decide exactly what it's worth to me."

Nothing, she thought as she turned away. His proposal wasn't worth one damned thing.

This time he didn't try to draw her back. He let her climb the stairs to his bedroom without saying another word.

Rafe swung gently to and fro in the hammock, staring out the undraped window. Night changed the tempo of the city's pulse without altering its restless rhythm. Cars growled, revved, raced, paused and cruised. Lights blinked on in some windows while others winked off. Somewhere a siren howled, muffled by walls and distance.

Here was home. Rafe enjoyed travel; he liked seeing new places, trying new things. The green of a wandering country lane, the rush and rapture of the ocean, the majesty of mountains and the silence of desert—all had a place in his heart, but none were at the center of it the way Chicago was. After a trip for business or pleasure he always settled into the sights, sounds and scents of this city like a child snuggling into his own familiar bed.

Tonight the city held no comfort for him.

All his life Rafe had seen dollar signs in people's eyes when they looked at him. It was an inescapable part of being a Connelly. Even basically decent people were sometimes more conscious of his family's wealth than they were of anything else about him.

He'd been eight when he first realized that some people disliked him simply because his father had money. He'd been as indignant as only an eight-year-old can be. His father had told him that most people had to deal with something along those lines. Whether you were black or freckled, fat or skinny, had a rich father or a funny name—whatever was different, that was what people noticed first. Most of them got past it if you gave them a chance.

On the whole he'd found that to be true. But it was also true that some women never saw beyond what his wealth might bring them, if only he could be persuaded to share some of it. Or all of it, along with his name.

The funny thing was, it had never occurred to him that Charlie might be one of those women. Not until she'd jumped to the conclusion that he was trying to buy her. Now that she'd put the idea in his head, he couldn't get rid of it.

*You're a fool to want to marry a woman who's more interested in what you own than what you are.*

Was that the most important fact about him to Charlie? What he owned?

When he'd offered a settlement, he'd been thinking about the power that money confers. Earlier she'd asked him if he would try to take custody of their child away from her if she didn't marry him. That had smarted, but after thinking it over, he could see that she might feel powerless. He'd thought to reassure her by giving her money of her own, money he didn't control. Instead he'd made her furious...and made himself doubt.

Charlie didn't know how to fight, though. She held tight to her temper the way she held on to all her emotions, as if relaxing her grip might leave some stray feeling out where people could see it and use it against her.

She needed to surprise herself more.

Well, he could help her with that. God knew he surprised himself with her. It was only fair if she was off-balance with him, too. And it would be good for her to loosen some of that too-tight control she put on herself.

She hadn't been controlled in bed. She hadn't been thinking about his money then, either. She'd burned for him, dammit. He wasn't wrong about that. Charlie might keep her emotions under lock and key most of the time, but when she let them out they were as real and honest as a thunderstorm.

He'd screwed up. Big-time.

Rafe scowled and shifted, making the hammock rock. The fact was, she'd scared him. He hadn't liked that, hadn't wanted to admit she had that much power over him, so he'd stayed away. He'd done his damnedest to shut her out of his mind, secretly glad for the business trip that took him out of Chicago for the next few months.

He knew how women felt about men who don't call. It was high on their list of Unforgivable Male Sins. Whatever Charlie said now, he had hurt her.

Calling her a month later didn't count, he admitted. That had been a matter of pride and conscience. He'd known there was a chance their lovemaking could have resulted in complications, and his own good opinion of himself hadn't let him duck that responsibility.

Maybe he'd wanted to talk to her again, too. Maybe he'd wanted that every bit as much as he'd wanted to stay away from her, and maybe it had hurt when she didn't return his call. Not a lot, he assured himself. But it had hurt a little bit.

He put his hand against the wall and gave a push, setting the hammock to swinging again. Things were majorly complicated, all right. He'd hurt her. She'd betrayed his father. What kind of marriage could they have when they didn't trust each other? When they each had good reason not to trust?

At the back of his mind he'd always thought that if he ever *did* get married, he would want what his parents had—something real and solid. They'd hit some rough patches, but they'd come out stronger in the end. Not many people had what they did. Too often marriage made people mean or crazy or unhappy. He supposed that had been another reason he'd steered clear of it. He hadn't wanted to marry unless he could do it right. He hadn't wanted to try for that and fail.

His mouth thinned. He hadn't failed yet. Hell, he hadn't managed to talk her into marriage yet. One thing at a time, he told himself. She'd wanted him once. He was pretty sure she still did, so he had that on his side. God knew he wanted her, too. Sometimes he wasn't sure which he wanted more—to shake her or kiss her—but even when the shaking sounded really appealing, he still wanted to kiss her.

Charlie would end up in his bed. That much he promised himself. The trust business, though… He sighed. That was going to take a lot more thought.

It would be a helluva lot easier to trust her if she'd just tell him what was going on. If he knew *why* she'd done what she had… When you got right down to it, he didn't know much about her. He wouldn't even have known her parents were dead if it hadn't been in her personnel file at Connelly Corporation.

Oh, he knew one or two of her secrets now. He brooded over that as the hammock rocked gently. He'd had to do some digging to find her, and wouldn't she be mad if she knew that? She'd had some rough times as a kid, Charlie had. But dammit, she didn't have to make a big secret out of everything.

It would be easy to learn more. Between him and Dix, there wasn't much that couldn't be pried out of various records, including the ones at the police department. But he knew what her reaction would be if she found out he'd gone behind her back that way. You don't go about building trust by hacking into a person's past.

Hell. He was going to have to do this the hard way, wasn't he?

# Five

In another part of Chicago, in a twelfth-floor room at a large hotel, Edwin Tefteller held a cellular phone to his ear. The drapes were drawn. The radio, tuned to a classical station, played just loudly enough to muffle any sounds of the city that might leak in through the walls.

He was a smallish man, only five foot six, but trim and very erect. His face was soft, clean, round. The skin was firm enough to suggest that his receding hairline had arrived prematurely. The neat little mustache beneath his nose was sandy brown, like the thinning hair on his head. His white dress shirt was of decent quality and moderate price, like his dark shoes and slacks and the conservatively striped tie knotted at his throat. The one small note of vanity or extravagance was sounded by his glasses, which had a designer frame. The lenses were clear glass, but no one could tell that by looking.

All in all, he looked like a man who ate his vegetables, flossed after meals and paid his bills on time, a man who could sail through an IRS audit without breaking a sweat. And he was. Most people looked at him and thought "accountant."

They were wrong.

Edwin's index finger tapped the little cell phone with restrained impatience. At last a voice came on the other end. "This had better be important. It's after one-thirty in the morning. My wife gives me hell when the phone wakes her up."

"I do not make a habit of calling about trivial matters," Edwin said. "You have violated our agreement."

"I don't know what you're talking about."

Edwin sighed. Employers preferred to consider him a tool. On the whole, it was convenient to allow them to think of him this way. Had they realized how much of their affairs he knew or inferred, it would have made them uneasy. But while Edwin might permit employers to underestimate him, he did not allow them to take him for a fool. "I have an exclusive contract with you, Mr. Kelly. I work alone. Always. I believe I made that clear at the outset."

"I'm aware of the terms of our agreement," Jimmie Kelly growled. "Especially the godawful amount of up-front money you demanded."

"I am relieved to hear it. Perhaps you can explain why the same bumbler who botched the first attempt was allowed to interfere in *my* contract, then."

"I still don't know what you're talking about. And Palermo's no bungler."

"He failed to kill the Masters woman once. That is why you contacted me, isn't it?" Edwin let a small silence fall. There was a great deal more to the situation than that, but it wouldn't pay to advertise his knowledge at this point. "That, and you appreciated the dispatch with which I took care of the earlier job with the private investigator. I, in turn, appreciated the dispatch with which you paid my fee. I am disappointed by your disregard of our agreement this time, however. I will not tolerate sharing a contract with others.''

"I told you I'd pull Palermo off the Masters job. If my word isn't good enough—"

"Today at 4:43 p.m., Rocky Palermo tried to run down Charlotte Masters with a '98 Buick—stolen, I assume. If your chief enforcer was not acting on your orders, you have a disciplinary problem.''

There was a tiny, betraying pause before Kelly exploded. "Damn right there's a problem! He's supposed to be keeping track of her for you, not trying to take her out. I'll straighten him out.''

"You do that," Edwin murmured. Palermo had, of course, acted on orders. The Kellys' chief enforcer wasn't in Edwin's class, but neither was he stupid. No doubt Jimmie Kelly thought he could refuse to pay the other half of Edwin's fee if his own man made the hit. It was a mistaken assumption, but in some ways Kelly was a simple man.

"I was prepared to complete the job tomorrow night, quietly and without fuss. Your man's blundering attempt alerted her that her whereabouts were known. Naturally, she has disappeared. I stand to lose a great deal of time tracking her down a second time. I cannot and will not tolerate having my contract interfered with again.''

"Dammit to hell, I've told you I'd take care of it.''

"You will understand, I'm sure, that I must refuse to share my information with you now. I would hate to have to eliminate Mr. Palermo, but if he were to interfere again, I would be forced to.''

The silence was longer this time. "I want to be kept informed.''

"I will let you know when I am prepared to complete the job. I will not tell you where the target is." Kelly hadn't found the woman. Edwin had. He saw no point in tempting his employer into misbehavior again.

Kelly needed to assert his authority with trivial demands and veiled threats. Edwin allowed him that. Employers wished to feel they controlled their tool. And they did, as long as they dealt with him according to the terms of their agreement.

After the call ended, Edwin put the cell phone back in his briefcase. Kelly had dealt with him squarely the first time, when he had killed the detective. Now, however, he was trying to save a few dollars. Edwin's mouth curved in dry humor as he carefully unknotted his tie. It was amazing, really, what avarice would tempt people into. One wouldn't think that one of the top killers in the world would have to worry about being cheated, but now and then a client considered himself so powerful that he could rewrite their deal after a job was completed.

Edwin did not kill clients, even when they were difficult. It would be bad for business. Instead he acquired information. In this instance it shouldn't be difficult to ensure that the Kellys dealt with him properly. One phone call to the police or to Grant Connelly would cost them a great deal more money than they owed Edwin.

He unbuttoned the top button of his shirt and hung up the tie, then took a file folder from his briefcase and sat at the table. The folder held a neat sheaf of papers with a color photograph on top—a woman's face, unsmiling. He picked it up.

Charlotte Masters was wearing a high-necked blouse—tasteful and modest, Edwin thought. Her hair was smooth, unfussy; though the color was a bit showy, it was her natural color, so Edwin didn't hold that against her. She was tidy, a trait he esteemed. He'd learned that while investigating the apartment she'd abandoned after Palermo botched the first hit.

Edwin's mouth pursed in distaste. Amateurs annoyed him. Palermo was a professional criminal, but having killed in the course of his duties did not make him a professional killer. He was certainly not a marksman. Hubris or envy of his betters had led him to attempt a shot few professionals would have tried. He deserved to have failed.

He set the photo down and studied the next paper in the pile, a floor plan of Charlotte Master's old apartment. One could learn a great deal about a target's habits from the way they arranged their living space. Additionally, of course, he had acquired details from investigating her belongings that had helped establish her habits, preferences, possible contacts. Some of the papers in the folder had come from the orderly files in her desk.

She was efficient, honest, responsible—altogether an admirable woman. Of course, she did have a weakness. Her brother. Brad Masters had been a burden on his older sister ever since their parents' deaths. He had provided the lever the Kellys had used to coerce her into betraying her employer.

But few people possessed the strength to completely sever outside ties the way Edwin had done. All in all, she was a worthy quarry.

There was a knock on the door. As matter-of-factly as another man might save an open file on the computer before responding to an interruption, he put the file away and removed a small, snub-nosed gun from the briefcase. He was expecting room service, having ordered his dinner earlier. But he assumed nothing. After covering the gun with a hotel towel, he moved to the door. "Yes?" he said pleasantly.

When the voice on the other side of the door confirmed that it belonged to room service, he arranged the towel so that it looked as if he'd been drying his hands, and opened the door. The waiter remained cheerfully unaware that a gun was trained on him the entire time he was in the room. He left with an adequate, if not generous, tip, and Edwin sat down to his meal—a salad with the dressing on the side, broiled salmon, and a baked potato, dry.

Forty minutes later, the tray holding his dishes sat outside the door and the folder was open once more. He had several possibilities for locating his target, but the most certain was the way he had found her the first time: the brother. Eventually she would contact him.

He lingered over her photograph. A pretty woman. Edwin appreciated beauty, but didn't admire it. No, it was her other qualities he esteemed. She deserved him, he thought. Not an amateur like Palermo. Suffering was messy, the mark of a poorly executed job.

Unlike Palermo, he was an excellent marksman. A bullet in the brain would assure that the admirable Ms. Masters didn't suffer. She would be dead before she realized what had happened.

# Six

Charlotte scrunched her head deeper into the pillow, reluctant to leave her dream behind. But it was drifting away already…something about a project at the office, an important project she had to finish….

The office, she thought fuzzily. Was it time to get up? If so, her alarm would tell her soon. She always set the alarm. Not once had she been late since she started working for Grant.

Her eyes flew open. No office. No job working for Grant Connelly. No job at all, she realized as her sleepy brain caught up with memory. She stared up at the ceiling, and it was the wrong ceiling. Not the one above her own bed in her apartment—because that, too, was gone.

Everything. Everything she'd worked so hard for was gone.

She flung the covers back and threw herself out of bed, blinking furiously. She would *not* give in to self-pity.

The light streaming in the wide, high window in Rafe's

bedroom told her she'd slept late. She glanced at the clock and grimaced. It was nearly ten. Normally she was a morning person, but she'd had to adapt her schedule to work at Hole-in-the-Wall.

She had to get back there. Today. She needed her backpack. She needed her money, too. Rafe had dragged her out last night with a total of twenty-two dollars and thirty cents in tips in her pocket.

Fourteen minutes later she'd done what she could to make herself presentable—pretty much a lost cause with no makeup, blow-dryer or clean clothes. She settled for wearing yesterday's skirt with another of Rafe's sweatshirts and headed downstairs, prepared for an argument.

He wasn't there.

Well. She put her hands on her hips. This was convenient, she told herself, not annoying. Rafe certainly didn't need to let her know what he was doing every minute, and she didn't need an argument. She poured herself a glass of milk and sat down at the table with the telephone directory.

Rafe slammed into his apartment over an hour after leaving it, sweatier but no more relaxed than when he'd left. Usually a good run cleared his mind. Not today.

Nothing worked the way it was supposed to with Charlie around, he thought in disgust, pulling off his sweatshirt as he headed upstairs for a shower. The T-shirt he'd worn beneath it was damp. He'd pushed himself pretty hard at the park, for all the good it had done him. He was no closer to getting a grip on the trust thing than he had been last night.

Maybe a hot shower would—wait a minute. The door to his bedroom door was open. Charlie must be awake at last.

The least he could do was share his frustration with her, he decided.

He stopped in the doorway. His bed was made. The sweats he'd loaned her were folded and placed neatly in the middle of the bed. Charlie was nowhere in sight.

He raced back to the stairs. "Charlie!" he bellowed. "Dammit, you'd better be here!"

She wasn't. His heart was pounding harder than it had during his run by the time he finished a hasty, pointless search of the apartment. Keep calm, he told himself. There were no signs that she'd been forced to leave, no indications of a struggle. Or violence.

Had she left because of the kiss he'd forced on her last night? Had he scared her that badly—or made her too mad to think straight? But she didn't have anywhere to go, or any money to get there.

Unless she'd taken some of his.

He dashed back upstairs. His wallet was right where he'd left it last night—on the bathroom floor next to his pants. He didn't bother to look in it. Charlie might be able to persuade herself she was justified in borrowing money from him, but she would never have put the wallet back on the floor after rifling it.

No money, no car, no clothes besides what she wore on her back—and with a hit man looking for her. "Dammit, Charlie," he muttered, his fists tight at his sides. "Where are you?"

Charlotte pushed the buzzer and waited, her foot tapping. She just hoped Rafe was back from wherever he'd gone earlier. She didn't fancy waiting around in the tiny foyer while he ran his mysterious errands. The other people in the building were likely to call the police if she hung around too long.

She shoved the sleeves of his leather coat back up—they kept slipping down and swallowing her hands—and shifted her backpack to the other shoulder. He was just going to have to trust her with a key. He'd forced her to come here, after all, so the least—

"Yes?" came a tinny voice from the intercom.

"It's Charlie. I—"

*"Stay there!"*

"Rafe?"

No answer. She stared at the intercom. Now what?

Moments later she heard feet thundering down the stairs. Alarm quickened her heartbeat. Whatever had upset Rafe must be urgent if he hadn't wanted to wait for an elevator. His apartment was on the fifth floor.

The door to the service stairs crashed open and he burst out of it at a dead run. "For God's sake, where have you been?" He grabbed her shoulders.

"What's wrong? What's happened?"

"You take off without a word and you ask me what's wrong?"

She frowned. "You're yelling."

"Damned right I'm yelling! You go off without leaving a note, without making any effort to let me know if you've been abducted or killed—"

"I'll be sure to leave you a note if I'm killed or kidnapped. Look, you're digging holes in my shoulders. And *you* didn't leave *me* a note when you left the apartment."

"I don't have a hit man trying to kill me!" He was still much too loud, but his fingers stopped playing holepuncher. "Dammit, Charlie—"

The elevator doors opened. A skinny woman with blue hair and a large rat on a leash—well, it was probably a dog, but it looked like a rat—stood in the elevator. She gave Rafe a dubious glance.

He switched his grip to Charlotte's hand and dragged her into the elevator, glaring at the woman. She and her rat stepped out quickly.

As soon as the elevator doors closed, Rafe dropped her hand. They rode up in stiff silence. On Rafe's part the silence might have been generated by anger. For Charlotte it came from sheer bewilderment.

He'd yelled at her. He was furious. He'd raced down those stairs as if he'd been frantic about her. She didn't understand. A man who climbed out of a woman's bed without a backward glance didn't go ballistic with worry just because she didn't leave him a note. Even given her current circumstances, his reaction didn't make sense.

A small motion inside her womb gave her the answer. She touched her stomach. Of course. Rafe had been worried about the baby, not her. He was serious about wanting this child. The thought should have reassured her. Instead her spirits sank. *Oh, no,* she thought, her eyes closing. *It can't matter. I couldn't be such a fool....*

The elevator doors opened. He grabbed her arm. She jerked it away and glared at him. "Quit dragging me around like a suitcase!"

"If you were a suitcase you'd stay where I put you." He headed for his door. "Come on, or I'll reach for your handle again."

She huffed out an exasperated breath and followed him. "Your courting technique lacks a certain something."

He yanked his door open and stormed inside. "I've got it in mind to be a husband, not a widower! What the hell were you thinking of? What could possibly be important enough to risk your life for?"

"This." She swung her backpack off her shoulder. "And I didn't risk my life. I called Nikki—"

"Your backpack?" He glared at the innocuous canvas tote. "*That's* what you were so desperate to get?"

"Everything I own is in that! My money, my ID, my—"

"You want money?" He dug out his wallet, pulled out a wad of bills—and threw them at her. "Here! You've got money now!"

Bills flew everywhere. Some fluttered to the floor at her feet. One landed on his shoe. Others scattered randomly on the floor between them, expensive green and white confetti. She stood frozen, staring at him, unable to believe he'd just thrown the entire contents of his wallet at her.

He scowled back at her.

Slowly she stepped forward. She unzipped her backpack and knelt in front of him, shoving the dratted sleeves of his coat up again. Then she began to empty out the contents, one by one.

"*This* is what was so important." She pulled out her mother's copy of *Little Women.* "I needed the money, yes." Other books followed—her high school yearbook, her address book, an old photo album, a very old volume of Mother Goose stories that her grandmother had read to her mother. "Believe it or not, rich man, it's hard to get by in this world without money."

She paused to stroke the jeweler's box she pulled out next. Most of the velvet had worn off. Inside were her mother's wedding ring, her father's watch and the tiny diamond earrings she'd bought with her first paycheck from Connelly Corporation. "But I needed these things more than the money."

Tilting the backpack, she emptied out the rest of her possessions—which included a hairbrush, toothbrush, toothpaste and shampoo. Extra pairs of panties and socks. A few more mementos, including the fancy gold-plated fountain pen Grant had given her for Christmas last year. Last she pulled out the things in the outside pocket: her birth certificate and the envelope containing all that was left of her savings; two hundred thirteen dollars.

She sat back on her heels and stared up at him, stony faced. "That's everything I own in this world now. And yes, it would have been worth risking my life to get these things back, but I didn't. I called a woman who works at Hole-in-the-Wall and asked her to bring my things to me. We met at the Irving Park El station so she wouldn't know where I'm staying."

Rafe was looking down at the small pile of objects at his feet with a sort of horrified fascination. He grimaced, scrubbed a hand over his face and met her eyes. "Why didn't you tell me why you needed your backpack?"

After the way he'd acted when she tried to get him to go back for it? She shook her head in disbelief. "Why? What good would it have done?"

He sighed, knelt and began gathering her treasures, slipping them into the backpack with more care than she'd thought he possessed. "Next time tell me if you need to go somewhere," he said quietly. "Don't go off alone. I don't want you risking yourself that way. If I can't go with you, I'll get someone else to. Hey." His hands paused. A grin spread over his face. "I gave you this."

He held up the tacky souvenir he'd brought her from Hawaii last year—a plastic hula dancer with bare bumps for breasts and a grass skirt that had been shedding steadily for months.

Her face heated. "I keep it to remind me of you," she said, snatching it out of his hand and stuffing it in the backpack. "Lewd, crude and obvious."

He was still grinning, damn him. "You like me."

She rolled her eyes and tucked *Little Women* back where it belonged.

"You may be mad at me, but you like me. If you didn't, you wouldn't…"

When he didn't finish the sentence she glanced up. This time he held a packet of letters tied by a blue ribbon, a slight frown on his face.

She grabbed the letters away, too. "Have you no sense of private property? Those are personal."

"You shouldn't put things at my feet if you don't want me to see them." But he helped her pick up the rest of her things without further comment, then sat back on his heels. "Ah, about the money I threw at you…"

She raised both eyebrows. "What about it?"

"That was childish of me."

"I agree."

"Yes. Well…" He pushed to his feet, glanced at the door—which still stood open—made an exasperated sound and stalked over to close and lock it. Then he started to pace.

Her eyes followed him. He was wearing a pair of jeans so old they were white in interesting places and a dark blue turtleneck with a frayed hem. He looked more like an un-employed stuntman than an heir to one of Chicago's big-gest fortunes.

He looked delicious. She swallowed, shoved up a sleeve and zipped the backpack.

"The thing is," he said, stopping abruptly, "I don't want you to think... That is, after what I said last night you might—I didn't throw money at you because I was trying to buy you, dammit!"

"I know that. You're an idiot, but not that much of an idiot."

His mouth stretched in a thin, exasperated line. "How do you do that?"

"What?"

"I'm standing, you're on the floor, and you still manage to look down your nose at me."

"It's a gift." She stood and took off the too-big coat, draping it over her arm. "Since you don't want me to go out by myself, perhaps you'd like to go shopping. Your sweats are comfortable, but the fit isn't great."

"We can go shopping, but not today."

"Look, you don't get to have everything your way. I'm not talking about a major shopping trip—just a few essen-tials. I can't keep wearing the same clothes every day. And I need some prenatal vitamins."

"Prenatal vitamins?" He frowned. "Are those some spe-cial kind?"

"They have extra nutrients the baby needs."

"Damn. I didn't think of that. Dix will be here later with some of your things. I told him to be sure to bring all your shoes— I know women have a thing about shoes. Maybe you can explain that to me sometime. My sisters sure love to buy shoes. It's their second-favorite thing, next to choc-olate. But I didn't think to tell Dix to look for some special kind of vitamins."

She blinked, trying to keep up with the main point. "What do you mean, Dix will be here with my things?"

"He's going to stop by your old apartment today. Not the crummy room and a bath that's your most recent old apartment. The one where we...ah, the one you had before."

She knew what he'd almost said: the one where they'd made love. No, he probably thought of it as the place where they'd had sex. Her mouth thinned. "And just how is he going to get in?"

"That shouldn't be a problem." He rubbed his chin. "They have prenatal vitamins at drugstores, don't they? I can have some delivered. Anything else you need right away?"

"I don't think so. Are you just going to leave your money all over the floor?"

"I'm trying to figure out how to give some of it to you without getting it thrown in my face."

Her lips twitched. "I don't throw money around. Offer me a blunt object, though, and see what happens."

He snorted and began gathering the bills. She found herself just standing there watching him. He looked so good to her. *And he isn't even trying. I look at him and I want him. He doesn't even have to do anything.* She wasn't sure if it was him or her own wayward hormones she resented more.

Her mouth tight, she went to hang up his coat.

"What did you tell your friend?" he asked, reaching for the empty billfold he'd dropped on the floor during his little temper fit. "The one who brought you the backpack."

"Nikki saw you drag me out of there last night, so I had to account for your odd behavior. I made up this ridiculous story about two boyfriends. There's this poor but honest fellow I broke up with before coming to work at Hole-in-the-Wall, and a rich, abusive man I'm hiding from."

"Which one am I?"

"Poor but honest. You have some self-esteem problems," she added. "I left you because your jealousy was driving me crazy. Nikki loved it. Here, you missed a twenty.'' She held it out.

''I don't suppose you... No, I'll have to find some other way.'' After pocketing the twenty he added, ''The bit about the abusive boyfriend. Was that to explain why someone might come around looking for you?''

Her eyebrows went up. ''Very good.''

''I'm not stupid. It won't be enough for your friend to keep quiet, you know. Too many others saw me at Hole-in-the-Wall.''

''That's why I also told her you were taking me back to Jamestown, New York. That's your hometown, you see. With the best intentions in the world, Nikki is incapable of keeping a secret. She'll tell one or two people in confidence, and pretty soon the story of our romantic elopement will be common knowledge at Hole-in-the-Wall. If anyone does come looking for me there, he'll think I've left the city.''

He nodded thoughtfully. ''That may help. I've another bit of misdirection in mind, too. I thought it might be best if people think your baby is...well, if they think my father is responsible.''

She sputtered. ''No way. Absolutely, positively no way.''

''The Kellys know you're pregnant. It's only logical for them to keep an eye on the father of your baby in order to find you. I don't want them looking for you here, and my father...well, you *were* his secretary.''

''Executive assistant,'' she said coldly.

''Whatever. The point is, people are likely to believe the story. He, uh, has something of a history.''

She knew what he meant. In addition to the twin sons, now grown, who had so recently come forward to join the family, there was Seth. Seth Connelly had been raised by Grant and Emma from the age of twelve, but he wasn't Emma's son. Many years ago Grant had had an affair with his secretary. Gossip said that he and Emma had been separated at the time of the affair, the marriage in trouble, but somehow it had survived.

The secretary's name was Angie Donahue. After handing over custody of her son eighteen years ago she'd left without a backward glance...until recently. She was also the niece of the head of the Kellys' family-run criminal organization, and the daughter of another of the bosses.

Charlotte wished with all her heart Angie had stayed out of sight. "Rafe, that was years and years ago. I promise you, your father has never been anything but professional and respectful in his dealings with me."

He gave her an exasperated look. "I know that. But the Kellys don't. And, given Angie's connection to them—well, they'll probably buy it. Maybe it will keep them looking in all the wrong places."

"But your mother...it's not worth it."

"Look, I wasn't asking for your vote. I've already called my mother this morning, and—"

"You didn't!" She stared at him in horror.

"And my grandmother." He grimaced. "Now there's a sacrifice. Talk about being put through the third degree! She'll know exactly how to go about things, though. She plans to deny everything. According to her, that will get the gossips buzzing, but the story won't really stick. After we're married everyone will agree they never believed a word of it. If—"

The buzzer sounded.

"Damn. Hold on a minute." Rafe went to the intercom and pushed the button. She couldn't hear what the other person said, but Rafe's response was clear enough, if puzzling. "She turned up...yeah, that's what I thought, too. Come on up." He punched the off button.

"Tell me that's not your mother, coming to strangle me."

"You're in luck. That was Lucas Starwind."

"The detective your father hired?"

He nodded. "When you pulled your disappearing act this

morning, I called Luke to help me find you. He was supposed to come over later today anyway. We've been working together on some things.''

''What sort of things?''

''We're both trying to find out what the Kellys are up to, though we're coming at it from different angles.''

''Oh, you're trying to find out what the tech from Broderton's Computing did, aren't you?'' Eager, she took a few steps closer. ''I went into the office on weekends, but couldn't figure out what he'd done to the system. Have you made any progress?''

He gave her a funny look. ''Some.''

His expression stopped her short. ''I wanted to undo whatever damage I'd caused. Maybe trying doesn't count when I failed. But I did try.''

There was a knock at the door. Rafe glanced at it and sighed. ''We'll talk later.''

He checked through the peephole before opening the door. ''Come in. You know Charlie already, don't you?''

''We've met.'' The man who entered was tall—about Rafe's height, maybe a little more. His hair and eyes were dark. So was his expression. She'd met Luke Starwind twice when he'd come to the office to give Grant a report. She hadn't liked him much. He was too controlled, too distant...*too much like me,* she thought, and her mouth turned down.

He gave her a cool, appraising glance. ''Ms. Masters. You've been hard to find. For an amateur, you're pretty good at vanishing.''

''Not good enough, apparently. Can I get you something to drink, or shall we go straight to the interrogation?''

''Coffee would be good.'' He turned to Rafe, dismissing her. ''Fill me in. How did you find her?''

''He didn't find me,'' Charlotte said, irritated at being spoken of as if she weren't there. ''I made it back here all by myself, without so much as a pair of handcuffs as motivation.''

''I meant how did he find you yesterday, not this morning. I take my coffee black,'' he added pointedly.

She had her mouth open, ready to offer a polite suggestion about what he could do with the coffeepot, when Rafe's hand landed on her shoulder.

''Whoa, champ.'' He slid an amused glance from her to the detective. ''Much as I'd enjoy watching the two of you go a few rounds, we've got a lot of territory to cover today. I'll make the coffee.''

# Seven

Charlie put the coffee on.

Rafe shook his head. He should have known that as soon as he said he'd do it, she'd be bound and determined to take over.

"Sorry," Luke said in a low voice while Charlie was in the kitchen. "I shouldn't have made that crack about coffee. She's got quite a mouth when she's irritated, doesn't she?"

"Charlie bristles up like a porcupine if you put her on the defensive. Before I start, do you have any news?"

"Nothing worth mentioning. Are you ready to—" He glanced at the kitchen. "Never mind. You can fill me in on your progress later."

Rafe grimaced. He wasn't crazy about secrets the way Charlie was, but for now he'd have to keep a few. "Let's sit down."

The two men moved to the area Rafe's sisters insisted on calling the conversation pit, where a couple of chairs faced the couch. He sat with his legs spread and frowned at the empty fireplace, organizing what he needed to tell the P.I.

Pretty much everything, he decided. He wouldn't mention proposing—that was personal. What about the letters in her backpack? Those damned letters she was hanging on to, the ones tied together with a pretty blue bow? Love letters, he supposed, scowling. From some man named Brad Fowler. He'd seen the return address.

Deer Lodge Prison.

Was Brad Fowler the reason Charlie had cooperated with the Kellys? Had she been involved with this crook, and that was the hold they had over her? Dammit, he could find out who the man was easily enough…but he'd decided not to hack into her past.

Some sense made him glance at the kitchen. She was standing in the doorway.

Difficult woman, he thought. Cute as could be in that short skirt and his sweatshirt, but difficult. She was in a snit about something. She didn't say anything, just stood there, her arms crossed, and listened while he brought Luke up to date about the way he'd tracked her down, the car that had almost hit her and her excursion that morning.

Maybe he should have told Luke about the letters, too, but he didn't. He wanted Charlie to tell him about them, dammit. About Brad Fowler.

She vanished briefly about the time Luke started asking questions about Hole-in-the-Wall and whether anyone there would be able to identify Rafe. When she reappeared, she had two mugs of coffee.

"Do you prefer to hear things secondhand, Mr. Starwind?" she asked sweetly as she handed Luke one of the mugs. "Or would you like to ask me some questions, too?"

Oh, so that's what was bugging her. She thought they were playing "boys' club—girls keep out." At least, he hoped that's what she assumed.

This trust business was about to get tricky.

"I've got questions," Luke said. "Are you ready to answer them?"

Her glance darted off Rafe and veered quickly back to Luke. "That depends on what you ask."

"Why do the Kellys want you dead?"

Her hand jerked. She narrowly avoided getting scalded by the hot coffee in the mug she still held. Rafe gave Luke a hard look, stood and took the cup from her. "Come on. Sit down."

She let him steer her to a place on the couch beside him, but she didn't sit very close. Not close enough for him to touch. When she answered Luke's question she was looking at him, not Rafe. "I suppose they want revenge. They shot at me as I was leaving police headquarters, so they must have thought I'd told the police what I knew."

"You're the key witness against Angie Donahue."

"I guess so." She didn't look happy about it. Rafe wasn't happy about it, either.

"Can you identify any of them other than Angie?"

"No. That is, there was just the one man who contacted me. I'd know his voice if I ever heard it again, but I never saw him. Lieutenant Johnson at the Special Investigative Unit said a voice identification wouldn't stand up in court."

"How did this man contact you?"

"I've been through all this with Lieutenant Johnson."

"Someone in the department has put a lid on everything connected to your testimony. All we know is that you used the tech the Kellys told you to use, and that you implicated Angie Donahue."

"I really don't know anything that will help."

"Charlie." Rafe leaned toward her. "You said you'd been going in on weekends, trying to undo what you allowed them to do. You haven't been able to. Help us fix things now."

She met his eyes and nodded jerkily. "All right, though I don't think it will do you any good. The first time they contacted me was back in May. I was on my way home, hurrying because it was dark. There were people around, though, so I wasn't really worried. Until *he* came up behind me.'' Her fingers twitched, closing on air then opening again. ''He told me he had a gun, warned me to keep walking and not turn around. He wanted me to arrange for a particular technician to work on the computers at the office. He said…'' She swallowed. ''I refused, of course.''

''You turned him down?'' Rafe asked sharply.

''At first. But when I got back to my apartment…I was going to call the police. I *was*. But he—he'd left something there that changed my mind.''

''What?''

She shook her head.

''For God's sake, Charlie. If they have some hold over you, tell us what it is so we can help.'' *So I'll know whether or not I can trust you.*

''They don't. Not anymore. The police…took care of things.''

''We need to know what they used to force your cooperation.'' Rafe hesitated, then added softly, ''*I* need to know.''

''They…threatened someone important to me.'' She looked down at her lap, where her hands were holding tightly to each other. ''I can't tell you more than that. I'm sorry, but I can't.''

Rafe leaned back, frustrated and disappointed.

Luke took over the questioning. He kept at it for nearly an hour, coming back to the same things over and over, but in the end he admitted she was probably right—she didn't know anything useful. She couldn't provide a link to any of the criminals except Angie Donahue. And Angie wasn't talking.

''There's some good news, anyway, from your point of view,'' Luke said after emptying his mug for the second time. ''Angie's lawyered up. As long as she plays the game by their rules, the Kellys are obliged to support her. Ordinarily they might not go as far as killing off the primary witness against her. In her own right, Angie is small potatoes. But her uncle is the head of the family, and her father has risen pretty high in the organization, too.''

''When do you get to the good news?'' she asked dryly.

''They won't try as hard,'' Rafe said abruptly as things clicked into place. ''That's what you mean, isn't it, Luke? There no urgency to silencing Charlie because the bosses aren't personally threatened. They're doing this as a matter of—well, call it family ties. Or good employee relations.''

Charlie made a choked sound that might have been a laugh.

''That's one way of putting it.'' Luke put his empty mug on the table. ''If Ms. Masters were able to incriminate one of the top people, they'd make killing her a priority. She'd have to go to a safe house—''

''I am not going to trust my life to the police,'' Charlie put in quickly. ''The Kellys could have informants on the force.''

''As things stand, it may be okay for you to stay here for now. The police think Rocky Palermo was responsible for the attempt on your life.''

''Who is he?''

''The Kellys' chief enforcer. He takes care of their dirty work. The cops are keeping an eye on him, but that doesn't mean you can be careless. No more solo expeditions like the one this morning. Aside from the danger from the Kellys, there's the little matter of the outstanding warrant for your arrest.''

All the blood drained from her face. ''Oh, God.''

''I take it you didn't know.''

She shook her head violently. ''They—the lieutenant said Grant didn't want charges pressed. He said…'' Her voice wobbled and she held her hand to her mouth as if trying to cram the shakes back inside.

''Dammit, Luke! Don't you have some widows and orphans you can go kick? Charlie.'' Rafe put a hand on her arm. She was stiff, resisting his touch. He ignored that.

"The warrant is just a technicality. It's for being a material witness. They issued it when you vanished."

"The police don't like it when their key witness does a fade." Luke studied Charlie, then shifted his gaze to Rafe. "They don't like it when people harbor someone with a warrant out, either."

"Luke," Rafe growled, "if you don't put a sock in it, I'm going to have to do it for you."

Luke's eyebrows lifted. "I'm not trying to scare her. There's a solution. A good lawyer can go to the cops, get them to drop the charges in exchange for her promise to appear to testify as needed. The police can contact the lawyer when they need her. I can't do it," he added irritably, as if Rafe had asked him to. "A lawyer can act for her without getting in trouble for not revealing her whereabouts."

She'd gotten some color back. "I don't have money for a lawyer."

"I do," Rafe said. He ran his hand down her arm to her hand, closing his fingers around hers. "No arguments this time, Charlie."

She looked down at their joined hands and swallowed. "I'll pay you back."

"No, you won't. It's an investment. I don't want my kid going to jail before he's born."

"Since you put it that way…" She looked up. "Okay. We'll do it your way this time. Just don't think of this as the start of a trend."

"Heaven forbid." Relieved, he grinned at her.

The buzzer sounded again, and relief leaked right back out of him. *Great timing, Dix.*

"You expecting anyone?" Luke asked.

"Dix," Rafe said without looking away from Charlie. They were about to hit the sticky part, and he still didn't have a clue how to handle it. "You want to buzz him up for me, Luke?"

The P.I. hesitated a second, then stood. "Sure."

A frown was tugging at Charlie's mouth. "Dix is the friend of yours that helped you find me, isn't he? The hacker."

"Ah, look, Charlie..." He dropped her hand to run his through his hair. "Damn. I can't come up with a good way to do this. I have to ask you to wait down here while we're working. We'll be in my office."

At first she didn't get it. He could tell because she just looked puzzled, then annoyed.

Then all the expression drained out of her face. "Oh. Of course. You're working on the problem with the corporation's computers, and your hacker friend is helping you." She used both hands to smooth her skirt—though from what Rafe could see, there wasn't enough of it to wrinkle— and stood. "I'll go practice my knitting while you men are busy."

Her voice was so polite, her shoulders so straight, her smile so small and brittle. She was breaking his heart. "If it was just me," he began, rising. "If there weren't so many others involved—"

"I quite understand. Naturally you couldn't let me be privy to what you're doing. I'm responsible for the problem."

"No, dammit, you're not. The Kellys are responsible. You're—"

"An accomplice. Though your father was kind enough not to want me prosecuted for it."

Luke turned away from the intercom. "He's on his way up." He glanced from Rafe to Charlie. "Is there a problem?"

"Not at all," she said.

"Yes," Rafe said at the same time. "I mean no. Charlie will be working with us today."

Luke's expression didn't change. After a moment he said, "That could be a problem, all right."

\* \* \*

She was getting used to him calling her Charlie. Maybe she was starting to like it.

"You have two big computers *and* a laptop?" She shook her head. "Men and their techno-toys."

Charlotte was sitting cross-legged on the floor of Rafe's office. His laptop rested in front of her on a stack of green-and-white printouts. Rafe sat at a desk crowded with an impressive array of computer equipment, including three monitors displaying three different—and to Charlotte, equally indecipherable—screens of code. Cables crawled across the floor, connecting two scanners and three printers to one or the other of the two CPUs under Rafe's desk.

"I need the laptop when I travel. When I'm working here, I use one computer for downloads, the other for confidential work. It isn't hooked up to anything. That's basic security." Rafe flashed a grin at his friend. "There are too many people like Dix who are too curious for my own good."

"Nah," Dix retorted amiably. He lounged in an armchair in the corner. A board resting across the arms of the chair held his laptop. "Not like me. I'm the best."

Charlie was beginning to like Dix. When Rafe had told him that she would be working with them, he hadn't turned a hair, unlike Rafe's other friend. Before leaving, Luke Starwind had tried to talk Rafe out of letting her be part of the investigation. Maybe she couldn't blame him for being suspicious. He had given Rafe the name of a criminal defense attorney Charlie could use, and promised to contact him on her behalf. That didn't mean she had to like the man. Or trust him.

But Rafe trusted her. In spite of everything, he believed in her. She hugged that knowledge to herself like a child with a Christmas secret.

"So why haven't I read about you?" she asked Dix, smiling so he'd know she was teasing. "The hacker who was caught last month for getting into some top-secret files got great press."

He gave her a slow wink. "Little girl, I don't get caught. That's why I'm the best."

Rafe snorted. "No, that's because you've got better sense than to break into the Pentagon's system just to prove you can."

"Hey, man," Dix said. "Quit interrupting. I'm trying to flirt with your girlfriend."

"Work now, flirt later. Charlie, do you understand what you're looking for?"

"I think so. Files accessed after hours, frequently used access codes—the same sort of thing I was looking for on my own, but you've narrowed the possibilities."

"Okay. If you have any questions, ask Dix. He likes to show off."

She called up the first of the files she was supposed to check and began.

Rafe had run several diagnostics without turning up signs of tampering or any obvious problems. There were some flagged areas, though. She was slogging through user records. Rafe—well, she wasn't clear on exactly what he was doing. Something involving a special program he was writing, but he'd spoken of it in such technical terms he'd lost her. Fortunately, she didn't have to understand his job to do hers.

By two o'clock her back ached and her stomach was growling. The two men were obviously not plagued by the physical discomforts of lesser mortals. Aside from tossing each other an occasional question or comment in terms so technical they might as well have been Martian, they'd been silent the whole time.

Enough was enough. She yawned and stretched. "I don't know about you two, but I'm hungry."

"If you're offering to fix something," Dix said, "I'm accepting. I'm not picky. I'll eat anything I don't have to cook."

"I'll see if I can find some sandwich fixings. Rafe?"

No answer. He didn't even twitch.

Dix chuckled. "When he's really into a program, it's not easy to get his attention. Pain works. Though you do have to be fast on your feet if you use that approach."

"I'll try something a little less drastic first." She wadded up a piece of paper and lobbed it at Rafe.

It hit him on the neck. He swatted at it, as if a bug had bit him, and went right on working, his fingers flying over the keyboard. She laughed.

His fingers stopped. His head cocked to one side. "You don't do that often enough."

"What—throw things at you?"

"Laugh out loud." He swiveled. "Are you going to make sandwiches?"

"You did hear! Why didn't you answer?"

"It isn't that I don't hear things when I'm working. It all just goes somewhere else, where it won't interrupt my train of thought."

She smiled, amused. "Where does it go?"

"Damned if I know." He stood and stretched. "Tell you what. I'm ready for a break anyway. I'll make the sandwiches and you can put away the clothes Dix brought."

"Put them away where? You were going to clear out a couple of drawers for me, remember?"

"Move some of my stuff around. You'll do better at finding places for things than I would, anyway."

He asked Dix a question in Martian, and the two men were deeply involved in one of their jargon-laden conversations before Charlie left the room. She smiled as she went down the hall, wondering if either of them would remember to fix the sandwiches.

Two bulging garbage bags sat on the floor of Rafe's bedroom: packing, man-style. She wondered if Rafe even owned an iron. She couldn't afford to send everything to the cleaners just because it was wrinkled. Of course, a great deal of her wardrobe wouldn't fit anymore. She put a hand on her stomach, savoring the firm swelling. The baby stirred.

Something else was stirring inside her. It felt very much like hope.

Maybe, just maybe, she and Rafe could work out some kind of future together. He seemed to have forgiven her for her part in the Kellys' schemes without knowing how they'd forced her to cooperate. She thought he'd forgiven her for not telling him about the baby right away, too.

Maybe, she thought as she knelt beside one of the trash bags, some of his anxiety this morning *had* been for her. Maybe he really did care. Caring wasn't love, but it was a start.

He trusted her. He *believed* in her. Yes, the wiggly feeling inside felt very much like hope. Or happiness.

She worked the twist-tie loose and looked inside. Shoes. All her shoes were in there, dumped on top of jeans and sweaters. Her smile widened. There were advantages to a man who'd grown up with sisters, she thought, pulling out her favorite gray pumps.

Brad had grown up with a sister. It hadn't seemed to do him much good.

Her smile faded as she tensed against the familiar anxiety. Automatically she started pulling things out of the bag, making neat piles.

Charlotte had never been able to decide whether she'd done too much for Brad, or too little. Had she been too harsh, lectured him too often? Or had she just never said the right things? He was so different from her, so volatile. Her hands smoothed a sweater as a deep sadness welled up. The one thing she and her little brother had in common, other than the same set of parents, was a hunger for fine things. Perhaps if she'd been able to rise above her own material longings...

She shook her head and made her hands move briskly, unpacking, then changing into pants and a sweater of her own. Sometimes she was able to convince herself that Brad's descent into a mad, bad world wasn't her fault, that nothing she could have done would have helped him make different choices. Sometimes she couldn't. But she had been so very young when their parents died. Whatever mistakes she might have made, they were past altering now.

The biggest mistakes had been Brad's. She didn't fool herself about that. He'd been young when he made them, yes, but not too young to understand the consequences. Not too young to be tried as an adult.

He was paying for those mistakes now, but he shouldn't have to pay with his life.

Lieutenant Johnson had kept his word. In exchange for her testimony he'd arranged for Brad to be secretly moved to a different prison. Even she didn't know where he was. At least now she knew for sure that the lieutenant had kept as quiet about it as he'd warned her to be. *Tell no one he's been moved,* the SIU officer had said. *If the Kellys find him, he's dead.*

It hadn't been a difficult secret to keep…until now. She grimaced and opened the other trash bag. She'd moved to Chicago after Brad was sentenced. No one here knew her brother existed. It had seemed simpler that way, easier than answering a lot of questions about him…and, she admitted with a grimace, she'd been ashamed. Not of Brad, exactly. Of everything that she'd come from. The chance to reinvent herself had been irresistible. But now…

Now she thought she could tell Rafe about her brother. She frowned, her hands growing still. She'd refused to tell him earlier because she hadn't trusted him. Oh, not that she thought he would sell her brother out to the Kellys. But he had a nasty habit of doing what he thought was best and running right over anyone who objected. Look at the way he'd dragged her out of Hole-in-the-Wall last night.

And he'd told Luke Starwind everything. Charlie didn't exactly distrust Starwind, but she didn't exactly trust him, either. Not enough to put her brother's life in the man's hands.

Rafe apparently told Dix everything, too. And she wanted to trust Dix. She would have, if it had been just herself, just her own secrets she was keeping. If it weren't her brother's very life at stake, she would tell Rafe everything.

That was what he had said, too, wasn't it? When he'd told her she had to stay away while he and Dix tracked down what the Kellys had done to the computers. "If it was just me," he'd said. "If there weren't so many others involved..."

It had hurt.

Had she hurt him by refusing to trust him?

She chewed on her lip and thought about how good she'd felt when he changed his mind and decided to trust her. She thought about hope.

The wiggle-worm in her womb did a slow roll.

Making her mind up all at once, she pushed to her feet. She would make him promise, she thought, hurrying out of the room. Before she told him, she would have his promise not to repeat it to anyone—not Dix, not Starwind, not even his father. He might not like it. He might make an unholy pest of himself trying to change her mind. But he would keep his word if he gave it. She was sure of that.

The office was empty. She smiled as she went by. Apparently he and Dix had remembered the sandwiches. She went down the stairs carefully, since her socks didn't offer much traction on the iron risers.

They didn't make much noise, either. Certainly not enough for the two men to hear her coming, not when Rafe's voice was raised enough for her to hear him from the kitchen.

"Dammit, Dix, don't give me a hard time about this."

Her feet slowed but didn't stop. Maybe this wasn't a good time, if he and his friend were arguing. But if she didn't speak up now, she was afraid she'd talk herself out of it. It was too easy to keep things secret.

"...don't like it, that's all," Dix was saying. "She's a sweet little thing. I don't like lying to her."

*Lying?* Her feet kept moving, but she didn't notice. Her mind had gone numb.

"I didn't lie to her."

Dix snorted. "No, but you fancy-danced your way around the truth pretty good. She doesn't have a clue what's going on. She thinks she's really doing something, going through all those access records."

"That's where we found the clue. If she finds it, too..." Rafe's voice drifted off. "I need to know. If she spots the same thing we did—"

"Is that what this is about? You're testing her?"

Charlotte's feet kept right on moving. They carried her right up to the kitchen doorway. Then they stopped.

Rafe was leaning against the counter scowling at Dix, who stood a few feet away. He started to answer, then he saw her. Consternation and guilt spread across his face like a snail's slimy trail.

Hope lumped up in a cold, hard ball. And died.

"Charlie," he said, straightening. "Charlie, I can explain—"

She bolted.

# Eight

He caught her, of course. Easily. She didn't even make it to the stairs before his hand landed on her shoulder, jerking her to a stop.

So she flung herself around and punched him. Right in the face.

That shocked her so much she froze. Her knuckles tingled. There was a red mark on his cheek, a mark she'd made.

He rubbed it. "Not bad, but you'd do better to aim for a less bony part of me next time. Noses are good. A nose won't hurt your hand the way a cheekbone will."

"Everything's a joke to you, isn't it?"

"Would you rather I hit you back? Look, I know at this point anything I say can and will be held against me, but I'd still like the chance to explain."

She folded her arms across her chest. "Go right ahead." Why not? He wasn't going to let her go until he did. So she waited, stone-faced, for him to explain why it had been necessary to trick her. To test her.

Test, not trust. Oh, what a fool she was. Over and over, she made a fool of herself with him.

Now that he had her attention, he didn't seem to know what to do with it. He looked away, rubbing his hand over his head as if he could rub some sense into it. "You looked so sad when I said you couldn't be around when Dix and I were working," he said at last. "I hated that."

"And you've made me so much happier by lying to me. Wonderful plan." She wanted to hit him again. Or cry. But she'd be damned before she let him see that, so she turned away.

Of course he stopped her. This time he grabbed her arm. "I was trying not to hurt you. Maybe I screwed up, but what do you expect? I don't know what I'm doing here! How can I do the right thing when I don't have a clue half the time what that is?" His voice was rising. "And you don't help. You want it all your way."

"Me?" Temper brought her around to face him once more. The hand she'd hit him with was beginning to throb. "I'm not the one who keeps physically dragging someone else around to get my way!"

"But you want the trust thing all your way, don't you? I'm supposed to trust you, and you're not supposed to have to tell me a damned thing!"

She'd been going to. She'd been ready to. Now... "I don't care if you trust me or not," she said, and at that moment she meant it. "I don't trust you, so it really doesn't matter how you feel about me, does it?"

Temper sparked in his eyes. His hand tightened on her arm. Then let go. He whirled and slammed his palm against the wall. "Dix!" he yelled. "Come tell this damned complicated woman what we're doing! Tell her everything! I'm going out!"

By the time Dix came out of the kitchen, the front door had slammed behind Rafe.

\*    \*    \*

Rafe drove, paying no attention to where he went.

Charlie wasn't going to let him touch her any time soon. If he couldn't touch her, how could he persuade her to marry him? Hell, he'd be lucky if she didn't run again.

That would be all he needed, he fumed. To have to track her down again, praying with every hour that passed that he found her before the Kellys did. She wouldn't skip right away, though. She'd want to find out what was going on. Dix would be filling her in right about now.

Contrary to what he'd let Charlie believe, they already knew what the Kellys' tech had done. Broderton had planted a "back door" in the Connelly computers, one that allowed them untraceable access to the system. At least, it was supposed to have been untraceable. Rafe had found it and modified a program that logged user access to let him track the tech's activities. For the past four days he and Dix had been able to monitor everything the Kellys' tech did. The man—they assumed it was Broderton, the tech who had planted the worm in the Connelly system and had since vanished—was trying to get into a special partition in the mainframe where the most sensitive material was stored.

So far he hadn't been able to. The partition was heavily protected. Rafe had added some extra bells and whistles, so the data there should be safe—for a time. But what exactly the Kellys wanted with that data remained a mystery.

Which was why Rafe and Dix were working frantically on creating their own version of Broderton's worm. Rafe wanted to make it work in reverse—to follow the link the Kellys' tech opened right back to *their* computer. While Broderton tried to get into the secured partition, Rafe would be downloading every bit of data he could grab from the Kellys' system. Even crooks had to keep records. You couldn't manage any system without them. If Rafe was lucky, the tech might be using a computer that held those records—records of the crime family's activities that could be used to stop them once and for all.

Maybe. If everything went well. But Rafe's chances of turning the tables on the Kellys would vanish if the criminals had any idea what he was attempting. If he was wrong about Charlie…if the hold they had over her was stronger than her honor…

Someone had tried to kill his brother ten months ago. Someone was still trying to kill Charlie, and the Kellys were connected to both attempts. Rafe didn't know how, he didn't know why. He just knew they had to be stopped.

Maybe Charlie had told the truth when she said she wanted to fix what she'd allowed to happen. Maybe she could be trusted with his brother's life. He wanted to believe that.

And maybe she'd be so blind with hurt and anger because he'd tricked her that she would run again, and get herself—and their baby—killed.

Dammit. He couldn't keep her locked up. Tempting as that sounded, it wasn't a practical solution. He'd have to hope that whatever passed for reason in that convoluted brain of hers would accept that she was better off with him than on her own right now.

When you got right down to it, he didn't know why he was so angry with her. Charlie didn't trust him. So what? He'd known that. He'd been over the reasons for it in his mind plenty of times. She was a difficult, closed-up woman who didn't trust easily, and he'd already messed up once with her.

Now he'd screwed up again. Big-time. What was that saying about the road to hell and good intentions?

Rafe heaved a large sigh. Charlie needed to feel useful. He'd tried to give her that, but without gambling everything that the secrets she held on to so tightly wouldn't make her betray them all. He'd wanted to give her a chance, he told himself as he headed back up Lake Shore Drive. What was so wrong with that?

But giving someone a chance wasn't the same as trusting. Not when he gave with one hand and held back with the other. The look in her eyes when she'd come into the kitchen, silent as a ghost and almost as pale, that stayed with him. It kept him churned up after the anger faded.

He didn't think he'd ever been this confused in his life.

So maybe it shouldn't have surprised him when he realized where he'd wound up. But it did. He pulled up in his brother's parking space in the garage used by Connelly Corporation, shut off the engine, then just sat there, his mouth pulled into a thin, disgusted line.

Coming here wasn't a bad idea. He needed to fill his father in. He just wished it had been an actual decision, not some automatic-pilot trick he'd played on himself. Bad enough that he couldn't figure out what was going on with Charlie. Being clueless about his own actions was a real pain.

At least his blasted subconscious hadn't sent him to his parents' home. He did not want to run into his loving, all-too-perceptive mother. His phone call this morning would have primed the pump on her curiosity, and he did not want to be bombarded with questions. He wasn't in the mood for dealing with any females at the moment.

Rafe heaved another sigh, swung open the door and climbed out.

The woman who sat at Charlie's desk these days was named Martha ''something or other.'' She was sharp as a tack, a cute little Puerto Rican spitfire. He hated seeing her where Charlie was supposed to be, so he took extra care to be nice. ''Afternoon, Martha. I stopped by to see if you've changed your mind about running off with me.''

She gave him a look over the top of her reading glasses. ''My husband and I are free this weekend.''

He shook his head. ''No offense, but I doubt he'd be my type.''

She laughed and waved at the door behind her. ''Oh, go

on in. Your father doesn't have anyone with him right now.''

Rafe was frowning as he pushed open the door. The first time he'd seen Charlie at that desk she hadn't wanted to play with him at all. She'd looked so dubious about him, sitting there with her sunshine hair all smooth and pretty and her mouth all primmed up. So he'd asked her out. And he hadn't been teasing, though a second after the words came out, he'd pretended he was. It had been better that way. He didn't—

"Did you come to see me or to stare out my window?"

"Hi, Dad." Rafe turned toward the big desk and the big man who sat behind it. "I thought I'd better bring you up to date."

"You've made progress?" Grant leaned back in his chair.

Progress? Mostly of the backward sort. Rafe grimaced. His father wasn't asking about his matrimonial plans. "Some. This isn't a plain, garden-variety virus Dix and I are working on, you know. More of a worm with legs. The subroutines alone—"

"Never mind the technicalities. I won't understand them. You're sure the Kellys can't get into anything they shouldn't, in the meantime?"

"They can't get into the partition." Rafe moved restlessly around the office. Charlie had worked for his father for over two years. Grant Connelly probably knew her as well as anyone, and better than most. "They can wander around the rest of the records pretty freely if they decide to, but their tech hasn't shown an interest in anything but the partition since we've been monitoring him."

"How much longer will you need to finish that fancy program of yours?"

"Another week, maybe. Could be more."

Grant drummed his fingers on the arm of his chair. "For

the life of me I can't figure out what would be worth this much trouble to them. Starwind suggested it might be some kind of money-laundering scheme.''

Rafe shook his head. ''Luke's good at what he does, but he doesn't know computers. Nothing that's behind the partition would help them pass money secretly through your accounts.''

''And money laundering wouldn't explain the attempt on Daniel's life last January.''

''No.'' Rafe brooded over that. No one had been able to come up with any scenario, however far-fetched, that connected the Kellys' interest in the Connelly computers to what had seemed to be a purely political assassination attempt when Daniel inherited the Altarian throne.

But there was a dead man who'd found some kind of connection. Tom Reynolds.

Grant thrummed the arm of his chair again. ''One way or another we have to find out what they're after. What are your chances of pulling this off?''

''Good, as far as hitching a ride back to their computer goes. I can't guarantee we'll find anything useful. Broderton is no slouch. The worm he planted in your computers is a devilishly clever piece of work. If he's in a position to advise them—''

''Spare me,'' Grant said dryly, standing. ''You may admire your alter ego's technical prowess, but I can't summon appreciation for anyone connected to the Kellys. And something tells me you didn't come here to talk about Broderton, anyway.''

''Not entirely.'' He looked out the window, down at the floor, then finally met his father's gray eyes. ''Mom told you that I found Charlie, I guess. That she's staying with me.''

Grant nodded.

''I decided to let Charlie in on what's going on. Everything." When his father didn't respond, he shoved his hands in his pockets. "You must wonder why. Considering she's the reason the Kellys were able to plant the worm in the first place."

"I suppose you have a reason."

"Probably." Rafe sighed. "I wish I knew what the hell it was. Listen," he said, beginning to pace. "You didn't press charges against her. What do you think—was she forced to do it? She won't tell me anything. Not one damned thing. Do I know where she went to school? What her childhood was like? No and no. How about what the Kellys threatened her with? No. What she thinks she's going to do if she doesn't marry me? Hell, no."

He stopped and glared at his father. "She wouldn't tell me the sky was blue without a subpoena. Why are women so blasted unreasonable?"

"It's the estrogen. Makes their emotions jumpy, so they think that's normal. And if you tell your mother I said that, I'll disown you." Grant went to the small wet bar in the corner and poured himself and his son a shot of scotch, neat. "I take it things aren't going smoothly with Charlotte."

Rafe gave a short laugh. "You could say that." He accepted the drink, eyed it briefly, then tossed it down.

"Good God. That's no way to treat seventeen-year-old whiskey."

The burn robbed him of breath for a moment. Whether the alcohol cleared his mind or not, it worked wonders for his sinuses. "I'm in an excessive mood."

"So I see. Do you want to tell me why you really came here?"

"Not especially." He studied the empty shot glass, turning it around and around. When he'd told his parents he was going to marry Charlie, his mother had looked worried and asked him if that was what he truly wanted. His father had simply nodded as if he'd been expecting it.

Probably he had. Grant Connelly knew his sons pretty well.

Rafe moved restlessly to the window. From up here the city looked busy but orderly. Down on the streets, noise and confusion took over. Rafe liked being able to have it both ways—the lively, in-your-face bustle of the streets, and the chance to pull back into his own space when the crowds and clamor got to him.

He felt a lot the same about his family. He loved them, couldn't imagine life without them, but they were a close, pushy bunch. He needed to be able to get away from them as much as he sometimes needed them around. That's why he didn't work for Connelly Corporation.

Charlie didn't have a family. Maybe that was why she was always pulling back, opting for distance and order. She didn't know how to handle the up-close-and-personal.

He frowned at the distant, orderly scene below. "When you first found out what Charlie had done, you were mad as blue blazes. But you didn't want her charged as an accessory. In fact, you put pressure on the police so they wouldn't charge her."

"I didn't want her to go to jail. I've always liked Charlotte. I consider her a woman of high principles. But sometimes when principles and need clash, need wins. I'd like to know what need the Kellys used against her."

So would he. If he could just be sure, absolutely sure, it hadn't been money... "I thought she might have told you."

"I haven't spoken with her since the police brought her in for questioning after Reynolds was killed."

Rafe considered pouring another shot, then decided against it. He hadn't come here to drink. Or to talk about Broderton and the Kellys, as his father had pointed out. "I guess I was wondering how you feel about me marrying her.''

"She's carrying your baby. It's the right thing to do." Grant sipped his scotch. "More importantly, how do you feel about it?''

"She's making me crazy. I don't know what to do about it. She turned me down, you know."

His father hesitated. "I'm sorry to hear that. Will she agree to a joint custody arrangement?''

Rafe waved that aside. "She's going to marry me. I haven't worked out how to persuade her, but I will."

"I'm not sure what you want me to tell you, then. Are you looking for advice on how to persuade her?''

Rafe wasn't sure what he was looking for, either. Nothing he could imagine putting into words. *How did you and Mom work things out after she found out about Seth? How did you put the pieces back together after you'd made a royal mess of them?* But they had never talked about that sort of thing. His parents had separated, his father had had an affair and then they'd gotten back together, and Rafe didn't have the foggiest idea how it had all gone wrong or been put right again. Or how to bring up a subject that was off-limits.

He tried asking obliquely. "How do you get a woman to trust you?''

"By being someone she can trust.''

Rafe flicked his father a hard look. There had been a time when Grant hadn't been someone his wife could trust, but somehow he'd gotten past that. Somehow he and Rafe's mother had gone from fractured to strong and solid, and Rafe would have appreciated a more substantial hint on how to work that bit of magic.

"Never mind," he said abruptly. "I'll work it out." He glanced at the door, hesitated, then asked one more question. "Has Charlie ever mentioned someone named Brad Fowler to you?"

"Fowler." Grant gave the name a few moments' thought. "No, I don't believe so. But she never said much about her personal life. She's a very private person."

No kidding. Rafe turned to go. "Thanks for the drink."

"Rafe."

He paused at the door, looking over his shoulder. "Yeah?"

"In many ways you take after your mother. As your sister Maggie would say, you're a 'people person.' You enjoy getting your way, but you lack my, ah, tendency to try to control others. You're like me in one way, though. Once you've made up your mind you want something, you go after it with everything you have. It's not a bad trait, but I can tell you from experience it can make you blind sometimes."

Rafe frowned, puzzled and annoyed. "If you have a point, I wish you'd make it."

"You're determined to marry Charlotte."

"You agreed it's the right thing to do."

Grant smiled faintly. "Yes, but I don't think that's why you're hell-bent on getting married."

"I'm not hell-bent on getting married. I don't want to be married. I do want my child, and I want him or her to have two parents who live together."

"And Charlotte? Do you want her, too?"

"She didn't get pregnant all by herself," Rafe growled. "Of course I want her. That doesn't mean I'm crazy about marriage. It's the right thing to do, that's all."

"Hmm. Well, like I said, there's nothing wrong with going after what you want. But you need to decide if you're using the woman to get the baby, or using the baby to get the woman. Neither one is likely to work out well."

After his son had left, Grant stood by the window for several minutes, sipping his scotch and thinking.

At sixty-five, Grant Connelly looked like what he was— a man who possessed money and power, and was comfortable with both. He favored suits tailored for him, Italian shoes and frequent manicures, all of which put an attractive gloss on the predator beneath. A man didn't climb to the top of a competitive, often ruthless heap and stay there for nearly forty years without his own share of ruthlessness— and that tendency he'd mentioned to his son. Emma had told him more than once that his habit of trying to control those around him arose from sheer, bloody arrogance, the unconscious assumption that he was always right.

But a good businessman knows when to call in the experts. After a few minutes of frowning contemplation he moved back to his desk, picked up the phone and called his wife.

# Nine

Rafe left his father's office in a worse state of confusion than he'd been in when he'd arrived. Damn, but he hated it when his dad turned all wise and cryptic. Why couldn't he just come out and say what he meant?

Using the baby to get the woman. Using the woman to get the baby. What was that supposed to mean? Rafe didn't see any reason he couldn't have them both. That was the whole idea.

Right now, though, he was about as far from becoming a reluctantly married man as he'd ever been. He'd be lucky if Charlie was speaking to him when he got home. If she did speak, he thought gloomily, she'd be using that polite voice of hers. The one that meant she was up in her tower, safely distant from all the noise and confusion.

If he had to live with all this confusion, she would just have to get down in the messy middle of things, too. It was only fair.

Charlie did like things tidy, though. By now she would

have found some nice, neat label to hang on him, something along the lines of Tricky—Don't Trust. His father thought he needed to prove he could be trusted, but Rafe didn't have time for that. Charlie was a stubborn woman. She'd hang on to that label she'd stuck on him halfway to forever if he let her.

The thing to do, he decided, was to be every bit as tricky as she thought he was—and then some.

"You sure I can't get you something before I go?" Dix asked. He stood at the door to the office with his laptop in one hand and a ferocious frown on his face. "Some juice, maybe?"

"Quite sure, thank you." Charlotte kept her head bent over the printout Dix had given her earlier. It listed the name and a brief précis of all the files stored within the partition the Kellys' tech was trying to get into. Somewhere in these files was the answer. It had to be.

"You should eat something."

"I will," she assured him. "I'm not hungry yet, but I'll fix something later." *Leave. Please leave now.*

"Okay. See you tomorrow." Still he hesitated.

She glanced up finally and met his eyes. "I *will* be here tomorrow. I promised I wouldn't leave, and I'm not a fool. I came here because I had nowhere else to go, and that's still true."

His frown didn't go away, but he nodded and, at last, he left. She listened to his steps on the stairs and took a deep breath—the first unobserved breath she'd had since Rafe slammed out of the apartment.

Dix looked tough. He talked tough. But he was a real marshmallow, she'd discovered. He'd been driving her crazy all afternoon, sneaking worried looks at her, as if he thought she was going to fall apart. Good grief. She was perfectly fine. Just because she and Rafe had had an argument…that was no big deal. They'd argued before. Perhaps she had been rather emotional, but she'd had plenty of time to calm down. Rafe had been gone for hours. She...

Was shaking. With a sense of betrayal Charlotte looked at the trembling hand holding a pencil. She couldn't write. She could barely hold the pencil.

Her eyes closed. There was a horrid, jittery feeling inside her, as if she'd drunk three pots of coffee in a row. Or was sitting in the dentist's chair with her mouth wedged open, watching helplessly as the drill came closer and closer. The dreadful feeling had been coming over her in waves all afternoon. It would retreat for a while and she'd think she'd finally pulled herself together—then, just as she was managing to concentrate, it would start shaking its way out again.

She set down the pencil with a sigh. It was very upsetting. Work had always been her sanctuary. Before moving to Chicago she'd handled the bookkeeping for a few small businesses. She didn't know how she would have made it through Brad's arrest and trial if she hadn't had all those soothing columns of figures to submerge herself in every night.

Why wasn't work helping now?

Pregnancy hormones, she thought, pushing to her feet and moving to Rafe's desk. She'd read that they caused a lot of emotional swings. She just had to ride this mood out. Sooner or later she'd settle down again. In the meantime, she could darned well get some work done. Whether it soothed her wasn't as important as contributing to the effort to catch the Kellys.

She sat in Rafe's chair and bent to slide a CD into its drive.

Why had he done it? Why had Rafe told Dix to tell her what he and Dix were really working on?

Her hand paused in midair. Her mouth turned down. This wasn't the first time that thought had intruded on her concentration. Deliberately she completed the motion.

The CD contained software to link to the Connelly computers. She waited through the dialing beeps, tapping her fingers impatiently.

She just couldn't make sense of Rafe's abrupt turn-around. He'd carefully kept the truth from her—and now that she wasn't blinded by emotion, she could understand why. She'd wanted him to trust her on some emotional level, but that would be irresponsible. Logic as well as feeling confirmed that Rafe couldn't be in league with the Kellys. If they had been able to use him, they wouldn't have needed their elaborate machinations to gain access to the Connelly computers. He could have handed them whatever they wanted, and no one would ever have been the wiser.

The same couldn't be said of her. Rafe had every reason to doubt and very little to trust.

*Test, not trust.*

Charlie's fingers stilled as anger spiked through her again. He should have left it alone. After asking her to stay downstairs when he and Dix were working, he should have let the subject drop. He shouldn't have pretended to trust. He...

Had changed his mind.

She bit her lip. Rafe had been so furious that he'd attacked an unsuspecting wall—and then he'd yelled at Dix to tell her everything. Why? It wasn't as if he were the sort to cave in under opposition. Oh, no. Normally you couldn't change that man's mind with a two-by-four. He was hard-headed, confident, so sure he was right....

But maybe he wasn't sure with her.

Charlie's heartbeat picked up. The shaky feeling was back, stronger than ever. Damn him, he was messing with her mind and she wanted him *out*. She wanted to have her thoughts to herself again. Why couldn't he leave her alone, even when she was alone? She—wasn't alone. At the sound of voices downstairs, her heart jumped. One of them was Rafe. She knew his voice, even if she couldn't make out the words from up here. Her heartbeat settled back to normal.

But who was with him? She heard a male voice, and a female one, too. A scraping noise, as if something was being moved. Laughter, and—what was that? *Drums?*

More voices. A muffled thud.

What in the world was the dratted man up to? Surely he wasn't giving a party! Well, whatever he was doing, she was not going to gratify him by going downstairs to find out. She didn't want to see him, speak to him or think about him. She'd stay up here and by damn, she would get some work done.

She called up a directory. Downstairs someone was tuning up an instrument. With an extreme effort of will Charlie managed to focus on the screen, even to make a little progress. She was almost able to tune out the strange sounds coming from downstairs—the buzzer sounding, more scraping sounds as if furniture was being moved, people talking...

"Charlie!" Rafe called. "Stay up there a few minutes longer, okay? Don't come down yet."

She was in the hall when the tiki music started playing. Tiki music?

Rafe stood at the foot of the stairs. He was wearing the same dark blue turtleneck and torn jeans he'd had on earlier, but he'd added something. Flowers. Two gaudy tropical leis hung around his neck.

He grinned. "I knew telling you to stay put would bring you running."

Her mouth flattened. She almost turned around and went back up the stairs. Too predictable, she told herself.

Besides, by then she'd seen too much to turn back.

Most of the lights had been turned off. The music came from a trio of musicians wearing sarongs and flowers. Or maybe the men's costumes weren't called sarongs. Whatever the name for the cloth around their hips, it was short and flowered and left a lot of coppery skin bare. One of the men was playing drums; another played some sort of flute, while the woman strummed a stringed instrument. Another man—this one older and fully clothed in a white dinner jacket and dark slacks—was setting the table. Not the dining table. The coffee table. Which had been moved in front of the fireplace...and the palm tree.

A real, live palm tree leaned over the coffee table. Pots of exotic flowers circled it. The man in the white dinner jacket was lighting candles, and a fire burned in the fireplace. The sweet scent of flowers mingled with spicy, unfamiliar aromas from the food the waiter had set out.

She stood on the last step and stared. "You *are* having a party."

"You could call it that." He held out his hand. "Or you could call it an apology."

Her heart was beating too hard. She could feel it pounding in her throat, keeping time with the drums. She swallowed and ignored his outstretched hand. "I don't understand."

"You know what I'm apologizing for, so it must be the manner of the apology you don't understand." The smile hung on his lips as he dropped his hand back to his side, but his eyes were dark. Serious. "I've been too narrowly focused, you see. I kept thinking you're too secretive, that you won't tell me anything. But I've learned some things about you in the past two years."

The smile eased into his eyes. "For example, I know you enjoy Italian food, Mexican food and the opera. You had a dog named Beau when you were thirteen—you told me that when I mentioned the dog I had when I was a kid. I know you like pretty clothes and a clean desk, and you're nuts about organizing things. You've got the sexiest mouth I've ever seen, and you've never been to Hawaii."

The sexiest mouth? Her tongue came out to touch her lips. She realized what she was doing and cleared her throat. "Ah, Hawaii. I mentioned that last year. That's why you sent me that silly doll when you went there on a business trip.''

He nodded and lifted one of the leis over his head. ''I nearly sent you a postcard—you know, the sort that say, 'Thinking of you, wish you were here.' Because I was, and I did. But I didn't want to be thinking about you. It bugged me. So I sent you the doll instead.''

He moved even closer, so that only inches separated them. His voice dropped. ''I also know you're honest to a fault. You don't lie, you don't cheat or steal or bend the rules. If you say that whatever hold the Kellys had on you isn't an issue anymore, then it isn't. I wish you'd trust me enough to tell me about it, though.''

He paused, giving her a chance to speak, to tell him. She firmed her lips against the urge to do so. All along she'd been too easy for him. She'd fallen into bed with him. She'd let him drag her back to his apartment. And now—now, she thought with a flutter of panic, she was close to forgiving him for everything. For anything, so long as he kept looking at her that way.

No. She wasn't so weak, so foolishly female. A few pretty words proved nothing. He'd known her for two years, just as he said. And for two years he'd found her eminently resistible. Rafe wanted his child, he wanted to have things his way, and he didn't mind seducing her to get it. Her jaw tightened, locking the words inside.

''No?'' he said softly. ''Well, I can't blame you. I'm sorry I didn't trust you earlier.'' He settled the lei over her head, and the heady scent of jasmine drifted up to tease her. ''I didn't take you to Hawaii with me last year, Charlie. My mistake. Let me bring Hawaii to you tonight.''

She liked the hula dancer. Rafe smiled at her astonishment, and at the suspicious look she cast him. She was sure she had his number. She thought she knew how the evening would end—with him trying to get her into bed.

And Lord knew that was how he wished it could end.

She was like wine, Charlie was, flowing sweetly through his veins and making him ache. But for tonight, at least, neither of them would get what they wanted. He wouldn't seduce her because that was what she was expecting. And she wouldn't keep him tucked neatly in whatever mental pigeonhole she'd assigned him.

The way past Charlie's walls was to keep her off-balance.

In the meantime, he was enjoying her reactions. By the time the hula dancer finished and the waiter removed the salad plates and began serving the main course, Charlie was in trouble. She wasn't being polite at all.

She fussed at him, telling him he was an idiot and this was absurdly extravagant. Her eyes were glowing. He agreed and urged her to try the *moloka'i,* the famous sweet rolls from the islands. She shook her head, took a greedy bite, swallowed and said she didn't even want to think about how much all this had cost. And her eyes were soft, beginning to dream.

She made a face when she tried the poi, but the lomi-lomi salmon and guava chicken went over big. The real hit of the evening, though, arrived as they were finishing dessert. Just when he'd decided the theatrical agent hadn't been able to come through, the last act showed up.

Charlie *loved* the sword dancers.

She watched, mouth open, as the two muscular young men in grass loincloths and fancy headdresses pranced and gyrated and tossed swords back and forth in Rafe's darkened living room. And Rafe watched her.

"Equal opportunity ogling," he said, leaning close to be heard over the pounding drums. "I watched a pretty woman wiggle her hips while we ate our salads, so it's only fair you get to look at a couple of naked men."

She ducked her head and glanced at him sideways. "Nearly naked," she corrected, a smile nipping at the corners of her mouth, as if she knew a secret that pleased her.

Maybe she'd noticed that he'd been looking at her, not the hula dancer.

Or maybe that sideways glance was the come-hither his body wanted it to be. Down, boy, he told himself. No point in raising hopes—and other things—that weren't going to be fulfilled tonight.

Naturally, his body paid no attention to reason. He leaned back and shifted, trying to ease the increasing pressure his jeans were putting on a sensitive part of his anatomy.

After the drums and the dancers had crashed into a grand finale, he applauded, though he had no idea if the performance had been any good. He'd been too busy watching Charlie. Judging by the way she was making her palms sting, though, she thought they'd been great. He smiled. "Want to honeymoon on Oahu?"

Her eyebrows twitched and her mouth tried to get prim again. "Rafe—"

"We'll talk in a minute," he promised, rising. "I've got to reward these fellows for a great show."

He ushered out the performers and the waiter, suitably enriched for their efforts, and hit the last light switch on his way back to Charlie. The room faded into nearly complete darkness. Candles still flickered on the table, but the fire had died down to a few small flames licking along the remains of the logs. Most of the light came from the big, undraped window where Charlie now stood—city lights filtered by the fronds of his new palm tree.

Charlie was looking out the window with her arms hugged across her chest. Battle stations, he thought, smiling. She was primed and ready to repel his advances.

"I hope you've got a green thumb," he said when he reached her.

"What?" Her hair was rebelling against that tight ponytail she'd pulled it into. Lots of wiggly bits had already escaped. Absently she tucked one of the escapees behind her ear. "A green thumb? Why?"

He liked the way all those loose curls tickled her face

and frisked around on her neck. He wanted to play with them. He shoved his hands into his pockets instead. "Because I'll probably kill it," he said, nodding at the palm. "I don't have a good track record with plants."

"Oh. Well, I don't know much about palm trees, but I can find out. There are probably resources on the Net about that sort of thing. Gardening books, too. There are bound to be books about palm trees. Or tropical plants. At bookstores, I mean, not the Internet. Or libraries. I—" She grimaced. "I'm babbling."

"Yeah. It's cute." Unfortunately, shoving his hands in his pockets had put more strain on his jeans right where he didn't need it. He pulled his hands out again. One of them immediately took advantage of that freedom to touch a playful wisp near her cheek. "I like your hair this way."

She frowned, but it wasn't very successful. Her eyes were too luminous in the glow from the fire and the city for effective frowning. "Messy, you mean?"

"I like you messy." His thumb got the idea to stroke her cheek. Such soft skin she had. "I like you tidy, too, but that may be because it makes me fantasize about messing you up. Did you know that when you're working, you get this little vee of concentration right here?" He smoothed the spot between her brows with one finger. "It makes me nuts."

Her laugh was unsteady. She took a step back. "You *are* nuts."

Her lower lip couldn't decide if it wanted to turn up or down. Her breath seemed to be in a hurry, which had a delightful effect on her breasts. His gaze lingered there, then returned to her face.

She was biting that undecided lower lip, but her eyes were steady and wide open when they met his. And it hit him suddenly. He could have her. Tonight. *Now.* If he put out his hand, touched her, pushed just a little, she would topple. She wanted to topple. Whether Charlie knew it or not, she was ready to be seduced into doing what they both wanted.

His breath stuck in his chest. His hands grew warm. His pulse took over his body, a hard throbbing that rushed from groin to stomach to neck. All along he'd told himself he would have her in his bed soon—but this wasn't soon. This was *now*. The sudden certainty of her acceptance was a lure he wasn't sure he could resist.

So why he said what he did, he had no idea. "Maybe you should go upstairs."

She blinked. "Excuse me?"

"I'm having a hard time remembering that I wasn't going to seduce you. That's not supposed to be part of the program, but I'm very close to changing my mind." Or whatever passed for his mind at the moment.

"I see." Her eyelids dipped. The tip of her tongue touched her upper lip, then retreated back inside her mouth. "Apparently we were on the same wavelength for once. You weren't going to seduce me, and I wasn't going to let you. The thing is..." She put her hand squarely on the center of his chest. "I did change my mind."

"Ah..."

"Your heart is beating hard. You haven't been running, and I know you aren't afraid." She looked up at him. "So you must want me."

But he *was* afraid. The realization jolted him—what could he possibly be afraid of? He pressed his hand over hers, trapping it against the rapid thud of his heart. "Yeah. I want you."

"You don't sound happy about it."

He wasn't. He didn't like tasting the sour backwash of fear when there was nothing to be afraid of. But he was more aroused than angry. "Let's see if we can make me happy, then."

Slowly, giving her time to change her mind—knowing she wouldn't, and so damned turned on by the knowledge he could have pushed inside her that very second—he pulled her to him.

# Ten

She had time.

Rafe moved his hands deliberately along the curve of her back, drawing her to him, giving her an eternity of seconds to tell him no, that he'd misunderstood or she'd changed her mind and she wasn't going to do this. Time enough to feel each of his fingers through the scant protection of her sweater, to thrill to the heat and pressure along her breasts and belly as their bodies touched. Plenty of time to wonder why he was angry—and just when she'd lost her mind.

She wasn't going to stop him. She wanted this, wanted him. Her heart was pounding as if it was trying to break free of the safe cage of her ribs and dance naked in the air.

Then his mouth was on hers. Hot, still angry—and oh, so welcome. Time shifted, slanted, becoming a dizzy rush of seconds slipping summer-warm through her blood as she tasted him again.

His mouth was as deliberate as his hands had been, his lips and tongue laying claim to hers insistently, as if she might still deny him. Her arms went around him as she sought the places she'd tried so hard not to remember in all the long nights since he'd left her. The hard slope of his shoulder. The dip of his spine, outlined by muscle. The way those muscles moved beneath her hands as his arms went tight around her, and his mouth turned greedy.

When their lips at last parted, they were both breathless. She tucked her head in the spot that seemed made for it, the warm hollow between his neck and his shoulder, and breathed him in. Her pulse sang. Between her legs, she throbbed.

He wrapped one hand in her hair and rested his head against hers. "I don't think I'm going to make it upstairs."

"No," she agreed, and then, because she had to, she added, "There's just one thing..."

His fingers tightened in her hair. "You're not changing your mind again."

"No. At least...I don't want to." She wasn't sure she could. She might be able to resist the sweet insistence of her body. She might find the strength to refuse the promised completion of his body. But his scent... How could she have come to need the simple smell of him in only one night? "But I have to be sure we understand each other. That it's...like last time. No expectations."

His head jerked up. "What the hell does that mean?"

She raised her head so she could meet his eyes. He was staring down at her, haughty as a king confronted by lèse-majesté. For some reason his arrogance didn't bother her this time. Instead, she wanted to soothe the tight muscles around his eyes. "The same thing it meant when you said it five months ago."

"Everything's changed since then." His hand left her hair, dropping to cup the swell of her stomach. "You're expecting my child. That gives me the right to expect some things from you. You damned well ought to expect certain things from me, too."

Temper nipped. "Like marriage, you mean." She pulled

back, but his arms tightened, holding her in place. "As far as you're concerned, our relationship is defined by the baby I'm carrying."

"I think you think you just said something significant, but damned if I know what you're getting at. Of course the baby changed things."

"What if it wasn't yours?"

His eyebrows snapped down. "If you're trying to tell me I'm not the father—"

"No." Aching in too many ways, she closed her eyes. He had no idea what she was trying to say. What she wanted him to say. "I'm not trying to tell you that."

"Good. Because I wouldn't believe you. Dammit, Charlie." The words were rough, but his voice softened. The arms around her gentled until he was holding her again, not pinning her in place. He sighed. "Why do you have to be so complicated?" His hand came up to urge her head back onto his shoulder.

She let him have his way, since it put her right where she wanted to be. "I suppose you're not?"

"I'm a simple man," he assured her, stroking her hair.

She almost laughed. Simple? Rafe was the most complex, confusing man she'd ever known. But the slow stroke of his hand stirred her, and the deep ache of her body gripped her too tightly for laughter.

He nuzzled the hair away from her ear and kissed the top of her jaw. "I'm just a man, after all, and we're pretty basic creatures, verging on simpleminded at times. Like right now. I'm having a hard time thinking of anything except ravishing you. Thoroughly. On the couch, or upstairs in my bed. Or on the stairs on the way to my bed. Or all three."

"On the stairs?" A laugh did make its way out, brief and shaky. She lifted her head to smile into his eyes. "I don't think so. That sounds terribly uncomfortable."

"Okay." He dropped a quick kiss on the corner of her mouth, then another on her cheek. "We'll skip the ravish-

ing on the stairs. Two out of three works for me. For now.''
He drew his hands down along her arms to capture her
hands. "Have we talked enough to satisfy your female need
for words? Can we go on to the kind of communication a
crude male like me understands?''

His words were casual. His smile was lightly mocking,
though whether it mocked her or himself she didn't know.
But his eyes held heat and hunger and a need she had no
defense against.

The important part of what he was telling her was word-
less, so she answered the same way. She pressed herself
against him, going up on tiptoe so she could reach for his
mouth with hers.

Rafe met her more than halfway.

He groaned. His arms were tight around her, his mouth
demanding. And she gave herself up to the moment—and
him.

When his mouth left hers to trace her jaw, seeking the
pulse in her throat, she shivered and arched her neck. His
tongue traced that arc while his hands chased the shivers
his mouth created. Time broke into soap bubble moments,
floating and fragile, that burst, one after another, showering
her with sensation.

His mouth on hers, his tongue dancing, thrusting. Her
hands hunting for skin beneath the soft knit of his shirt.
His hand finding her breast beneath the sweatshirt, caressing, teasing. The need building, the empty place waiting
for him, calling for him.

"Too many clothes,'' she gasped in a moment when her
mouth was, briefly, free.

"And too vertical,'' he agreed. Her feet left the ground
as he swung her up in his arms. She might have told him
she was too heavy if he'd given her a chance. But his mouth
stopped any protests before she could make them.

Then he was lowering her to the couch, coming down
on top of her, nestled between her legs. He kissed her wild,
kissed her boneless, then tore his mouth away. "Is there

anything I should know?" He smoothed her sweatshirt up over the swell of her belly. "I don't want to hurt you. I don't want to do anything wrong."

She smiled. "My breasts are a little tender. Other than that, you can't hurt me. When I'm farther along..." But that was in the future, and only dreamers concerned themselves with the future. All she and Rafe were offering each other was now. So she ran her hand down his side, around to his front—and up the full, hard length of him.

The cords in his neck went taut as his head went back. What he muttered might have been a curse or a prayer. His hips moved, pressing him firmly into her palm. "I'm not going to make it if you do that."

She squeezed gently.

"That's it. You're in trouble now." He pulled her hand away, pushed her sweatshirt up and tugged it over her head. He pushed her bra up without bothering to unfasten it—and bent his head.

His mouth was warm and sweet. First he licked, then gently closed his lips around her nipple. His slow sucking drew a tight band from breast to groin, making her moan. "You're right," she gasped. "Big trouble." She threaded her hands through his hair, but the ache was building too fast. Sweet as his mouth was, it wasn't enough.

His hands were busy, though, unfastening this and that, colliding with hers when she tried to help. Between them they managed to get her bra and his shirt off in spite of stopping to kiss whatever portion of each other's bodies they could reach, then her pants and panties.

He cupped her. She jolted and nearly tumbled him off. He slid a finger in. "I've thought of doing this so often." Two fingers, and he was looking at her. "The first time I saw you, looking so pretty and tidy at your desk, this is what I was thinking of doing." In and out. "Could you tell? Is that why you looked so disapproving?" His thumb lightly circled her clitoris and she bit her lip to keep back a cry. "Did you ever think about me touching you like this when you were sitting there with your blouse buttoned up to your neck?'' Out and in.

''No,'' she said, and grabbed his arm, holding on tight. ''Maybe. I don't know. Dammit, Rafe...''

''Maybe?'' Sweat darkened his hairline and his chest heaved, but he remained intent on his intimate teasing. ''I think you do know. I think you thought about me sometimes, nasty thoughts about things like this....'' And he put three fingers in this time. ''And this.''

Her hips bucked. She gasped, grabbed his zipper and yanked it down. ''Stop playing! I want you in me.''

He looked up at her face and grinned, though it was strained. ''Now there's an idea.''

He tugged his jeans and briefs off. Then he was on top of her, easing her legs wider, easing himself inside. And she was full at last, full of Rafe, holding him inside. She made a sound, a sob.

''Charlie,'' he said, leaning forward to rest his forehead on hers, taking some of his weight on his arms. His skin was hot and slightly damp. ''You feel so good, Charlie. So good.''

She reached up with both hands, threading her fingers through his hair, cherishing the line of his jaw. She was all but panting in her need for the rest of the act, yet couldn't bear to move past this moment yet, when he was fully hers.

Suddenly afraid—and not wanting to know what she feared—she lifted her hips. He groaned and began to move, one slow thrust at a time.

Slow didn't work for either of them for long. The power built, cycling back and forth between them—his strength, her suppleness, her hands clutching, one of them moaning. Climax hit like a fist, a gut-punch of pleasure. She cried out. He slammed into her one more time and threw his head back, every muscle of his body clenched as he spilled his seed inside her.

Slowly he sank down, carefully keeping his weight off her stomach. He ended up with one of his legs between hers, his body angled across her hips, the rest of him on the couch. Her eyes closed. Little tingles chased themselves up her legs. Aftershocks shivered through her most intimate muscles.

His head was next to hers. She felt his breath stir her hair when he spoke softly. "Charlie."

That was all he said, just her name. But the way he said it made her smile, eyes still closed, drifting in a moment she wished would never end. He drifted with her, holding her close as her heartbeat gradually settled back to normal.

Eventually he spoke again. "I hate to mention this, but I'm about to fall off the couch."

Amusement made her open her eyes and slant him a sleepy glance. "I guess you want me to move over. Let me see if anything's working yet." She lay utterly still for a few seconds. "Nope. Apparently not."

"Lazy wench." He shifted and she accommodated him, and she ended up mostly on top of him with their legs tangled together. His fingers sifted through her hair. There was a dreamy contentment in being quiet and close this way, the demands of their bodies temporarily subdued. She felt the baby move, and smiled.

"Charlie."

There was an odd note in his voice. She opened her eyes. "Yes?"

"Your stomach is moving."

"Properly speaking, it isn't my stomach that's moving."

"Sweet God," he said, and put his hand on her belly.

His voice, even more than his words, made her look at him. She'd never seen that expression before—not on Rafe's face.

"Will it do that again?" he asked. "Can you get it to move again?"

"No. I don't…" Something was clutching at her, a hard squeezing as if she were about to cry. Which made no sense. She swallowed. "I can't make the baby move when I want. Or stop moving, for that matter. That's a whole separate little person in there, and he or she does what she or he wants to. But the baby will probably move again if you wait awhile.''

He waited, his fingers outstretched, as motionless as if he were trying to coax some small, timid creature out of hiding. When the baby rewarded his patience by squirming, a grin spread over his face. "How about that.''

His delight made her unsteady, as if the shaky feeling that had plagued her all afternoon was coming back. Charlie swallowed and made herself breathe evenly. There was nothing wrong. There was no reason to feel panic nibbling at the edges.

"How does it feel to you when the baby moves?'' he asked.

"Pretty wonderful.''

"I guess it's not very big yet.'' He glanced at her face, frowning. "But it's going to get bigger. It's got to hurt. When the baby comes out, I mean.''

"Yes, it will.'' *I'm fine. This mood will pass. It's just another ride on the hormone roller coaster.* "I'm tough, though. I may scream a lot or curse, but I'll be fine.''

"I don't like it. There ought to be a better way, something that doesn't hurt. With all the advances in medical technology these days—''

She laughed, and it eased the tightness in her chest. "Oh, Rafe. They tried the 'no pain' approach in the fifties, drugging women into unconsciousness. Mother Nature's way really works best for both mother and child.''

His mouth twisted ruefully. "Am I getting carried away? All of a sudden everything is so real to me. I mean, I knew the baby was real. But before, we hadn't been introduced, me and the little squirmer here.'' His hand moved over her belly as if he could caress the life inside. "Now we have.''

Her eyes stung. She hadn't planned to become pregnant, nor had she carefully selected her baby's father. Yet for all her lack of planning, she'd chosen well. Rafe was a good man. He would be a good father.

"Hey." He touched her cheek. "What's wrong? You're getting damp."

She blinked the moisture away. "Hormones. They make me a little crazy sometimes."

The lift of his eyebrow said he didn't buy that, but he let it pass. "Why don't you know if it's a girl or a boy? I thought they could tell these days."

"Usually they figure it out when they do an ultrasound, but I haven't had one yet. My doctor was going to do one when I was twenty-four weeks along, but…well, I missed that appointment."

"Because you went into hiding." His voice flattened. "You need to see another doctor right away. And I don't want to hear any nonsense about how women have been having babies for centuries without a doctor. They didn't all live through it."

"Don't worry. I'm all in favor of modern medicine." She bit her lip and looked down at his hand, still spread possessively over her stomach. "But it isn't that simple. I don't dare send for my medical records. I don't know if they could find me that way. I don't know how they found me the last time."

Rafe's mouth tightened. "I'll take care of it."

"I'm sure you mean well, but what do you know about obstetricians and how—"

"I'll find out. But this is the wrong time for this discussion, isn't it?" All at once he stood and slid one arm under her knees and the other behind her back.

She was so startled she squeaked as she rose in the air. That annoyed her, so she frowned at him even as she threw her arms around his neck. "What do you think you're doing?"

"Amazing. You can look all prim and tidy even when you're naked and ravished." He dropped a kiss on her mouth, a little slow, a little sweet, a little bit of tongue. "I haven't forgotten the second part of my plans for the evening."

''The second...oh.'' For once, she was able to follow one of his lightning mood changes and understand. Rafe wanted to distract her. He didn't want her worrying about the Kellys and the unholy mess her life was in.

Oh, yes. He was a good man. The least she could do was play along. She moistened her lips. ''The part that takes place upstairs, you mean?''

''In my bed.'' He sounded thoroughly satisfied with the idea.

''As long as you've given up on the part involving—Rafe,'' she said firmly when he started walking, ''you are not going to carry me up all those stairs.''

''Want to bet?''

Rafe was very good with distractions. After losing the bet, Charlie didn't think about the Kellys or anything else for quite some time. But afterward she lay in his bed with his arm thrown loosely over her waist, holding her in place. His breath was warm against the side of her head, the tempo smooth and shallow with sleep.

But sleep was nowhere to be found for Charlie. She lay quietly in his arms for a very long time, staring dry-eyed at the darkness.

# Eleven

---

**R**afe was not a morning person. He didn't bound cheerfully out of bed at the crack of dawn, and didn't approve of those who did. Normally, though, especially near the end of a project, he woke up early whether he wanted to or not, his mind buzzing as it automatically picked up where he'd left off the night before.

He definitely wanted to pick up where he'd left off last night. But when he reached for Charlie, she wasn't there.

A sharp pang cleared the last traces of sleep. His eyes opened. Damn. He wished…a glance at the clock had him raising his eyebrows. It was three minutes after ten o'clock.

That explained why she wasn't beside him, he supposed. But he didn't like it. He'd wanted her there when he woke up. Scowling, he threw back the covers and padded, naked, down the hall to the bathroom.

She could have woken him up, couldn't she? If she'd gotten tired of waiting for him to wake up, she could have given him a shake. Or roused him in other, more pleasant ways.

Obviously she hadn't wanted to.

Rafe was in a thoroughly bad mood by the time he stepped under the shower. He'd thought last night was pretty special. Mind-bogglingly wonderful, in fact. Maybe she hadn't. That thought pinched at him in a place deep inside, the same place the fear had come from the first time he'd made love with Charlie.

His anger deflated in one slow exhalation. He put his hands on the side of the shower stall and leaned under the spray, not liking himself very much.

Maybe she'd wanted him there in the morning, too—that first morning, after their first time together. Maybe she'd been as crazy in love with him five months ago as he was with her right now.

Water continued to pound down on his shoulders and back. Rafe stood motionless. Dumbfounded. Just how long had he been falling in love without noticing? And what was he supposed to do about it?

His brain failed to come up with any suggestions. At last he shut off the water and shook his head, sending drops flying. This changed things. Explained things, too. No wonder he'd been so confused.

*Are you using the woman to get the baby...or the baby to get the woman? Neither one is likely to work.*

Rafe heaved an exasperated sigh. Damn. His father had known what was going on before he did. Grant Connelly had been right, too, in his annoyingly cryptic way. A man didn't use the ones he loved.

If she had been in love with him, even a little bit, he had hurt her badly when he climbed out of her bed and ran for cover.

Feeling like scum, Rafe grabbed a towel and rubbed himself dry, then went through the rest of his morning ritual. It was a wonder she'd slept with him again, he thought as he drew a razor along his jaw. Or maybe not. The razor paused. Why would a woman with Charlie's defenses give him a second chance?

He'd been ready to back off last night. *She'd* seduced *him.* Admittedly it hadn't taken much, but... Damned complicated woman. Grimly he finished shaving and rinsed the razor. The only explanations he could come up with for her change of mind didn't make him happy. If she hadn't cared deeply before, then she hadn't been badly hurt. Going for a second round might not have seemed too much to risk.

He didn't like that explanation because it meant he was the only one in love at the moment, but it could be worse. At least he would still have a chance to change her mind and her heart. It was the other possibility that had his jaw tight as he left the bathroom.

Maybe she'd cared too much and he'd killed her love, so now it didn't matter if she went to bed with him or not. He couldn't hurt her again because she didn't care at all.

The thought made him feel hollow and scared. He wanted to go downstairs and shake her and make her tell him how she felt, but he had enough sense left to know how well *that* would work. So he pulled on his jeans slowly, trying to figure out how to get a woman who never told him anything to tell him how she felt about him.

He was zipping his jeans when the smell reached him—yeasty, fragrant. Bread baking? And wasn't the scent of cinnamon mixed with it?

Cinnamon rolls. Charlie was making cinnamon rolls.

A woman might lose her head and have sex with a man she didn't care about—but she wouldn't bake him cinnamon rolls the next day.

Rafe didn't bother to grab a shirt on his way out of the bedroom.

"I had no idea you found cinnamon such an aphrodisiac."

"Absolutely. My reaction didn't have a thing to do with the fact that you're not wearing a thing beneath that robe.

But if you keep licking the crumbs off your lip that way, I'll have to demonstrate the power of cinnamon and yeast on my libido again.''

They were sitting on the couch, devouring the cinnamon rolls. She'd been taking them out of the oven when he came downstairs, which had struck him as perfect timing. He'd offered to thank her for the rolls. Since his hands had been inside her robe at the time, she'd taken his meaning. ''A simple verbal thank-you would be sufficient,'' she'd told him politely without making the least objection to what he was doing.

''I do intend to express my appreciation orally,'' he'd assured her, lifting her onto the kitchen table and nudging her legs apart. ''But not with words.''

''I—oh, my. I didn't...I had no idea you liked... cinnamon rolls—'' She'd gasped, her hands clenching in his hair. His mouth had been on her inner thigh by then. ''S-so much.''

Rafe smiled now, enjoying the memory and the moment. He loved looking at Charlie like this, all rumpled and glowing. She did tuck her tongue back in her mouth, but the sidelong glance she gave him was distinctly speculative. ''You're considering going back for seconds? Already?''

''I might be able to handle another cinnamon roll, too.''

She laughed, but shook her head. ''We'd better not. We've lost most of the morning already.''

Rafe nodded regretfully. At that moment only one thing seemed more important than making love to Charlie— keeping her safe. Which meant stopping the Kellys. Which meant he'd better get to work.

''Before you get lost in your programming,'' she said, rising and picking up their plates, ''I had a couple of questions. That is, if it really is all right for me to work on this with you.''

''It's more than all right,'' he said quietly. ''I want your help.''

She smiled, shy and pleased, and headed for the kitchen

with their dirty dishes. He smiled, too, as he followed her, amused by her incurable tidiness.

"I can't help with the actual programing, obviously," she said as she loaded the dishwasher. "So I've been going over the list of material stored in that partition."

"We've been over the list more than once." He poured the last of the coffee in his mug, sipped and made a face. It was cold.

"I assumed you had, but sometimes connections only become visible when material is sorted or classified in a particular way. At any rate, that type of thing is my strong point, so that seemed the best tack for me to take."

"Makes sense. Here, have one more." He added his cup to the dishwasher, then stuck in the empty carafe and got the machine running. When he turned around she was smiling that secretive smile of hers. "What?" he said, annoyed.

"You're cute when you're being domestic."

Cute. Great. So were teddy bears. He headed for the stairs. "So how have you organized the list?"

"First I'm eliminating everything that might be available elsewhere. They wouldn't have gone to this much trouble if they could get hold of whatever they're after somewhere else. I've been going over the corporate items first, of course." As they started up the stairs she added, "As I understand it, you, your father and the head of the computer department are the only ones who can access the partition."

"Theoretically true. In practice, Dad can never remember the protocol, which is rather involved. Mickey Tenjo—he's the corporate computer guru—and I are the only ones who really use it."

"Dix said you had an arrangement with the corporation that lets you store your own material in the partitioned area."

"Yeah." He glanced wistfully at the bedroom, but turned in at the office. "Security isn't Mickey's bailiwick, so it's a decent exchange. I get a secure off-site location for backups of some of my own sensitive material. They get an ultrasecure location for their most confidential stuff.''

''I'll need you to look over this, then.'' She handed him a neatly printed list. ''These are your files on the partition. I need to know if any of them are available elsewhere.''

''They all are,'' he answered absently as he sat in front of his computer and hit the power switch. ''They're copies of programs I've written for various clients, and related files. Obviously the client has at least one copy of the program.''

''Oh. I guess they wouldn't be likely prospects, then. Although...''

''What?''

''Well, this one.'' She tapped the file named Altinst. ''The précis says this is an encryption program. There are five of those listed, but this is the only one where the client isn't mentioned in the précis.''

''That particular client was especially security-mad. Didn't want any copies of the program anywhere. I have to keep one so I can do updates, of course, but in deference to their paranoia I...'' His voice drifted off. He frowned.

''What is it?''

''This may be just a coincidence, but...the client was The Rosemere Institute in Altaria.''

''Rafe.'' Her hand closed around his wrist. ''That's the kind of coincidence we've been looking for. Altaria has to be the key, doesn't it? The Kellys tried to have your brother assassinated—''

''We don't know it was the Kellys who tried to have Daniel killed. We know someone did, but the only solid link to the Kellys is Angie.'' And Charlie was the link to her. He drummed his fingers, thinking. ''I don't see a motive. The Institute is involved in cancer research. What possible interest could the Kellys have in cancer research?''

''Maybe that's a front. Maybe this Institute is really doing something else.''

"Hey." He grinned. "I just learned something else about you. You like spy thrillers."

"Don't joke. We need to find out for sure what this Institute is up to."

His fingers drummed again. Charlie was right—this was the only significant connection they'd found, and he'd be an idiot to ignore it just because it didn't make sense. "I'll call Daniel and ask him to check things out at his end. He's the king. They have to tell him what's going on."

She looked down, then away. The twist to her mouth was rueful. "Yes. Call your brother the king."

"I don't like the way you said that." He used his knuckles beneath her chin to tilt her face to him. "You prejudiced against royalty?"

A tiny head shake. "Never mind. Call Daniel, and I'll take a shower and get dressed."

Daniel wasn't an easy man to reach these days, but Rafe had his private number, which usually meant he only had to go through one intermediary. Gregor Paulus, the stiff and annoying personal assistant Daniel had inherited along with the throne, often answered the phone.

This time, though, Rafe lucked out and got his brother right away. "Hello?"

The protocol experts apparently hadn't had any better luck getting Daniel to change his telephone habits than their mother had. "I hope you didn't strain something," Rafe said solicitously.

"What are you talking about?"

"Answering your own phone like that. I know you're not used to doing things for yourself anymore. Probably have people around helping you get dressed, cut your meat, take a bath—"

Daniel's response was pungent and profane. Rafe grinned. His big brother was having a hard time adjusting to all the formal rigmarole that was so much a part of his new life. He figured he had a brotherly duty to be as annoying as possible and give Daniel a chance to blow off some steam.

"You didn't call just to make me mad," Daniel said after he'd expressed himself. "What's up?"

Rafe told him. Daniel was silent a moment. "I don't see a connection, either, but it's too much of a coincidence to ignore. I'll check with the scientists at the Institute and get back to you."

"Good enough. So, how's Erin?"

"Beautiful." A softness came into Daniel's voice when he spoke of his bride. "I hear you're thinking of taking the plunge, too."

"I'm working on it." Rafe frowned, still uneasy about the expression on Charlie's face when she referred to "your brother the king." There was something going on in that tricky mind of hers. "She's stubborn."

Daniel started to give him some big-brotherly advice. Fortunately, the intercom buzzed and Rafe was able to interrupt. "Got to go. Someone's here."

The identity of his visitor surprised him, though it probably shouldn't have. "Mom," he said, leaning forward to kiss her cheek. "Come in and warm up. Your nose is red."

Emma Connelly, née Rosemere, had never fully adjusted to the cold autumns and freezing winters of her adopted city. "You're not supposed to tell a woman her nose is red. Say, rather, that my cheeks are flushed."

"I never can remember all those female rules," he said sadly.

She pulled off her gloves and patted her son's cheek. "Brat. You remember exactly as much as you want to. Why are you running around without a shirt in this weather?"

"I'm building up my manly endurance," he said, moving behind her to help her off with her coat. "Once I get used to going shirtless in a heated apartment I'll try bathing in any icy fjord."

"Chicago has many amenities, but I don't think icy

fjords are among them. And that was a foolish question, wasn't it? You're living with a lovely young woman now. I suppose I should be glad you were wearing pants when you came to the door.''

''Ah…'' To his dismay, his cheeks heated. He turned to hang up the coat he'd taken from her.

''I've embarrassed you. Good. A mother likes to be able to do that now and then. Where is Charlotte?''

''Upstairs.'' He couldn't hear the shower, so she was probably getting dressed. With luck his mother would assume she was in the office working rather than cleaning up after a bout of hot sex. ''Can I get you something? I could heat up some water for tea.''

''No, thank you, dear. I can't stay long. I just dropped by to meet Charlotte.''

''Mom, you know Charlie.''

''That's right, you like to call her Charlie, don't you? I wonder which she prefers? I'll have to ask her. I know her as my husband's assistant, not as the woman you want to marry. The woman who's carrying my grandchild, although, owing to the situation she's in, some people believe it's my husband's child.''

His eyebrows lifted. ''You in a hurry? You've taken the gloves off pretty quickly.''

This time it was her cheeks that flushed. ''I didn't come here to fight.''

''Maybe you could give me a hint about why you did come here, then.''

''I'm worried about you.'' Nervous or agitated, she moved farther into the room. ''I've always tried not to be an interfering parent. Your father does enough of that for both of us,'' she added dryly. ''And I'm not judging your Charlie harshly, truly I'm not. The problem is that I don't know her well enough to have an opinion at all. I don't know anything about her—except that Grant likes her, she's pregnant with your child and she connived with Angie

Donahue to let the Kellys do something to the computers at the corporation.''

"You might trust Dad's judgment,'' he said quietly. "And mine. I like her, too.''

"But where is she from? What are her people like?'' She turned to face him. "And is that all you feel for her? You like her?''

"Actually, I'm crazy in love with her. But I like her, too.''

His mother didn't say anything for a long moment. Then she sighed. "Oh, my.''

He shook his head. "I'm going to have to quit trying to predict your reactions. Oddly enough, I thought you'd be happy to hear that, considering I'm going to marry her.''

"She's agreed, then?''

"No. But I'm making progress.'' She was in his bed now. That had to be progress, but he didn't think he'd go into that with his mother.

"How does she feel about you?''

"I'm not sure,'' he said curtly. "Look, you want to sit down and make yourself comfortable while you grill me?''

"I'm sorry. I am being a pain, aren't I?'' Instead of sitting she came closer and did one of those mother-things, smoothing his hair off his forehead. "I can't seem to help myself. I'm going to say one more thing, then I promise I'll stop pushing. I hope you won't take this the wrong way, but...Grant said that he thinks she came from a rather poor background. Poor as in impoverished,'' she added quickly. "I'm not concerned about her social standing.''

He had his doubts about that. His mother had done her best to adopt the democratic outlook of her husband's country, but she'd been born and raised a princess. "What are you concerned about, then?''

"Disparate backgrounds put a strain on a marriage. A woman who grew up lacking material comforts could easily become caught up in the Cinderella fantasy. I just want you to be sure she isn't more enchanted by the Prince Charming aspects of marrying you than she is by you.''

He had to smile. ''That has to be the most tactful way possible of asking if she's marrying me for my money.''

''Is she?''

Charlie's words came back to haunt him: *You're a fool to want to marry a woman who's more interested in what you own than what you are.* She hadn't meant it, he reminded himself. She'd been striking back at him for what she thought he meant. ''Since she's laboring under the impression she isn't going to marry me at all, I think it's safe to conclude she hasn't mistaken me for Prince Charming. Or Daddy Warbucks.''

She smiled. ''All right. I promised I'd let the subject drop, and I am.''

''Good.'' He put an arm around her shoulder. He'd gotten through that pretty well, he thought. ''Now come sit down and tell me what a bad son I am for not coming to see you lately.'' Some internal radar had his head turning. He smiled. ''Charlie. Look who's here.''

She was coming down the stairs, looking pretty and neat in a loose-fitting wool dress in a dusky green. The white collar added a scholarly touch that suited her, but her hair was all curly and damp from her shower. And the wool was stretched over the bulge of her stomach in a way that made him smile.

Charlie smiled, too, as she came down the stairs, but it was that terribly polite smile of hers. She was manning the barricades, prepared to repel enemy attack—courteously.

''It's good to see you again, Mrs. Connelly,'' she said as she reached the bottom of the stairs.

''Make it Emma, please.'' His mother moved towards her, holding out both hands. ''Otherwise, if my son has his way and the two of you do marry, we'll be calling each other Mrs. Connelly and confusing everyone.''

''Emma,'' Charlie repeated dutifully, allowing his mother to take her hands. ''I'm not...'' Her breath huffed out suddenly, and she grimaced. "This is horribly awkward. I want to apologize for all the trouble I've caused your family."

Emma Connelly didn't treat apologies as a matter of form. She studied Charlie's face a moment. "Yes, I believe you mean that." She gave Charlotte's hands a squeeze and dropped them, smiling. "Apology accepted. Now, I was just telling Rafe I really can't stay. I only stopped by to give him a hard time, and make sure you knew about the party on Thursday."

She blinked. "What party?"

"It's just a family get-together—casual, in deference to Rafe's preferences. Drinks and dinner followed by birthday cake and baby pictures. I couldn't resist having some kind of party. Rafe's been out of town on his last two birthdays."

"Mom has a thing about birthday parties," Rafe explained. "I should have known she wouldn't let me turn thirty-four in peace."

Charlie lifted her eyebrows. "You'll be thirty-four next Thursday? I'm only twenty-six. I think you're too old for me."

"Nonsense. Everyone knows women mature faster than men. We're about even now." Rafe was encouraged. Charlie had loosened up enough with his mother to tease him. He was about to encourage some female bonding by making a chauvinistic comment—nothing united women faster than having a male to abuse—when the phone rang.

It was a former client, panicking over a minor glitch. Rafe listened, explained that he wouldn't be able to fly out immediately, and still managed to hear pretty much everything his mother and his lover said to each other. They were being very polite. Charlie's stiffness didn't surprise him, but he'd expected his mother to do better. She was normally very good at putting people at their ease.

When his mother started gently probing Charlie about her family, Rafe decided he'd better end the call. Before he could, Charlie turned the conversation neatly on its axis by asking Emma about Rafe's family.

"There's something I'm curious about," she said. "Rafe's brother is the new king of Altaria. Doesn't that mean Rafe is—well, a prince?"

Rafe winced at the echo of his talk with his mother about Prince Charming.

Emma looked uncomfortable. "Not in American eyes."

"As far as Altaria is concerned, though, he would be a prince?"

"Yes, in Altaria he would be. He's a long way from inheriting the throne, however."

"Of course." Charlie looked unhappy. "I see."

Aha. Rafe disconnected at last. His mother would take Charlie's reaction the wrong way, but he knew what it meant—and what her "your brother the king" expression had meant earlier. Charlie was playing snob on his behalf. She'd decided she didn't measure up socially.

He wasn't about to let her get away with that nonsense, but the phone rang again before he could tackle that job. "Hello," he snapped.

"Bad day?" Luke's voice said dryly.

"It's had its up and downs. What's up?"

Luke's news was good, but his timing sucked. Charlie had obviously listened in, because as soon as he disconnected she asked him what was going on.

"Nothing important," he said easily.

"You were talking to Luke and you mentioned my name, so it has something to do with my situation. I'm entitled to know."

She wouldn't thank him for blurting it out now. He tried to dodge. "I'll tell you later. Now, about that birthday party, Mom—"

His mother picked that moment to take sides. "Rafe, you shouldn't keep things to yourself that involve Charlotte."

He gave up. "Good news, Charlie. You don't have to worry about being arrested. Your warrant has been revoked."

Nausea rose, stomach to throat. Charlie swallowed and walked Emma Connelly to the door with Rafe, smiling pleasantly. She'd almost made it. In another few moments Mrs. Connelly would be gone...and then there would be just Rafe to deal with.

Rafe. Who had told his mother he was in love with her.

Somehow she'd managed not to give herself away, but she was too miserable to congratulate herself on her acting ability.

Charlie hadn't meant to eavesdrop. Some trick of acoustics in the high-ceilinged apartment had carried the voices to her clearly at the top of the stairs, and she'd taken a quick step back out of sight. At first it had been a cowardly urge to retreat until Rafe's mother had gone. Then she'd heard what they were saying.

She rested a hand on the turmoil of her stomach and breathed carefully as Rafe helped his mother on with her coat. The easy, ingrained courtesy of the act seemed symbolic of all that stood between them.

Rafe hadn't had to check books out of the library to know that napkins went in your lap, which fork to use, how to write a thank-you note. Of course, he probably didn't know the proper protocol for visiting a family member in prison. She was one up on him there.

Oh, Rafe. She rubbed her stomach. Had he meant it? Was it possible that he was really in love with her? He might have just wanted his mother to believe that. It had never occurred to Charlie that he might feel something more than friendly lust for her. The idea was astonishing. Wonderful. Terrifying.

She needed time, she thought desperately. Somehow she had to slow things down. Everything was happening too quickly. She couldn't deal with it. Time was the answer, time to plan, to adjust, to understand what was best for both of them, what she could reasonably hope for.

Oh, but reasonably, rationally, there was so little hope. Even if he'd meant what he said…her whole body felt dizzy and strange at the thought. But it wouldn't really be *her* he was in love with. There was too much he didn't know.

His mother was worried about him. Well, she should be, Charlie thought bitterly. And just think how much more Emma Connelly would worry if she knew the warrant that had just been dismissed wasn't the first one that had been issued with Charlie's name on it.

Rafe shut the door and turned. "Now, what's bothering you?"

"Nothing. It was kind of your mother to make sure I was invited to your birthday party."

"Yeah." His eyes were slightly narrowed as if he was studying her. "She's a great lady, but she didn't exactly shine today. I think you make her nervous."

"Me?" That was so absurd she dismissed it immediately. "Rafe, I don't think I should go to the party."

"Why not?" he demanded. "If you claim you'll feel out of place—"

"Well, I will." Desperate for distraction, she began stacking the scattered sheets of the newspaper. "She said this was a family affair. I'm not family."

"Close enough. Let's get one thing straight. You are not going to use my accidental connection to royalty as an excuse not to marry me."

She blinked. "I don't know what you mean."

"I mean that we're in America, this is the twenty-first century and I don't want to hear any nonsense about how different our backgrounds are. Because you don't mean backgrounds, you mean social standing. And that's crap. You can mix and mingle with anyone. You wouldn't have been such a great executive assistant if you hadn't been able to handle the rich and the snobby."

His compliment warmed her. And made it hard to argue. "Your family isn't snobby," she said weakly.

"No, they're not. Though my mother did inhale a lot of noblesse oblige during childhood, she does her best not to let it influence her now. And the rest of us don't give a hoot in hell about social standing. Charlie." He came to her then, smiling that beautiful smile of his and cupped her shoulders in his warm hands. "I want you there. I want to celebrate my birthday with you."

Her heart was beating too fast and her resolve was melting even faster. "I—I don't have anything to wear."

"Okay. We'll go shopping."

# Twelve

"**Y**ou were very patient," Charlie said as she dumped two sacks on the couch.

"I was a saint." Rafe didn't bother to drop his three sacks. He collapsed in the big purple chair with them still in his hands. "You've got the stamina of an ox. Never has a woman fought so hard to avoid spending a man's money, but once you surrendered, you shopped like there was no tomorrow."

Her brow puckering, Charlie looked at the department store bags with dismay. "I didn't realize... I shouldn't have let you talk me into buying so much."

"You needed maternity clothes," he said for the one hundred twenty-fourth time that afternoon.

"I'll take some of it back. That black dress— I don't need a cocktail dress, for heaven's sake. And I certainly don't need four pairs of maternity slacks."

He looked at her and shook his head. "If you put me to the trouble of running around and buying back a bunch of stuff you've returned, I'm going to be mad." He let the shopping bags fall from his hands and stretched, legs out, arms over his head. "You know, Charlie, if I didn't know better I'd think you didn't have a single gold-digging bone in your body."

She bit her lip. Maybe she should have spent twice as much of his money instead of protesting every time he handed her something else to try on. Maybe she ought to be persuading him that she was after his money, so he wouldn't care too much and wouldn't be hurt. She wanted so badly to do the right thing...if only she knew what the right thing was.

"I'm plenty greedy," she said lightly. "I'm going to take everything upstairs and gloat over it before I put it away." She bent to pick up the sacks he'd dropped.

His arm snaked around her waist and dumped her over the arm of the chair and into his lap. "Yeah, you're a greedy woman." He nuzzled her hair. "That's okay. I loved the way your eyes lit up over that silk dress. You can thank me now," he added. "With words if you must, but if you'll cast your mind back to this morning and the way I thanked you for those cinnamon rolls, it might give you a clue what I'd prefer."

She was already fighting a smile. Putting her hands on his chest, she tried to ignore the spreading warmth and the interesting bulge beneath her rump. "Are you trying to make me feel like a kept woman? Buy me a few trinkets and I'm supposed to fall on my back and show my appreciation?"

"Your back, my lap, your knees—whatever works. As for making you a kept woman..." Banter died out of his voice and his eyes, leaving them serious and soft. "That's what I have in mind, Charlie. Keeping you."

Her mouth went dry. "Keeping the baby, you mean."

"That's what I thought at first, so I can't blame you for believing it now." His hands slid up her sides, pausing just below her breasts. "I was a little slow catching on. Did you overhear what my mother said this morning?"

"I—I don't—what do you mean?"

"You're a lousy liar, did you know that? You can keep a secret forever, but you can't lie worth beans. That's reassuring. I'm talking about Mom spouting all that crap about Cinderella and Prince Charming. You heard her, didn't you?"

Her mind went blank. She licked her lips nervously.

He nodded. "That's what I thought. Let me take this point by point. First there's that Cinderella nonsense." His fingers slid up a fraction, so that the sides of his hands pushed against the soft bottoms of her breasts. "You're about as far from Cinderella as a woman can be. If some prince tried to sweep you off your feet and carry you off to his castle, you'd turn up your nose, say no thank you very politely, and go right back to organizing your ugly stepsisters until the family business showed a profit. You are dead set on making it on your own, Charlie. Maybe you need to prove you can. The last thing you want is to have anything handed to you. My money is an obstacle to our marriage, not an incentive."

How did he know? How *could* he know her so well?

"Still nothing to say?" He smiled. "Okay. I'll move on to the important part. You heard what I said to Mom, too, didn't you?"

Panic rose, a great, dark beast pushing words out every which way. "Don't say it, Rafe. I can't hear that right now."

His expression darkened. "Tough. I don't just want the baby, Charlie I want you. I—"

Acting without thinking, she pressed her lips to his. The kiss was frantic, a little sloppy. He responded anyway, his hands tightening on her ribs. She opened her mouth, inviting more, craving the haste and the hunger. Her pulse throbbed in her throat as the liquid heat spread.

He tore his mouth away, catching her face in both hands.

His eyes were stormy, his mouth hard. "Damn you," he said, but then he kissed her again, harder, his tongue thrusting deeply inside.

Relief made her tender. It must be relief, this soft aching that sent her hands roaming gently over him, searching the places she knew he liked to be touched. Oh, such sweet, delicious relief....

"Let me," she whispered as she dotted kisses along his jaw. "Let me make love to you this time." She ran her hands along his shoulders, loving the firm, round shape of the muscles, then drew her hands down along his chest. Slowly she began unbuttoning his shirt.

He leaned back in the chair, his eyes hot and unsmiling, watching her as she unfastened his shirt and opened it.

Rafe's chest was perfect—not too lean, not too brawny, with just a sprinkling of hair right in the center. Charlie had always secretly loved the look of a tight male butt, but Rafe's chest had converted her. She ran her hands over him, enjoying the way his muscles quivered beneath her touch. Then she leaned forward and tickled one small, flat nipple with her tongue.

He sucked in his breath. Encouraged, she laid down a path with her mouth, testing the texture of the skin along his collarbone, comparing that to the smooth skin of his stomach just above his belt buckle.

His stomach muscles clenched. Hard.

She slipped from his lap, kneeling in front of him and watching his face. Slowly she unfastened his belt. Then the snap of his jeans. A muscle jumped in his jaw. As if they were connected, her heart jumped, too, pounding harder. Next, his zipper. She went very slowly there, drawing out the movement, brushing her fingers along the hard length beneath.

His eyes closed as his breath shuddered out. "You're killing me. You know that, don't you?"

"No, you have to live a little longer." She'd never set out to deliberately arouse a man this way. It was exciting.

Intoxicating. She freed him from his jeans and licked her lips.

He groaned. "I hope you mean that."

Her mouth curved up. Sweetness pulsed between her legs. Oh, yes, this was quite delicious. She leaned forward and tasted him.

He made a wonderfully guttural noise that aroused her spirit of experimentation. She ran her tongue up, down, and around, then settled in to see how wild she could make him. He didn't let her enjoy herself for long, though. His hands slid beneath her arms and lifted, and a second later she was sprawled across him, mouth to mouth.

He shoved her dress up, groaning when he discovered her panty hose but sliding his hand between her legs anyway. She jolted, the shock of his touch so strong it almost tipped her over the edge. His fingers moved back and forth, and the friction made her crazy. Moaning, she tore her mouth away from his and pushed back to stand on shaky legs in front of him—and slowly, very slowly, pull her panty hose down.

Oh, he liked that. His gaze followed her hands, and his whole body looked tense enough to shatter. With her panty hose gone she climbed back in his lap, straddling him, letting her skirt ride up. Reaching beneath, she guided him inside her.

The heat, the fullness—the sense of being filled by *him*—overcame her, and her breath hissed out between her lips. He wound one hand in her hair and tugged her face to his. Mouths joined, they began to move—slowly at first as she adjusted to him and the position, then faster. Until he seized her hips in an iron grip and took over, thrusting up into her over and over. He put his hand near the spot where they were joined and brushed her with his fingers. Her vision dimmed and her body bucked with the force of climax.

He was right behind her.

Dishrag-limp, she rested against him, her head on his

shoulder, aftershocks making her inner muscles clench every so often. Her mind floated, distant and unimportant.

"I survived," Rafe murmured close to her ear. "Amazing. But if you keep doing *that* I'll have to start all over again, and that will surely kill me."

"Doing what?" Another little aftershock rippled through her.

"That."

Oh. Her inside muscles. "I can't help it."

"You're blushing," he pointed out.

"I can't help that, either."

"The female mind never fails to astonish me. Why that would make you blush after you…" Mercifully, he didn't finish the sentence. Instead he pressed a kiss to her cheek and for a few moments they drifted together in dreamy silence. Finally she stirred. He helped her lift slightly, then rearrange herself so that she sat sideways across his lap, cuddled up to his chest.

After a moment she said, "I wonder how long the phone has been ringing."

"What phone?"

She giggled and put her hand over her mouth. She *never* giggled.

"I'm getting to you." He shifted her gently so he could stand and fasten his jeans. "Pretty soon you'll be running wild, scattering the newspaper all over the floor and forgetting to make the bed. God knows where it will end."

His voice was lazy, amused. He was smiling but he wasn't looking at her. "Now, where's the phone?" He glanced around as if it might wave at him.

"On the base unit on the hutch." She'd put it where it belonged during a brief fit of tidying before they left to go shopping. *It isn't that he's avoiding meeting my eyes,* she told herself. He was looking for the phone, that was all.

Even as he started toward it, the answering machine picked up. Charlie heard a voice she recognized from her years of working for Grant—Daniel Connelly, the oldest son. The king of Altaria. "Why the hell do you have such a long delay set before your blasted machine picks up?" his voice demanded from the speaker on the base unit. "Never mind. Rafe, call me right away. It's—"

Rafe picked up the phone. "I'm here. What is it?"

Though she only heard one side of the conversation, that was enough to destroy the languor from their lovemaking. She scrambled to her feet, dimly aware of the stickiness between her thighs, the chill rising from the floor beneath her bare feet. But that wasn't as important as whatever Daniel was telling Rafe. She watched his expression go from shock to stunned horror to dead-serious determination, and waited with growing fear.

At last he disconnected. "Dear God."

She took a quick step toward him. "What did he tell you?"

"Your hunch was right. They want the encryption program for the Institute. Get your shoes on." He moved quickly, scooping up her panty hose, tossing them at her and heading for the coat closet.

"But what do they want it for?" She scrambled into the panty hose as quickly as possible. "And where are we going?"

"To see my father and get that damned encryption program off the hard drive."

"But I thought they couldn't get to it." She stepped into her shoes.

"Nothing is foolproof enough. We can't take *any* chances, not with what's at stake."

What was at stake? "You said something about a virus. Why would the Kellys spend so much effort on a computer virus?"

"Not a computer virus." He handed her coat to her, his expression wholly grim. "A human one. Those ivory-tower innocents at the Institute are trying to create a genetically engineered virus that will target cancer cells in humans. Along the way they accidentally created another type of virus altogether. One that *causes* cancer—fast-growing and lethal. It's highly contagious and vectored through the air.''

Horror chilled her so powerfully that goose bumps popped out on her arms and legs. ''Dear God. You're thinking it could be used as a—a biological weapon.''

''Oh, yes. And the Kellys want to sell it to the highest bidder.''

# Thirteen

**R**afe had worked hard before. For the four days following that phone call from his brother, he worked like a man driven by demons.

With reason. Charlotte wasn't an overly imaginative woman, but she had to work to shut out horrific visions of what might happen if the wrong people got their hands on the killer virus. There were biological weapons aplenty already in existence, of course, but this virus was apparently a huge leap ahead of them because of its ease of delivery and transmission.

The scientists at Rosemere Institute weren't irresponsible. They'd been horrified when they realized what they'd created, and the Institute's director had immediately informed the former king. King Thomas had ordered all samples of the virus destroyed, along with every description of it and how it had been created. But according to the director, a well-funded lab could recreate the virus if they had access to the Institute's database. Much of the research, therefore, had been encrypted, using Rafe's program.

As soon as they'd told Grant Connelly about the virus, he'd summoned Luke Starwind. After some discussion, they had agreed with Daniel that the U.S. government shouldn't be brought in right now. The fewer people who knew of the existence of the virus, the better. If they had any reason to think the data was in imminent danger of falling into the Kellys' hands, that would have to change, of course. But for now only Rafe, Grant, Luke, Daniel and Charlie knew the truth.

Daniel had increased security at the Institute itself, Luke Starwind had stepped up his investigation, and Rafe had removed the program from the Connelly computers. He'd burned it onto a CD, but she didn't know what he'd done with that CD. Nor did she want to know.

Charlie had never felt so far out of her depth. She couldn't do anything to help Rafe; after the second day even Dix hadn't been able to help. Rafe wasn't sleeping enough. She wasn't sure he'd slept at all last night, but there was nothing she could do. So she cleaned and organized and cooked and worried. Rafe's apartment had probably never looked so neat.

Not that he'd noticed. He was so immersed in his work she wasn't sure he knew she was around, except late at night, when he finally came to bed. Then he made love to her with a quiet ferocity that overwhelmed her every bit as much as learning about the virus had—but in a far different way.

He scarcely spoke to her the rest of the time.

That was all right, she told herself as she pulled her hair back in a quick ponytail. She didn't expect him to lavish attention on her at a time like this, with so much depending on him. If he was silent and grim, he had reason. She wasn't going to jump to any self-centered conclusions. His mood had nothing to do with her and the words she hadn't let him speak.

She hadn't hurt him. Surely he didn't care enough to be really hurt, did he? If he did...if he'd meant what he said to his mother—

Charlie reached out blindly, grabbing a lipstick at random. As soon as she'd sleeked a little color over her lips she hurried down the stairs.

Dix was waiting for her in his favorite cap, a black leather jacket, black slacks and turtleneck. He lifted his pierced eyebrow. "Never saw a woman get ready that fast."

"I'm stir-crazy," she said lightly. "I haven't been outside this apartment in days." Four of them, to be precise. Ever since she and Rafe had gone to Connelly Corporation to erase the encryption program. Absently she smoothed the rusty-red sweater she was wearing. He'd bought it for her.

"You left a note for Rafe?"

She nodded. She'd told him she was going shopping, too, of course, but getting Rafe's attention when he was this far into his programming world wasn't easy. Dix had suggested she leave him a note in case he forgot what she'd said.

"Okay, let's go. But I'm warning you," he said with a ferocious frown. "Two stores. That's my limit."

Three stores later, he was not happy. "So what's wrong with that sweater?" he demanded.

"It just isn't right." Nothing had been right. Hastily she refolded the sweater and put it back in the stack. "It isn't personal enough."

"You want personal, buy him underwear," Dix muttered.

She bit her lip and looked around. She didn't even know what to look at next. Maybe something for the kitchen? He liked to cook. Where was the housewares department?

Oh, what was she going to do—buy him a blender? Frustration tightened her mouth. She turned back to the sweaters again.

"If you don't make up your mind soon, I'm gonna carry you out of here. I'm tired of the way that saleslady's looking at me."

"Maybe she isn't a Cubs fan." She knew what he meant, though. The woman had kept Dix in view the whole time. It reminded Charlie of the way clerks used to watch her, many years ago. Because she remembered how horrid that had felt, she started moving. "We'll try the next floor up. Maybe there's some techno marvel he doesn't have."

Dix fell into step beside her, but shook his head. "You said you didn't have much to spend. Everything in this place costs plenty. The techno toys sure won't be cheap."

She stopped and scowled at him. "What do you suggest, then? You've known Rafe a long time. Don't you have any ideas?"

"What do I know about this sort of thing? Buy him a CD. He likes music."

"Great idea," she muttered, moving ahead. "A lovely, thoughtful birthday present for a man like Rafe. A CD. Maybe we should go to the discount store and check out the blue light special."

He looked disgusted. "You think the value of a gift is what it costs?"

"No. No, I don't, but if I can't find something special, something personal, I can at least give him something that costs more than $19.95." Suddenly, to her horror, her eyes filled. "I don't know what to get him. How can I not know what to get him?"

"Whoa." Dix eyed her with alarm, then grabbed her arm and pulled her toward the escalator. "Time out. We're going to that ritzy tea shop on the second floor. We'll sit at one of those dinky tables and drink water that tastes like boiled rocks and let the hostess worry about me snagging the silverware. And you'll probably tell me what's wrong, whether I want you to or not."

"I'm sorry," she said, almost stumbling to keep up with him. "I don't usually...it's the stress. I'm not a crier."

"That's good, 'cause I do not *do* crying females. You get yourself dried up quick," he ordered her. And he continued to chide her and drag her gently along until they were sitting at "one of those dinky tables" in the tea shop.

"There," Dix said with relief after the waitress set cups of steaming tea in front of them. "Drink your boiled rocks. You'll be better in a minute."

She sniffed and smiled. Dix's technique was bracing but effective.

"Thank God you aren't one of those women who have to tell a man every little personal detail. I hate relationship talks. I don't want to hear about how you and Rafe aren't communicating."

"Okay." She sipped the tea. It was a soothing blend of chamomile and some other herb.

Dix frowned at his cup. "He's a good man," he said abruptly.

"Yes, he is," she agreed, a wave of sadness putting her dry eyes in danger. "He's wonderful."

"He doesn't get the money thing, though. He never thinks about whether a person has money or not—it doesn't matter to him. But when you've grown up rough, you can't ever see things quite that way." He met her eyes steadily. "I think you know what I mean."

She rubbed her thumb over the handle of the cup, looking down at the pale amber brew. "I didn't think it showed anymore."

"Mostly it doesn't. But I saw you at the dive where you were working. You talked fancy, but you knew how to handle yourself. You know the streets."

Her mouth curved in bitter humor. "I didn't ever work them, if you're wondering."

"Didn't figure you had. Too prissy by half." He took a sip of his tea, made a face and put it down. "God knows how you can stand this stuff. You ever wonder how someone like me got to be friends with someone like Rafe?"

"It has crossed my mind."

"I hacked into one of his systems when I was younger and a lot dumber, left a snotty note—to prove I could, you know. Just like the idiots who get caught hacking into SAC or the DOD. He tracked me down so fast it was embarrassing, thanked me for pointing out a flaw in his program, told me he'd kick my butt if I ever did it again, and we started talking. I'd still be a two-bit hacker if it weren't for him. Now I'm a consultant." He grinned. "Pays a lot better than leaving snotty notes."

"That sounds like Rafe." She smoothed her thumb along the handle of her teacup. "He gets mad, but he doesn't judge."

"Exactly. Now, I don't know what's wrong between the two of you—and don't you go telling me, either." He held up a hand as if she'd been about to burst into confession. "But I figure whatever isn't working, it's your fault."

"Gee, thanks." Miffed but amused by his unabashedly partisan support, she asked, "You don't think you might be a bit biased?"

"Of course I am. But after watching you today, I have to think part of the problem is the money thing. He has it, always had. You don't, never did. But like I said, there isn't a problem on his side. He doesn't think that way. So the problem's with you."

"In your limited way, you're right." She sighed. "But that doesn't give me a clue how to deal with it. And I don't think this is the time for me to—to bring any of that up, anyway, not with the pressure he's under."

"I don't know what's going on. I know something has changed, and this deal with the Kellys has gotten a lot hairier. I also know that whatever's wrong with the two of you is eating at him. I want you to fix it. You aren't quite stupid enough to be blaming yourself for not being born rich—"

"Another compliment. I'm overwhelmed."

"So I figure there's something else. Like maybe you're

blaming yourself for something you did because you didn't have money.''

She stiffened. That was entirely too close to the mark.

''So what you have to do is tell him about it. Even if it's bad. Especially if it's bad. If you don't level with him, you're not dealing straight and things will go right on being messed up. Damn,'' he said, pushing his chair back. ''I can't take this place another minute. Let's get out of here.''

She tried to pay for the tea. He gave her a disgusted look and told her not to insult him. After that, neither of them said much. She let him steer her out of the store and down the street to an El station.

Dix was right. Obnoxious and biased, but right. She'd been telling herself this wasn't the time, that Rafe had too much on his mind for her to bring up painful subjects, but that was a cop-out. She'd been protecting herself, not him, hanging on to the last remnants of a dream that wouldn't die, no matter how often she told herself it had.

She had to tell him everything. Today. The thought made her half-sick with dread, but she'd deal with that. ''Wait a minute,'' she said, noticing at last that they weren't going in the right direction. ''Where are you taking me?''

''To see my cousin. You wanted suggestions on what to get Rafe. I've got one.''

''I knew you were a hacker. I had no idea you were a con artist, too.'' Charlie punched the elevator button in the lobby of Rafe's building. ''I don't know how I let you talk me into this.''

''Didn't have to. You talked yourself into it just fine.'' Dix was grinning smugly as they stepped into the elevator.

''You caught me in a weak moment. I—'' A little pink tongue licked her face and she went all mushy inside. ''Yes, sweetie, we're almost there. You want to get down and run around, don't you?''

''He might have something else he needs to do.''

''He just did that.''

"Puppies do it a lot. You'll have to put newspapers down."

The elevator doors opened. She stepped out, cuddling Rafe's present close. "I shouldn't have done this. What made me think Rafe would want a puppy peeing all over? He doesn't have time to take care of a dog right now!" She stopped. Had she had some stupid idea at the back of her mind that if Rafe accepted a mongrel puppy, he'd accept her, too, as she really was? "I've lost my mind. We have to take him back."

"Keep moving." A hand at her back encouraged that. "You're not taking that puppy back. You're nuts about him. And my cousin has probably left the neighborhood by now. He's no dummy."

Dix's cousin had had three of the little darlings left. All were guaranteed to have no pedigree whatsoever. The one Charlie had lost her heart to looked like a cross between a beagle and a few dozen other breeds. He was a dirty white all over except for a big, brown patch over one eye.

"Rafe's going to think I've lost my mind," she muttered, trying to juggle an excited puppy in one arm while she pulled out the key. "You just don't give someone a puppy unless you're sure he wants a dog. It's thoughtless. I don't even know if his lease allows pets."

"You said someone else in the building had a dog." Dix took the key from her, stuck it in the top lock and started working his way down. "He'll like the puppy. Tell him you'll take care of it, train it."

"I don't know how." And what if she wasn't around? What if he didn't *want* her around after he realized the woman he might be in love with was a fabrication, that the prim and correct Ms. Masters didn't really exist?

Charlie's heart was pounding when the door swung open—pushed from the inside.

Rafe stood there glowering at her. "Where the hell have you been?"

Dix put down the puppy kibble he'd brought. "I'm out of here."

"Coward," Charlotte muttered, but he was already in the elevator.

Rafe's furious gaze zeroed in on the wiggly bundle in her arms. "Good God. What in the world are you doing with *that*?"

Oh, yes, this was a great idea. Rafe was obviously thrilled. Tears stung her eyes. "Here," she snapped, thrusting the puppy at Rafe and shoving past him. "And happy birthday."

Rafe shut the door and refastened all the locks. He was still so mad he wanted to choke her. Some of that mad, he admitted, had nothing to do with today and everything to do with what had happened four days ago, and the pain that didn't seem to grow any less as time went on.

Charlie didn't want his love. His body, yeah. She liked it just fine. His protection—she was reluctant about that, but she'd accept it for now. But not his love.

Turning, he absently began running one soft, floppy ear through his fingers. The puppy wriggled in delight and insisted on licking his chin.

Reluctantly he smiled. Ugly little runt.

Happy birthday, she'd said. His practical, logical Charlie had gotten him a puppy for his birthday? An ugly little mongrel puppy, which, from the look of things, wouldn't stay little for long. It was such a foolish thing to do. So unlike her. He looked up from his adoring present.

Charlie was speeding around the room, looking for something to clean or straighten. She had to settle for plumping some pillows. She'd already done everything else.

Had he really seen tears in her eyes? "I was scared," he said abruptly.

She didn't look at him. Those pillows were desperately in need of fluffing, all right. "I told you I was going shopping. I left you a note."

"Yeah, well...after you left I got a phone call from Elena Connelly—formerly Detective Delgado of the SIU. She'd been keeping us posted as much as she can on what the police discover."

Her busy hands stilled and she faced him, still holding one blue pillow. "There's news?"

"You know they thought the hit man was Rocky Palermo."

"The Kelly enforcer. Yes. Have they—has he gotten away from their surveillance?"

"No." His muscles tightened up again, making him sound curt. "They've had a tip from an informant. Word is that the Kellys hired another hit man after Palermo missed. This one's not part of the organization. He's got quite a reputation. According to Elena, he makes Palermo look like one of the losing contestants on Amateur Hour."

She stood frozen, no expression at all on her face, that pillow hugged tight to her chest. "They think this other hit man is the one after me?"

He nodded. "Why didn't you take a cell phone?"

"I didn't think of it. You didn't, either."

No, he hadn't. He'd been too focused on his work and had barely paid attention when she said she was going shopping. And he'd been furious with himself when he realized he'd let her and Dix leave without having any way to get in touch with them.

A small pink tongue recalled his attention. He looked down and idly played with the soft pad of one paw, then shook his head. Either the pup was deformed or he was going to be one big dog. "Thumbs."

"What?"

"I'm going to call him Thumbs." He scratched behind the puppy's ears, sending him into a frenzy of pleasure, and tried to make sense of a woman who didn't want his love, but gave him a puppy for his birthday. Her timing couldn't have been much worse. He glanced up. "Thank you for the birthday present, Charlie."

She moved closer, smiling hesitantly. "Dix bought the puppy food. He said that's his present."

Dix had also cleared out immediately. Smart man. Rafe sighed and held out the puppy. "We're going to talk, but not now. Here. You'd better put him in the kitchen with some newspapers."

She took the puppy, but her smile vanished. "Sure. I'll take care of him, don't worry. It was a dumb idea, Rafe. I'm sorry. I don't know what—"

"Charlie." He laid his fingertips on her lips. "Hush. The puppy's great. I can't stay and get acquainted right now, though. I've got to go. I should have already left, but—"

But he hadn't wanted to. Not until he knew she was okay.

Abruptly he turned and headed for the door.

"Why? Where are you going?"

"I finished the program. I need to install it on-site."

Rafe leaned his head back and let the cabbie worry about traffic and everything else. His head buzzed with programming language, street sounds and the look in Charlie's eyes when he'd said he would call the puppy Thumbs. He was too tired to make sense of any of it, too keyed up to doze off. But he was done. Somehow he'd crammed at least a week's worth of work into four days. The program was installed, and every test he'd been able to run told him it would work.

And Charlie was waiting back at the apartment. With Thumbs. A tired grin touched his mouth. Crazy woman.

Crazy him, for being so crazy about her.

The ghost of a grin vanished as the cab pulled up in front of his apartment building.

Picking up the mail on his way was automatic. Sorting through it in the elevator was equally mindless. Until he hit the long white envelope addressed to Charlotte Masters...from Brad Fowler, Deer Lodge Prison, Bridleton, Connecticut.

Fury seared away fatigue. He stared at the return address,

his mouth tight, jealousy and pain pumping through him with every heartbeat.

*This* time she would give him some answers.


Charlie gave the pepper mill a few more twists, then stirred the simmering soup. She'd wanted something that would keep if necessary. Rafe might want to sleep before eating—heaven knew he'd done little enough of that lately, and he'd be up tonight if the hacker accessed the Connelly system. She could watch the alarm thingee he'd rigged and wake him if—

She heard the front door open and close. "I'm in the kitchen," she called. Thumbs was curled up near her feet. She had to step over him to put up the pepper mill. "Is everything ready?" she asked, turning around.

He stood in the doorway. His eyes were shadowed, drawn with fatigue, hard. Without saying a word he came into the kitchen and slapped an envelope down on the counter beside her.

It was a letter from Brad. Sickly she realized the time for truth had arrived. Her hands were shaky when she reached for the dishtowel. "You want to know why I never told you about him, I suppose."

"Damned right I do." The glitter in his eyes scared her a little. "Is *he* the reason you cooperated with the Kellys?"

"Yes. I—"

"I knew it." He began to pace. "By God, I knew it. When I saw that bundle of letters you kept I wondered...but you're carrying *my* child. You're sleeping with me. And you're writing some other man—a convict, for God's sake!"

Her eyes closed. Oh, this ought to be funny. Rafe thought Brad was another man. But she couldn't find a grain of amusement to lighten the dread coiled in the pit of her stomach. "He's—"

"He's history, that's what he is! Starting right now, he's your past. I can't believe you gave him this address. No one's supposed to know where you are. No one. And you wrote this convict, this criminal lover of yours—''

''Your family knows where I am!''

''What does that have to do with anything? If you're going to tell me this guy is like family to you, I don't want to hear it!''

''He's not like family, he *is* family!''

He stopped.

She swallowed. ''Brad is my brother.''

An odd, blank look settled over his face. ''You don't have a brother.''

''I—I lied on my application at Connelly's.''

Abruptly he turned and walked out of the kitchen.

Slowly she followed.

Rafe was sitting on the big, apricot-colored couch, his legs sprawled, rubbing his face with both hands. When she stopped in front of him, he spoke without looking up. ''His last name is Fowler, not Masters.''

''My parents didn't marry until I was three, just before Brad was born. He carries our father's name. I don't.''

''I see.'' His voice was carefully level. ''And he works for the Kellys? That's why you did as they asked?''

''No! God, no, it wasn't like that. Th-they sent me the tip of his little finger.''

His head jerked up.

She swallowed bile. ''It was waiting for me in an express mailer the night their man contacted me.''

''I'm sorry.'' His voice was muffled. ''I'm sorry I accused you of...but I don't understand. How could you not tell me you had a brother? I knew you had secrets, but I never thought...how could you not tell me about something as important as that?''

''Because that wasn't the only thing I lied about.''

He dropped his hands between his knees and shook his head slowly, like a swimmer in deep water. ''You have more brothers? A sister or two? Your parents are alive and well and living in Florida under an assumed name?''

"No more brothers, or family of any sort. My parents were killed in a rollover when I was seventeen, just as I said on my application. I persuaded the court to let me have custody of Brad—he's three years younger than me—and I shouldn't have. I made a lousy guardian. He was in trouble all the time. When he was nineteen, he was arrested for selling drugs."

He said nothing at all.

Her hands were clenched together so tightly her fingers were starting to tingle. She had to finish now, get it all out in the open, or she'd lose her nerve. "I was arrested once, too."

"Yeah, I know. For helping your father with the numbers operation he was running. They dropped the charges, probably because you were a juvenile and your father said he'd made you do it."

Shock froze her. She couldn't speak, move, think.

His eyes widened. "That's it? That's your deep, dark secret? Jesus!" He collapsed against the back of the couch, his legs stretched out, slumped so deeply his head rested against the back of the couch. "All this time I've been waiting to hear something horrible—that you turned tricks or plotted armed robberies or something."

"You knew?" Her voice was high and unfamiliar. "How did you—how *could* you know?"

"I dug into your background some when you went into hiding. And don't go getting all huffy about it. I had to. How do you think I turned up your mother's social security number?"

"But juvenile records are *sealed*."

He gave her a get-real look. "Yeah. So?"

"How could you have found about my record and not known about my brother?"

"I saw a record of your arrest. For some reason the cops didn't put 'P.S. She has a brother named Brad' at the bottom of it." His eyes closed wearily. "I can't believe it. With all your defenses I thought there had to be something really horrible in your past. Turns out you couldn't even trust me enough to tell me you had a brother and got into a little trouble when you were sixteen.''

"It was more than a little trouble,'' she said stiffly. "And my father..."

His eyes opened. "I guess it must have seemed like great big trouble at the time. And your father did end up serving some time, a few months, anyway. Sit down, will you? My neck's getting a crick in it from looking up."

Dizzy, confused and vaguely offended by his easy dismissal of a past that shamed her, she sat on the edge of the couch.

He looped an arm around her and pulled her up against him. She lay there stiffly, unable to relax. He didn't seem to notice. "That's better. Now, tell me about your father. How did he wind up running numbers? Had he always leaned toward the crooked end of things?"

"N-no." She was so badly off-balance she didn't know what she was saying. "At heart he was a wanderer. He never could settle in one job, one place. But he was also a family man, so he took us with him." A bittersweet smile touched the corners of her mouth. "I'd lived in seventeen cities by the time I was twelve. Big cities, mostly. He wasn't much for small towns or the country."

"He took you with him, at least. He must have loved you."

"Yes." That was both comfort and a source of guilt. Her parents *had* loved her and Brad. And she'd loved them. Her grief had been hard and painful when they were killed. But the truth was that she'd resented them, too, and there had been times when she'd secretly wished her mother would stop following her father from city to city and dragging them along.

But her mother had never really grown up, no more than her father had. A sweet woman sometimes bewildered by the turns her life took, she'd never lost faith that her husband would someday make everything right. Jack Fowler had been a cheerful drifter, always convinced he would hit it big one day if he could just be in the right place at the right time. San Diego, L.A., Galveston, New Orleans, New York City, Boston. They were in Mobile for a few months, but that job hadn't worked out—they never did—then down to Miami.

"I was twelve the first time he strayed from the straight and narrow. He was working for a wealthy man in Miami. Odd jobs, mostly. Handyman work and filling in for the chauffeur. He wanted to give me and Brad a big Christmas that year, so he—he stole from his employer." The shame and guilt swept over her again. "We had a splendid Christmas, all right. A huge tree, lots of presents. The next day his employer—who, as it turned out, had ties to some unsavory people—fired Dad. Then he had him beaten. We left the city as soon as he was well enough to travel."

"That ought to have scared him into good behavior."

"For a while it did." Gradually she began to relax into his warmth. "Over the next few years he worked as a blackjack dealer, a horse trainer—that didn't last long, since he knew nothing about horses. He was a stand-up comedian and a sanitation worker, among other things. The only other time he dabbled in crime was when he tried his hand at running numbers. He was caught pretty quickly. He wasn't a very successful crook." Her smile was easier this time, if rueful. "His one real talent was forging whatever credentials he needed to get a job."

"A marketable skill, but not much use in the long run."

She slid him a sideways glance. "I used what I'd learned from him about that when I applied for the job with your father. Most of my work history is fabricated."

"Hmm. Sounds like Dad needs to tighten his personnel procedures." Rafe settled a little more, his legs outstretched. "How did you keep the Kellys from making good on their threat to your brother? He's alive and writing to you, so you must have done something."

"When I was shot at, I figured all deals were off. I

couldn't trust them not to do something to Brad—take off another finger, or worse—as a lesson to me. And I didn't want to die, or to let them get away with everything. So I made a deal with Lieutenant Johnson. In return for my testimony he pulled some strings and got Brad secretly transferred to another prison under another name. He's still carried on the records at Deer Lodge Prison, but his mail goes to the warden, who forwards it to wherever he is now. Just as his letters to me go to Deer Lodge Prison first, so the postmark and everything will make it look like he's still there.''

Rafe didn't say anything, and for a few minutes she didn't, either. It felt strange to have everything out in the open. He hadn't been shocked. He'd already known about her arrest, and that still made no sense to her. How could he have known and not spoken of it? How could it matter so little to him?

He'd been hurt, though. She'd hurt him by not trusting him with the truth. ''I've always been…intimidated by your family,'' she said shyly. ''Not by the money—no, to be honest, that's part of it. But only part. Your family—they're all so strong and honorable. None of them would just drift, doing whatever came easiest. There always seemed such a huge gulf between us. And I've always admired your father so much. I…''

She turned her head to look at him. And had to smile.

His eyes were closed. His mouth hung open, and his breath sighed in and out evenly. He was sound asleep.

Charlie eased away. Much as she would have liked to stay snuggled up to him, she was afraid she'd doze off, too. While she hadn't been running on stubborn instead of sleep as much as he had, she hadn't been sleeping well, either. And someone had to stay awake in case the ''hacker alarm'' went off.

She spread a throw over him and left him to his dreams, feeling the sweet, sharp bite of hope as her own dreams stirred stubbornly to life once more.

* * *

Eighteen blocks away, in a pleasant if generic hotel room, Edwin Tefteller hummed along with Pachelbel's *Canon* as he packed his favorite silencer in the specially designed briefcase that held his SIG Sauer.

He was looking forward to the evening.

It was always pleasant to discover that one's instincts, based on planning and research, had been correct. The brother had indeed proven to be the key to locating his target a second time. The parolee who handled the warden's mail at Deer Lodge Prison had been admirably quick about passing Edwin the return address on the letter Ms. Masters had sent her brother.

If truth be told, he was a bit disappointed in her. She'd seemed staunchly independent. Yet she'd gone to roost with her lover, abrogating her responsibility for her own welfare. But he was charitable enough to allow that women were hampered by their biology. Given an opportunity to depend on a male, particularly one who had impregnated them, they inevitably took it. Even the admirable Ms. Masters.

He'd been watching the apartment for the last three days while gathering information on Rafe Connelly. His target had stayed sensibly inside until today. He had very nearly had her three times while she wandered the stores with her companion, but each time someone else had moved to ruin the shot. When the two of them had gone into the El station, he'd come back to the hotel.

It was quite possible to kill someone on the subway or in a crowd, but there were a great many variables involved. Edwin preferred to control the setting whenever possible. That wouldn't be difficult with this job.

His suitcase was already packed. He went through the room, using a hotel towel to wipe down every surface he might possibly have touched. He doubted very much the police would dust this room for prints, but he hadn't risen to the top of his profession by leaving things to chance.

If there had been time, he would have arranged to rent

an office in the building across from Rafe Connelly's apartment and wait for his shot. The windows were large—an easy shot for a marksman of his skill. The only difficulty would have been acquiring the office. His employer, however, was applying a great deal of pressure. Franklin Kelly wanted the job done quickly. Edwin had decided to accommodate his employer's wishes.

Besides, there was a certain intimacy to killing someone in her home. Edwin enjoyed it when he was the last thing his targets saw. He wouldn't jeopardize a job or himself to indulge that preference, of course, but in this case his personal tastes fit neatly with the most efficient way of concluding the job. He was good with locks.

Finished with his final tidying, he folded the towel and put it with the other dirty linen. He didn't expect to have a problem with Rafe Connelly. The man was a computer programmer, not a martial arts expert. Not that Edwin was underestimating him. Connelly was fifteen years younger than Edwin and quite fit—the information Edwin had gathered indicated he indulged in such daredevil sports as hanggliding. A great foolishness, in Edwin's opinion, but it indicated a degree of athletic prowess, the ability to react quickly and a certain disregard for personal safety.

No, he wouldn't underestimate Rafe Connelly, Edwin thought as he closed his hotel door behind him for the last time. Nor would he give the man time to indulge his penchant for taking risks. He would shoot Connelly first, then Ms. Masters.

# Fourteen

Someone was shaking him. Rafe stirred and waved a hand, trying to shove them away.

"Rafe! Rafe, you have to wake up. The alarm sounded. The hacker is accessing the computers *now!*"

He was off the couch before his eyes fully opened. He took the stairs three at a time. "Get hold of Luke!" he called as he sat at his computer.

Dammit, Broderton had signed on early tonight. Rafe had planned to be at the corporate offices at the usual time the man hacked into the system—there was a measurable lag doing it this way, even with the fastest connection.

But his connection was damned fast. And his program—"Yes!" he cried. "Got him. I'm in."

"Already?" Charlie's incredulous voice came from the doorway.

"Broderton is good," Rafe said tersely as his fingers flew over the keyboard. "So's his worm. But mine is better."

Data was coming in. Rafe had it routed to the Connelly mainframe, but he had complete access to that. As long as Broderton kept the connection open... Rafe called up a file, and whistled under his breath. "Did you call Luke?"

"I'm ringing him now. He hasn't answered yet."

"As soon as you get him—"

"Luke? This is Charlotte. Rafe installed his program this afternoon and he's got an open connection to the hacker right now. He wants to talk to you."

He waved the phone away. "Tell him to get his butt over here. I'm into the Kellys' computer, not just Broderton's PC. And I'm getting plenty from it."

Just before 3:00 a.m. Broderton signed off and the connection was lost. Rafe, Charlie and Luke didn't know that, though. They were in a warehouse on the south side of Chicago that was owned by Connelly Corporation.

Grant Connelly was with them. He held a portable scanning device. "This is the one," he said tersely, and stepped back.

Luke had a crowbar the night watchman had found for them before Grant sent him away. He used it to pry open the large packing crate whose bar code matched the one given in one of the files Rafe had downloaded from the Kelly computers. The wood creaked and parted with a loud crack.

Charlie's job—holding the flashlight—wasn't really necessary, but she'd flatly refused to stay at the apartment while the men flexed their muscles and located what the Kellys had gone to such trouble to smuggle into the country. According to the file Rafe had found, this shipment of lace imported by Connelly's from an Altarian manufacturer contained something not listed on the cargo manifest.

It took Luke and Rafe together to tip the huge crate over on its side. The two of them dug through the contents with a complete disregard for the worth of the fine lace, ripping open the flat, heavy packages one at a time.

"Here it is." Rafe crouched beside the upended crate, holding a small, padded box. He opened it.

Inside were five innocuous-looking CDs.

"That's it?" Grant looked dubious. "Are you sure?"

"They didn't go to all this trouble to smuggle contraband music into the U.S.," Rafe said dryly. "But I'll check it just to be sure."

He'd brought his laptop with him, with the encryption program loaded on it. Half an hour before they'd left the apartment, Dix had shown up, handed Rafe the CD that contained the program and waited while Rafe loaded it on his laptop. He'd taken the CD with him when he left—all without asking a single question.

Charlie waited tensely while Rafe inserted one of the CDs. First he looked at a file without running the program that would remove the encryption; the screen showed garbage. Then he opened the file again, using the encryption program. "This is it, all right," he said grimly. "Not that I can understand one word in ten, but it's related to DNA encoding." He handed the CD to Luke. "The police will need these."

The police would not be told what was on the CDs, or about the copy of the encryption program that Rafe was even now erasing from his laptop's drive. But the existence of the CDs would tie the Kellys to a smuggling operation that had cost one man his life.

Grant frowned. "I'm not convinced we should let those CDs out of our sight. If they fall into the wrong hands...you said yourself any code can be broken."

"Eventually, yes. But this is one hell of a good code." Rafe's grin was tired but cocky. "Besides, these five CDs cover only a fraction of the Institute's database. Genetic research generates incredibly massive amounts of data. The Kellys have been smuggling these things out for some time—what we have here is a drop in the bucket, nowhere near enough for anyone to use to replicate the virus."

"The police can definitely use these to build their case

against the Kellys,'' Luke said. ''If you're sure they can't be used—''

''I'm sure.'' Abruptly Rafe pushed to his feet. ''Dad, it's time to get your friend the judge on the phone. The police will need to move fast to confiscate the Kellys' computer. The quicker and quieter a search warrant is issued, the better.''

Grant nodded grimly. ''I'll see what I can do.''

Grant drove them back to Rafe's apartment. Luke was to take the CDs—and the story of how they found them—straight to the police. Charlie and Rafe could expect a visit from the cops soon after that.

Rafe slept most of the way. Charlie, too, was exhausted—too tired to make conversation, but too wired to doze off.

Was it really almost over? Once the Kellys had been arrested, would they call off their hired killer—or be more determined than ever to see her dead for her part in their downfall? And Rafe—would they try to take vengeance on him?

She gripped his hand tightly the whole way.

Rafe woke just as they pulled up in front of his apartment building. He exchanged a few low-voiced words with his father, then he and Charlie climbed out.

The night was no more quiet than any other in this part of Chicago. Pedestrians were nonexistent, but cars cruised the street even at this hour. The air was knife-edge cold.

Rafe's arms were warm when he wrapped her in them. ''We've got a lot of talking to do,'' he murmured close to her ear. ''But I'm about to fall over, I'm so tired.''

''It can wait.''

''Falling over?''

She giggled, punch-drunk all of sudden with exhaustion and success. Rafe had done it. He'd stopped the Kellys. Somehow they'd find a way to make sure he didn't pay a terrible price for having taken on the mob. "I'm hoping you'll postpone falling down until you're near the bed."

"Bed," he said longingly. "I wish I could promise to do what I'm supposed to once we get there, but..."

"What you're supposed to do is sleep. We'll have time for other activities later."

"Other activities." He grinned. "I love it when you talk prissy."

Arms looped around each others' waists, they wobbled into the lobby like a pair of drunks. Rafe punched for the elevator, urging her to "talk prissy" some more. She giggled and he bent to nibble her neck in the elevator, pretending to be a great deal more turned on than was humanly possible at this point.

He unlocked the door. She went in first. "Uh-oh," she said. "Good thing we left the lights on or I would have stepped in it."

"Stepped in what?" Rafe asked.

"Looks like Thumbs got out of the kitchen. I don't know how. I could have sworn I had him barricaded in there." She sighed. "At least he didn't go on the rug."

"My fault, I'm afraid," said a soft tenor voice. And a round-faced man wearing glasses and a pleasant smile stepped out of the kitchen doorway. With casual ease he pointed the gun he held directly at Rafe—and stumbled.

Thumbs yelped. Something coughed. Rafe threw himself forward as Thumbs shot out from under the hit man's feet a split-second before Rafe collided with the man, taking him down. They rolled, Rafe's hand imprisoning the man's gun arm. Another coughing sound—oh, God, he had a silencer on his gun and was shooting!

Rafe shouted at her to get back. She danced over to the other side, away from the gun, looking around frantically for a weapon, any kind of weapon, but she'd tidied things up too well. There was nothing close by.

She wasn't needed. The scuffle was fierce but brief, and ended with Rafe sitting on the hit man's chest, pinning his arms at the wrists. His eyes had rolled back from a vicious series of punches.

"Get his gun," Rafe ordered.

Even half-conscious, the man was feebly trying to dislodge Rafe—and he'd held onto his long, wicked-looking gun. Charlie scrambled close and wrenched it from his grip. Once she did, she knelt beside him and put the barrel up to his temple.

He froze. "The trigger is extremely sensitive."

"Then you want to be extremely still. I'm scared, I'm shaking and the least little surprise might make my finger twitch."

He was wonderfully obedient.

Charlie held herself together while they waited for the beat cops to arrive. She kept her cool while they cuffed the hit man and read him his rights. More police arrived and she answered questions and more questions.

The hit man didn't speak at all except to mutter something about puppies and dog pee and planning. He looked quite bewildered as they took him away.

Even when Lieutenant Johnson arrived and she had to answer the same questions all over again, she held on to her composure by repeating silently that it was over, that the man who had almost killed Rafe and her was gone, and soon the cops would be gone, too. In spite of what she'd said to the hit man, she didn't start to shake until the lieutenant announced that they would have to go down to the station to finish making their statements.

Once she started, though, she couldn't seem to stop.

Rafe didn't exactly argue with the lieutenant. He just told him they weren't going anywhere. The lieutenant argued. Rafe put his arms around her and held on and ignored the man, who finally went away.

That's when she started crying.

Rafe looked alarmed. "Hey, Charlie, it's okay. Everything's all right now. You're just having a reaction to all the adrenaline your body didn't use. You're okay.''

''I didn't—he didn't—'' But the tears were coming harder and she couldn't get the words out. She wrapped her arms around him.

Rafe was priceless in many emergencies, but he was helpless with tears. He kept telling her she was all right— as if she didn't know that—and to stop crying, which was no help at all.

Finally she grabbed the front of his sweater in both hands. ''I-I'll cry if I w-want to!'' she choked out. ''Don't t-tell me to stop! You were almost *k-killed* tonight because of *me* and I *love* you and I damned well d-deserve to cry!''

His eyes went wide. ''You love me?''

She sniffed and sniffed again, but the tears seemed to have at last run their course. ''Of course I do! Why else would I put up with a stubborn, sloppy man who falls asleep when I'm baring my soul? And who tries to push me around and doesn't understand that I don't have a clue how to belong in his world, but—''

He gave a loud yelp—which woke Thumbs, who'd dozed off sometime between the arrival of the police and their exit—and grabbed her and whirled her around.

''Are you crazy?'' But she was laughing as they spun in a circle, her hands on his shoulders and her feet flying clear off the ground.

''Crazy about you.'' His voice went soft and full of wonder as he pulled her close. ''Charlie. You love me.''

She nodded and swallowed. ''I couldn't let you say it to me before because I didn't think it was *me* you'd be saying it to. There was so much you didn't know about me....'' She frowned. ''At least I thought you didn't know.''

''I'm going to hear about that for the next thirty or forty years, aren't I?'' He smoothed the hair back from her face, his eyes tender and happy. ''Charlie, I'm nuts about your prim-and-proper side—which isn't fake, you know. You really do get off on neatness. But I'm just as crazy about the wild, wanton woman you don't let out enough. The woman who does illogical things like get me a puppy for my birthday—a gift that saved both our lives.''

Her smile wobbled a bit. "It was so close. If Thumbs hadn't come out right then—"

"Life isn't horseshoes, so 'close' doesn't count. In case you didn't notice, I did not propose again. I'm not going to, either. You keep turning me down. I'm simply telling you that we're getting married as soon as possible. It's only reasonable, since you love me and all."

She bit her lip to hold back her laughter. "Rafe."

His gaze had drifted to her mouth with unmistakable interest. "Yeah?"

"You're forgetting something."

He frowned. "A ring? I'll get you one, don't worry."

She shook her head.

"The carrying-over-the-threshold bit comes later. No, I can't think of anything I've left out that needs doing at this point. Other than—"

She put her hand on his chest. "You're far too tired for that."

"Want to bet?" And he kissed her. Long minutes later he lifted his head, smiled down into her eyes and said softly, "Charlie, I love you."

And quietly, happily, she let go of those pesky dreams. It was easy to do. There would be other dreams to enjoy, different ones, but she didn't have to dream of love anymore. Now she had the real thing.

She had Rafe.

# Epilogue

*The day after Thanksgiving*

The bride wore a sarong. It was blue and brief, and made no attempt to camouflage the swell of her belly. Her hair was loose and curly, ornamented only by the white orchid tucked behind one ear. After the ceremony she tossed several leis to the guests instead of a single bouquet.

The groom was more traditional. He wore a tux. When the dancing started, though, he lost the jacket and let the tie hang loose before leading his new wife onto the dance floor.

"You looked sexy in that tux," Charlie said, casting his discarded finery a wistful glance.

"It's too warm in here for a jacket." Rafe pulled her into his arms and started them moving to the music. The band was playing "Blue Hawaii." Three inches of snow covered the ground outside, but his folks had turned the heat up in the ballroom to accommodate the bride's bare shoulders.

"I'm comfortable."

"Yeah." He ran one hand down her hip and, reluctantly, back up to her waist. "You sure are."

She smiled a private smile that hinted she was thinking things she wouldn't tell. "You'd be nice and cool if you'd worn the loincloth."

Charlie had suggested the groom ought to wear a grass loincloth like the sword dancers. Rafe still wasn't sure she'd been kidding. "I've created a monster," he said, and held her closer.

Charlie looped both arms around his neck and tilted her head back. "So, what do you think of marriage so far?"

"It's already changing me. I never used to be turned on by married women." He showed her what he meant with a kiss, long and deep and lingering. *His*. She was his now in the eyes of man and God, and the knowledge made him eager to switch from vertical dancing to the horizontal sort.

Someone tapped on his shoulder. "We're all enjoying the show, but I'm a little concerned that you've forgotten to breathe."

Rafe lifted his head slowly, smiling down into Charlie's eyes. At some point the band had stopped playing. No one was dancing anymore. No, the idiots were all standing around, watching and chuckling. And Charlie was blushing. "Damn voyeurs. Go away, Dix."

"No, I'm going to dance with the bride and you're going to pretend to be civilized and go talk to your guests. Move over."

Reluctantly he moved to the side of the dance floor as the musicians started playing again. He'd have to dance with several of the other ladies present, and it wasn't as if he didn't like them and want to dance with them, but...

"I'm not offering a penny for those thoughts," his father said with a chuckle. "The way you're watching her it's a wonder she doesn't spontaneously combust."

Oh, but she did. Rafe grinned. "I can wait. I guess I'd better start doing my duty and dancing with as many family members as possible. Where's Grandmother?"

"Giving Catherine's new husband a test drive, as she put it. Said she'd never danced with a sheik before."

Oh, yes. He saw now—the erect old lady beaming at the dark young man. "Pity Daniel and Erin couldn't make it," he said, snagging a glass of champagne off the tray of a passing waiter.

"They sent their apologies. Between taking on the duties of ruling a country and getting ready for the upcoming coronation, Daniel's stretched pretty thin right now." Grant chuckled. "It will be a wonder if he makes it to the ceremony without committing murder. Gregor Paulus is driving him crazy. I suggested that firing the man was a more politically correct solution than choking him."

Daniel had more on his mind than his irritating assistant. Rafe's mood sobered. The Kellys had all been arrested. It was one of the biggest sweeps of gang bosses in recent years, and the police were convinced their case was tight.

That case had been much strengthened when the hit man Rafe had caught decided to testify against his former employers. Edwin Tefteller seemed much more concerned about the black mark on his reputation than with the prison term he faced. He was determined to set the record straight. The Kellys had apparently violated their agreement with the hit man by sending Palermo after Charlie the first time. From that breech of contract, the hit man believed, all his own ills had sprung.

But no one knew how the CDs had been made and smuggled out of Altaria in the first place—or where the rest of the CDs were, or how many there were. And as he'd said, no encryption program was fail-safe. If the CDs fell into the wrong hands, eventually they could be decoded. A lab might be able to reconstruct the steps to creating the killer virus.

Then there was the Kellys' enforcer, Rocky Palermo,

who had managed to lose his police tail and vanish. All in all, there were a lot of loose ends. And they were all scary.

His father's annoyed exclamation broke into Rafe's troubled thoughts. "What is that little hussy of mine up to now?"

Rafe followed his father's gaze. His youngest sister, Maggie, was more or less dragging Luke out on the dance floor. "Looks like she wants to dance," he said mildly, but uneasiness grew as he watched. The moment Luke stopped resisting Maggie's blandishments and drew her into his arms, the two moved together with a physical harmony Rafe recognized all too well. The attraction was obviously strong—and mutual.

"Luke's a good man," he said, reminding himself.

"He's too old for her," Grant growled.

"Maggie doesn't seem to think so." And that wasn't what worried Rafe. The differences the calendar registered were far less important than the ones experience had carved into his friend. Luke was a good man, yes. But the shadow on his soul was large and dark, and Rafe didn't want his irrepressible sister damaged by that darkness.

So he made a point of dancing with Maggie next. After that he snagged his grandmother, then his mother. Then someone tapped his shoulder just as he was about to take one of his sisters-in-law out on the floor.

"I hope you'll excuse me," Charlie said apologetically to Elena. "But I bribed the band to play this song. It's rather special to me, and I'd like to dance to it with Rafe."

"By all means," Elena said, smiling.

So Rafe danced his second dance with his wife to the sound of "Dream a Little Dream." Her eyes were glowing, her cheeks flushed with pleasure. And her mouth was turned up in that secret-loving smile of hers.

He held her a little closer, smiling himself. He could let her keep a few secrets...for now. He had a lifetime to learn them.

\*     \*     \*     \*     \*

# Cherokee Marriage Dare

## SHERI WHITEFEATHER

## SHERI WHITEFEATHER

lives in Southern California and enjoys ethnic dining and visiting art galleries and vintage clothing shops near the beach. When she isn't writing, she often reads until the small hours of the morning.

Sheri also works as a leather artisan with her Native American husband. They have a son, a daughter and a menagerie of pets, including a pampered English bull-dog and four equally spoiled Bengal cats. She would love to hear from her readers. You may write to her at: PO Box 5130, Orange, California 92863-5130, USA.

To the editors on this series, thank you for your hard work and dedication. And to the other authors who made the Connelly family come alive – your emotional and creative support was truly appreciated.

# One

Maggie Connelly waited on Luke Starwind's doorstep. The Chicago wind blew bitter and brisk. She could feel the December air creeping up her spine like icy fingers. A warning, she thought. A prelude to danger.

Adjusting the grocery bags in her arms, she shifted her stance. Was she getting in over her head? Playing with fire?

No, she told herself. She had every right to get involved in her family's investigation. She needed to make a difference, to find closure. Her beloved grandfather was dead, and so was her dashing, handsome uncle. Their lives had been destroyed, and she needed to know why.

But her biggest stumbling block was Luke. She knew the former Green Beret would try to thwart her efforts.

Maggie tossed her head. Well, she had a surprise in store for him. She'd uncovered a valuable piece of evidence. And that was her ace in the hole, the card up her sleeve. He couldn't very well shut her out once she revealed the winning hand fate had dealt her.

Luke opened the door, but neither said a word.

Instead, their gazes locked.

Maggie took a deep breath, forcing oxygen into her lungs.

The man stood tall and powerfully built. Jet-black hair, combed away from his forehead, intensified the rawboned angles of his face. He possessed a commanding presence, his features strong and determined—high-cut cheekbones, a nose that might have suffered a long-healed break, an unrelenting jaw.

Luke was a jigsaw puzzle she'd yet to solve, each complicated piece of his personality as confusing as the next. Everything about him rattled her senses, and made her want to touch him. Not just his body, but also his heart.

His reclusive, shielded heart.

Did Luke know that he had a romantic side? A masculine warmth hidden beneath that stern, rugged exterior?

Maggie had asked him to dance at her brother's wedding reception, and now she could feel every gliding motion, every smooth sultry sway. He'd rubbed his cheek against her temple and whispered a Cherokee phrase, something that had made him draw her closer to his beating heart. She'd never been so tenderly aroused.

"What are you doing here?"

Instantly, Maggie snapped to attention. After that sensual dance, he'd avoided her like the plague, returning to his hard-boiled self.

But why? she wondered. Because she'd made him feel too much?

Refusing to be intimidated, she shoved the groceries at him. "I came to fix you dinner, Starwind. So be a gentleman, will ya?"

Flustered, he took the bags, nearly dropping one in the process.

Maggie bit back a satisfied smile. She'd managed to catch Mr. Tough Guy off guard. That in itself rang like a small victory.

He moved away from the door, and she swept past him, curious to see his home.

The spacious, two-story town house showcased a stone fireplace and nineteenth-century furnishings, each piece sturdy and functional. A little battered, she supposed, but the rustic antiques made a personal statement. She assumed Luke had chosen them, as they suited him well.

She noticed the absence of knickknacks and lived-in clutter. Apparently Luke surrounded himself with the necessities of life, rather than objects that sparked sentiment. A person's home reflected his emotions, Maggie thought. And although Luke's town house was located in the heart of the city, it made her wonder if he'd been raised on a farm or a ranch. The oak floors were polished to a slick shine and padded with braided area rugs.

She zeroed in on the kitchen and headed toward it, knowing Luke followed. He set the groceries on a tiled counter, and she familiarized herself with his spotless appliances and practical cookware. The windowsill above the stainless-steel sink was bare, no potted plants, nothing to water or care for.

Something inside her stirred—a wave of sadness, an urge to brighten his rough-hewn world. To make Mr. Tough Guy smile.

He frowned. And for an instant she feared he'd just read her mind.

He leaned against a pantry-style cabinet, watching every move she made. Maggie unbuttoned her coat and told herself to relax. The man was a top-notch private investigator.

It was his nature to study people and make analytical assessments. Plus, she thought, releasing the breath she'd been holding, he was attracted to her.

Their bodies had brushed seductively on the dance floor; their hearts had pounded to the same erotic rhythm. *A qua da nv do.* The Cherokee words swirled in her head. What did they mean? And why had he said them with such quiet longing?

Maggie hung her coat behind a straight-back chair in the connecting dining room. Luke's gaze roamed from her cashmere sweater to the tips of her Italian boots, then back up again.

"What's going on?" he asked. "What are you up to?"

"Nothing," she responded a little too innocently. She wasn't ready to drop the bomb. First she would ply him with pasta. And a bottle of her favorite wine.

Luke crossed his arms. He wore jeans and a dark-blue sweatshirt, attire much too casual for his unyielding posture. In his left ear, a tiny sterling hoop shone bright against dark skin. The earring defined the native in him, she thought. A man who remained close to his Cherokee roots.

She unloaded the groceries and realized he intended to stay right where he was, staring at her while she prepared their meal.

"I'm surprised you know how to cook," he said.

She shot him a pointed look. "Very funny." Maggie knew how Luke perceived her. No one took her endeavors seriously.

She was the youngest child in one of the wealthiest, most powerful families in the country. Her elegant mother hailed from royalty, and her steely-eyed father had made his fortune in business, transforming a small company into a global corporation.

But Maggie had yet to earn the respect often associated

with the Connelly name. The paparazzi deemed her a spoiled, jet-setting heiress. The tabloid pictures that circulated made her seem like nothing but a party girl. It was an image she couldn't seem to shake, no matter how hard she tried.

And while Maggie's personal life was dissected in gossip columns, Luke kept a tight rein on his.

Why was he so detached? she wondered. So cautious? Why would a handsome, successful, thirty-nine-year-old choose to protect his heart?

She didn't know much about Luke, but she'd done a little digging, asking for information from anyone who knew him. And although she hadn't been able to unravel the mystery surrounding him, she'd learned a few unsettling facts. Luke had never been married or engaged. He didn't participate in meaningful relationships, and most people, including women, described him as guarded.

Maggie held his watchful gaze, searching for a flicker of happiness, a spark of joy. But his eyes seemed distant. Haunted, she thought, by undisclosed pain.

Could she make him happy? Could she hold him close and ease the tension from his brow?

Deep down, she wanted the chance to try. But she doubted he would welcome her efforts. Especially when she told him that she intended to help him with her family's investigation.

Lucas Starwind, she knew, wouldn't appreciate the Connelly's youngest daughter working by his side.

A little over an hour later Luke and Maggie sat across from each other at his dining-room table. The lady was up to something. He knew she'd been questioning people all over town about him. And now here she was, enticing him with a home-cooked meal. Young, beautiful, impulsive

Maggie. The Connelly baby. The free-spirited jet-setter. Something didn't add up.

But, then, Maggie was far from predictable. She carried herself like a muse, like the goddess of dance, flaunting a playful sensuality Luke wasn't accustomed to. She wore her light-brown hair in a natural style, and her eyes were the color of a tropical sea. Long, lithe curves complemented all that unchained beauty.

She had a temper, too. Just enough to ignite his blood.

But Luke didn't like the idea that they wanted each other. She was too young for him—much too young. Seventeen years spanned between them, a lifetime in his book.

He glanced at the food she'd prepared—antipasto salad, lasagna and a loaf of oven-warmed bread. It was a cozy, charming meal. The kind of dishes a sidewalk café would serve. Even the ambience seemed intimate. Maggie had provided a scented candle, and it burned between them like a melting jewel.

But this wasn't a date, and in spite of the wine sparkling in his glass, Luke was in complete control of his senses.

Maybe not in complete control. But close. As close as his body would allow while in Maggie's presence. As long as they weren't touching, he would survive her proximity. No more dances, no more warm, gentle seductions. Luke couldn't take another bewitching. Not after what he'd said. What he'd felt.

He glanced up and caught her watching him. Waiting, he supposed, to see if this cozy dinner had affected him, if it would make him easier to deal with. He knew she was plotting something. Those blue-green eyes shimmered with what he'd come to think of as muse magic—enchantment that could steal into a man's soul.

Luke frowned, disturbed by his train of thought. Maggie

Connelly was a woman, not a muse. And he was too practical to get caught up in mythical nonsense.

Then why had she inspired him to hold her close? To sway flawlessly to the music? To whisper words he hadn't meant to say? Luke hadn't spoken the Kituwah dialect since he was a boy.

He shook his head, intent on clearing his mind. Dwelling on that moment wouldn't do him any good. He still had this other business with Maggie to contend with—whatever the hell it was.

"Level with me," he said. "Tell me what's going on."

She reached for her wine. The light from the chandelier cast an enchanting glow. Luke ignored the gilded streaks in her hair, the gold that gleamed like a treasure.

"I'm going to help you solve my family's case."

He clenched his jaw. So that was it. The grad student wanted to amuse herself by playing detective. No way, he thought. No damn way. Tom Reynolds, his experienced partner, had been killed while working on this investigation. The last thing Luke needed was an amateur sleuth—a gorgeous female—dogging his heels, getting herself into all sorts of trouble.

"This isn't a game, Maggie." He drilled her with a hard stare. "People are dying out there."

"You think I don't know that?" She bristled before her voice turned raw. "King Thomas was my grandfather. And Prince Marc was my uncle."

And both men were dead, Luke thought. Killed in a boating accident that hadn't turned out to be an accident at all. "I'm sure you're well aware that the Kelly crime family is responsible for what's been going on. And they have ties in Altaria." He leaned against the table. "This is a sophisticated operation. An international crime ring. There's someone in the royal household who's a key player in everything that happened."

"And that's why this matters so much to me. I have a right to know why members of my family were killed. Altaria is a second home to me."

He pictured her in Altaria, sunbathing on the white sandy beaches, strolling the cobblestoned streets, breathing in the cool, clean air. Altaria was an independent kingdom on the Tyrrhenian Sea, just off the southern coast of Italy. Yes, he thought. Maggie Connelly belonged to that world, to the picturesque island that captured the essence of her youth and royal blood. He didn't doubt that she had been King Thomas's favored grandchild.

"This case is too dangerous for sentiment." And he wasn't about to put her in the center of a critical investigation.

"My grandfather and my uncle are gone," she countered, pushing her plate away. "And I need closure."

Luke heaved a rough sigh. If there was one thing he understood, it was the thirst for justice. But Maggie's situation was different from his. She wasn't responsible for the despair in her family. "I can't let you get involved." He had a darn good idea why King Thomas and Prince Marc had been killed, and the danger was still out there. A danger that threatened Mother Earth. Biological warfare wasn't child's play.

She set her chin in a defiant gesture. "I'm already involved. I have a piece of evidence, something I'm sure is related to this case."

Silent, he studied her for a moment. Pretty Maggie—the free-spirited coed, the high-society party girl. She had to be bluffing. There was no way she could have uncovered vital information. "Really, Nancy Drew? And what might that be?"

Irked by the mockery, she met his gaze head-on, her eyes suddenly more green than blue. Like one of those mood rings, he thought with a spark of humor. The lady did have quite a temper.

"A few weeks ago I found a CD in a lace shipment from Altaria," she said, knocking the amusement right out of him. "The software is encrypted, so I couldn't read the file, but it doesn't take a genius to know that it was smuggled out of the country."

Luke's entire body tensed.

Another pirated file.

Damn it, he thought. Damn it all to hell. Maggie's discovery was enough to get her killed. "Who else have you told about this?"

"No one."

"Good." At least she had the sense to keep quiet. Unable to finish his meal, Luke set his fork back on the table. This case was tying his stomach in knots. "What were you doing nosing around at the warehouse?" She wasn't involved in the Connelly import business.

She sent him a tight look. "I wasn't nosing around. I custom ordered some lace for a dress. When it arrived, the warehouse forwarded the package to me."

A package that had accidentally contained one of the stolen files. Luke shook his head. Maggie had gotten herself tangled up in biological warfare over a dress. Somehow that made perfect, idiotic sense. "You're going to turn that CD over to me and forget that you ever saw it."

"Oh, no, I'm not. I'm keeping it until you agree to let me help you with the investigation."

She tilted her head at a regal angle, and Luke cursed beneath his breath. Women in Altaria couldn't inherit the throne, but that didn't make Maggie Connelly any less of a princess.

Her oldest brother, Daniel, had inherited the throne. Although his very public, very lavish coronation was scheduled at the end of the month, he'd already taken a private oath before the United Chambers, becoming king of the small, sovereign nation. And now King Daniel had stolen files to worry about, information that had been smuggled out of his country. He doubted the monarch would appreciate his sister withholding evidence.

Luke had the notion to wring Maggie's royal little neck. "You're not getting away with this," he said.

"And neither are you," she retorted.

Their gazes locked in a battle of wills. Luke cursed again, only this time out loud. In that long-drawn-out moment, he knew he had met his match.

And now, damn it, he had to figure out what to do about her.

The Connellys' Chicago mansion was a classic Georgian manor, located in the city's most fashionable neighborhood. The brick structure sat like a monument, surrounded by a sweeping lawn.

Luke had been escorted to a sitting room, but he didn't feel like sitting. Instead he stood beside a marble fireplace, waiting for Maggie's brother Rafe. Overall, she had eight brothers, two sisters, a graceful mother and a powerful father, but Rafe was the one Luke had been working with on the Connelly case.

Leaning against the mantel, he glanced around the room and shook his head. He couldn't imagine growing up in a place like this. Luke had found his own measure of financial success, and he appreciated antiques, but everything in the Connelly mansion was too grand for his taste.

A moment later he moved his arm, realizing it was dangerously close to what looked like a priceless vase. Ming

Dynasty, Qing Dynasty. He didn't know the difference, but knocking the damn thing over wasn't the most prudent way to find out.

Rafe entered the room, and Luke moved forward to greet him. Rafe Connelly was anything but the computer nerd Luke had expected before they'd met the first time. He was athletic and hardworking, charming when he felt like it and fond of casual clothes and fast cars. Luke respected him immensely. And if anybody could turn Maggie around, he could. Although Rafe was levelheaded, he shared a bit of Maggie's impulsive nature. Luke assumed she wouldn't resent her brother's intervention.

"Any luck?" Luke asked.

The other man shook his head. "She's upstairs in her room, hissing like a cat. There's no way she's going to relinquish that CD. Not without a compromise."

And I'm the compromise, Luke thought. Me and the investigation. "Did you tell her what's on the CD?" he asked. Rafe had recently uncovered the existence of the pirated files, as well as the lethal material they contained.

Rafe gave him an incredulous look. "Not without consulting you first."

They both fell silent, their expressions grim. They had discussed the severity of this case, the need for secrecy. Luke gazed out a French door. He could see a crop of distant shrubbery blocked in each wood-framed pane.

He turned back to Rafe. "What the hell are we going to do?"

"I don't see that we have much choice. If we don't allow Maggie to get involved, she intends to go snooping around on her own." The other man pulled a hand through his wavy light-brown hair. "I swear, I could brain her."

Luke knew the feeling. And he also knew what Rafe was getting at. Maggie was in more danger on her own than she was working by Luke's side. And her having possession of one of the CDs made it even more critical. "I don't need this."

"I know. I'm sorry."

Once again they fell silent. Luke thought about Tom Reynolds, who had been shot to death while on the investigation. His stomach clenched. If he hadn't been out of town at the time, he could have given Tom the backup he needed.

"You'll have to keep a close eye on Maggie."

He looked up and slammed straight into Rafe's dark-blue gaze. Was the other man blaming him for Tom's murder? Or was it a reflection of his own guilt he saw?

They stood in the center of the room, the finery closing in around them. Luke knew what came next. He knew exactly what Rafe was going to say.

"I'm asking you to protect my sister, Luke. To treat her as if she was your own flesh and blood."

He locked his knees to keep them from buckling. His own flesh and blood. A pain gripped his heart. The ever-constant ache that reminded him of what he'd done. Tom Reynolds wasn't the only death he was responsible for. Twenty-seven years before, he'd let a beautiful little girl die. He would never forget the day her body had been found. The muggy summer day a farmer had discovered her, bruised and battered—tortured by a vicious attack.

"Promise me you'll protect her."

"I will," Luke vowed. "I promise." He would keep Rafe's sister safe. With his life, he thought. With the only honor he had left.

The other man broke the tension with a grin. "It won't be easy. Maggie's one headstrong female."

Luke couldn't find it within himself to smile. But he rarely could. His joy had died twenty-seven years ago.

"Yeah. I've already locked horns with her. I know what I'm up against."

"You're going to have to fill her in about what we've learned so far," Rafe said. "I don't want to give her an excuse to go poking around on her own."

Luke squinted. "Fine. But first I want you to lay some ground rules. Tell Maggie that I'm the boss. This is my investigation, and whatever I say goes."

Rafe agreed. "I'll brief her, then send her down in a few minutes."

He headed toward the French door. "Have her meet me outside. I could use some air."

"Sure. And Luke?"

He turned, his boots heavy on the Turkish carpet. "Yeah?"

"Thanks."

Luke only nodded. Protecting Maggie Connelly scared the hell out of him. But her brother had entrusted him with the responsibility. And that was something a Cherokee man couldn't deny.

# Two

Maggie exited the house, then shoved her hands in her coat pockets to ward off the chill. Luke stood quietly, a lone figure surrounded by a winter garden, his face tipped to the sky.

In the distance, boxwood shrubs created a maze—a mystic castle of green. The maze was Maggie's favorite spot at Lake Shore Manor. To her, it had always seemed dark and dangerous. Haunted yet beautiful.

Like Lucas Starwind.

He wore black jeans and a leather jacket, the collar turned up for warmth. On his feet, a pair of electrician-style boots crunched on the frozen grass. As she approached, he turned to look at her.

She continued walking, and when they were face-to-face, she waited for him to speak.

But he didn't. Instead he let the wind howl between them.

Maggie had never met anyone like Luke. He had an edge,

she thought. A dark and mysterious edge, like the maze. She used to play hide-and-seek there as a child, and as much as the twists and turns had frightened her, they had thrilled her, too.

Luke, she realized, produced the same staggering effect. He looked powerful in the hazy light. His cheekbones cast a hollow shadow, and his eyes bore permanent lines at the corners. From frowning, she decided, or squinting into the sun. In his hair, she could see faint threads of gray, so faint they almost seemed like an illusion.

"Are you cold?" he asked. "Do you want to go back inside?"

She shook her head. The air was sharp and chilled, but she didn't want to break this strange spell.

"It's going to snow," he said. "By Friday. Or maybe Saturday."

The weathermen claimed otherwise, but Maggie didn't argue the point. Luke seemed connected to the elements. She attributed that to the loner in him, to the man who probably spent countless hours alone with a winter sky.

Although Maggie wanted to touch him, she kept her hands in her pockets. Luke wasn't the sort of person you placed a casual hand upon. But, then, she knew what sparked between them was far from casual.

"Did Rafe talk to you?" he asked, looking directly into her eyes.

"Yes. He said I'm supposed to listen to whatever you say." That, of course, had rubbed her the wrong way. Rafe had made her feel like a child rather than a grown woman. Then again, she had behaved badly in front of her brother, her Irish temper flaring.

"That's right. You're supposed to follow my direction, and I'm supposed to keep a close eye on you."

"Really?" Somehow that pleased and irritated her all at

once. She liked the idea of spending time with Luke, but she didn't appreciate having him as her keeper.

He lowered his chin, glaring at her through narrowed eyes. "Do you have a problem with that?"

"No." She decided she would turn his guardianship against him. She would use every opportunity she could to make him smile. To save that tortured soul of his.

"Good. Then I need some information from you."

An angry breeze blew his hair, dragging it away from his face. He had a natural widow's peak, which gave him a rather ominous appeal. Like the maze, she reminded herself. The silver earring caught a glint of the gray winter light.

"How many residences do you have?" he asked.

"Me or my family?"

"You, Maggie. Where do you sleep?"

The question had been posed in a professional voice, but there was still a note of intimacy attached. She couldn't seem to ignore the tingle it gave her.

"I have a room here," she told him. "But most of the time I stay at a loft downtown. I own the building." It was her sanctuary, her home and her studio. Maggie was an artist. She painted because she needed to, because the images she created stemmed from her emotions.

Luke shifted his stance, and she imagined painting him where he stood, the wind ravaging his hair, daylight reflecting the torment in his eyes, the silver earring catching a glint of gray from the sky.

A muscle ticked in his jaw. "Do you have a current lover? Someone who has access to your loft?"

A sensuous shiver streaked up her spine. "No." She wanted him as her lover. She wanted him thrusting inside her, clawing at her with the heat and power she knew he possessed. She met his gaze, felt her heartbeat stagger. "Do you have a current lover, Luke?"

He squinted, causing the lines around his eyes to imbed themselves deeper. "This isn't about me."

She tossed her head, but the image she'd created in her mind wouldn't go away. "So you get to pry into my life, but I have to stay out of yours?"

"That's right. And do you know why that is, Maggie?"

She didn't respond. There was no need. Clearly he intended to enlighten her.

"You're too young and too emotional," he said. "You don't observe the world through calculating eyes. You wouldn't have the slightest idea if the person following you was a cameraman or a hit man. So it's my job to know where you are and who you're with."

Counting silently to ten, and then to twenty, she suppressed the urge to fire her temper at him. "Which basically means I'm a thorn in your side."

"You're not exactly the partner I would have chosen."

Maggie saw a shadow cross his face, and she knew he was thinking about Tom Reynolds. Luke had left town for a while after his partner's funeral. He had seemed enraged at the time, barely in control of his pain.

"You're emotional, too," she said.

"Not like you. I'm not playful one minute and pissy the next."

No, she thought. He was *never* playful.

"Come on." He motioned to the courtyard, his demeanor stern and strong and businesslike. "Let's sit down, and I'll fill you in on the case."

Ten minutes later, they occupied a glass-topped table, each with a hot drink in front of them.

Maggie's mocha cappuccino tasted rich and sweet, flavored with a splash of raspberry syrup. Luke drank his coffee strong and black. Which suited him, she thought.

He lifted his gaze and looked directly into her eyes. For

an instant she held her breath. Lucas Starwind never failed to accelerate her heartbeat.

"We're dealing with the possibility of a biological weapon," he said.

The air in her lungs rushed out. "That's what's on the CD I discovered? Some sort of scientific formula that could kill people?"

He gave a tight nod. "We've recovered six CDs in all, including the one you have, but there's more out there. The files they contain were pirated from the Rosemere Institute."

"That doesn't make sense." Maggie's grandfather, King Thomas, had founded the Rosemere Institute in hopes of discovering a cure for cancer. "How could the Institute have anything dangerous in their files?"

"Because they've been focusing on viral genetic research," he explained. "The idea is to tailor a virus that will destroy cancer cells without debilitating the patient the way radiation and chemotherapy do."

Waiting for Luke to continue, Maggie placed her hands around her coffee cup, drawing warmth from the porcelain.

"Last year the Institute made a breakthrough in their research," he said. "But they also explored a number of dead ends. And one of those dead ends led to the accidental creation of a virus that stimulates a fast-growing cancer. A virus that's vectored through the air."

Momentarily stunned, Maggie stared at him. "They created a cancer? Did King Thomas know?"

"Yes. He made sure the original virus was destroyed, along with the final codes needed to fabricate it. But if a top-quality lab had all of the Institute's data, they could figure out the final codes and re-create it."

"How many of the CDs are still missing?"

"Enough to worry about. Whoever has them intends to

sell them on the black market. That's what this whole scheme is about.''

Her pulse pounded in her throat. Biological warfare wasn't what she had expected. "So this is why King Thomas and Prince Marc were killed?''

Luke paused, gauging Maggie's expression. She looked pale, sad and worried. He decided now wasn't the time to tell her that Prince Marc had most likely been involved in stealing the files. In a roundabout way, her uncle's treachery had cost him his life.

"Rafe and I aren't clear on all the details," he said. "We know the Kelly crime family is responsible, and even though they're in prison now, they still have ties in Altaria.''

She lifted her coffee with both hands. "So solving this case means recovering the rest of the CDs and putting the Altarian traitors behind bars?''

"That's exactly what it means.''

A moment of silence stretched between them, but Luke assumed she needed to absorb the harsh reality of what she'd just learned.

The courtyard didn't provide much of a wind block. Maggie's hair blew wildly around her shoulders, each light-brown strand tipped with gold. She wore a camel-colored coat, the collar lined with a faux-print fur. The effect was stunning. And distracting, Luke thought.

She seemed vulnerable, and that made him want to touch her.

She replaced her cup with an unsteady hand. "This is so awful. King Thomas founded the Institute because his wife died from cancer. He was trying to do something good for mankind, not destroy it. He loved his queen very much. It broke his heart to watch her suffer.''

Luke nodded. He had seen firsthand how terribly cancer patients suffered, how the disease ravaged. He had lost his father to colorectal cancer. But Luke wasn't going to tell Maggie about his past or the ache that came with it. The burden was his, and his alone. And so was the broken promise he'd made to his dad.

He stared at his coffee, into the void of nothingness. He wanted to drop his head in his hands and mourn the mistakes he'd made.

But he couldn't. There was no turning back. He had to live with what he'd done, face himself in the mirror every day and despise the reflection.

"Are you all right?" Maggie asked.

Instantly, he locked away the pain. "Of course I am."

Their eyes met and held. Hers were a pale wash of blue, flecked with tiny sparks of green. Her incredible, ever-changing eyes.

"Are you sure?" she pressed. "You seem troubled."

"It's a troubling case," he responded.

"Yes, it is," she agreed, her gaze never wavering from his.

Once again he longed to touch her. They sat side by side, their shoulders nearly brushing. He resisted the urge to lift his hand, to stroke her cheek, to feel the warmth radiating from her skin.

Luke reached for his coffee and sipped the bitter brew. This investigation was too critical to get sidetracked by a beautiful woman. Especially since she was the lady he had vowed to protect.

Rey-Star Investigations was located in a dramatic tower overlooking the city. Maggie took the elevator to the ninth floor and entered Luke's office through double-glass doors.

A blue-eyed blonde sat behind a mahogany reception desk. Focusing on a computer screen, she pursed her racy red lips, forming a provocative pout.

She was stunning—in a bombshell kind of way. A sweater, the same notice-me shade as her lipstick, stretched across her ample bosom.

Maggie frowned, irked that Luke had a blow-up doll working for him. She cleared her throat and waited for the receptionist to acknowledge her.

The blonde looked up and flashed a thousand-watt smile. That, too, managed to irritate Maggie. Apparently the other woman, who probably shared Luke's bed whenever he beckoned, didn't see her as a threat.

Clearly Luke wasn't as lonely as he appeared.

"May I help you, Ms. Connelly?" the receptionist asked.

"Yes, thank you." She wasn't surprised the other woman had recognized her. Maggie's celebrity rarely went unnoticed. "Is Mr. Starwind available?"

"I'll let him know you're here."

Within minutes Maggie was escorted into Luke's office. He stood beside a window, gazing out at the city. The room was furnished with an ebony desk, leather chairs and a lacquered bar. A slim marble table held a bronze eagle, its enormous wings poised in flight. Stone and metal, she thought, with a blend of masculine elegance.

Luke turned and met Maggie's gaze. Dressed entirely in black, he looked as striking as the decor.

He shifted his gaze to his receptionist. "Thank you, Carol."

The blonde nodded and closed the door behind her.

Luke and Maggie stared at each other for what seemed like an endless amount of time.

"She's quite the bombshell," Maggie said finally.

He moved away from the window and sat on the edge of his desk. "Who? Carol?"

Yes, Carol, she thought, wondering why he bothered to play dumb. "I wasn't aware busty blondes were your type."

He crossed his arms, his mouth set in an unforgiving line. "So you analyzed her, did you?"

"Women notice other women," she replied in her own defense. "We're quite observant in that regard."

"Really? Then why don't you give me your evaluation of her?"

Maggie removed her coat and flung it over a chair. Luke remained where he was, perched on the edge of his glossy desk.

"Let's see." She walked to the bar and poured herself a cherry cola. Rattling the ice in her glass, she took a sip. "Carol takes long lunches, wears cheap perfume and keeps her boss entertained on cold winter nights. She has an average IQ, and buys more clothes than she can afford."

Luke uncrossed his arms and tapped his chin in an analytical gesture. "That's very interesting, but you're wrong on every count. First of all, she works her tail off. Second, most perfumes, cheap or otherwise, give her a headache. She also happens to be sharp as a tack, frugal to a fault and happily married to a man who adores her."

Maggie wanted to sink into the carpet. "I suppose they have children?"

He nodded. "Two little boys. Whose pictures are prominently displayed on her desk. But you didn't notice them. Just like you didn't notice the absence of a fragrance or the gold band shining on her finger."

Mortified, she lowered herself to a chair. "I'm a lousy detective, aren't I?"

"The worst."

Maggie winced. Blond hair. Big breasts. Luke's bed. Her evaluation had stemmed from a catty scratch of jealousy. Which was something she had never experienced before.

"I'm sorry," she managed to say, thinking she owed Carol an apology as well.

He shrugged, and they both drifted into what she considered uncompanionable silence. She certainly wasn't doing a very good job of making Lucas Starwind smile. And that was something she would have to remedy. Maybe not today, but soon.

"So, am I going to work with you here at the office?" she asked.

"Don't you have finals this week?"

"I can come by afterward."

"Then you're welcome to use Tom's old office."

"Thank you." She wished this wasn't a baby-sitting effort on his part. Maggie preferred to earn her keep. But that rarely happened. No one gave her any credit, not even her own family.

Thoughtful, she studied her companion. Sooner or later the brooding detective would figure her out correctly. He would see her for who she really was. Wouldn't he?

"What is your type, Luke?"

He blinked. "What?"

"Your type of woman," she clarified.

He drilled her gaze, and their eyes clashed. Her pulse skipped like a stone, and she decided they were perfect for each other. No other man challenged her the way he did. Or made her care so deeply. She needed him as much as he needed her.

"I don't have one," he responded steadily.

Oh, yes you do, she thought. And I'm her.

Detective work, Maggie decided, didn't live up to its TV image. They weren't tailing bad guys, lurking in trench coats on a shadowy street corner or dodging bullets in a high-speed car chase. Instead they faced mounds and mounds of paperwork.

It was Saturday afternoon, a light snow blanketed the

ground, and she and Luke were holed up in his town house, poring over files, cataloging information about individuals and corporations known to have even the slightest association with the Kelly crime family. Luke was searching for someone, anyone, who might have an interest in the missing CDs. Locating a potential buyer, he claimed, could lead them to the Altarian traitor.

"Aren't the files encoded?" she asked. "How can they sell encrypted CDs?"

"The encryption can be broken. Not easily, but it can be done. The Kellys tried to get the encryption program from the Connelly Corporation computer system, but they failed."

"Does the Chicago P.D. know about the cancer virus? Didn't Rafe have to tell them when they arrested the Kellys?"

"No," Luke responded. "He didn't have to tell them. He led the police to believe the Kellys stole valuable data relating to the Institute's purpose—a cure for cancer. The fewer people who know the truth, the better. We don't need an international scandal on our hands."

Maggie nodded, then studied Luke's profile. He sat beside her in his home office, tapping away on a laptop.

"Why don't you send some undercover agents to Altaria?" she suggested. "There must be someone you can trust to keep an eye on things over there."

"I've already done that. I've got some former military men on it. Guys I served with. I planted someone at the castle and at the Rosemere Institute. And I've got another man watching the textile mill."

Maggie thought about the CD that had been accidentally forwarded to her. If the syndicate had discovered their error, her life would have been threatened. She understood how dangerous this case was, and she appreciated Luke for his skill and dedication. "Sounds like you've got everything under control."

"I'm trying to stay one step ahead of the game." He rolled his shoulders and nearly bumped her arm. The desk they shared was barely big enough for two. "But unfortunately the men I sent to Altaria haven't uncovered any leads."

He stopped typing and turned to look at her. His face was close enough to see the detail of his skin, the faded scar near his left eyebrow, the slight shadow of beard stubble. She was tempted to touch him, to run her fingers over those stunning cheekbones. As an artist, she was fascinated by his features. As a woman, she couldn't help but admire his rugged appeal.

"I need to tell you something about Prince Marc," he said.

Instantly Maggie braced herself. There was always something to be said about her uncle. Prince Marc had been a charming, dashing playboy. Considered one of Europe's most eligible bachelors, he'd juggled lovers the way he'd juggled his finances. He'd also fathered a daughter out of wedlock, but unfortunately hadn't proved to be much of a parent.

Nonetheless, Maggie had loved him. He was still her blood.

"Prince Marc had an association with the Kellys," Luke announced.

For a moment she only stared. Her uncle, the free-spirited prince, had been involved in organized crime? A man the media often compared her to?

Her stomach knotted. "In what capacity?"

"He owed the Kellys money. His gambling debts were eating him alive." Luke sighed. "We believe he was part of the smuggling scam, Maggie."

"That can't be." She jumped to her feet, paced a little. "He was murdered in the same speedboat accident as the king. They were together."

"Think about it. Prince Marc hadn't originally planned on being on the boat that day. He'd gone with his father at the last minute. Therefore, he wasn't the intended hit."

She stopped pacing. "So what's your theory?"

"Prince Marc needed to get out from under his gambling debts, so he formed an alliance with the Kellys. In fact, I think they killed King Thomas because they wanted Marc, a man they could easily manipulate, to take the throne."

"But they accidentally killed Marc instead." Which meant that her uncle hadn't known that the Kellys meant to murder the king. But someone at the castle did. Someone who had kept the Kellys informed of the king's whereabouts, someone who had sent a hit man to the dock to tamper with the boat.

She blinked, fighting tears she wouldn't dare cry in front of Luke. King Thomas had been her salvation, the only person in the world who truly understood her, who knew how diligently she struggled to earn her family's respect.

Frivolous Maggie. The temperamental artist. The spoiled Connelly baby. No one seemed to care that she was earning a double major in business and art.

Damn it, she thought, missing the king's keep-your-chin-up encouragement.

She worked as hard as she played. Harder, she decided, staring at the stack of paperwork on Luke's desk. She'd studied for finals in the midst of all this. And now she had to contend with images of her traitorous uncle.

Weary, she shifted her gaze to Luke. He rubbed his temples and went back to the laptop. She could see the strain on his face, the headache forming beneath his brow. He worked hard, too. Only he never gave himself a break. He never had any fun.

Maggie gazed out the window, at the perfectly beautiful winter day, at the snow Luke had predicted. "Let's get out of here," she said. "Let's ditch these files and go build a snowman." With a big, carrot nose, she thought, and a smile made of twigs.

He gave her an incredulous look. "I'm not going to waste valuable time goofing around. I've got a schedule to keep."

Not easily deterred, she moved away from the window and devised a brilliant plan. One way or another, she and Luke were going to play in the snow. "How about lunch? You have to eat, don't you?"

He shrugged. "I suppose."

"Then let's go out for lunch."

He agreed, albeit reluctantly, to take an hour off for a meal. Precisely one hour, he stipulated, sounding like the ex-military man that he was.

Maggie buttoned her coat and slipped on a pair of kidskin gloves. Luke reached for a leather jacket, then pulled a hand through his hair, smoothing a few stray locks into place.

Dressed for the weather, they exited the house, and he locked the door behind them. As he turned and strode toward his SUV, Maggie knelt to the ground. And then, as quickly as her hands would allow, she formed a snowball.

Rising, she took aim and heaved it. The snowball sailed through the air and hit Luke in the back, dissolving into a white burst as it made the connection.

He spun around, and Maggie swallowed her triumphant smile.

The first thing out of his mouth was a curse. The second was a complaint.

"Damn it. I dropped the keys." He kicked the fresh powder. "And now I've got to dig through this mess to find them."

She offered to help, thinking he had to be the biggest grump on earth. The snow wasn't that deep. How far could the keys have gone?

Luke put on his gloves, and they sifted through the powder, neither uttering a single word. Disgusted, Maggie turned her back and searched in another spot.

And that was when a huge clump of snow fell right on top of her head.

Stunned, she wiped away the moisture dripping onto her face. The sound of keys jangling caught her attention. She turned and saw Luke standing above her, a dastardly grin on his handsome face.

"You've been had," he said, shoving the keys back into his pocket, where they had apparently been all along.

"Oh, yeah?" Maggie wanted to hug him breathless, but instead she packed another snowball, making her intentions clear.

Instantly he ducked for cover, choosing a battle station on the other side of the car.

The war was on.

# Three

Maggie peered around the tailgate, but saw neither hide nor hair of Luke. Her hide and her hair, on the other hand, were drenched. He'd outsmarted every maneuver she'd tried so far.

Where was he? Under the vehicle? Wedged against a tire? She had an arsenal of snowballs ready to go, just waiting for him to show his sneaky face.

Determined to win, she opted for another tactic. The damsel-in-distress ploy ought to work. A macho guy like Luke should fall for that. Her brothers usually did. Men, she thought with a feminine gleam in her eye, were natural-born suckers.

"It's time to quit," she called out. "I'm freezing, and I want to go inside."

She continued to peer around the SUV, armed with a carefully packed snowball. Testing the weight in her hand, she smiled. It was, in her estimation, a solid sphere of ice.

"Luke!" she called out again. "This isn't funny. I'm exhausted, and you have the keys to the house."

"Nice try, princess," a deep voice said from behind her.

She turned and saw Luke aiming a bucket of snow at her. Still clutching her ammunition, Maggie let out a girlish squeal and took off running.

Bucket in hand, he chased her.

They danced around a tree, back and forth, like foolhardy kids. There was no time to think, to stop and admire the husky sound of his laughter or the way his dark eyes crinkled when he smiled.

She was having too much fun to analyze the moment. And so was he.

Maggie tossed the snowball at him. It sailed past his shoulder and splattered against the tree. White flecks glistened against the bark, the edges icy and sharp.

Luke moved toward her, slowly, teasing her with the bucket, giving her a chance to turn tail and run.

Instead, she did something to catch him off guard. She charged him, full force, intending to knock the ammunition out of his hand.

The bucket went flying, and so did she.

When she tackled Luke, he lost his footing and took her down with him. Arms and legs tangling, they rolled, like snowmen toppling to the ground. Maggie's breath rushed out in gasping pants.

He ended up on top, his weight sinking into hers, powdery flakes fluttering around them. He wiped the snow from her face, his gloved hand brushing gently.

"Are you all right?" he asked.

"Yes." She touched his face, too. Then ran her hands through his hair, combing the dampness away from his forehead.

Their eyes met and held. Without speaking, they stared at each other, their emotions frozen in time.

It could have been a dream, she thought. A fantasy drifting on the edge of reality. If she looked past him, she would see a rainbow, an arc of gems shooting across the December sky.

He whispered her name, and the jewels grew brighter—diamonds, rubies, emeralds falling from the heavens.

Maggie and Luke moved at the same time, in the same instant. She drew him closer, and he lowered his head.

The wind whipped over them, and they kissed.

Desperately.

He sucked on her bottom lip, caught it with his teeth. The imaginary rainbow blurred her vision, sending sparks over every inch of her skin.

Thrusting his tongue into her mouth, he clasped both of her hands in his, taking possession, staking his claim.

Maggie wanted to possess him, too. To make Lucas Starwind hers. To take everything that he was and wrap him tightly around her heart. He tasted like heat and snow, like ice dripping over a long, dark, dangerous candle, the wick igniting into a flame.

A gust of cold air sliced over them, but neither noticed.

They kissed, again and again, questing for more—nibbling, licking, absorbing every thrilling sensation.

Luke released her hands, and they went after each other. She unzipped his jacket; he unbuttoned her coat. He slid his hips between her legs; she bumped his fly.

They were making love in their minds, mimicking the rocking, rubbing motion with their bodies. Maggie clung to the man in her arms. This was, she thought, the most wildly erotic moment of her life.

Until a neighbor's car door slammed.

Luke shot up like an arrow. Then he cursed, clearly chastising himself for losing control.

"You're going to catch pneumonia," he said, fumbling to rebutton her coat.

Maggie didn't think that was possible. She was as warm as sealing wax. And she wanted to melt all over him. But she knew the opportunity had passed.

Luke was Luke again. Tough. Tense. Guarded.

"Come on." He reached for her hand and drew her to her feet. "You need a hot bath. And something to eat."

She needed to kiss him again, she thought, but she didn't argue. She rather liked being protected by the big, tough detective. He actually swept her into his arms and carried her to the front door.

Luke Starwind was dark and dangerous. Exciting. When she'd slid her hands over those sturdy muscles, she'd felt the holstered gun he kept clipped to the back of his belt. It seemed, somehow, like an extension of his body, like part of the man he was. The Cherokee warrior, she thought. The former Green Beret.

He fumbled with his keys. Maggie put her head on his shoulder as he stepped over the threshold. Feeling delightfully feminine, she pressed her lips to his neck and smiled when he sucked in a tight breath.

He deposited her in the master bathroom, where a sunken tub awaited—an enormous, dark-green enclosure surrounded by rugged antiques. She caught a glimpse of his four-poster bed and tried not to swoon. His house was growing on her.

Feeling as boneless as a rag doll, she allowed him to remove her coat.

"Will you start a fire?" she asked, wishing he would undress her completely.

He didn't, of course. Her coat was as far as he went.

"Yeah. I'll heat up a can of soup, too."

"Thank you." She pressed a delicate kiss to his cheek and felt him shiver. "You're cold, too," she remarked.

"I'll dry off in the other bathroom."

He backed away and thrust a towel at her. Maggie accepted the offer, thinking how incredible using his soap was going to be.

She eyed a bulk of terry cloth hanging behind the door. "Can I wear your robe, Luke?"

"What?" He followed her gaze, a frown furrowing his brow. "No," he responded, his voice strained. "I'll get you a pair of sweats."

"All right." She shrugged as if his robe held little consequence. When he was gone, she decided, she would slip it on. Just for a second. Just to feel it caress her bare skin.

Luke washed his face, towel-dried his hair and slipped on a T-shirt and a pair of old, comfortable jeans. Next he built a fire and headed to the kitchen to heat some soup. He tried not to think about Maggie soaking in his tub, sleek and naked, her skin warm and flushed.

He'd behaved like a kid, goofing around in the snow, letting Maggie pull him under her playful spell. But worse yet, he'd lost complete control, kissing her until his body ached with a hot, feverish lust.

Dumping the soup into a pot, he added the required amount of water and reminded himself that Maggie was off-limits. Way off-limits. The last thing he needed was to get involved with a woman practically young enough to be his daughter. Luke rarely took a lover, and when he did, he made damn sure his partner was mature enough to handle a sex-only relationship.

Then again, he doubted free-spirited, frolic-in-the-snow Maggie was looking for a lifelong commitment. He'd seen

pictures of her in the society pages with her former beau—
a twenty-something Italian race-car driver. A live-for-the-
minute European playboy.

Which made Luke wonder what Maggie saw in a crusty,
pushing-forty P.I. like himself.

"Luke?"

Squaring his shoulders, he turned to acknowledge her.
She stood in the doorway, her freshly washed hair combed
away from her face, her blue-green eyes sparkling.

Luke squinted through a frown. What spell was she about
to cast? And how could a woman look downright breathtaking in a pair of standard-gray sweats?

His sweats, he reminded himself.

"That smells good," she said.

"It's ready." He reached for a cup. "Do you want crackers?"

When she nodded, he pulled a box from the cupboard.

Minutes later, they sat in front of the fire, sipping tomato
soup. Flames danced in the stone hearth, warming the room
with a flickering gold light. Maggie spooned up soggy
crackers and watched him through her magical eyes.

"Tell me what you said, Luke."

Confused, he shook his head. "What are you talking
about?"

"When we danced at Rafe's wedding reception. You said
something to me. Something in Cherokee."

He fought to steady his pulse. *A qua da nv do. My heart.*
He would never forget those words or the moment he'd said
them. "I don't recall saying anything."

She scooted closer. They sat cross-legged on a wool rug,
just a few feet apart. Her hair had begun to dry, and the fire
bathed her in an amber glow. She looked young and soft,
her skin scrubbed free of cosmetics.

"But you have to remember. They sounded so pretty."

She struggled to repeat the phrase. "I can hear them in my head, but I can't pronounce them."

He could hear them in his head, too. Could feel them pounding in his chest. "I'm sorry. I just don't remember."

Maggie glanced down at her soup, and Luke frowned. He knew his lie had hurt her feelings.

But how could he tell her that for an instant in time she had actually become part of his heart? He didn't understand why he'd felt such a tender, almost haunting connection to her. And he never wanted to go through something like that again. She had no right to touch his heart, not even for an instant.

"I bought a book about the Cherokee," she said. "I curled up one night in bed and read about your ancestors. It's a fascinating culture. So beautiful. So noble."

He placed his empty cup on the mantel. "I'm only half Cherokee." And he was neither noble nor beautiful.

Maggie watched him, and he felt self-conscious under her scrutiny. He knew she was studying his features—eyes lined with well-earned crow's-feet, a nose that had been broken on the worst day of his life, a jaw as hard as granite.

"It's still part of your legacy, Luke."

"So you bought that book because of me?"

"Yes." She tilted her head, her hair falling to one side. "The chapters about the Trail of Tears made me cry. All those people being forced to leave their homeland, starving and freezing and dying on the way."

Something inside him nearly shattered. In some small way, she had cried for him. "I'm Eastern Band Cherokee. My ancestors hid in the Great Smoky Mountains in order to escape removal." Men, women and children, he thought, whom the army had pledged to hunt down like wild dogs. But he supposed Maggie had read about that, too.

"Where do your parents live?" she asked, her voice still filled with emotion.

"My dad's dead."

"Oh. I'm sorry." She glanced at the fire. For a moment, they both fell silent.

He knew she was going to ask him about his mom next. Somehow, that hurt even more. His mother's sheltered, fragile lifestyle was a constant reminder of the pain his family had endured.

"Is your mom close by?"

"No. She lives in the country." In the same house where he grew up. The same quiet little farmhouse where the kidnapping had taken place.

"What does she look like?"

Like a woman who'd lost everything that mattered, he thought. "She's fair-skinned, and her hair is sort of a silvery-gray. It used to be brown."

Maggie smiled. "I bet she's pretty."

He swallowed the lump in his throat. "My dad thought so."

She finished her soup, placing the empty cup beside his. Uncrossing her legs, she drew her knees up. Her face was a wash of golden hues from the fire, her eyes a watery shade of blue. He wondered how many times a day they changed color.

"Do you have any brothers and sisters?"

The question hit him like a fist. He clenched his stomach muscles to sustain the impact. "No," he said as his heart went numb.

Not anymore.

The next day Maggie awakened to the sound of a screeching telephone. She pushed through the mosquito netting that draped her brass bed and squinted at the clock.

Groaning, she nearly knocked the phone off the dresser. Who called at five o'clock on a Sunday morning? On her private line, no less?

"This better be important," she said into the receiver.

"It's Luke."

A shiver shot straight up her spine. She'd worn Luke's sweats home yesterday. And needing to feel connected to him throughout the night, she'd also slept in them. The fleece-lined fabric brushed her skin like warm, masculine hands.

His hands, she thought as she heard him breathe into the phone.

"What's going on?" she asked, trying to sound professional. Clearly an early-morning call from Luke related to business. As far as she knew, he didn't make personal calls, at least not to her. "Did you get a breakthrough in the case?"

"No. But I picked up your bodyguard at the airport, and we're on our way over. So get out of bed and put on some coffee. He's moving into your place today."

Maggie shot up like a rocket, nearly tearing the mosquito net from the ceiling. Her bodyguard? "You're not going to sic some big, burly brute on me." In spite of her family's wealth and celebrity, she did her damnedest to live a normal life. Which meant no maids, chauffeurs, cooks or bodyguards. She cleaned her own house, drove her own car and fixed her own meals. Granted, her house was a two-million-dollar loft, her car was a Lamborghini and she purchased her food from a gourmet market, but she was still self-sufficient.

"I have the most sophisticated alarm system ever devised," she went on. "I don't need a bodyguard."

"Too bad. Your brother already agreed with me that Bruno should move in with you until this case is solved."

Her brother. She should have known Rafe had a hand in this. He and Luke seemed to think she was some sort of helpless female. "What kind of stupid name is Bruno?" She pictured a no-neck, muscle-bound Gestapo guarding her front door.

"I've seen Bruno in action, Maggie. And I'm not changing my mind about hiring him. We'll see you in fifteen minutes. And if you don't let us in, we'll break in, proving to you how useless that alarm system of yours is. You don't even have a security camera."

She fumed. She raged. She paced the floor with darts in her eyes. Luke was going to suffer for this. And so was Bruno. She would make the bodyguard's assignment a living hell, ditching him every chance she got.

Maggie washed her face and brushed her teeth, but she didn't change her clothes or put on a pot of coffee. If Luke wanted freshly brewed coffee, she would gladly kick his rear all the way to Colombia, where he could pick his own damn beans.

Luke and Bruno arrived in the estimated fifteen minutes. Luke buzzed her, and she pressed the remote and opened the security gate at the entrance of an underground parking structure, then shot out of the loft and waited at the indoor elevator that led to her living quarters. The industrial building had been remodeled to suit her needs, but she'd kept the old-fashioned, gated elevator because she liked its vintage style.

She heard the elevator ascending, and when it stopped, her jaw went slack.

Luke's companion was on a leash.

Bruno, it appeared, was a dog. The most powerful-looking creature she'd ever seen.

"That's my bodyguard?"

Luke and the beast exited the elevator. "He's not what you expected?"

"You know damn well I thought Bruno was a man."

The dog didn't react to his name or to the sharp tone in Maggie's voice. Luke, however, had the gall to arch an eyebrow at her. Apparently he didn't care that he'd ruffled her feathers at five in the morning.

"Now why would I hire another man to move in with you? Hell, Maggie, I could have done that myself."

Then why didn't you? she wanted to ask. Why didn't you become my personal bodyguard? My roommate?

Because he'd given the job to Bruno.

She shifted her attention to the dog. He stood about thirty inches tall and probably weighed a good two hundred pounds. Heavy-boned, with a fawn-colored body, his muzzle bore a dark mask.

"What is he?" she asked.

"An English mastiff."

She studied Bruno's serious face. She doubted the big dog would ever roll over with his paws in the air, begging for a belly rub. Maggie patted his head, deciding she would have to loosen him up. Teach him to do dumb doggie things. The poor fellow behaved like an armed guard with a rifle up his butt.

"There's no point in standing in the hall," she said, inviting Luke and Bruno into her home.

The first thing Luke noticed about Maggie's loft was the skylight. Dawn blazed from the ceiling, sending lavender streaks throughout the room.

Her decor was bold, yet decidedly female. A variety of textures, ranging from watered silk to carved-and-painted woods, made up the living room. Leafy plants grew from clay pots and scented candles dripped melted wax. The oak floors were whitewashed, and one entire wall was covered with a mural of mermaids rising from the sea.

Instinctively, he knew Maggie had painted it. He felt the enchantment flow over him like a cool, sensual wine.

Moonlight and mermaids. He turned to look at her, and saw that she watched Bruno instead.

Luke let out the breath he'd been holding, shrugging off the sexual pull.

"Is Bruno one of those German-trained dogs?" she asked. "The ones that compete in international trials?"

"You mean Schutzhund? No, he's not." Luke had decided a Schutzhund-titled dog wasn't what Maggie needed. "Bruno is familiar with the perils of everyday life."

Maggie met his gaze. He moved away from the mermaids and focused on familiarizing her with the dog. "I'll teach you his verbal commands. He'll respond to you without a problem." A business associate of Luke's supplied dogs to police and military canine units, as well as private citizens. "Bruno has been trained to protect women. He's stopped kidnappers and stalkers right in their tracks. He'll keep you safe."

She regarded the mastiff with a curious expression. "Does he fetch?"

For a moment Luke could only stare. He'd provided her with one of the most expensive, sought-after protection dogs in the world, an animal that adapted to a new environment without the slightest hesitation, and she wanted to know if he retrieved tennis balls?

"Bruno is a bodyguard, Maggie."

She ran a manicured hand through her night-tousled hair. Luke had no idea why she was still wearing his sweats, but he thought she looked as wildly erotic as one of the naked mermaids.

"Can he shake? Or high-five?"

"He's a personal protection dog," Luke reiterated, clenching his jaw.

"I'm well aware of that. But I don't see anything wrong with teaching him to do a few doggie tricks. He deserves to have a little fun."

Luke caught Maggie's gaze and saw a spark of mischief brewing in those muse-magic eyes. "Don't you dare ruin this animal." He envisioned her encouraging a two-hundred-pound, muscle-bound mastiff to sit up and beg for table scraps. "I don't want you distracting him from his job."

"I hope he knows how to kiss. All dogs should kiss."

Good Lord. Luke glanced at Bruno. The canine sat, watching his new mistress. The dog had been taught *not* to lick people's faces, which made perfect sense to Luke. "I'm pretty sure he drools. Will that do?"

She smiled like a siren. "It's a start."

Maggie brewed a pot of coffee, and they spent the next three hours going over Bruno's commands. Luke offered to come by every night after work to help her exercise the big dog.

Maggie seemed pleased, and he warned himself not to get too attached. No hugs, no kisses, no foreplay in the snow.

"Are you and Bruno ready for the grand tour?" she asked.

"Sure."

The loft was six thousand square feet of artistic inspiration. Bruno had plenty of corners and shadowy areas to explore.

They went from room to room, and Luke found Maggie's home strangely alluring, particularly her bedroom.

A mosquito net draped her unmade bed. He pictured her sleeping there, her hair fanned across satin pillows. The color scheme was warm and inviting, the textures rich and smooth.

Bruno sniffed, taking in every scent. Luke could smell a heady blend of candles, incense and French perfume.

In that intoxicating instant he wanted to break his self-imposed rule and kiss her. Pull her onto the bed and run his hands all over that long, luscious body.

"Come on," she said. "I want you to see my work."

He drew a rough breath and followed Maggie to her studio.

The walls, he noticed, were splattered with paint, as if she'd attacked them in an emotional rage. Art supplies littered the floor. Canvases were stacked everywhere. Floor-to-ceiling windows illuminated the enormous room.

Her work reflected her moods. A life-size watercolor of a wood nymph was blatantly sexual, whereas the portrait of a baby dragon projected sheer whimsy. Each piece was inspired from fantasy or folklore, portraying mythical creatures.

He wondered if she'd ever painted a muse. He decided not to ask.

"This is my latest series," she said, displaying three canvases for him to view.

He studied the paintings, analyzing each one before he moved on to the next. The first one depicted a wide-eyed little boy peering at a leprechaun. The second was a fair-haired toddler with a fairy on her shoulder.

And the third painting had Luke nearly dropping to his knees.

His breath shot out, and he curled his fingers to keep from touching the beautiful, haunting, heartbreaking image.

"She could be my sister," he whispered. The profile of a young girl filled the canvas, jet-black hair blowing around her face, a tiny winged horse fluttering from her outstretched hands.

He turned to look at Maggie, who watched him through silent eyes. "How did you know?" he asked, his voice breaking. "How did you know that we buried her with her favorite toy?"

A tiny winged horse.

# Four

"**Y**our sister?" Maggie placed her hand on his shoulder. "Oh, God, Luke. I didn't know you had a sister. Or that she died."

Then she couldn't have known about the winged horse, he thought. Her painting was simply a coincidence or an omen or a connection that had no logical explanation.

Luke drew a breath. "Can we go outside? I need some air."

"Of course."

They took the elevator to the roof where Maggie had created a patio. A barbecue pit was formed of stone, with chairs gathered around it. Snow melted on the ground, and the wind blew mildly.

Luke stood near the rail and scanned the sweeping lake-front view. He could see the Art Institute and the glass-and-steel structure of the Connelly Tower. He assumed Maggie enjoyed the city traffic and the sound of the el train.

He turned to look at her. Bruno remained by her side, already protecting her. That gave Luke a measure of relief.

"Will you tell me about your sister?" she asked.

He knew he couldn't hide the truth. Not now. Not after his reaction to Maggie's painting. "Her name was Gwen. I used to call her Lady Guinevere." He gazed at the fire pit, his heart clenching with the memory. "She loved legends and fables and pretty fairy tales."

"What happened to her, Luke?"

"She was murdered," he responded. "And it was my fault."

Maggie reached for a chair, her breath catching. "You can't mean that."

"When my father was dying, he asked me to protect her." To be the man of the house, he recalled. The young warrior. "But I didn't keep her safe. I let a stranger come into our home. He kidnapped Gwen, and then he killed her."

Maggie's face paled, and Luke sat across from her, preparing to tell her everything, every detail that made him ache.

"I was twelve and Gwen was eight. Our father had died three months before, and Mom was visiting a friend in the neighborhood. She had been grieving very deeply, and this was the first time she'd socialized since his death."

As Luke spoke, his mind drifted back in time, back to the day that had destroyed what was left of his family.

Gwen, dressed in pink shorts and a white top, had played on the porch. She'd made a castle out of a cardboard box for the king and queen she'd cut out from a coloring book. The winged horse sat next to her, waiting to soar across the sky. The air was warm, the sun setting behind the hills in a reddish-gold hue.

Luke watched his sister from the screen door, then went

into the kitchen to toss a couple of TV dinners in the oven. He chose fried chicken for Gwen and meat loaf for himself. The mashed potatoes always tasted fake, but his mother wouldn't be back in time to cook what he considered real food.

But that didn't matter, he thought, because he was glad she'd gone out. She still cried a lot, and he never knew what to say to make her feel better. Luke missed his dad, too.

Ten minutes later, he heard Gwen talking to someone on the porch. Luke went to the door and saw a fair-haired man crouching next to his sister.

"His car broke down in front of our house," she said as the man raised to his full height. "I told him nobody was home but you and me."

The quiet stranger was tall, with narrow shoulders, skinny arms and lean hips. His skin was pale, his eyebrows as blond as his hair. Luke thought the guy looked frailer than a man should.

Gwen got up and came toward the screen door. "Can he use our phone? He needs to call a tow truck."

"Sure." Luke figured the guy didn't know how to fix his own car. He didn't seem like the mechanic type. Plus, it was obvious he'd gotten lost and was too embarrassed to admit it. Their old farmhouse was on a dirt road, miles from the main highway.

"I really appreciate this," the man said.

"No problem." They went inside, and Luke showed him to the den. He pointed to the phone, which sat on a cluttered rolltop desk. The Yellow Pages were next to it. "Try Harvey's Garage. I'm pretty sure they have a tow truck."

"Thank you. I will."

Luke turned away to see what Gwen was doing. She'd gone into the kitchen, and he figured she was going to bug him about dinner, which would seem rude in front of the stranger.

Within seconds, a burst of pain exploded in the back of Luke's head. He knew instantly the man had hit him with a heavy object, possibly even a gun. He tried to call Gwen's name, to tell her to run, but the stranger hit him again. And this time, the force knocked him down.

His face crashed against the corner of a table. And then he felt the sickening warmth of blood running from his nose and into his mouth.

His sister dashed into the room. He saw her feet, then heard her panicked scream—just once before the world went black.

For a moment, Maggie and Luke remained silent, the wind stirring around them.

His eyes were dark and filled with pain. She longed to touch him, to bring him close to her heart.

He met her gaze, and she thought about how much he was hurting. She couldn't imagine the horror of losing a sibling. Maggie had grown up with a houseful of brothers and sisters, and she adored them all. "I'm sorry," she said.

"Two days later, a farmer found Gwen's body in an empty field. The weeds were so high, he nearly tripped over her." Luke's voice broke. "The lot was for sale, and he was looking for a place to buy. But he found my sister instead."

Maggie's eyes filled with tears. She pictured the little girl she had painted, dumped in a field of weeds. She had no explanation why her painting resembled Luke's sister. The dark-haired child and the tiny winged horse had stemmed from her imagination.

"The things that bastard did to her. And I trusted him. I let him into our home."

"You couldn't have known he was dangerous. Or that he preyed on children."

Luke released an audible breath. "The police caught him, but that didn't bring closure. Not to me. When I testified at his trial, I sat there envisioning what he did to Gwen and thinking how much I wanted to kill him."

"Is he still in prison?"

"Yes. He was up for parole in September. I attended the hearing. I wanted to make damn sure that bastard wasn't paroled. There's no such thing as a rehabilitated pedophile." He gazed out at the city. "But no matter what I do to make things right, I still feel like I have blood on my hands."

"What happened to Gwen wasn't your fault, Luke."

"Yes, it was. And so was Tom Reynolds's murder."

"Your partner?" Maggie tried to comprehend his logic. "You were out of town when Tom was killed."

"That's exactly my point. I was at the parole hearing while my partner was being ambushed. If I had been here, I could have given Tom the backup he needed."

So much unwarranted guilt, she thought. So much pain. Lucas Starwind wanted to save the world all by himself. "You're one man. There's only so much you can do."

"There's no way you can understand how I feel. You haven't lived my life."

But she wanted to. She wanted to live inside him, to be part of him. She looked into his eyes and saw the emptiness she wished she could fill.

Placing her hands on her lap, she felt them tremble. Heaven help her. She knew what was happening.

Maggie was falling desperately in love, losing her heart to a reclusive, tortured man.

"Are you cold?" he asked.

She blinked. "What?"

"You're shivering."

Because I'm in love, she thought. And afraid I won't be able to keep you. Their paths had crossed, but Luke seemed determined to remain alone, to punish himself for tragedies that were beyond his control.

Maggie glanced at the melting snow, at the slush around her feet. How could she help him? How could she bandage wounds that refused to heal?

"Come on," he said. "We'll go inside and warm up."

Once they were back in the loft, Luke poured two cups of coffee. He doctored hers with sugar and cream, and she found the strength to smile. Already he knew she liked her coffee light and sweet.

Bruno remained by Maggie's side. She pictured all of them—man, woman and dog—living together, happy and content.

Luke frowned, and she realized how hopeful her fantasy was. Luke was investigating her family's case, and Bruno was her temporary bodyguard. They weren't exactly a family.

"I can't stay too much longer," he said.

"It's Sunday. Don't tell me you're working today."

"No."

"Then what are you going to do?" she asked, wishing he wasn't so evasive. He'd told her about his sister, but she knew her painting had stunned him into revealing that part of his life.

He sipped his coffee. "There's just someplace I have to be."

"Where?" she pressed.

"Nothing that concerns you."

Maggie sighed. Luke's dismissal hurt. Everything he did concerned her. He was the man she loved, the dark-eyed warrior who had stolen his way into her dreams. And Maggie believed in pursuing dreams. "Why won't you tell me?"

"Because it's personal."

How personal? she wondered, suddenly suspicious. Was he seeing another woman?

Of course he was. What other explanation could there be? Men weren't always the most honest creatures. Even her father had stepped out on her mother. Although it had happened over thirty years ago, and her parents had been separated at the time, the mighty Grant Connelly had still cheated. Maggie's half brother Seth was proof of the affair.

"I can't believe you're doing this to me."

Leaning against the counter, Luke continued to sip his drink. "Doing what?"

"Cheating," she snapped. "Dating someone else."

He arched an eyebrow. "Since when have you and I been an item?"

She narrowed her eyes, deciding she would tear his lover's hair out. Strand by strand. "You kissed me."

"That's not exactly a commitment."

Hurt and anger rose, brimming like a volcano. "Are you seeing someone or not?"

He almost smiled, telling her that he found her envy amusing. That ticked her off even more. Luke treated her like a crush-crazed teenager, like a girl who wrote his name all over her notebook, doodling hearts around it. True, she thrived on the lure of romance, but that didn't make her immature.

"Damn it. Give me a straight answer."

He cocked his head. "Your eyes change color. Did you know that? They're blue when you're sad or worried. And green when you're spewing that Irish temper of yours."

"Don't change the subject," she retorted, even though she was flattered that he'd looked that closely at her eyes.

His near smile turned to a frown. "Okay. You want the

truth. Here it is. I visit my mom on Sundays. I drive out to the country because she won't come to the city.''

So the "other woman" was his mother. Now Maggie felt foolish. But people in love were allowed to act foolish, weren't they? "Doesn't she like the city?"

"She's agoraphobic."

Maggie stepped forward. "She's afraid of open spaces?"

"That's the literal explanation, but it's more complicated than that. She's afraid of going places that will cause her to panic, places away from home."

"Why?" was all she could think to ask.

"I'm not sure. But I think it's because she wasn't home when Gwen was kidnapped. So her way of feeling safe is to stay home, to be where she thinks she should have been that day."

Maggie drew a breath. Did Luke blame himself for his mother's phobia? Did it make him feel even more responsible for his sister's death? There was so much hurt in his family, so many sad, empty hearts. "Is she under a doctor's care?"

He shook his head. "When it first happened, I didn't know that she was having anxiety attacks. All I knew was that Gwen was dead, and my mom didn't want to leave the house anymore. She didn't tell me that she was panicking in public situations." He set his empty cup in the sink. "Once I learned what agoraphobia was, it was too late. She refused to discuss her condition with me."

"Does she go out at all now?"

"A little bit, but never very far. She has a live-in housekeeper. Someone who shops and runs errands for her."

Someone, Maggie suspected, Luke had hired.

He checked his watch. "I better hit the road. It's a long drive." He reached down and patted the dog, then looked up at Maggie. "Don't go anywhere without Bruno."

"I won't." She walked Luke to the door. He turned, and they stared at each other, but only for a moment.

When he entered the elevator, she watched him depart, wishing she had the courage to tell him that she loved him.

Maggie headed for her studio, Bruno on her heels. She gazed around the room and locked onto the painting she'd yet to title—the watercolor of the little girl who looked like Gwen.

How did you know? Luke had asked her. How did you know that we buried her with her favorite toy?

Maggie studied the tiny horse fluttering from the child's outstretched hands. She remembered painting it, feeling each delicate wing come to life.

"Are you Gwen?" she asked the painting, tears filling her eyes. "Did you slip into my subconscious because you wanted me to fall in love with your brother? To touch his heart? To heal his soul?"

Maggie wanted that, too. But she didn't know how to reach Luke, how to prove that they belonged together.

Bruno cocked his big, fawn-colored head, and Maggie smiled through her tears. "I'll think of something," she said to the dog, the child and the tiny winged horse. "I'll find a way to make Luke mine."

On Monday morning, Maggie entered Rey-Star Investigations attired in an emerald-green suit and gold jewelry. Bruno, the dog she'd come to think of as a big, furry accessory, strode beside her. She'd bought him a jeweled collar that made him look less like a bodyguard and more like a pampered pet.

Carol glanced up from her computer and smiled. "Hello, Ms. Connelly. Oh, my, who's your handsome friend?"

Maggie introduced Bruno and explained that Luke had

gotten security clearance for the mastiff to accompany her to the office.

"May I pet him?"

"Of course."

Carol came around her desk to fuss over the dog.

Bruno gazed up at the buxom blonde and drooled.

When Maggie entered Luke's office, she was smiling. He, on the other hand, sat at his desk, wearing his usual scowl.

She removed her overcoat. "Good morning."

He lifted his gaze and looked her over, those dark eyes traveling from the top of her head to the tips of her Italian pumps. "You're late," he said.

"Bruno wanted to sleep in."

"Very funny." He glanced at the dog, then back at her. "In the future, I expect both of you to be on time. Now go to your own office and get to work."

She thought about the files on her desk, the drudge of paperwork. "I'm having a cup of tea first." After releasing Bruno from his leash, she walked over to the bar and pressed the red spigot, filling her cup with hot water. Digging through an assortment of teas Luke kept on hand for his clients, she chose chamomile, hoping it would soothe her nerves. She'd stayed up most of the night plotting her strategy. And this morning she intended to enforce a carefully developed plan.

She sweetened her tea, then took a seat and crossed her legs. Eyeing Luke over the rim of her cup, she studied him. He looked like what he was—a former Green Beret, mature, highly skilled, superbly trained. Not that she didn't admire his military background or the fact that it made him a more effective P.I., but it also made him a difficult civilian to deal with.

Luke was an expert at unconventional warfare. Which was why she had devised a challenge with which to bait him. All is fair in love and war, she thought, placing her cup on the edge of his glossy black desk.

"I'd like to make a deal with you," she said.

He released an impatient breath. "I suppose you want to come in at ten instead of nine every morning."

"This doesn't have anything to do with me working here."

"Then what's it about?" He checked his watch, telling her that she was wasting valuable time.

"I want the opportunity to heal that tortured soul of yours."

He looked up from his watch, his narrowed gaze latching onto hers. "What the hell are you up to? Is this a joke?"

"No." This is my heart, she thought. Everything I have to give. "Let's face it, Luke. You're a tense, troubled man. If you're not angry, you're sad."

He gave her a pointed look. "And you're going to turn me into Mr. Chipper?"

Maggie couldn't help but smile. "Not exactly."

He leaned back in his chair. Today he wore various shades of gray. The gunmetal tie and a charcoal jacket reminded her of a rainstorm. He would never be Mr. Chipper.

"I'm going to teach you to stop punishing yourself," she said. "To live life and have a little fun."

"As opposed to suffering with inner demons?"

"That's one way of putting it."

"I see. And what do I have to do in return? Sign my name in blood?"

"No." She reached for her tea and took a dainty sip, giving herself a moment to form the words. Suddenly her heart pounded so hard, she feared it would burst through her blouse. "I'm offering you a dare. A marriage dare," she added, emphasizing the challenge.

He came forward in his chair. "Excuse me?"

"You have to promise to marry me if I can make you stop hurting. If I can save you from your pain." He needed so desperately to live, she thought. To experience hope and joy and the beauty love had to offer.

Luke couldn't decide if she was on the level, so he assessed her body language, and when that didn't help, he went right for her eyes.

They were as green as her suit, which told him nothing. Rather than reveal her emotions, they reflected the color she wore. He wondered if she had camouflaged herself on purpose.

"A marriage dare?" he asked, struggling to comprehend her logic.

"Yes," she responded, giving nothing away.

Luke leaned his elbows on the desk. Maggie Connelly could have just about any man she wanted yet she'd zeroed in on him. Why? What made him so appealing?

The challenge, he realized. She thrived on challenge, and he was the biggest contest of all. The aloof detective, the confirmed bachelor. She considered him the unattainable prize.

"I accept," he said, deciding he'd beat her at her own game. "But I'm adding another clause. I'll promise to marry you if you can save me, but you have to do it before the stroke of midnight on New Year's Eve."

She gave him an incredulous look. "That's less than a month away."

"Take it or leave it, Cinderella. Those are the terms."

Maggie chewed her bottom lip and glanced at Bruno. The dog looked back at her. "I want it in writing, with Bruno as our witness."

She was turning to a dog for support? Clearly she was in over her head. "No problem. You type up the contract, and I'll sign it."

"Once you commit, you can't back out," she said.

"I won't need to," he told her.

She headed to her office to draw up the contract, and he returned to the file on his desk. Not even a muse named Maggie could save Lucas Starwind from his demons.

# Five

Luke, Maggie and Elena Delgado Connelly gathered around the table in the conference room at Rey-Star Investigations, studying the reports Elena had given Luke months ago.

Elena was the Special Investigative Unit detective the Chicago P.D. had first assigned to the case, and although she was no longer on active duty, Luke had asked her to come in. He intended to check and recheck the facts, giving Maggie the benefit of discussing the case with Elena—the only cop who had been entrusted with the truth about the cancer virus.

The women, of course, already knew each other on a personal level. During the course of the investigation, Elena had become a member of the Connelly clan, falling in love with and marrying Maggie's twenty-seven-year-old brother, Brett.

Luke shifted uncomfortably in his chair. He didn't intend

for that to happen to him. In spite of the "marriage dare," he wasn't going to marry Maggie Connelly. Nor was he going to fall in love. Or have babies, he thought, glancing at Elena's four-month-old daughter.

Madison Connelly sat on her mother's lap, chewing the corner of a manila envelope. Luke was doing his damnedest to ignore her, but she kept watching him, mimicking his every move.

He'd never felt so self-conscious in his life.

He ran his hand through his hair; she reached for the fancy headband in hers. He frowned; she made an odd little scowling face.

"I bought a book on child development," Maggie said, causing Luke to glance her way.

What was she up to now? he wondered. Trying to add a baby clause to the marriage dare?

"Within two months Madison might be crawling," she went on, smiling at her niece. "Or giving it her best shot."

"She already is," Elena proclaimed. She laughed and bounced the baby, who seemed enthralled with the conversation. "Sometimes she actually manages to move backward."

Like a diaper-clad caboose, Luke thought, chugging along in reverse.

"So how does it feel to be a full-time mommy?" Maggie asked her sister-in-law.

"I don't know if I can describe it." Suddenly the other woman looked soft and dreamy with her tawny-brown hair and pastel-colored sweater. "I loved my job, but Madison and Brett are my life. Family means everything."

She rubbed her cheek against her daughter's head. The tender gesture made Luke's heart ache. He had vowed long ago not to have children. He couldn't face each day wondering and worrying if his kids were safe. Gwen's kidnapping had taught him a painful lesson he'd never forget.

As the child leaned into her mother, he noticed the syrupy expression on Maggie's face. Luke decided he'd had enough.

"Excuse me, ladies, but do you think we could get back to work?"

All three females narrowed their eyes at him. He assumed his tone of voice, rather than his actual words, had irked little Madison. He almost apologized, then chose to hold his ground.

This was a business meeting not a baby convention.

Elena recovered first. She opened a file and glanced at the contents inside. Handing it to Maggie, she said, "This is Rocky Palermo."

"The Kelly hit man?"

Elena nodded, and Luke leaned over Maggie's shoulder, grateful their meeting was back on track. The man in the picture was broad-faced, his black hair scalped in a military-style cut. The scar that ran down the side of his neck protruded like a pale vein.

"Take a good look," Luke told her. "He could show up anytime, anywhere. Rocky is the Kellys' prime enforcer." He saw her shudder, so he touched her hand, running his fingers over her knuckles. "He's responsible for killing King Thomas and Prince Marc."

"Even in disguise, Rocky could be recognizable," Elena added. "He's willing to change his appearance, but not to the degree of altering his physique. He's proud of those muscles and likes to show them off."

"That figures. A conceited hit man." Maggie lifted the picture and held it next to her face. When she lowered it, baby Madison squealed.

That started a game of peekaboo with Maggie at the helm

and Elena beaming with maternal pride. Luke found himself in the middle, not knowing what to do. The baby shifted her gaze to him, searching, he assumed, for his approval.

She was a pretty little thing, a munchkin with a cap of black hair and expressive blue eyes. She wore a girlish ensemble of lace, denim and bows. Tiny white shoes, polished to a perfect shine, encased her feet. Frilly socks flared at her ankles.

Somehow, she made Rocky Palermo seem insignificant. She'd reduced the hit man's picture to a goofy, hand-clapping game.

Luke decided she deserved the attention she was getting. He flashed her a masculine smile. She rewarded him with a toothless grin.

And at that moment, at that surprisingly tender moment, he wondered how it would feel to be a father.

But as an image of Gwen's bruised and battered body came to mind, he drew a rough, gut-clenching breath.

Turning away, Luke glanced out the window. A gray haze covered the sky, floating across the city like a dark cloud.

There was no point in fooling himself. He could never handle being a parent.

Maggie opened the door, and Luke entered her loft. She'd given him the security code to the parking structure and a key to her home, but he hadn't been inclined to use either.

He frowned at her, an expression she'd come to know well.

"You're not ready," he said, stating the obvious.

Maggie stood before him in a silk robe. She'd done her hair and makeup, but she hadn't chosen her wardrobe yet. "I just have to get dressed." And she was nervous about their outing. Today she was meeting Luke's mother.

She glanced at her half-eaten breakfast on the dining-room table. Without thinking, she picked up her plate and set it on the floor.

Bruno gobbled up the remains, and Luke's jaw nearly dropped.

"You've been feeding that dog table scraps? Damn it, Maggie, I told you not to give him any junk. I promised his trainer you'd keep him on a strict diet."

Maggie knew the dog would be returned to his trainer once this case was over, but she couldn't resist spoiling him. "Eggs aren't junk. They're protein."

Luke eyed Bruno critically. "He looks like he's put on a few pounds. That's not good, you know. Mastiffs tend to get obese." The detective studied the dog from another angle. "You're not giving him snacks, are you?"

"No," she lied. She'd taught Bruno to shake. He was a fast learner with a fondness for corn chips and jelly beans.

"Are you sure?"

"Yes." She picked up the plate. The dog had lapped it clean. Still feeling anxious, she headed to the kitchen and poured Luke a cup of coffee, hoping that would placate him.

He accepted the offer and told her to hurry up and get dressed.

Maggie turned away, then spun back around. "Why did you invite me to go with you this morning?" He'd called at seven, asking if she wanted to meet his mother. The unexpected invitation had nearly stunned her speechless.

"It was my mom's idea."

"Really? She wants to meet me?"

"Why wouldn't she? You're famous."

Maggie's hope deflated. Mrs. Starwind was expecting a celebrity, someone she'd read about in the gossip columns. "You didn't tell her about our agreement, did you?"

"Our agreement? You mean that crazy marriage dare? Of course not. Now put on some clothes so we can get going."

Getting dressed wasn't a simple task. Maggie paced her room, hurt by Luke's indifference. He wasn't taking her seriously. True, daring him to marry her had been a bold proposition, but in the process, she'd offered to heal his heart. Couldn't he see what that really meant? Wasn't it obvious that she cared about him? Short of admitting outright that she'd fallen in love, the marriage dare was the best she could do.

She reached for a sweater, then discarded it onto the bed. Seven outfits later, she still couldn't decide what to wear. Luke's mother wanted to meet the glamorous Maggie Connelly, yet Maggie wanted to present a genuine image, not the heiress the media had created. Then again, if she showed up looking too casual, Mrs. Starwind might be disappointed.

A knock sounded. She opened the door a crack.

Luke peered at her through the narrow space. ''Are you okay? It's taking you forever.''

She glanced at the clock. Thirty-five minutes had passed. ''I'm accessorizing.''

He rolled his eyes. ''This isn't a fashion show. Just throw on some jeans.''

Easy for him to say, she thought. He was ruggedly handsome without the least bit of effort. Scuffed boots and faded Levi's added to his appeal.

Bruno appeared at Luke's feet. Sniffing curiously, he nudged his way into the room, pushing the door wider.

Maggie shot a quick glance over her shoulder and winced. Her bed was filled with designer rejects.

But when she turned back, she saw that Luke wasn't paying attention to her fashion fiasco. His gaze was fixed on her body.

Her robe had come undone, exposing her bra and panties.

Maggie froze, struggling to catch her breath. Suddenly the air turned hot and muggy. Silk clung to her skin like steam from a torrid summer rain. Beneath the skimpy bra, her breasts tingled, her nipples rising to taut peaks.

She wanted to kiss Luke, to draw his mouth to hers and devour him. But instead she let him look, hoping he would touch.

He did.

He lifted his hand and rubbed his fingers over her lips. She licked his thumb and watched him shudder.

And then they stared at each other. A stretch of silence ensued, but their gazes never faltered.

Finally he moved his hand to her neck, and then to her robe. When he brought his other hand forward and closed the silk garment, his fingers brushed her nipples.

Deliberately. Accidentally. She wasn't sure.

"Get dressed," he whispered before he turned and walked away.

Maggie leaned against the door, her knees nearly buckling. How was she supposed to emerge from her room acting as if nothing had happened?

For the next fifteen minutes Luke sat on the sofa staring at the mermaid mural. Because he was tempted to touch the painting, to run his hands over each sensual siren, he tried to think of something casual to say when Maggie came out of her room. Something to douse his desire, something to ease the tension.

But he couldn't focus on anything except the heat running through his veins.

"Are they calling to you?"

"What?" Luke's heart bumped his chest. He turned away from the mural and saw Maggie. He hadn't heard her approach, yet she was there, like an apparition.

"The mermaids. Are they calling to you?"

"Yes," he answered honestly. And so was Maggie. Suddenly his mind was filled with an image of making love to her in the ocean, moonlit water lapping their skin. He could almost feel the warmth, the wetness, the motion of sliding between her legs.

"They called to me, too," she said, lowering herself to the sofa. "One night when I couldn't sleep, I read about mermaid sightings in the nineteenth century. And at dawn I started that mural."

"Who sighted them?" he asked, wondering if she believed the sea creatures were real.

"There are documented accounts from schoolmasters and explorers, but mostly they came from fishermen. In some cases, the mermaids had been caught in herring nets or tangled in fishing wire."

Luke glanced at the mural, then back at Maggie. "Did the fishermen set them free?"

She nodded. "In one instance, on the Isle of Man, they kept a mermaid for three days, but she wouldn't eat or drink, so they released her back into the ocean. They said she was very beautiful, perfectly formed. Above the waist, she resembled a young woman, and below she was a fish, with fins and a huge spreading tale."

"What about mermen?"

"There have been sightings of them, too." She met his gaze, her eyes a clear shade of aqua. "Someday I'm going to paint lovers from the sea. A merman, with a mermaid in his arms."

Luke had to catch his breath. "How will they make love?"

She smoothed her hair, combing her fingers through the golden highlights. She looked long and lean, dressed in jeans and an embroidered blouse that seemed as delicate as dandelions.

"They'll become human. And they'll join the way people do."

"Why will they become human?" he asked, mesmerized by her imagination.

"Because they've been touched by magic."

Luke moistened his lips. "How often will this spell occur?"

"Once a year, but only for an hour. So every time it happens, they'll be frantic for each other."

He pictured them, the enchanted lovers from the sea, tangled in each other's arms, caressing and kissing, their damp bodies feverish with lust. They would make love in the water and then on the shore, stars shimmering in the sky and sand glistening on their skin.

It was, Luke realized, the same fantasy he'd had about Maggie.

He met her gaze and saw his own hunger shining back at him.

They didn't speak, but there didn't seem to be anything to say. Their eyes said it all. They both wanted the same thing.

This was madness, he thought. No matter how seductive, how incredibly erotic Maggie was to him, she wasn't the appropriate lover for a man his age.

"I was seventeen when you were born," he said, suddenly thinking out loud.

She blinked. "What?"

"Nothing. Never mind." He stood, forcing himself to gain his composure. "We better go."

She came to her feet, then tilted her head. "I'm an adult, Luke."

Barely, he thought. She'd taken her first legal drink just the year before, and he'd downed his first legal beer in what seemed like a lifetime ago.

He grabbed his jacket, and Maggie reached for her purse, a tan shoulder bag that matched a pair of snakeskin boots. She'd accessorized all right, right down to the diamond studs winking in her ears and the gold bracelets shining on her wrists. Her jacket was vintage leather, a fringed number from the late sixties. The decade before she'd been born, Luke reminded himself. She had no recollection of hippies, Vietnam or men walking on the moon.

Luke might have been a kid then, but he remembered all of it. That era had been too emotional to forget. Times were turbulent, but his family had been happy.

Feeling oddly nostalgic, he ushered Maggie into the elevator. They reached the parking structure and climbed into his SUV.

Hours later, they traveled on a country road.

Maggie peered out the window at the barren orchards, the winter wheat fields and the empty pastures going by.

"It's really peaceful here," she said.

"Yeah."

She shifted in her seat and turned to look at him. "It must make you homesick."

"Sometimes." When he reached far enough into the past, he thought, to the years his father and Gwen had still been alive. "But I'm used to the city now. To the traffic and the road noise and all that."

"You've become an urban Indian," she said.

"Maybe, but I haven't forgotten the old ways." He respected what his ancestors believed—that the universe was created for more than just man. Everything had a life force, making a significant contribution to the tangible and intangible world, to the earth and the heavens above. "My dad taught me about the early Cherokee."

"Did he teach you what an early Cherokee wedding was like?" she asked, watching him through her magical eyes.

He almost said no, that his father had never explained a traditional marriage ceremony. But somehow he couldn't lie.

"The wedding takes place in the center of the council house," he explained, "near the sacred fire. A priest prays and the bride and groom exchange gifts. Then they—"

"What kind of gifts?"

"The groom gives the bride venison and a blanket. Nothing a modern girl like you would want," he added, trying to downplay the marriage dare.

"And what does the bride give the groom?" she persisted, undaunted by his comment.

"Corn and a blanket. But she also gives him a black-and-red belt that she made herself, and he puts it on during the ceremony."

"What happens next?"

"They drink from a double-sided wedding vase, then the vase is broken. The broken fragments are returned to Mother Earth, and a white blanket is placed around their shoulders, symbolizing their union. White denotes peace and happiness to the Cherokee."

Maggie sat quietly for a moment. Luke could feel her watching him, so he kept his eyes on the road. He didn't want to think about the wedding he didn't intend to have.

"That sounds like a beautiful ceremony," she said. "I like the idea that both the bride and groom are shrouded in white."

He nodded, then glanced at his shirt, realizing how often he wore black—the color the Cherokee associated with death.

Everything in Luke's world was dark, everything except Maggie Connelly. She was charming her way into his life. And quite frankly, that scared the hell out of him.

He turned onto another country road. ''We're almost there,'' he said. He was bringing Maggie home to meet the only family he had left.

Suddenly that seemed much too significant.

# Six

Luke turned into a graveled driveway, then parked beside a cozy old farmhouse. With its flourishing evergreens and Early American charm, it seemed to Maggie too serene to be the location of a kidnapping, yet twenty-seven years before, a child had been taken from there.

She glanced at the house, and for an instant she imagined Gwen kneeling on the porch, playing with paper dolls and a cardboard castle.

*Lady Guinevere.* Maggie had finally chosen a title for the painting, but she didn't have the courage to tell Luke. He hadn't mentioned the picture since the day he'd first seen it.

"This used to be a dairy farm," he said, interrupting her thoughts. "But that was a long time ago, before my parents bought it."

Rather than respond, she sent him a nervous smile, and

he paused to study her. "You seem uncomfortable. Are you worried about meeting my mom?"

"A little," she answered truthfully.

"You don't have to walk on eggshells around her. She doesn't go to parties or social functions, but she can handle having company at home. She isn't crazy. Agoraphobia is an anxiety disorder not a mental illness."

"I never thought she was crazy. I'm just concerned about making a good impression."

"Really? You? The sister of a king?"

"Yes, me." The heiress the media had manufactured. "I might not live up to her expectations."

He reached for the denim jacket he'd tossed in the back seat. "Are you kidding? She already thinks you're special."

Because I'm a celebrity, Maggie thought. Because I was born a Connelly.

They exited the SUV and walked to the back of the house. Luke unlocked the door and they entered through a service porch.

"We're here!" he called out as they proceeded to the kitchen, where the counters were laden with food.

"Oh, my." A woman in a knit pantsuit bustled around the stove.

Maggie assumed she was the housekeeper since Luke hadn't described his mother as a redhead with a teased and sprayed hairdo.

Luke made an introduction. Her name was Nell. She appeared to be in her midsixties, a former waitress with a husky voice and a quick grin. Maggie liked her immediately.

Nell shook her head, spinning the miniature Christmas ornaments dangling at her ears. "You shouldn't bring a guest through the back door, Luke." She flashed her ready smile at Maggie. "Now, isn't that just like a man? Of course, he's a handsome one, so we'll forgive him."

"You must be talking about my son," a softer voice interjected.

All eyes turned to Luke's mother, who had stepped quietly into the room. Dana Starwind stood tall and thin, with silver-gray hair and a smooth complexion. She looked fragile yet strong, her delicate features set amid stunning bone structure. She must have been breathtaking in her day, Maggie thought.

Maggie moved forward, and with mutual interest, they studied each other.

After a proper introduction, the other woman asked, "Did Luke tell you how much I wanted to meet you?"

"Yes, but I hope you don't believe everything that's been written about me."

"You're a graduate student, earning a double major in business and art."

Maggie's pulse quickened. "That part is true." The part most people ignored. The tabloid pictures of her on a yacht in the south of France usually generated the most interest, particularly since her bikini top had come undone—an accident that had been made out to seem like a deliberate, party-girl striptease.

"Dana's an artist, too," Nell said.

"It's a hobby," Dana corrected quickly. "I paint to keep busy. But I saw your work in a magazine. It's exceptional."

And that, Maggie realized, was the reason Luke's mother had been so eager to meet her. Nothing could have pleased her more. "Thank you. I would love to see your work, too."

"Then come to the living room," Dana said with a tinge of shyness. "Nell insists on framing my paintings."

An array of watercolors depicted scenes from nature—flowers blooming in a formal garden, a bowl of lemons in a patch of sunlight, a stream splashing over shimmering rocks. The snowcapped mountains could have been Switzerland, Maggie thought, the vineyards from France, the row of chestnut trees flourishing on Tuscany soil.

"They're all beautiful," she said. Clearly Dana traveled in her mind, creating the world as she imagined it.

Each soul-inspired painting blended with the country charm of the Starwind home. Farm-made furniture complemented historic antiques. Patchwork pillows decorated a pre–Civil War settee, and an old butter churn sat between two straight-back chairs. The entire setting, Maggie thought, brimmed with magic and warmth.

Yet, the absence of family photos told another story. Pictures of Gwen were still too painful to face.

Maggie glanced at Luke. He sat next to his mother. The affection between them was obvious, but so was the ache they shared.

While they made small talk, Nell swept into the adjoining dining room, clearly enjoying her role as the housekeeper. She filled a buffet table with homemade entrées and colorful side dishes.

Proud as a country peacock, she encouraged everyone to eat. Maggie chose a little bit of everything, knowing the feast had been prepared in her honor.

Luke filled his plate as well. "Nell loves to cook."

As they gathered around a sturdy oak table, Maggie smiled at the redhead. Nell cooked and Dana painted—hobbies that gave the two older women purpose. They seemed like good friends, closer than she had expected them to be.

"Mom and Nell used to work at the same diner," Luke said, as if he'd just read her mind.

"Really?" She shifted her gaze to Dana. "You were a waitress, too?"

She nodded. "But that was forty-five years ago."

"It's also how she met Luke's daddy." Nell fanned herself with a napkin. "Goodness, but was that man a looker."

Dana smiled, her brown eyes shimmering. "I fell instantly in love. Jacob Starwind was a truck driver from North Carolina. He was from the Qualla Boundary, the Cherokee reservation," she clarified. "But he worked for a company that had locations in Winston-Salem, Pittsburgh and Chicago. It was a good-paying job, and he was grateful to have it." She reached for her water and took a small sip. "He traveled all over the United States. And whenever he made a delivery in this area, he'd stop by the diner."

"They caused quite a scandal," Nell put in. "An Indian man and a white woman. This was the fifties, mind you, and interracial relationships were still frowned upon back then."

"That's true." Dana glanced at her longtime friend. "My reputation suffered, but I didn't care. I wanted Jacob more than I ever wanted anything. Nell was the only one who didn't judge me."

Nell waved her hand. "That's because you never judged me." She turned and winked at Maggie. "I had a reputation in those days, too."

"I'll bet you did." She pictured the snappy redhead wearing her uniform a tad too tight and flirting shamelessly with the local farm boys.

"Nell was always around when I was a kid," Luke said.

And she was, Maggie realized, the friend Dana had been visiting when Gwen had been kidnapped.

Dana toyed with a three-bean salad. "Eventually the gossip settled down about Jacob and me. He asked me to marry him and had his route changed so he could live here. It was difficult for him to leave the reservation, but in the old days a Cherokee husband would take up residence with his wife's clan. And since my family lived in Illinois, Jacob thought that was the proper thing to do."

"He must have been an honorable man." Maggie gazed at Luke. "Like his son."

He didn't look up from his plate, but Nell and Dana exchanged a feminine glance. And at that moment, Maggie knew they saw what was in her heart.

Hours later, as they said goodbye, both women hugged her. It was, she thought, the acceptance she needed.

"I'll come back again," she told Luke's mother. Next time they would talk about art and literature and the beautiful places they both loved—the European countrysides Dana painted but had never visited.

The following afternoon, Luke entered Maggie's office. It still seemed strange to see a woman occupying Tom Reynolds's desk. The room smelled like hothouse flowers instead of Tom's ever-constant cigarette smoke.

She looked up and smiled. An oversize cappuccino cup sat next to her Rolodex, and a jade paperweight rivaled the color of her eyes.

"I have an assignment for you," he said. "I want you to ask your family about Gregor Paulus. I'm looking for anything, even the most minor detail, that might give us a better understanding of his relationship with Prince Marc."

"He was my uncle's personal assistant."

"I know. But I haven't been able to zero in on the dynamics of their association. Was Paulus Marc's confidant? Or was it strictly a professional relationship?"

"Do you think Paulus is involved?" she asked. "Do you think he's the Altarian mob contact?"

"He's on my list of suspects." Luke took a seat in one of the leather chairs across from her desk. "But I haven't come up with anything linking him to the Kellys. If he was part of the CD-smuggling scam, then Prince Marc brought him into it."

"Why would Marc do that?"

"I don't know. That's why I want you to talk to your family about Paulus. I just can't seem to get a handle on him."

"No problem." Maggie came to her feet, then crossed to the bar. Dispensing the cappuccino machine, she filled her cup. Next she opened the refrigerator and added a swirl of whipped cream to the hot beverage.

When she returned to her desk, she sat on the edge of it, giving Luke an enticing view of long, shapely legs ending in a pair of wicked-looking pumps.

The intercom buzzed. Maggie leaned across the desk to press the button, and as she did, her skirt rode farther up her thigh. Luke told himself not to stare, but he gathered an eyeful anyway.

"Yes, Carol?"

"Is Luke with you?"

"Yes, he's right here."

"Good. I picked up something on my lunch hour both of you need to see."

Maggie stood, and Carol came into the office carrying a copy of a current supermarket tabloid.

The blonde placed it on the desk. The movie star on the cover didn't mean anything to Luke, but as he scanned the minor headlines, he caught Carol's concern.

Connelly Heiress Obsessed With Private Eye.

The word that came out of his mouth was a quick, vile curse.

The story was on page four, along with several photographs of Maggie and him kissing in the snow. The pictures weren't professional quality, which meant someone in his neighborhood must have snapped them for a lark, and then realized who Luke's companion was. He wondered how much the bastard had sold them for.

"I'm sorry," Maggie said.

"It's not your fault."

"Are you going to sue?" Carol asked.

"No." He dragged a hand through his hair. "It'll blow over."

"I already warned building security to be on the lookout for reporters and cameramen," Carol said, proving her loyalty as a trusted employee.

"Thanks."

She went back to work, leaving Luke and Maggie alone with the tabloid.

Maggie read the article, while he restrained his temper. He wanted to smash his fist into the wall, but he knew behaving like a hothead wouldn't do any good.

"It says I come to your office every day because I can't get enough of you. Supposedly we're carrying on quite an affair."

He blew out a rough breath. The story also described him as the first "older man" she'd taken up with. That made his stomach churn.

"At least they didn't report that I'm helping you on the case. Of course, they would never suspect that. No one thinks I have half a brain, let alone enough intelligence to assist a respected P.I."

"We were kissing, Maggie." Mauling each other, he thought. "That's all they're interested in."

"Then maybe this is a blessing in disguise. In fact, maybe we should start attending social functions together."

"You mean give credence to the trash they printed?"

"I'm in less danger if the Kelly hit man thinks I'm your lover instead of your temporary business partner, right?"

Luke frowned. She had a valid point, but he didn't like the idea of dragging their lives through the mud, even if it created a believable cover for their association. And then there was that marriage dare. "You're not going to use this as leverage, are you?"

Maggie gave him an incredulous look. "You think I'm going to try to win the dare by seducing you in public?"

He shrugged. What did it matter? She wasn't actually serious about marrying him. She'd devised the dare as a challenge, as a creative way to get his attention. And he had accepted it to teach her a lesson, to prove she had no business trying to change him.

"We'll start this evening," she said, reaching for her cappuccino. "You can escort me to an art show I was invited to. I'm tired of staying home every night anyway."

"Fine," he responded, expecting to be bored out of his skull. He appreciated the kind of art he could understand, but there were plenty of wacky sculptures and paintings out there he could never relate to. Luke knew damn well he didn't fit into Maggie's avant-garde world. They didn't belong together, and no amount of phony dating was going to turn them into real-life lovers.

Luke had never drooled over a woman, but this just might be a first.

Maggie's cocktail dress was the size of a postage stamp. The silver fabric shimmered over every lethal curve, exposing a hint of cleavage and more leg than she had the right to own. A sparkling necklace and a pair of stiletto heels completed the killer package.

Even Bruno couldn't keep his eyes off her.

She smiled at Luke. "Are those for me?"

"What? Oh, yeah." He'd forgotten about the roses. Bringing her flowers seemed like the proper thing to do, even on a fake date. He handed them to her and noticed the dress turned her eyes a moonlit shade of blue.

"Thank you." As she walked into the kitchen to retrieve

a vase, her shoes clicked across the floor, as sleek as silver bullets.

Suddenly it was the sexiest, most dangerous sound he'd ever heard.

She returned with a single rose, the stem snapped short. Moving closer to Luke, she pinned the bloodred flower onto his lapel. He felt as if he'd been branded.

"Shall we go?" she asked, reaching for a wrap that matched her dress.

He merely nodded.

She tossed her head. Her hair was long and loose, golden highlights spilling around her face. "We can take my car." She handed him the keys to her Lamborghini. "It's more showy, and we're trying to get noticed tonight, right?"

Minutes later, Luke slid behind the wheel. Maggie owned one of the six hundred and fifty-seven Countach Anniversario models ever made—a vehicle capable of traveling 183.3 miles per hour.

"I like to move fast," she said.

He pictured making fast and urgent love to her. "So do I."

They flew into traffic and reached their destination in record time. The gallery was located in a historic building with multipaned windows and a brick walkway. Inside, lights burned brightly. A winding staircase led to three spacious floors.

Other guests milled in and out of showrooms. A waiter held a tray in front of them, and Maggie accepted a flute of champagne. Luke declined a glass of the bubbly in lieu of a harder drink from the bar. Maggie took his arm and led him to the first display.

A lone statue stood in the center of a stark white room. They moved closer, and he noticed the sculpture depicted a naked woman; her head tipped back, her long, lithe body arched. A bed of rose petals lay at her feet.

Maggie fingered the flower on Luke's lapel. He wanted to pull her tight against him.

The next room showcased a trio of paintings, each more sensual than the last.

"Damn," was the only word he could manage. He couldn't take his eyes off a painting that focused on a woman kissing a man's navel. Only his bare stomach and the waistband of his jeans were visible, making the image mysteriously provocative.

She sipped her champagne. "A nameless, faceless man. He could be anyone."

"Yeah." And Luke was imagining Maggie's mouth on his stomach. "You should have warned me."

"What? That this show is a collection of erotic fine art? It must have slipped my mind."

Like hell, he thought. She'd done it on purpose, and her ploy had worked. Desire gushed through his veins.

But at this point he didn't care. He was going to take what he wanted. Immune to the fact that they were in a public place, he grabbed her by the shoulders and kissed her—hard. So hard he nearly lost his breath.

She kissed him back, and he explored the hot, impulsive sensation, running his hands up and down her dress. Hungry for more, he toyed with the idea of devouring her in one quick bite.

Fast, he thought. He wanted it fast. The way an addict injected a drug or an alcoholic downed a forbidden drink.

And then he realized he was dangerously close to spilling his vodka on the marble-tiled floor.

Pulling back, he stared at Maggie. Her eyes were a fiery shade of blue, her lips still slightly parted. The silver dress reflected sparks of light, like a chandelier casting vibrant rays.

"Don't trick me again," he said. "Don't set me up for another seduction."

"But that's part of enjoying life," she challenged.

And part of the dare, he thought, realizing she had just won the first round. She sent him a triumphant smile, and he had the notion to grab her, to tip her head back and taste her all over again.

"Maggie?" a feminine voice said behind them. "Darling, is that you?"

They both turned. A well-preserved blonde in a black dress clung to the arm of her young, brawny escort.

Instantly, the irony hit Luke. He figured the couple had at least seventeen years between them, just like him and Maggie. Suddenly this game, this dare, seemed morally wrong.

"Delilah." Maggie reached out to hug the blonde. "It's so good to see you."

"You, too." Delilah tilted her head. She wore her hair in an upswept style, showing off the gems at her ears and the jewels at her throat. "You must be the private eye," she said to Luke. "Maggie's handsome obsession."

"That's what the tabloids say."

The blonde laughed. "I have an obsession, too. Let me introduce you to him."

Luke shook hands with the young man and wondered if the guy was receiving stud-service pay or if he dated Delilah for free.

When the couple moved on, Luke drained his glass, swallowing the last of his vodka. Maggie was still sipping eloquently on champagne.

"Delilah is a patron of the arts. She has an amazing collection."

"Of what?" he asked sardonically. "Twenty-five-year-old men?"

She glared at him. "That was her husband."

"And that's supposed to impress me? Some young gigolo marrying a rich divorcée?"

"First of all, Delilah isn't a divorcée. And second, she and Kevin live in an estate *both* of them paid for. She didn't marry him for his body, and he didn't marry her for her money." Maggie looked him straight in the eye. "And since neither one of them can have children, they plan on adopting an orphan from Bosnia."

Luke caught the information right in the gut. He rarely, if ever, misjudged people. It was his business and his nature to look beyond stereotypes. "I'm sorry," he said. "I had no right to insult your friends."

"That's okay. I did the same thing when I met Carol. So I guess we're both guilty of jumping to conclusions."

With a forgiving smile, she took his hand and led him toward another incredibly erotic piece of art, intent on drawing him into her world.

# Seven

Maggie's childhood room had been redecorated since her youth, but it still felt like home. French doors led to a balcony that overlooked the gardens. She stared at the view, picturing herself as a child hiding in the maze and pretending to be braver than she was.

"Maggie?"

She turned to the sound of her mother's voice.

As always, Emma Rosemere Connelly was the image of beauty and grace. She wore her blond hair in a French twist, and a strand of pearls accented a classic Chanel suit. Maggie had never seen her mother looking unkempt or frazzled.

"Are you all right?" Emma asked.

She nodded and perched on the edge of the bed. "Did you see the tabloid article, Mom?"

Emma sat in a velvet side chair. "I heard about it, but I certainly wasn't inclined to read it."

"Dad isn't upset?"

"He doesn't intend to confront Mr. Starwind if that's what you're worried about. Luke already called and apologized."

Maggie didn't know whether to be pleased or angry. She appreciated the fact that Luke respected her honor, but she didn't want him apologizing for their relationship or downplaying the emotion between them.

"We already knew that you and Luke were attracted to each other."

She reached for a pillow. "You did?"

"We saw you dancing with him at Rafe and Charlotte's reception. The way he held you, the way you looked at him…well, it wasn't hard to miss."

"I'm in love with him."

"Oh, my." Emma placed a jeweled hand against her heart. "Are you sure? This isn't just one of your impulses, is it?"

"No." She met her mother's gaze with a candid stare. "This is the real thing. And I've never been so frustrated in my life. If we're not snapping at each other, we're fantasizing about tearing each other's clothes off."

"Well, then."

Emma coughed delicately, and Maggie bit back a smile. She never failed to surprise her family with her blatant, if not inappropriate, honesty. "Tell me what it was like when you first fell in love with Dad."

The older woman sighed. "It was wonderful. But it was turbulent, too. Grant was such a dynamic man. So proud, so strong." She fingered a pearl at her ear. "And much too crass for the likes of my family. As you know, my parents were heartbroken, as well as angry, that I didn't marry another royal. I was a princess. It was my duty to form a strategic alliance for my country."

"But instead, you gave up your title and married a rugged American."

"Yes." Emma smiled. "I was headstrong in my youth, too."

"Do you ever regret your decision?" she asked, curious how her mother had coped with the knowledge that her husband had slept with his former secretary. "You and Dad did have some problems."

"I've never regretted marrying the man I love. And our troubles happened long before you were born. A lifetime ago." Glancing at the balcony, Emma paused as though tempering painful memories. "A person has to learn to forgive, to work through the hurt."

"What about your sacrifice?" Maggie asked, trying to envision her mom as a young, headstrong princess. "All those years away from your family?"

"That was the most difficult part. And now, of course, I'm grateful I had the chance to make peace with my father before he died." Five years before, Emma had gone back to Altaria to make amends with King Thomas, bridging the gap between the Connellys and the royal family.

Glancing at the pillow on her lap, Maggie toyed with the lace edge. Her mother must be devastated by Prince Marc's treachery. Maggie had already questioned Emma, as well as other family members, about Marc's association with Paulus. "Luke is going to solve this case."

"I trust that he will," Emma responded. "And I'm also aware that you're determined to help him. That worries me, Margaret," she added, using her daughter's formal name.

"Luke promised Rafe that he would keep me safe."

"I know, but you're so reckless at times. You have to be careful and listen to what Luke says. He isn't just a private investigator. He was a Special Forces soldier. He has experience in these sorts of matters."

"I won't defy him. I just want to be part of this, to make a difference." Maggie tilted her head. "What do you think of Luke, Mom?"

The other woman clasped her hands in her lap. "He's a good man. Your father and I like him."

"Good. I'm glad." She sent her mother a confident smile, even though her heart was beating triple time. "Because sooner or later, I intend to marry him."

The following morning Maggie's car phone rang. She pressed the speaker button. "Yes?"

"It's Carol. Are you on your way to work?"

"Yes." And she was running late as usual. She glanced at Bruno. The dog rode shotgun, staring out the Lamborghini's tinted window. "We should be there in about five minutes." She approached a yellow light and sped through it. "Maybe four."

"Luke's in a foul mood, Maggie."

She checked her rearview mirror, spotted a cop and slowed down. "Why? What's wrong?"

"Another tabloid hit the stands today. And it has Luke fuming."

Shoot. "Thanks for the warning, Carol. I owe you one." She ended the call and proceeded to the office, reminding herself to breathe. Of course Luke was upset. He wasn't used to being in the limelight. He hadn't lived his life under public scrutiny.

"Well, he better get used to it," she told the dog. "Particularly since he's going to marry a Connelly."

Bruno grinned at her, and she patted his head. She'd fed him steak and eggs for breakfast, with a scatter of corn chips on the side. He was adjusting to her devil-may-care lifestyle with ease.

She pulled into the parking lot and wondered if she should have dared Bruno to marry her instead.

The moment she exited the car, a camera flashed its glaring bulb in her face. She squinted at the photographer, a squirrelly little man who touted himself a "royal watcher."

While he continued to snap her picture, she let Bruno out on the passenger side, giving him a subtle command. The big dog bared his teeth. The cameraman jumped back, slipped on a grease spot and fell flat on his rear.

Maggie waved to the "royal watcher" from the parking-lot elevator. Bruno snarled until the door closed.

At the reception desk, Carol had the phone glued to her ear. She gestured toward Luke's office, letting Maggie know he was waiting for her.

She nodded, removed her coat and gloves, then proceeded to the lion's den.

Luke was pacing, so she stood silently, allowing him to stalk the perimeter of his cage, hoping he would get the agitation out of his system.

Finally, he stopped. "A love triangle," he said, spewing the headlines like an expletive.

Maggie unhooked Bruno's leash, but the dog didn't leave her side. "I don't understand. A triangle implies there's a third party."

"It says Claudio and I are fighting over you."

"Really?" She tried not to smile. Claudio Di Salvo, a free-spirited playboy on the international racing circuit, wouldn't dream of fighting over a woman.

Luke stared her down. "Are you still seeing him?"

She managed a casual shrug. "We're still friends, if that's what you mean."

"What kind of friends?"

Maggie took a seat, thrilled that Luke appeared jealous of her former lover. She wanted him to feel possessive of her, to think of her as his. "Are you asking me if I still sleep with him?"

"You know damn well that's what I'm asking."

She crossed her legs, feigning indifference. Bruno, her faithful companion, chose to lie at her feet. "I don't think that's any of your business."

"The hell it isn't. I have a right to know just how much of this article is true."

Maggie picked up the tabloid off his desk and breezed through it. The pictures of her and Luke kissing were plastered across a page, along with a cozy shot of her and Claudio at a casino in Monaco. She read the text, and then went on to check her horoscope. On a whim, she checked Luke's horoscope, too, wondering if their signs were compatible.

Finally, she looked up, meeting his piercing gaze. "Actually, none of it is true, but Claudio won't mind. He gets a kick out of these sorts of things."

"Well, hooray for Claudio."

"Honestly, this is no big deal. My affair with him was quite casual, you know."

"How European of you," he said, his voice tight and cynical. "But if you don't mind, I'd just as soon not hear the details. I've had enough of Claudio for one day."

Because you're jealous, she thought. And you're worried that he was better suited to me.

She closed the tabloid. Claudio had been her first and only lover, and although he had satisfied her physical needs, their relationship had lacked an emotional bond. Maggie craved true intimacy—the kind she hoped Lucas Starwind could give her.

"I don't sleep around," she said, suddenly concerned about his opinion of her. "And I would never pit one man against another."

Luke saw the discomfort in her eyes and realized how

unfair he was being. "Is that how I made it sound?" He
leaned forward. She smelled like flowers, like spring on a
winter day. "I'm sorry. I didn't mean to blame you. I'm
just not used to all of this."

"I know. It's like living in a fishbowl."

He reached out to touch her cheek, felt the softness of
her skin. Was he falling for her? he asked himself. This
young, beautiful muse?

Yes, he thought, drawing his hand back. He was falling
down a mountain. Running headlong into a speeding train.
And sooner or later he'd end up with emotional scars. How
long could he keep a woman like Maggie interested? How
much time would pass before she got bored? Before his
graying-at-the-temples appeal wore off?

He went around to the other side of the desk, determined
to put a barrier between them. "We better get back to
work," he said, forcing himself to focus on business. The
Connelly case was going nowhere. Luke had a list of suspects and no substantial leads.

"Did you talk to your family about Gregor Paulus?" he
asked.

"Yes." She reached for her briefcase, placed it on her
lap and opened it. Glancing at her notes, she said, "I wasn't
able to reach Princess Catherine. She's the one who probably knows Paulus the best."

Luke nodded. Princess Catherine, the recent bride of a
sheikh, was also Prince Marc's illegitimate daughter.
"Where is she?"

"On a holiday with her husband."

"Will she be at the coronation rehearsal?" he asked,
knowing Maggie and her family would be traveling to Altaria within the next few weeks.

"Yes. Are you going, Luke?"

"It depends on what happens with this case. I've got

plenty of people keeping an eye on things in Altaria.'' He scrubbed his hand across his jaw, wishing something would turn up. ''Tell me what you learned about Gregor Paulus.''

''Overall, he isn't a very likable man. He's overbearing, so much so that he argues over trivial things. The king intends to fire him after the coronation. Paulus lied about several small domestic matters, and my brother isn't going to put up with that.''

Luke had heard most of this before. ''What about Paulus's relationship with Prince Marc?''

''Prince Marc treated Paulus well, but still considered him an employee, or a servant, if you will. Paulus knew his place, and he never tried to step out-of-bounds where Marc was concerned.''

''So they weren't friends?''

''No.''

''Was Paulus your uncle's confidant?''

''Maybe. No one is sure what they discussed in private. Of course, Princess Catherine might be able to tell us something pertinent, but she isn't available for an interview right now.''

''Then we'll wait.''

''Who else is on your list of suspects?'' she asked.

He conjured a mental image of the names imbedded in his brain. He counted them like sheep before nodding off to sleep each night. ''The security personnel at the Rosemere Institute, the scientists who discovered the cancer virus, the owner of the Altarian textile mill that manufactured the lace. And besides Gregor Paulus, there's a slew of people employed in the royal service who could have discovered that Prince Marc was associated with the mob.''

''But you have a hunch about Paulus?''

''I suppose you could call it that.'' Luke leaned back in

his chair. "What do you think of him, Maggie? What's your gut instinct?"

She blinked, shuffled her notes, then smoothed her skirt. Nervous, he thought. Or embarrassed that she didn't have an opinion of one of their key suspects.

"I never paid much attention to him."

"I see." He brought his hands together, forming a steeple. "And what do you think his observation of you would be?"

"That I'm rich and spoiled. That the only things that matter to me are designer clothes, fast cars and good-looking men."

Intrigued, he watched her hair spill over her shoulders. "Why would he think that about you?"

"Because that's my reputation," she answered simply.

Luke had to admit that her reputation was easy to believe. Or it had been before he'd started spending time with her. Now he didn't know what to think.

"You shouldn't work here anymore," he said.

She frowned at him. "You can't take me off this case. You—"

"I'm not. But you can assist me without coming into the office every day. You're causing too much of a stir. Pretty soon the other tenants are going to start complaining about all the photographers hanging around." And she was, he thought, a nine-to-five distraction he didn't need.

"Take the rest of the day off," he told her. "I'll come by tonight to help you reorganize your home office."

"This isn't fair."

He ignored her protest. "I'll bring your files. I've got plenty of work to keep you busy. You can follow up on Tom's old notes. Maybe he stumbled upon something I missed. Something besides the information that got him killed."

"But I like working here. I like being around you and Carol."

She pouted, and Luke realized how young she really was, how headstrong yet vulnerable. He worried she might cry. He didn't think he could handle that, so he gave her a stern look, hoping it would rile a temper rather than tears. "Don't fight me on this, Maggie."

She made a face at him and grabbed her coat. Outside, the weather turned damp. Suddenly he could hear a gush of rain.

"You're going to miss me, Lucas Starwind. It's going to be boring around here without me."

She dropped her gloves. He picked them up and handed them to her. He didn't doubt for a minute that he'd miss her. And that was exactly why he was shooing her away. He didn't like the idea that she had become so important in his life.

# Eight

Maggie told herself not to cry, but as rain pounded against her windshield, tears flooded her eyes. If she lost the dare, she would lose Luke.

Sniffing like a heartbroken teenager, she steered her car down a water-slicked highway. Bruno sat beside her, patient and gentle as a lamb. She couldn't imagine life without the big dog. Or a day without Luke.

Damn him. He was pushing her away, closing himself off, shielding his heart from what he was afraid to feel. And there didn't seem to be anything Maggie could do about it. Except bawl like a baby.

Hours later, she arrived on Dana Starwind's doorstep, dripping with rain and wiping her nose.

"Oh, honey." Dana ushered her inside, then gasped when Bruno tromped in as well.

"He won't hurt you. He's my bodyguard."

"He certainly looks big enough for the job." She paused

to study the rain-sodden pair. "Let's get both of you dried off."

While Dana removed Maggie's coat and wrapped her in an oversize towel, Bruno watched with interest. When the older woman knelt, the dog lifted his paw to shake her hand. She smiled, took his muddy foot and wiped it clean. Like an expectant child, he offered his other paw, then allowed her to go to work on his back feet.

They proceeded to the kitchen where meatballs simmered in a pot of sauce. The scent of garlic, oregano and basil danced through the air. A loaf of Italian bread sat on the counter.

Nell came in from the pantry, took one look at Maggie's red-rimmed eyes and began preparing meatball sandwiches with slabs of mozzarella melting in the center. It seemed as though she believed a home-cooked meal had the power to comfort a saddened heart.

Bruno sat in a toasty corner, sniffing and hoping for his share. But he didn't need to wait long. Nell fed everyone, including the dog.

They gathered around a small fifties-style table in the kitchen, dripping sauce on a vinyl tablecloth and drinking colas spiked with grenadine. It was, Maggie decided, food for the soul.

After their meal she helped the women clean up. There was no automatic dishwasher. They accomplished the task with a sinkful of suds, rubber gloves and two checkerboard-print towels.

No one asked why she had been crying. Instead they welcomed her into a routine that made her feel as if she belonged there. She still sported the chic designer suit she'd worn to the office that morning, but that didn't seem to matter. Maggie was one of them. She was part of Luke's family.

A short while later, while Nell retired in an easy chair with a book, and Bruno dozed on a carpet by the hearth, Dana took Maggie to the room she used as a studio.

A braided area rug padded the floor, and a blank canvas rested on a lone easel, waiting for a stroke of color.

Maggie glanced at the eyelet curtains. And because she felt a softness, a gentleness in the air, she sensed this room had once belonged to Gwen.

Dana crossed to a wood shelf and brought back a handful of tiny figures.

"Luke made them," she said.

Maggie reached for one and studied it. Fine and smooth, the stone carving depicted a howling wolf, its head tipped to the sky. "It's beautiful."

"They're all wolves." Dana held them protectively. "They represent the A-ni-wa-ya, the Cherokee clan Luke's father belonged to. In the old days, the Wolf Clan raised wolves, training the pups like dogs."

"When did Luke make these?"

"Years ago, when he was a boy."

Before Gwen died, Maggie realized. "What was he like back then?"

Dana smiled. "He loved being outdoors. He had a horse named Pepper, and he would ride through the fields, whooping and hollering. He was tall for his age, and his hair was long, just past his shoulders."

Maggie pictured him, the boy who carved wolves, racing in the wind, scents and sounds from the earth stirring his young, vibrant soul. She could even hear his laughter, the freedom that rang from his chest.

"You're the first girl he's brought home since high school."

Startled, Maggie looked up. "I am?"

"Yes." Dana placed the wolves back on the shelf, then

closed Maggie's hand around the one she held, silently telling her to keep it. "I know there have been women in his life, sexual partners, I suppose. But he's never mentioned a name or brought anyone here. I gave up on the idea of becoming a grandmother long ago."

Suddenly the wolf in Maggie's hand felt warm and alive. She brought it next to her heart. "I dared him to marry me."

Now it was Dana's turn to startle. "Oh, my. How did he react to that?"

"He accepted the dare, but only because he doesn't think I can win. I made him promise that he had to marry me if I could make him stop hurting."

Luke's mother glanced at the window. Rain slashed against the glass, pounding in a steady stream. "He doesn't want to stop hurting, does he?"

"No. Your son blames himself for everything bad that's ever happened. He carries the weight of the world on his shoulders."

"Because of Gwen," Dana said softly. "Did he tell you about her?"

"Yes." And she had painted the little girl without knowing it. She had created an image of Gwen with the winged horse that had taken her to heaven.

"Luke loved her so much. He was such a good big brother. He would have given his life for her." The other woman paused and a breath shuddered through her. She met Maggie's gaze, a gray light filtering between them. "But, then, that's what happened, isn't it? Somewhere along the way, he did stop living."

"So did you, Dana."

"I—" Her excuse faded, and she sighed. Twisting her hands together, she glanced at the blank canvas. "You won't give up on us, will you, Maggie?"

"No," she promised. "I won't give up."

Both women stood silently then, listening to the downpour and wishing for a rainbow.

At 12:00 a.m. Maggie entered the parking structure below her loft and saw Luke's SUV. Surprised, she took the elevator to the first floor and unlocked her door, wondering why he was there at this hour and why he'd finally made use of the key she'd given him.

Bruno went in ahead of her and got her attention, leading her to the couch. Luke was sprawled across it, fast asleep. His holstered gun, a weapon that seemed out of place in her artistically designed home, sat on the engraved coffee table.

Maggie moved closer. Luke looked hard and strong, even in repose. His hair fell in an inky-black line across his forehead, and shadows cut across his face, defining his rugged features. His shirt was partially untucked and he'd removed his boots, but his belt was buckled, his jeans zipped. They were an old, faded pair of Levi's, fraying at the seams.

Unable to stop herself, she smoothed his hair.

He jerked and came awake.

"Maggie?" He squinted at her. "What time is it?"

"After midnight."

"Damn." He sat up. "I didn't mean to sleep that long. I just closed my eyes for a second."

"That's okay. What are you doing here?"

"I brought the files by after work, but you weren't here, so I left them." He rolled his shoulders and tucked in his faded denim shirt. "I went home, but when you didn't return my messages, I came back."

She wanted to stroke his cheek, but she knew he wouldn't understand the tender gesture. She kept seeing him as his mother had described him—young and beautifully free. "You were worried about me?"

He shrugged. "I figured you were visiting a friend or

something, but I wanted to be sure. It was raining pretty hard.''

"Why didn't you try my cell?''

"I did. And your car phone, too. You didn't answer.''

"Oh.'' She dug through her purse and flipped open her phone. The battery, as usual, was dead. "I guess I forgot to charge it.'' And she hadn't thought to check her car phone for messages. She wasn't used to having people fret over her. Her family had accepted her independence long ago.

"You have to be more careful, Maggie.''

"Bruno was with me.''

"I know. But still, it really bugged me when I couldn't reach you.''

She sat beside him on the couch, her heart swelling. "Thank you.'' She touched his arm and felt the hard-earned muscle beneath his sleeve. "It matters that you care.''

He frowned, intensifying the lines at the corners of his eyes. "You're my responsibility until this case is solved.''

He couldn't say it, she thought. He couldn't admit that he cared, not even a little.

Maggie watched as he picked up the 9mm, reached behind him and clipped it to the back of his belt. She didn't want to be his responsibility; at least not in the way he meant it. But, then, he was a former Special Forces soldier. It was his nature to keep a level head, to focus on whatever mission he had been given. And at the moment her safety was part of his assignment.

"Will you stay here tonight?'' she asked, not wanting to let him go. "You can sleep in one of the guest rooms, and in the morning I'll fix breakfast. I cook a pretty mean omelette.''

"No. I can't.''

"Can't or won't?''

"It isn't a good idea.'' He grabbed his boots and shoved

them on. They were as timeworn as his jeans. "Us sleeping under the same roof." He tied the laces on his boots, knotting them twice.

She watched him, imagining his hands on her body, his heart beating next to hers. "I fantasize about you," she said. "When I'm lonely, I touch myself and think about you."

She heard his breath catch, and the reality of her words hit. She had just told him her deepest, most intimate secret. Instantly shamed, she hugged herself for comfort, wanting to die a thousand deaths.

She felt herself blush, knowing two rosy spots colored her cheeks. "I'm sorry. I didn't mean to say that. I—"

He lifted his gaze and slammed straight into hers. Neither moved. They sat, staring at each other, the air between them as jagged as a shard of glass.

Luke's entire body shuddered. He was too shocked, too aroused to think straight. If he didn't leave, if he didn't force his legs to carry him to the door, he was going to drag Maggie into his arms. Push his tongue into her mouth, tear at her clothes, bury himself between her legs.

Deep, he thought. Deep and wet between her legs.

"I have to go." He shot up like a rocket and nearly tripped over the dog, feeling big and boyish and stupid.

"I'm sorry," she said again.

"Don't apologize." He jammed his hands in his pockets and tried to act casual. "People do that. They…you know, fantasize." Flustered, he removed his hands from his pockets, suddenly worried that they would call attention to his distended fly.

"Do you?" she asked, gnawing on her lip.

Luke felt like a sexually starved teenager, a kid too shy to admit that he had normal, healthy urges. "Sometimes. Especially if it's been awhile since I've—" He paused, searching for the appropriate term. When nothing but raunchy words came to mind, he settled on, "Been with some-one."

"Oh." She grabbed a decorative pillow and twisted the tassel. "Has it been awhile?"

Determined to avoid her gaze, he glanced at the wall, then caught sight of the mermaid mural. Cursing to himself, he shifted his gaze again. That erotic painting wasn't helping. "Yeah. It feels like it's been forever."

"For me, too," she admitted.

In the next instant they both fell silent. She hugged the tasseled pillow to her chest, and he glanced at the white-washed floor, trying to think of a way to change the subject.

"I put the files in your office," he managed to say, gesturing to the computer room down the hall.

"Thank you. I'll sort through them in the morning."

"Great. Well, I better go. It's getting late." He checked his watch, then realized he wasn't wearing one. This had to be, he thought, the most awkward, strangely sexual moment of his life. He was still fully aroused, still turned on by what she'd told him.

She walked him to the door. They stammered through a goodbye and, when the elevator descended, he dropped his head against the wall and let out a rough I-should-have-spent-the-night-with-her, she's-all-I'm-going-to-think-about, how-in-hell-am-I-going-to-sleep breath.

Maggie couldn't sleep. She tossed and turned in bed, stared at the ceiling, watched the clock and thought about Luke. The rain had started up again. She could hear it pounding on the roof.

The phone rang, and she nearly jumped out of her skin. Nothing but bad news came in the middle of the night.

She answered the call, fearing the worst.

"Maggie, it's me." Luke's husky voice came over the line. "I didn't wake you, did I?"

"No. Is something wrong?"

"I can't sleep."

She snuggled deeper under the covers. "Me, neither."

Silence bounced between them before he said, "I've never had phone sex, have you?"

"No." She focused on the rhythm of the rain to keep her pulse from running away with her. "Is that why you called?"

"Yeah, but I don't think I'm going to be very good at it."

Did he want her to say something erotic? To start the forbidden game? She wasn't sure what to do. She couldn't exactly tell him what she was wearing. Her flannel pajamas had cartoon characters all over them. They were her silly, cold-weather indulgence.

"I wish you would have stayed here," was the only thing she could think to say. It was, after all, how she felt. She missed him terribly, and now the rain sounded lonely and sad.

"Me, too. But deep down, I know better."

"I haven't made things easy on you," she said, aware of the fire, the fine line between passion and anger, that fueled their reactions to each other. "How many times have I accused you of being with someone else?"

"I would never do that, Maggie. I would never hurt you deliberately."

"Thank you. That means a lot to me." In her heart she knew he was an honorable man, but she needed to hear him say it, to admit in some small way that he cared.

"I was jealous, too," he said. "And things like that never mattered to me before. I've never been in a committed relationship."

"But you should be, Luke. You need someone." You need me, she thought, the woman who loves you, the woman who dreams about you every night. "You should have a wife and children."

His response was quick. Too quick. "I'm not the husband type. And I'd make a terrible dad."

"No, you wouldn't." Maggie could see him holding an infant against his chest, whispering softly in the Cherokee language. The dedicated father, the protective warrior. "A child would be lucky to have you."

"Do you want kids?" he asked, his voice suddenly rough with emotion.

"Yes. But I hadn't given it much thought until I met you." She adjusted the phone. "I want your babies, Luke. Think of how beautiful our children would be." She glanced at the window. She'd left the blinds open, inviting the city lights to filter in, to slash watery hues across the room. "Come over and make a baby with me."

He was silent for a moment, and she knew he was imagining them together, his body spilling into hers.

"We can't let that happen," he said. "You know we can't." He released a heavy sigh. "This is crazy. I'm standing in front of the fireplace at two in the morning, talking about making babies."

It wasn't, she realized, the kind of conversation he'd anticipated. It was deeper, much more intense than he'd bargained for. "I thought you were in bed."

"No. I'm too restless to lie down."

She pictured him, a crackling fire sending golden waves over his skin. In her mind's eye, his chest was bare and frayed denims rode low on his hips. And his hair, that midnight hair, would be tousled from dragging his hands through it.

Her heart went soft. Tough, detached Luke. He'd called

because he needed her, because he couldn't bear to sleep alone. "Climb into bed," she said, wishing she could hold him. "And we'll keep each other company."

"Okay." She heard a smile in his voice. "But you've got to talk dirty to me."

She laughed. She knew he was kidding. At this point, all they would do was cuddle and listen to the rain.

Dawn stole its way into Luke's room, and he awakened with a cordless phone jammed against his ear. He listened for a dial tone and heard nothing but stillness coming from the other line. He was still connected to Maggie's phone, but she was asleep.

What they'd done last night seemed even more intimate than sex. Remaining on the phone had been romance in its purest, most innocent form. And that, he thought as he sat up and shoved off the covers, was dangerous.

"Maggie?" he whispered her name into the receiver, recalling the tender emotion they'd shared.

*Come over and make a baby with me.*

For an instant last night, he'd been tempted. But then reality had set in, and he knew he couldn't give that much of himself. Nor could he live the rest of his life worrying about keeping his children safe.

"Maggie?" he said her name again. But this time when she didn't respond, he ended the connection, pressing the power button. A shiver sliced through him, and suddenly he felt as if he'd just severed a limb.

No, he told himself. Don't you dare form that kind of attachment to her, that kind of gut-wrenching need.

Luke leaned over and placed the phone on the dresser, and it rang a second later. He didn't answer it, not right away. Preparing to hear Maggie's voice, he sat on the edge of the bed. He caught his reflection in the mirrored closet door, thinking he looked like hell. He'd slept in his jeans, and a shadow of beard stubble peppered his jaw.

Finally he answered the phone. "Hello?"

"Good morning, Lucas."

The woman on the other end of the line was his mother. He cleared his mind, or at least he tried to. Maggie still dominated his thoughts. "Hey, Mom."

"I wanted to catch you before you left for work."

"No problem." He opened the blinds, insisting he wasn't disappointed that the call wasn't from Maggie.

"I'm going to see a doctor," she said.

"Why? What's wrong? Are you sick?"

"It's been twenty-seven years since I've traveled more than a few blocks from my home," she responded. "That's not a particularly healthy way to live."

Stunned by her admission, he rose, carrying the phone into the kitchen. Suddenly he needed a strong dose of caffeine. She hadn't referred to herself as agoraphobic, but she'd said it in her own way.

As he opened a can of coffee, his eyes turned watery. He wanted to blame that uncharacteristic reaction on lack of sleep, but he knew better. "I'm so glad. I want you to be healthy."

"I've made your life so difficult," she said. "You've sheltered me from the outside world, but I can't keep expecting you to do that."

He frowned at the coffee grounds he'd spilled on the counter. "I don't begrudge our relationship. I love you, Mom." Luke was the one at fault, the one who hadn't protected Gwen that day. Dana Starwind had nothing to feel guilty about.

"Oh, Lucas." She made a sad, sighing sound. "I love you, too. And that's why I should have made this decision years ago."

"Don't blame yourself for something you couldn't control."

"I'm through making excuses," she said.

Her voice turned stronger, and he pictured her squaring her shoulders, drawing strength from somewhere deep within.

"There's plenty of help out there," she continued in the same determined voice. "I've seen TV commercials about the medication they give people who feel the way I do. It wouldn't hurt for me to try something."

How long would her bravado last? he wondered. Would she panic later? He had seen her at her frailest, battling the fear and overwhelming grief that kept her chained to the house.

"I'm going to ask Maggie if she'll take me to the doctor. And I think I'll bring Nell along, too. She's been dancing around the house all morning. Prattling about all the things we'll be able to do. Nell wants to go on a cruise. Goodness, can you imagine me on one of those floating casinos?"

He was still stuck on the Maggie part. What had the Connelly heiress said to influence his mother? To make her reevaluate her life?

"I warned Nell not to jump the gun," she said.

She paused, and Luke knew the idea of a cruise made her nervous. Hell, just going to the market made her nervous.

"I'm not fooling myself," she went on. "This isn't going to be easy. I don't expect to turn into a world traveler overnight. Besides, my main concern is attending your wedding."

"What?" He dropped the coffeepot into the sink. The glass carafe bounced but didn't shatter. "I'm not getting married."

"You never know. You might. And I need to prepare for a big social event like that."

Luke's next breath clogged his lungs. When he picked up the coffeepot, his hands were anything but steady.

*Come over and make a baby with me.*

"I'm not getting married," he reiterated. And he wasn't going to make babies with a woman almost half his age. He was too old and too ornery to be a husband and father. Maggie's affection for him would blow over soon enough. "There isn't going to be any wedding, Mom."

"Oh, my. Listen to yourself, Lucas. You sound more afraid than I do."

He shoved the coffeepot in place, refusing to believe he was basing his decision solely on fear. Even, damn it, if his heart was slamming against his ribs and his mouth had gone unbearably dry.

# Nine

The Shaky Shamrock wasn't a dive, but it wasn't a trendy bar, either. It was, in Luke's opinion, an Irish-owned pub that provided a pool table, a stingy dance floor and a working-class environment that normally put him at ease.

Here, he thought, a guy could get friendly with a bottle of vodka and forget his troubles. But only if he wasn't waiting for trouble to arrive.

Where the hell was Maggie anyway? Couldn't she ever be on time?

Luke eyed the clear liquid in his glass, then downed the alcohol and signaled the waitress. One more wouldn't hurt. If anything, it would take the edge off.

Marriage. Babies. He didn't want to think about any of it.

Five minutes later, Luke finished another drink, then sucked on an ice cube. And because he'd heard that sexually frustrated people chewed ice for a diversion, he spit it back into his glass and shelled a peanut instead, hoping no one noticed.

The pub was getting crowded. Couples squeezed onto the dance floor, gyrating to cover tunes played by a local band. Four college-age guys wagered on a rowdy billiards game, laughing above the music. The bartender, a big Irishman with a potbelly and thinning red hair, kept a steady flow of alcohol moving while currency exchanged hands.

Maggie, the recognizable celebrity, came through the door alone—her faithful bodyguard Bruno having been left behind for the evening—and turned every head in the place. And no damn wonder. Beneath a zebra-print coat, she wore a leather dress that made her look capable of handcuffing a man to his bed. Sleek and shiny, the black garment hugged lean curves, stirring even the most staid imagination. And those spiky-heeled boots. Luke envisioned pulling her onto his lap and tangling his hands all through that gorgeous hair.

Talk about needing to chew ice.

He stood, and she walked over to the table. "Am I late?" she asked.

Luke didn't take his eyes off her. "You know you are."

She removed her coat, and he came around to do the gentlemanly thing and push in her chair. And that was when he noticed that her dress was backless.

She turned to look at him. "Is something wrong?"

"No." Nothing that didn't make him a healthy, all-American, hot-blooded male. "You want a drink?"

He could sure as hell use another one. Was it his sixth? he wondered. His seventh? Eighth? Hell, at this point, he didn't care.

"A glass of white wine would be nice," Maggie said, drawing his attention back to her.

Bypassing the waitress, he ordered directly from the bar.

One of the pool players gaped at Maggie, and Luke sent the guy a hands-off stare.

When he returned to the table, she reached for her wine. He sat across from her and watched the way she handled the glass, her fingers sliding up and down the stem. How could someone so young be so damn seductive?

"Do you come here a lot?" she asked.

He shrugged. "Now and then. I don't go out that much."

She looked around. "It's cozy. Kind of rough." Her lips curved into a feminine smile. "I like it."

He guzzled his drink and went after a handful of peanuts. Cozy and rough was the way he wanted to paw her right now. He knew she wasn't wearing a bra. He'd gotten a good look at her naked back and the intriguing shape of her spine.

"So what's on your mind, Luke?"

Sex, he wanted to say. As much of it as I can get. "The case."

She scooted her chair closer to the table. Vintage rock blared from the amplifiers, filling the room with strumming guitar licks, a thumping bass and the pounding of a rhythmic drum. He wondered how she'd react if he asked her to do a private strip show for him tonight. Slide down a metal pole, the whole bit.

"Well?" she asked.

He wanted a lap dance, too. One of those slow, sultry—

"Luke? What's going on with the case?"

"Maybe we should discuss it outside." Where he could inhale a strong gust of city air. Gasoline fumes and factory smoke ought to clear his head right up.

A bit bleary-eyed, he grabbed his jacket. He was drunk and horny, and she was dressed like a dominatrix and sipping a ladylike glass of wine. The odds, he decided, weren't in his favor.

Maggie stood, and Luke helped her with her coat. Once

they were outside, he scanned the parking lot for his SUV. Finding it right where he'd left it, he leaned against the hood. Amber streetlights cast a buttery glow, softening the December night. A damp chill nipped the air. He blew a breath just to see it fog and disappear.

Maggie eyed him speculatively. "How many have you had, Luke?"

"I lost count awhile back, but I remember what I was supposed to tell you about the case. The guy who owned the Altarian textile mill died. Keeled over from a heart attack."

Long, loose hair tumbled around her face. She batted at the breeze-ravaged strands impatiently. "Are you sure he wasn't murdered?"

"Positive. And this really sucks, because he was one of our prime suspects. Those CDs were smuggled out of his mill."

"What about his employees? Could one of them be tied to the mob?"

"It's highly unlikely. We did background checks on all of them. Nothing surfaced, but we didn't expect much. They're just working-class folks."

She slipped her hands in her pockets. Her coat billowed in the wind, snapping like a faux-fur flag. He knew she favored those fake animal prints. She wasn't the sort who went after real fur, even if she could afford it.

"And that's it?" she asked. "That's why you asked me to meet you here?"

"Yep."

"We could have done this over the phone."

Oh, sure. The phone. Where he'd spill his guts about how much he needed her. Or admit that he didn't want to fall asleep without hearing her voice. "Bars are safer."

"For whom?" she asked, taking his keys away.

For guys who are trying to remain single, he thought. "Where's the Lamborghini?" He swept the lot for her vehicle. "I like your car."

"I took a cab. I usually do when I meet a date." She nudged him into the passenger side of the SUV.

Well, hell. He deserved to get his ass kicked, he supposed. She'd been expecting a pleasant night on the town. A little dancing, a little kissing, some warm conversation. "Crummy date, I guess."

"I've had better." She got behind the wheel and started the engine.

He closed his eyes. This was proof, he decided, that he'd make a rotten husband. Proof that he wasn't father material.

Or maybe, he thought, trying to humor himself, this proved that Maggie Connelly was the kind of woman who drove a levelheaded man, some poor unsuspecting sap like Lucas Starwind, to drink.

Three days later Luke and Maggie fixed dinner together in his kitchen. He browned hamburger meat for the tacos, and she diced tomatoes and onions, her eyes watering from the latter.

Luke would never forgive himself for getting drunk the other night. He had no right to do that while Maggie was still in his care. His inebriated state could have put her in danger. What if Rocky Palermo had shown up? How effective would Luke have been against the hit man?

"I'm sorry," he said.

She blinked through the onion-tears. "For what?"

He resisted the urge to dab her eyes. "For the crummy date the other night."

"Oh, Luke. How many times are you going to apologize for that? You deserved to let off a little steam."

Not if it meant putting her in danger, he thought. "I won't do it again. I won't put you in a position to look after me."

"You're making too much of it. All I did was drive you home. You managed to get yourself to bed."

Where he'd conked out soon enough. "I'm still sorry."

"No problem." She scooped the onions into a bowl. "Do you want to hear about what happened with your mom?"

"Yes. Please." He turned the burner down a notch. Chili spices rose in the air, filling the kitchen with a south-of-the-border flair. Maggie had taken his mom to the doctor earlier that day. He hadn't pressed her for details, but he was hoping she would supply a few.

Maggie went to the refrigerator and removed a head of lettuce. "The doctor gave Dana a prescription for an antidepressant. He explained that some antidepressants are effective in controlling anxiety disorders. The key is finding the right one for her."

"So it's a hit-and-miss kind of thing?"

Still holding the lettuce, she leaned against the sink. "More or less. But he also recommended group therapy. She needs to interact with others who are going through the same thing." Maggie sighed. "You wouldn't believe how many people are afflicted with social phobias. Housewives, executives, movie stars. Some people, like your mom, become housebound, while others appear to function normally when they're actually panicking inside."

Luke nodded. He knew his mom had faked her way through it at first, hiding her fears from him. "What a hell of a way to live."

"Dana is bound and determined to get through this, to do whatever she can to face the world again. And she knows it's not going to be easy. She's not expecting miracles. The toughest part for her will be going places alone. She's relied on you and Nell for so long—"

"I enabled her, didn't I?" he cut in, his stomach clenching.

Maggie met his gaze. "She needed you, and you were there for her. That's not enabling someone. That's loving them." She blinked, her eyes still watery. "You did the only thing you knew how to do, Luke. You protected her."

"But it wasn't enough. I didn't insist that she get help."

"You can't force someone to get help. They have to be willing. And in spite of group therapy and medication, your mom still might suffer from this disorder. There's no guarantee that all of her fears will go away."

But at least now she has a chance, he thought. Because of Maggie—a twenty-two-year-old girl with a heart the size of Texas. He stepped forward. "Thank you for caring."

She set the lettuce down and reached for him. He took her in his arms and guided her head to his shoulder. She felt soft and warm. He stroked her hair and let himself enjoy the luxury of holding her.

Maggie looked up at him, and Luke's pulse tripped. She didn't fancy herself in love with him, did she? She was still young enough to confuse lust with love, still rebellious enough to want a man who was no good for her.

Suddenly the marriage dare didn't seem like a game.

Did it matter? he asked himself. This wouldn't last, not for either one of them. He was too old and set in his ways to get wrapped up in a woman, and she was too young and free to saddle herself with a hard-boiled P.I. forever. She would get over him in no time.

Stepping back, he released her, grateful they hadn't given in to the urge to sleep together. That, he decided, would complicate things, forming a physical attachment they didn't need.

He turned to stir the meat, giving himself something to

do. He would win the dare and that would be the end of it. Midnight on New Year's Eve would come soon enough.

She might be a rich, impulsive Cinderella, but he sure as hell wasn't Prince Charming.

"Do you want me to grate the cheese?" he asked, trying to slip into a casual, meaningless conversation.

"We bought the kind that's already grated."

"Oh, that's right. I forgot." He wasn't used to shopping with someone else or spending so much time with a woman. "I'll set the table." He grabbed the plates and silverware and carried them into the dining room.

Standing in front of the window, he gazed out. Dusk settled in the sky. Rain drizzled on and off, leaving moisture in the air. The neighbor's roof twinkled with strings of holiday lights. Luke turned to glance at his tree, then saw Maggie standing behind him, placing a tray of taco fixings on the table.

"It's beautiful," she said.

He knew she meant his Christmas tree. "Thanks." He'd decorated it with leather-wrapped feathers, hand-engraved silver conchas and strands of turquoise beads. The Indian ornaments reminded him of who he was and where he'd come from. In spite of his urban lifestyle, he never wanted to forget that he had Cherokee blood running through his veins.

"Do you ever go to the reservation to visit your father's family?" she asked.

"Not as often as I would like." Because he had gotten so involved with the city, with the high-profile cases that absorbed his time. "My grandparents are gone, but I still have some distant relatives there." People he barely knew, he realized.

"I'll bet the land is breathtaking."

"It is," he responded, picturing the serenity of the Qualla

Boundary. The rolling pastures, the high meadows, the winding streams. "It's the gateway to the Great Smoky Mountains. It's prettiest at dawn, when the sun shines through the mist."

"I'd love to see it someday. I've never been to North Carolina." Maggie smiled, and he wondered why he felt lonely all of a sudden. Was he missing her already? The enchanting Cinderella he couldn't claim?

A few minutes later Luke and Maggie sat down to dinner. Halfway through their meal the phone rang. He got up to answer it. And then his pulse jumped.

The man on the other end of the line was one of his contacts in Altaria. Finally, they had a lead on the Connelly case.

He hung up the phone and returned to the table. "I'm leaving for Altaria in the morning," he said. "The chief of security at the Rosemere Institute is on the verge of a break-down. He's ready to crack."

"And you're going to be there when he does."

"Damn straight."

Maggie met his gaze head-on. "I'm going with you."

Her eyes, he noticed, flashed like emeralds. He knew there was no point in arguing, in insisting that she fly over next week with the rest of her family, who would be arriving for the coronation rehearsal. Maggie was determined to remain by his side, to help him solve the case. And that meant getting on a plane with him tomorrow.

"Fine, but Bruno is coming along, too." Luke wasn't about to let Maggie accompany him without her bodyguard. Of course, that wasn't a problem. Altaria didn't quarantine dogs and cats from America, as long as the proper veterinary certificate was provided, and Bruno's medical records were in perfect order. "Just remember, when we get there, I'm in charge. Whatever I say goes."

She agreed, and he reached for his water, promising himself he would do anything, absolutely anything, to keep her safe.

The jet was equipped with everything money could buy—a luxurious living room, a fully stocked bar, sleeping quarters adorned with silk sheets and downy pillows. Maggie sipped a glass of plum wine and nibbled on sushi. She was used to traveling in style, particularly when en route to Altaria. The remote island was only accessible by yacht or private jet as the airstrip was too small to accommodate commercial flights.

She glanced at Luke, who sat beside her on an Italian sofa. Studying his notes, he seemed unfazed by their luxurious surroundings. Then again, he was an experienced flyer and this was, in spite of its glamorous trappings, still a plane.

Bruno yawned from a cozy corner, and Maggie smiled. They made a compatible trio.

Luke looked up. "I hope the security chief has plenty to say. We need a break in this case."

"Especially since one of our prime suspects just died," she said, thinking about Cyrus Koresh, the man who had owned the Altarian textile mill. "Are you sure we don't have anything linking Cyrus to the Kellys?"

"Nothing but the fact that the CDs were smuggled in lace shipments from his mill. He didn't have a record or any known criminal activity. Of course, he was ambitious as hell."

"He must have socialized with someone in the mob," she put in, reaching for a vegetable roll.

"He belonged to the same country club as Gregor Paulus. It could be a coincidence. Plenty of prestigious Altarians belong to the club, but my gut tells me that Paulus is the one who brought Cyrus into this mess.'' Luke stretched his legs. ''You know what the ironic part is? Cyrus's wife died from cancer.''

''Really? Then why would Cyrus agree to smuggle a cancer virus onto the black market?''

''I don't think he knew what was on those CDs. Someone offered him a chance to make some cold hard cash, and he took it.''

''And now he's dead.''

Luke nodded. ''He already had a weak heart, and the stress from the smuggling scheme probably did him in. Whoever else is involved in this must have told him that your brother Rafe discovered what was going on.''

''Which meant Cyrus would be under suspicion.''

''Exactly.''

''The Royal Guard don't know about the cancer virus, do they?'' she asked.

''No. They're aware that files were stolen from the Institute, but they don't know those files contained a potential biohazard. The king thought it was best to keep quiet about that. He didn't want to create a state of panic. We can't afford any leaks.''

And with good reason, Maggie thought. They weren't just going after the mob; they were trying to save the world from biological warfare. ''What do you think the bad guys are doing?''

''Besides dying from heart attacks? Lying low, I would imagine. Or falling apart like the security chief at the Institute.''

''I'm still worried about Daniel,'' she said, recalling the assassination attempt that had been made on his life.

''The king is being protected by the Royal Guard.''

''I know.'' She finished her wine, then managed a reminiscent smile. ''It still seems strange to think of Daniel as a king.'' She remembered her oldest brother as an all-American teenager, slipping past the Connelly cook to swipe a drink from the milk carton, and now he was ruling a nation, a devoted wife by his side.

''You're the one I worry about,'' Luke said as he placed his notes back into a leather briefcase. ''It's dangerous for you to be working with me, Maggie.''

''I'll be fine.'' She had two protectors—a big, burly dog and a former Special Forces soldier. ''How long were you in the military?'' she asked, envisioning Luke as a young, passionate warrior.

''Ten years.''

''Did you enlist when you were eighteen?''

''Yes. I thought about going into law enforcement when my tour ended, but I changed my mind.''

She sensed he had become a P.I so he could investigate unsolved crimes, helping families who needed closure. And somewhere along the way, his skills had led him to high-profile cases.

''We've got a long day ahead of us, Maggie. You should try to get some rest.''

''I am sleepy.'' From the wine, she suspected. She glanced at the bedroom compartments, but decided to nap right where she was. Reclining on the couch, she put her head on Luke's lap and gazed up at him.

With a gentle caress, he stroked her cheek. She imagined unbuttoning his shirt and sliding her hands all over that massive chest.

He toyed with her hair, and a heated shiver slid down her spine.

''Close your eyes,'' he whispered.

Dreamy, Maggie snuggled against his body. But when she turned her head to get more comfortable, she heard Luke suck in a rough breath.

The side of her face was nestled against his fly, and suddenly he was aroused.

That makes two of us, she thought as she drifted into a sweet, sensual sleep.

# Ten

Dunemere, the Rosemere family's beach house, faced a rugged coastline. Luke and Maggie stood on a balcony and watched the ocean rise into foaming waves. He thought about the mermaids Maggie had painted and decided that if the sea creatures existed, they would choose to frolic in Altarian waters.

The island, with its sparkling white sand, swaying palm trees and jagged mountains, was indeed a sight to behold.

"I better get ready." Luke turned and entered a suite decorated in chintz, warm woods and mellow pastels. Maggie's suite connected to his, an unlocked door the only barrier that separated them at night.

Moonlit nights, he thought, lulled by the sea.

Maggie sat on the edge of his bed, and he cast her a curious look. "What are you doing?" he asked.

"Nothing," she responded a little too innocently.

Luke knew damn well she was waiting around to see if

he'd strip in front of her. He removed a dark suit from the closet and hung it on a wooden valet. "Scram, little girl." He shooed her away with a dramatic gesture. "Go raid the cookie jar or something."

"Very funny, old man."

They both laughed, and for the first time since they'd met, their age difference seemed almost insignificant.

Almost, he reminded himself. Seventeen years was nothing to scoff at.

She rose, came toward him, grabbed his shoulders and kissed him smartly on the mouth. "Good luck with the security chief," she said.

"Thanks." It took every ounce of willpower he owned not to toss her onto the bed and ravish the hell out of her. She wore a filmy dress that flowed around her like a sheer curtain. He assumed she had some sort of flesh-colored bodysuit on beneath it. The naked illusion was enough to drive him mad.

He watched her walk to the door that divided their rooms. And once she was gone, he let out the breath he'd been holding.

Less than an hour later Luke was seated across from Rowan Neville, the security chief at the Rosemere Institute. The office was clean and organized, with a large desk and metal file cabinets. Nothing appeared to be amiss, nothing but the man himself.

Neville smoked nervously, lighting one cigarette after another. His graying blond hair framed a ruddy, wind-burned face. His tie was so tight, he looked as if he might choke.

Luke eyed him from across the desk. He had been informed that Neville quit smoking twenty years ago. Yet here he was, employed at a cancer-research facility and putting himself at risk for the disease.

Luke presented a document with the royal crest. "The

king sent me here to discuss the Genome Project with you,'' he said, referring to the name of the research that had accidentally created a virus.

Neville flinched, then took another drag, inhaling as if his life depended on tobacco, tar and nicotine. "The scientists would know about that. You can speak to them."

"The king wanted me to talk to you. He's had someone watching you, Rowan, and he's curious about your odd behavior." Luke sat back in his chair, creaking the leather. He studied the other man, keeping his expression blank. "You've rushed out of the office early every day this week. Why the hurry to get out of here?"

"I needed to get home to my family."

"Why?"

After Neville stamped out the cigarette butt, he fidgeted with the empty pack, clearly craving another. "Because last Saturday I saw the man who threatened to kill them."

Luke's heart leaped to his throat, but he didn't move a muscle. "What man?" he asked.

"The one with the scar." Neville touched his neck, drawing with his finger the scar by which Rocky Palermo was known. "He forced me to do what I did. They needed me, you see. I helped design the security system, and I was able to alter it. No one has clearance to enter the lab at night, not even the scientists."

Luke finally moved, leaning toward the desk. "But you rigged it so someone could get into the lab?"

"Yes. There were two men. One kept me at gunpoint, and the other worked in the computer room. This happened on ten different occasions. The archived data they were after wasn't stored in the same computer. They had to keep coming back, checking different files."

"Give me a description of them," Luke said. "Every detail."

"I can't. They always wore ski masks. I never saw their faces."

"But you saw the man with the scar?"

"Yes, but only a few times last year when all of this first started. He wasn't one of the masked men."

"How can you be sure?"

"Because he was wider than they were. Broader in the shoulders."

Luke scrubbed his hand across his jaw. Either Rowan Neville was a skilled liar, covering his tracks by pointing the finger elsewhere, or he was truly running scared, fearing for his family's safety. "But you saw the scarred man last Saturday?"

He nodded. "At the pier. I was with my children." Pausing, Neville took a breath. "He had a mustache and longer hair, and he wore a turtleneck sweater, so I couldn't see the scar. But the way he was built, the way he walked, I knew it was him." The security chief frowned. "I know it sounds crazy that I recognized a man who didn't look the same, but he threatened my children. That's something a father doesn't forget."

It didn't sound crazy, Luke thought. Rocky often appeared in disguise, but his muscles and cocky stance were hard to miss. Then again, Neville was in a panicked state. He could have mistaken another bodybuilder-type for the hit man. "Did he see you?"

"Yes, but I turned away quickly. He didn't follow me. He was with another man. They were talking quietly."

Luke showed Neville some photographs. The security chief identified Rocky Palermo instantly, but when Luke presented a picture of Gregor Paulus, Neville studied it for a while. "This could be the other man who was at the pier. He was tall and thin like this, but he wore a hooded jacket and dark glasses. It looks like him, but I can't be sure."

Luke decided he would get his computer tech to enhance

the photographs of Palermo and Paulus, creating images of them in the manner Neville described. "I'll be in touch," he told the other man. "This is a private investigation. For now I'm the only person you'll be dealing with."

Neville fidgeted with the empty cigarette pack once again. "I'm still worried about my children. And now that I've told you what I know, they might be in more danger. Will you speak to the king about protecting my family?" he asked, his voice edged with what sounded like genuine fear.

"Yes," Luke responded solemnly. He knew Rowan Neville had two rosy-cheeked little girls. "I will."

Two days later Luke and Maggie shared dinner in Luke's suite, a meal provided by a maid—a woman who had been a loyal Dunemere employee for years. Nonetheless, Luke had investigated the domestic staff, including the maid. She and the others had turned up clean, but Luke continued to sweep their suites for bugs just the same. No one, in his opinion, was above reproach.

Silent, he toyed with his fork. He'd misjudged the man who had killed his sister, and Gwen had paid for Luke's mistake. He would never take anyone at face value again.

"Don't you like the food?" Maggie asked.

He glanced at his plate. The meal, consisting of maple-glazed salmon, sautéed chanterelles and cream biscuits, was fit for royalty. And that, somehow, reminded him of Gwen and her cardboard castles.

"It's great," he responded.

"How would you know? You've barely tasted anything."

That, he supposed, was true. He'd picked at the spinach and lentil salad, but he'd bypassed the wild-rice griddle cakes relished with golden caviar and sour cream. Forcing himself to focus on his meal, he cut into his salmon. Now wasn't the time to think about his dead sister.

The fish practically melted on his tongue. He moaned, and Maggie smiled.

"It's almost better than sex, isn't it?"

Luke laughed. Trust Maggie to make him feel better. "Almost," he agreed.

"I guess you've never gotten orgasmic over food before," she said, teasing him.

"No. I can't say that I have." He took another bite, and suddenly the mood shifted. What seemed like an innocent meal was now laced with more than the flavor of maple glaze and peppered cream.

A fire blazed in a gilded fireplace, and outside, the wind howled a haunting melody. Luke sensed the ocean was rising, crashing wildly upon the shore.

Over the candlelit table Maggie met his gaze. Her eyes shimmered like jewels. Muse magic, he thought. The lull of enchantment.

Unable to stop himself, Luke glanced at the bed, knowing Maggie would lie with him if he asked her to.

Heat shot through his veins, as blinding as the fire. He grabbed his water and did his damnedest to douse the flames. If he took Maggie to bed, the addiction would set in, and he would never want to let go.

And that, he thought, as the iced liquid slid down his throat, scared the hell out of him.

"I need to brief you on what's happening with the case," he said.

"Oh, of course." She blinked, as though waking from a fog. "That's why we agreed to dine in your suite."

He nodded. They needed to speak privately, to make certain they weren't overheard. "Rowan Neville identified Rocky in the altered photograph, but he wasn't able to identify Paulus." Luke sat back in his chair. "Let me rephrase that. Neville thought the altered picture of Paulus looked 'a lot' like the man who was with Rocky at the pier. But he wasn't a hundred percent sure.''

"It's the only lead we have, Luke. None of your other suspects could be confused with Paulus. You know it was him.''

"Most likely, yeah.''

"Most likely?'' she challenged. "Did you talk to my brother about this?''

"You mean the king? Yes, I did. And he agreed that we should keep a close eye on Paulus.'' Luke held up a finger to stop Maggie's protest. "We don't have a positive ID on him. Neville can't testify that he saw Gregor Paulus with Rocky Palermo. Hell, his identification of Rocky isn't even airtight. The hit man was in disguise.''

"So we're just going to sit around and wait?''

"Not exactly.'' Luke scooped a forkful of the chanterelles into his mouth. He wasn't a mushroom connoisseur, but they were damn good. "The king suggested that we devise some sort of sting operation.''

"Really?'' Her eyes all but glittered. The muse magic had returned with a vengeance. "We're going to trap Gregor Paulus?''

"Figuratively speaking. It won't be you and me pulling this off. It will involve an undercover agent.''

Her eyes dulled. "So what's the plan?''

"I haven't worked out the details yet. I'm kicking around the idea of baiting him with a potential buyer for the pirated files. As far as I can tell, those CDs haven't turned up on the black market. Their hacker is probably trying to crack the encryption code. Those files aren't worth nearly as much in code, but at this point Paulus would probably welcome a quick, painless sale.''

"Are you sure he even has the CDs?'' she asked. "They

were shipped to Chicago and hidden somewhere by the Kellys."

"After the Kellys were busted, Paulus probably sent Rocky after them. They wouldn't have taken the chance of leaving them there."

Luke finished his meal, then eyed the dessert on a nearby serving tray. Deciding to indulge, he reached for a parfait glass and tasted the tapioca and cranberry swirl. Pleased, he made a mental note to compliment the chef.

Maggie sat back in her chair and gave him a serious look. "We don't need an undercover agent," she said. "I can handle the sting operation."

He nearly choked on the pudding. "Excuse me?"

"Think about it. I'm perfect for the job."

Before he could respond, she continued, "I'll convince Paulus that I have a potential buyer, but I want in on the deal." She leaned forward a little. "And here's the beauty of it. Paulus has access to some of the CDs, and I have access to the rest. Plus I can get ahold of the encryption program. Together we can sell all the files and make a fortune."

"And why would he believe that you're on the level?" Luke shook his head. "Hell, Maggie, you're practically living with me. The whole world thinks we're lovers. And Paulus knows damn well that I'm investigating this case. He's not an idiot. They killed your grandfather, your uncle, my partner. We're knee-deep in this."

"And that's exactly why it will work. I have a wild reputation. Like Prince Marc," she added. "The media used to compare me to him. And he was part of the smuggling scam."

"He owed the mob money. You're a twenty-two-year-old artist with a trust fund."

"For your information, I won't have access to my trust

fund until I'm thirty.'' She flipped her hair over her shoulder. ''And I can play up that angle. I can say that I need more than the petty cash my stingy family tosses my way. Paulus can skip town after we unload the CDs, and I can defy my parents with my own money, pulling the wool over their eyes in the process.''

Luke couldn't believe what he was hearing. ''What about your relationship with me? How are you going to explain that away?''

She sent him a seductive look. ''I've been using you to get access to the CDs. And, of course, you've fallen prey to my charms.''

He grabbed his water and took a swig. Did she realize the danger she would be putting herself in? People they cared about were dead. Rowan Neville's innocent children had been threatened. Armed guards were protecting the king. And Maggie wanted to walk headfirst into a hornet's nest, with nothing but her youth and feminine wiles. ''Get this ridiculous scheme out of your head right now. I won't consider it, not even for a second.''

She pushed away from the table, rattling the dishes. ''I know I can make it work.''

Luke stood and came toward her. She stared at him defiantly, with her head held high, her chin thrust forward.

''It's a good plan,'' she said. ''And if you helped me refine it, we could catch Paulus.''

''It's dangerous,'' he countered. ''And even if I thought Paulus would fall for it, I wouldn't let you do it.'' Damn it. He cared about her, more than he could say. What would he do if something happened to her? How could he go on?

''That isn't—''

''Don't say another word.'' Frustrated, he backed her against the wall, silencing her argument. And then he realized how close they were. Their faces were inches apart, their bodies almost brushing.

She was still angry. She hissed like a cat, and he lost control. Tugging her head back with her hair, he kissed her, catching her startled gasp as he covered her mouth.

She clawed, then rubbed against him, bumping his zipper with grinding hips. Their tongues mated desperately, and all of his fantasies crashed and tumbled in his brain. Making love to her on the shore, both of them rolling frantically over the sand. The striptease he'd imagined when he'd gotten drunk. The hot, gritty lap dance. He wanted all of that and more.

Ending the kiss, he shackled her wrists in his hand and held her arms above her head. He knew he should step back, release her, kill the urge to tear off her clothes. Maggie Connelly was trouble. She messed with his emotions. She challenged his heart. And she was too young, he thought. Too reckless. Too free.

She met his gaze, her eyes flashing. She looked like a vixen, hot and ready, her hair falling like rain.

"Do it," she said. "Take what you want."

He knew she was baiting him, taking his weakness and using it against him, but suddenly he didn't give a damn.

The need was too strong.

Her dress was red silk, adorned with a row of tiny, jeweled buttons. Luke grabbed the collar and pulled the fabric. Buttons popped as the garment tore, exposing a bra nearly the same color as her skin.

He kept tearing until he saw her panties. She wore a garter belt and hose, and the sultry lingerie turned him on even more. It was as if she knew, as if she'd been preparing for this moment since the night she'd asked him to dance. The inevitable seduction. The unholy surrender.

"Take everything off," he told her. "I want to watch you

undress.'' And then he wanted to ravage her, to make her come, to feel her melt in his arms.

She removed the tattered dress, then unhooked her bra, letting it fall to the floor. When she touched her nipples, Luke's entire body trembled.

Anxious and aroused, he watched. She discarded her shoes, a pair of red leather pumps with spiked heels. The garter belt and hose came next. And after she took off her panties, she slid her hand between her legs. But only for second. For one wild, erotic second.

Luke wasn't in the mood to wait, to play a slow, sexual game. This fantasy was unbridled and swift.

He dropped to his knees, grabbed her hips and pulled her against his mouth.

She bucked on contact, but she wasn't shy. She dragged her hands through his hair and encouraged him to taste her, rubbing and making throaty little sounds.

Young. Free. Reckless.

Licking and kissing, he teased her with his tongue, absorbing the slick, womanly flavor. He knew she was close. He could feel the moisture, the heat, the tangle of electricity.

He looked up at her and saw that she looked back at him. "Luke.'' She breathed his name, and suddenly her eyes glazed.

He intensified each intimate kiss, and she climaxed, shuddering violently. He kept his mouth there, tasting her release. And when her limbs went molten, he rose to catch her so she could fall gently into his arms.

Maggie felt as if she were floating. And then she realized Luke was carrying her to bed. She kissed him, brushing his lips softly.

"Sometimes when I look at you, I have to remind myself to breathe,'' he said. "You're all I think about.''

Still dazed, she blinked. She hadn't expected such romantic words, not when he'd just driven her to madness.

She touched his face, skimming her fingers over those rugged features. "You're my lover now." My heart, she thought. The man I love.

He pushed the quilt away and placed her on the sheet. It was cool and inviting against her skin. When she reached for him, he shook his head.

"Not yet," he said, nipping her bottom lip as he kissed her. "We need protection." Luke headed for the bathroom, and Maggie smiled.

Naked and aroused, she scooted against the headboard, feeling delightfully wicked. The lights were on, and the table was cluttered with discarded dishes. Yet the setting seemed perfect.

Luke returned with his shaving kit. He rifled through it, secured a foil packet and placed it on the nightstand. Maggie watched as he undressed hastily, tossing his shirt onto the floor. When he unzipped his trousers, she pulled him onto the bed and they tumbled over the sheet, kissing and dragging off his pants and briefs.

His body boasted power and strength. Sliding her hands over broad shoulders, she followed the ripple of muscle down his stomach to stroke his sex.

He was unbelievably hard, with a bead of moisture pearling at the tip. She lowered her head and kissed him there, tasting the saltiness with her tongue.

His stomach muscles jumped. "Don't do that," he warned.

Maggie didn't listen. Stroking him, she took him in her mouth. In sudden surrender, he lifted his hips and said something unintelligible—a groan, a prayer, a curse—she couldn't be sure. But it didn't matter. Tonight he was hers. Every rough plane, every raw, rugged inch.

He didn't let her claim him for long. He was, she realized, much too eager to engage in the final act. To make love. To join with her.

Luke tore into the condom, sheathed himself and nudged her thighs apart, taking control once again. She let him have what he wanted. She gave willingly—her body and her heart.

He was tender yet rough. Anxious yet somehow patient. He pleasured them both, thrusting deep and then withdrawing, over and over, heightening the sensation. She arched to meet him as he tongued her nipple. And those hands, those skilled soldier's hands, were everywhere, sending slow, dreamy shivers over her skin.

"I don't want this to end," he said. "I want to be inside you forever."

He spoke of sex, but she told herself it was love. She needed so desperately for him to love her.

She could hear the ocean, like a seashell against her ear. Or was it her pulse pounding at her throat? He pressed his forehead to hers, and for a moment the world stilled. There was nothing but them. Lovers who could have risen from the sea.

Overwhelmed, Maggie kissed him. She longed to know his heart, to heal his spirit. This beautiful man, she thought, with the dark eyes and the dark, reclusive soul. Emotion, hers and his, swirled like a mist. She could feel it rise and float over them, a haunting they couldn't see.

They clasped hands, and he increased the rhythm.

Deeper. Stronger.

The maddening, lethal rhythm. The explosive heat.

This was more than sex, she told herself as her body quaked. So much more, she whispered as Lucas Starwind threw back his head and climaxed, spilling his seed.

# Eleven

Even without an alarm clock, Luke awakened before dawn. He sat up and watched Maggie sleep. He thought she looked damn good in his bed. Night-tousled hair tangled around her face, and a pale-blue blanket covered her nakedness.

Smoothing her hair, he kissed her forehead. She made an incoherent sound and turned onto her side. He smiled, leaving her alone. She wasn't a morning person, that much he already knew.

Luke went about his usual routine. He washed his face, brushed his teeth, pulled on a gray sweatsuit and headed to the wet bar, grateful the suite provided an array of caffeine choices, including a no-frills brand of American coffee.

After putting on a pair of running shoes, he took his coffee onto the balcony, then sat at the glass-topped table and waited for the sun to rise, enjoying a misty view of the private beach.

Finding comfort in the wind and sea, Luke sat for hours,

studying the sky. Glittering beams of red and gold broke through the clouds, finally introducing the Mediterranean sun.

"I thought I'd find you out here."

He turned to see Maggie wrapped in a white silk robe, her eyes still sleepy, her hair tousled. She came toward him and when she leaned against the balcony rail, he caught the faint outline of her naked body beneath the thin material.

She looked enchanting as ever. A muse who inspired the arts—poetry, dance and song. She inspired lust, too, he thought. Fantasies he couldn't seem to control.

His sex stirred. "I want you," he said. "Right here. Right now."

"Do you?" She sent him a sultry smile and opened her palm. A foil packet shimmered in her hand. "I had the same idea, only I came prepared."

Reaching for her, he pulled her onto his lap and kissed her hard and quick. She tasted like mint, as cool and refreshing as the morning air.

She opened her robe and brought his head to her breast. He licked her nipples, then caught one with his teeth and tugged, just a little, just enough to make her moan.

Sliding his hands down her body, he caressed every curve, stroking her belly. She squirmed, and he moved lower.

When he plunged a finger deep inside, she gasped. She was wet and slick and eager. While the ocean rolled quietly upon the shore and clouds floated softly across the sky, Luke and Maggie went crazy.

She streaked up his sweatshirt to scrape her nails across his chest; he bit her neck and sucked the tender spot like a vampire.

He couldn't think, but he didn't want to. She was naked and straddling his lap, her white robe billowing like wings. All that mattered was her. Tasting, feeling, living out the lust.

He lifted his hips and tugged down his sweats. The moment he was free, the very instant the male hardness nudged her thigh, she tore into the condom, slipped it on him and sank onto his length.

He closed his eyes, and she rode him until he thought he might die—from beauty, from bliss, from emotions that slammed into his soul.

Her climax triggered his, and they shared a mind-blowing release, kissing and panting.

When it ended, when he could breathe again, he opened his eyes and knew he would never be the same. Not from the sex, but from her. She'd changed something inside him, and because he wasn't quite sure what it was, he told himself not to panic.

He wasn't going to marry her.

Pulling himself back to reality, he adjusted his sweats, feeling a bit awkward about removing the condom. "I hate these damn things."

She belted her robe. "I'll get on the Pill. I've taken it before."

During her affair with Claudio, he supposed. Luke didn't argue. He wanted the opportunity to spill inside her and not have to worry about conception.

If he wasn't going to marry her, then they weren't going to have children.

They went back to his suite. He discarded the condom, then resisted the urge to pace, recalling the night she'd asked him to come over and make a baby. He'd actually been tempted then.

And damn it, he was tempted now. He wanted to claim her, plant the seed of life so she would be connected to him forever.

Yet the idea of being a husband and father scared him senseless.

"Should I order breakfast?" she asked.

"Not for me." He knelt to tighten his shoelaces. "I'm going for a run." Something he did every morning before he showered. He wasn't avoiding her purposely, but today of all days he needed to clear his mind, to stop thinking about a commitment he didn't intend to make.

"Will you take Bruno along? He's probably anxious to get out."

"Sure."

Maggie opened the door to her suite and called the dog. The loyal mastiff appeared instantaneously. She patted the canine bodyguard and then gave Luke a gentle, heart-stirring kiss.

"I'll wait to eat until you get back," she said.

"Okay," he responded, trying to sound casual, even though his mind was still spinning.

Luke retrieved Bruno's leash and turned away. And with the dog by his side, he headed for the beach, wishing the Connellys' youngest daughter hadn't dared him to marry her.

The following afternoon Maggie and Luke interviewed Princess Catherine, gathering information about Gregor Paulus. They'd chosen to conduct the meeting in a relaxed environment, so they sat on a redwood deck at Dunemere that provided a soothing view of the sea.

Luke drank coffee, while Maggie and Princess Catherine sipped chamomile tea sweetened with honey. A platter of blueberry scones went untouched.

Studying Catherine with an appreciative eye, Maggie noticed changes in the other woman. Emotional changes that made the young princess more beautiful than she already was.

Love, Maggie decided, had given her feisty, headstrong cousin a graceful air of contentment. The dashing sheikh, Kajal bin Russard, she had married was truly her soul mate.

The way Luke is mine, Maggie thought, glancing at her lover.

"Was Gregor Paulus your father's confidant?" he asked the princess.

"Yes. Gregor was quite devoted to my father."

"So Prince Marc would have entrusted him with just about anything?"

She nodded, placing her tea back on the table. "Yes, I believe so."

"Will you tell me what you think of Paulus?" he asked.

"Truthfully, I don't like him." A strand of Catherine's auburn hair lifted in the wind. "Not in the least," she added, intensifying her statement. "When I was a child, he did his quiet best to diminish me in my father's eyes."

Maggie suspected that Prince Marc had been too self-involved to notice.

"And now?" Luke asked. "How does Paulus treat you now?"

"He tried to manipulate me soon after my father was killed. I was supposed to go out on the boat that day, but I couldn't make it, so Father took my place." She paused to sip her tea, to breathe a gust of sea air. "Gregor preyed on my guilt. He made certain that I knew he felt the prince died because of me."

"Bastard," Luke muttered.

"Quite," the princess agreed before he could apologize for the profanity. "But I don't allow Gregor to intimidate me anymore. These days he keeps his distance."

"Thank you for your time. I know how difficult all of

this has been for you," Luke said. "But I have one more question. Can you tell me why Prince Marc was driving the king's speedboat? Particularly since he wasn't originally scheduled to be on it that day?"

"King Thomas preferred to have someone else in the family drive. Because he was getting on in years and his eyesight was failing, he didn't take the boat out by himself anymore. But that wasn't something that was widely known."

"So you were going to pilot the boat before your father stepped in?"

"Yes. And I'm sure you can see how Gregor used that against me."

A short time later Maggie escorted her cousin to the limousine that waited to take her back to the palace.

They hugged and then looked into each other's eyes. There wasn't much more to say. Princess Catherine had been informed of her father's treachery, and she was coping with the knowledge, leaning on the man she loved for support.

Maggie returned to Luke and found him standing on the deck, gazing at the ocean, his hands thrust in his pockets, his jacket billowing in the breeze. She wished that he would lean on her for support, that he would trust her to help him trap Gregor Paulus.

"Prince Marc was a weak man," he said without turning.

She stepped closer. "Yes, he was."

Luke still watched the sea, concentrating, it seemed, on the rise and fall of each wave. "Which is exactly why he relied on someone like Paulus."

"You have a theory, don't you?"

"Yeah." He finally turned, his hair falling onto his forehead. "I think Paulus pulled Prince Marc into this."

"How? Marc is the one who had an association with the mob."

"True, but I suspect that it was Paulus's idea to approach the Kellys about pirating those files from the Institute."

"How?" she asked again. "Paulus couldn't have known about the cancer virus."

"Marc probably told him about it when it first happened. And later, when Marc told Paulus that he was in trouble with the mob, Paulus devised a plan to appease the Kellys and get the prince out of hot water."

Maggie sighed. "And Marc went along with it because he was too spineless to face the Kellys on his own."

"Exactly. He let Paulus do his dirty work for him."

She met Luke's gaze, determined to convince him to allow her to help. Gregor Paulus was a force to be reckoned with, but with a carefully developed plan, she knew she could trap him. "You have to let me—"

"No!" He cut her off before she could finish her plea. "You're not going undercover. Do you hear me? You're not."

"Why are you being so stubborn about this? All I'm asking for is a chance to approach Paulus. I'll wear a wire, and you can be somewhere nearby, just in case there's trouble. And on top of that, I'll keep Bruno with me." Who in their right mind would try to hurt her with a two-hundred-pound mastiff by her side? "Why do I have a canine bodyguard if I can't use him?"

Luke glared at her. "Paulus is severely allergic to dogs. There's no damn way he would have a reasonable conversation with you if Bruno were there. And I'm not going to be listening with an earpiece while the woman I'm sleeping with is risking her neck. Let it go, Maggie. It isn't going to happen."

At a standoff, they stared at each other. With her tempe

flaring, she shot poisoned darts from her eyes to his. She ought to defy Luke and go after Paulus on her own. Prove to the stubborn detective that she was capable of much more than he'd given her credit for.

"Don't even think about it," he said.

"I don't know what you mean," she retorted.

"The hell you don't. It's written all over your face."

As a strand of her hair blew against her cheek, she shoved it away. Deep down, she knew that trapping Paulus without Luke's help would be next to impossible, but she had the right to fantasize about it, to imagine herself glorifying in personal triumph.

"I'm keeping my eye on you, Maggie."

Fine, she thought. If he was going to watch her like a hawk, then she would use this to her advantage and spend every waking hour right under his suspicious nose, concentrating all of her energy on winning the marriage dare.

She was mad as hell, but she still wanted to be Lucas Starwind's wife. She couldn't help it if she'd fallen in love with a macho, overly protective jerk.

After an exceptionally long, invigorating shower, Luke stepped out of the stall and wrapped a towel around his waist. Maggie sat at the vanity mirror, wearing a terry-cloth robe and applying her makeup. Apparently she'd bathed in her own suite, then moved all of her creams, lotions and cosmetics onto his countertop.

"What are you doing?" he asked.

"Getting ready." She stretched her eye, lined it with a creamy brown pencil, then smudged the line with a cotton swab.

He moved toward one of the double sinks. "Why didn't you finish getting ready in your own bathroom? Why'd you haul your stuff over here?"

"Because I'm moving in." She turned to face him. "I don't understand why we need two suites. We're sleeping together now."

But that wasn't the same as living together, he thought. Watching her settle into his domain made him feel as if they were in a committed relationship. Or, heaven help him, married.

"Your family is arriving tomorrow," he said. "And I don't think it would be proper to share a room while they're here."

Her jaw dropped, and she looked at him at if he'd just sprouted gills and a tail. "Good grief, Luke. My family isn't from the Dark Ages."

"You're still their baby." And he was the older man who ravished her every night, who couldn't seem to get his fill.

"We're consenting adults," she countered. "And being up front about what's going on is certainly more mature than sneaking into each other's beds. Besides, my parents are staying at the palace."

But some of her brothers and sisters intended to stay at the beach house. Her *married* siblings, he realized. Every damn one of them had settled down. In fact, Maggie was the last unmarried Connelly.

Preparing to shave, he lathered his face, frowning into the mirror.

"So, what's the verdict?" she asked.

He contemplated their situation further, scraping a disposable razor across his jaw. "We're keeping both rooms. I can't sleep with you while your family is here. It just isn't right. We'll have to learn to behave ourselves."

Maggie raised her eyebrows. "No wild moans in the middle of the night? No more early-morning romps on the balcony? I don't think that's possible."

He looked at her, and after several seconds of complete silence, they both burst out laughing. Wild moans. Early-morning romps. He supposed they did have the tendency to get carried away.

"Come on, Luke. Don't be so old-fashioned about this," she said when their laughter faded. "Let's move in together."

"I can't do that. Not in good conscience." Even if her family suspected that they were lovers, he wanted them to know that he wasn't using her, that his feelings for her were based on more than just sex. "This is my way of respecting you, Maggie. Please don't take that away from me."

"Oh." Her voice went soft, her eyes glassy. He could see that he'd touched her heart.

"So, will you work with me on this?" he asked.

She nodded, and he knew that if his face wasn't covered in shaving cream, she would have kissed him.

"I promise to behave," she said. "But I'm not giving you up after this trip is over."

"I know." They would remain lovers for a while, he thought. But it wouldn't last forever.

Luke returned to the mirror and finished shaving, looking forward to a night on the town. Maggie had offered to take him on a tour of Altaria, treating him to her favorite places.

He drove the European SUV they'd rented, and she gave him directions, guiding him down narrow roads flanked with cobblestoned sidewalks and buildings rife with old-world charm.

They stopped at a quaint little café, and Luke allowed Maggie to order, then wondered what he'd gotten himself into when the appetizer was served. The marinated olives and zucchini seemed normal enough, but he refused to try the stuffed squid, eyeing the suction cups with displeasure.

Maggie tossed her head and laughed, and he knew she'd ordered it to tease him. Where food was concerned, he wasn't nearly as adventurous as she was.

On an outdoor, heated patio, they drank Chianti and talked, their conversation as vibrant as the wine.

Luke studied his companion. Her hair, loose and straight, fell past her shoulders. She wore slim-fitting jeans and a denim blouse. Her buckskin jacket was smooth and feminine. Beautiful, he thought. *Bella,* just like the Italian waiter had called her.

Their entrées arrived, and they dined on eggplant, roast chicken and potatoes seasoned with mouthwatering spices. Luke wanted to lean across the table and kiss Maggie, but decided that dragging his sleeve through a side dish of pasta wasn't the most gentlemanly way to steal a kiss.

After their meal, he took advantage of the opportunity to touch her. They strolled, hand in hand, down imperfect sidewalks, stepping over cracks and chips in the stone. Stars lit up the night, the Big Dipper pouring silver specks across a royal-blue sky.

Maggie guided Luke into an ice-cream parlor. They ordered two melon sorbets, then resumed their walk, eating the refreshing dessert along the way.

"What do you think of Altaria?" she asked.

He finished his sorbet. "I love it." And he loved this moment, this carefree evening with her.

"Let's go there," she said, indicating something across the street. "I've always wanted to see what it was like."

He turned, expecting an old stone church or another historic building. But instead she pointed to a magic shop, a tiny establishment with ancient symbols on the door.

Healing crystals dangled from serpentine chains, and candles flickered, sending jasmine-scented smoke through the air. An older woman with long gray hair and watchful eyes hovered near a glass case. The proprietor, Luke thought. A local Gypsy who probably read tea leaves and tarot cards.

He met the old woman's gaze, and suddenly his breath lodged in his throat. He could feel her power, the energy that flowed through her veins.

And because he was a superstitious man, a Cherokee who knew magic existed, he tried to break eye contact, but found himself trapped.

She removed a tiny glass figurine and handed it to him. "Terpsichore," she said. "The muse of dance."

He glanced at the fragile glass figure. The goddess held a gold lyre, and on her head she wore a crown of leaves.

"Terpsichore knows what's in your heart," the old woman said.

*A qua da nv do. My heart.*

He'd lost his heart the first time he'd danced with Maggie, and now the Gypsy wanted him to admit that he'd never gotten it back, that Maggie, his muse, had claimed it for good.

I don't need this, he thought. I don't need someone prying into my mind. Or trying to convince me that I'm falling in love.

He handed the figure back to her, but she refused to accept it. "Keep it," she said, turning away from him.

Feeling unsteady, Luke considered leaving the muse on the counter, but quickly changed his mind. He didn't know anything about the old woman's culture, but in his, it was rude to refuse a gift.

Unsure of what else to do, he headed straight out the door, leaned against the building and pulled a much-needed gust of air into his lungs.

"What was that all about?" Maggie asked, rushing after him.

"I don't know," he lied, even though the tiny muse glowed in his hand.

Later that night Maggie sat next to Luke on his sofa, a pillow between them. Her family would be arriving tomorrow morning, which meant she wouldn't be seeing much of Luke, and just the thought alone made her miss him.

But worse yet was his detached behavior. She feared he was reverting to his reclusive self. He seemed disturbed by the incident with the Gypsy. Maggie didn't understand why, and he hadn't offered an explanation.

"What did you do with the muse?" she prodded, moving the pillow.

He motioned to the bedroom. "It's on the dresser."

"I wonder why the Gypsy gave it to you."

He shrugged. "I have no idea."

She studied his profile. A golden light from the fire bathed his skin, intensifying the razor-edged slant of his cheekbones and strong, determined cut of his jaw. "Did you even know who Terpsichore was before the Gypsy mentioned her?"

"Sort of. I knew that there were nine muses, and that they were goddesses from Greek mythology, but I didn't know their names."

"Pegasus was from Greek mythology, too," she said, thinking about Gwen's winged horse. "In fact, when Pegasus was a colt, the goddess Athena entrusted the muses with his care."

"I know." He turned to look at her. "Pegasus was so excited to meet the muses that he struck the side of Mount Helicon with his hooves and caused two springs to gush forth. Springs of inspiration or something."

Maggie nodded. Luke seemed to know the story quite well. "Did you read to Gwen about Pegasus?"

"My mom did. But I always thought the idea of a winged horse was pretty cool, so I paid attention, too."

Now Maggie understood. The muse figurine probably reminded him of Gwen. And that was why the Gypsy's unusual gift had unnerved him. "So many mystical things have happened," she said. "I painted Gwen without knowing it, and now the Gypsy gives you a muse. All of this must mean something."

"I don't know. I guess. I'm trying not to make a big deal out of it."

"Don't be sad, Luke. I think Gwen is watching over you. Like an angel."

He met her gaze, his dark eyes suddenly struck with emotion. "Thank you," he whispered. "That was a nice thing to say."

She reached for him, and they embraced. And because she felt his heart pounding next to hers, she shivered. She wanted to tell him that she loved him, but she wasn't sure if this was the right time.

Maggie drew a nervous breath. This had to be the right time. Once her family arrived, she wouldn't get the chance. There would be no more stolen moments, no more candlelit dinners or romantic strolls on the beach.

Luke would probably spend his days discussing the sting operation with Rafe. And while they were devising a plan for an undercover agent to trap Paulus, she would be busy with her sisters.

No, she thought, there would be no time for confessions of love.

Luke nuzzled her neck, and she felt her pulse quicken.

"There's something I need to tell you," she said softly.

He ended their embrace. "What is it?"

She looked right at him. "I love you. And not just as a friend. I love you the way a wife loves a husband."

He went perfectly still, and when he finally spoke, his voice sounded raw. "You just think you do. What you're experiencing is some sort of youthful infatuation."

Hurt, she squared her shoulders, preparing to defend herself. "Please don't talk to me like I'm a fickle-hearted teenager. I'm a grown woman. And I love you, whether you believe it or not."

He shook his head. "I don't believe it."

Drawing strength from her pride, she did her damnedest to keep her eyes dry. She wouldn't cry in front of him. Not now. "Why would I have dared you to marry me? Why would I have offered you that kind of commitment?"

"Because you *think* you love me. You're confused."

"Damn you." Her temper rose, and unable to stop the blast of anger, she socked his arm. The least he could do was acknowledge how she felt. "You're a jerk, you know that?"

He grabbed her wrists before she could pummel him again. And then he straddled her, pinning her to the couch. "I have no idea what in the hell to do about you, Maggie. You're driving me crazy."

You could love me back, she wanted to say. You could open your stubborn heart.

They stared at each other, and for a moment she thought that he might kiss her, that his frustration might turn to passion. Or, she prayed, to an admission of love.

But it didn't.

Breaking eye contact, he released her. "Go back to your own room, Maggie. Get some sleep and forget about this."

"You're asking me to forget about the way I feel? To convince myself that I don't love you?"

"Yes," he said. "I am."

# Twelve

**T**he Connelly siblings weren't a quiet bunch. They were, in Luke's opinion, an interesting gene pool sired by Maggie's father, Grant.

Three out of the eight boys had been conceived with women other than Maggie's mother, Emma. Thirty-six-year-old twins, Chance and Douglas, sons Grant hadn't been aware of until this year, were products of a relationship he'd had before he'd married Emma. Thirty-two-year-old Seth, on the other hand, had been produced from an affair Grant had had with his secretary while his marriage to Emma had been on shaky ground.

Grant and Emma, now completely loyal to each other, weren't staying at the beach house, but there were enough Connelly heirs present to keep Luke's head spinning. Through the lively conversation and rustle of linen napkins, no one seemed to notice Luke's discomfort. He sat at the cherry-wood table, doing his damnedest to dodge eye contact with six-year-old Amanda, or Mandy, as she was often called.

The child watched him, and he didn't know why. Luke couldn't read kids. He'd spent a lifetime analyzing his peers, yet children managed to elude him. But as far as he could tell, Mandy was the apple of her daddy's eye and quite enamored of Kristina, the woman twenty-seven-year-old Drew Connelly had married.

"Where's Aunt Maggie?" the little girl asked Luke.

He finally turned and met Mandy's curious gaze. "She's in her room. She isn't feeling well." Or more than likely, he thought, she was avoiding him.

"What's wrong with her?"

"She has a headache."

"Did she take some aspirin?"

"Yeah, I suppose she did."

A maid served their salads, and Luke breathed a sigh of relief. Mandy would be too busy eating to chat.

Serving bowls of ranch dressing were passed around the table. After Mandy doused her salad, Luke accepted the dressing, poured some onto his greens and then handed it to Seth, who thanked him with a polite nod.

Luke considered Seth the black sheep of the family. His mother, Angie Donahue, the secretary Grant had dallied with, had turned Seth over to Grant and Emma when he was a hard-edged, scrappy twelve-year-old. Unable to control the wild youth, they'd shipped him off to military school, where he'd learned to distance himself from his prominent family.

But these days, Luke noticed, Seth seemed right at home with the Connelly clan. He'd overcome plenty, including the heart-wrenching knowledge that his mother had come back into his life for the sole purpose of aiding the Kelly crime family in the smuggling scam.

As Luke picked up his fork and concentrated on his salad,

Seth leaned toward his wife, Lynn. They bent their heads together like the newlyweds they were.

Damn it. There were too many married couples at the table, he thought. Too many happy, madly-in-love Connellys.

"How come you're frowning?"

Luke turned to see Mandy, her head tilted, white-blond bangs dusting observant green eyes.

"I wasn't frowning. I was eating."

"Nuh-uh. You were making a face like this." She furrowed her brow and turned down her lips, exaggerating a bitter scowl.

He wondered if he looked that surly all the time. "I guess I've got some things on my mind."

"What?" she asked.

"Nothing that concerns you," he responded.

"Grown-ups always say stuff like that." Quite properly, she adjusted the napkin on her lap. "But they don't fool me. I'll bet you had a fight with Aunt Maggie. You probably gave her a headache."

At this point, Luke decided that Miss Mandy was six going on forty. "You're pretty smart for a kid." And he was a first-rate heel. He'd hurt Maggie's feelings last night, refusing to believe that what she felt for him was real.

But he didn't want her to be in love with him. Nor did he want to face the fact that he might be falling in love, too.

"I saw you dancing with her," Mandy said.

His chest constricted. Terpsichore. The muse of dance. "You did?"

She nodded. "At Uncle Rafe's wedding. I could tell she liked you. I was going to help you guys be together, but my dad and Kristina said I already did enough matchmaking. They got married because of me."

He couldn't help but smile. Amanda Connelly was an angel, an adorable little girl with invisible wings.

*Don't be sad, Luke. I think Gwen is watching over you. Like an angel.*

Maybe she was, he thought as Mandy grinned at him. Maybe she was.

After dinner, Luke went into the kitchen and asked the maid if she would prepare a plate for him to take to Maggie.

He carried the tray upstairs and received a boy-has-our-little-sister-got-you-whipped look from three of Maggie's brothers. In return, he sent the Connelly men a hard stare. Single guys were supposed to rib married ones, not the other way around. But that hadn't stopped Rafe, Seth and Drew from chuckling.

Luke knocked on Maggie's door—the door in the hallway rather than the one that connected their rooms.

She answered, clearly surprised to see him. She wore a satin robe, and her hair was coiled into a hasty topknot, damp tendrils falling from the confinement. She smelled like sunshine on a breezy, winter day.

"I thought maybe you could use a little food," he said.

"I was going to order something later."

"Oh, well…I can take this back." He shifted uncomfortably, picturing himself passing her brothers again.

"No. That's okay. You can come in."

He entered her room and set the tray on a nearby table. "How's your head?"

"Better, thank you."

Because he didn't know what else to do with his hands, he shoved them in his pockets. Her nipples were hard. He could see them pearling against the satin robe. He suspected that she'd just stepped out of the tub, which accounted for the flowery scent clinging to her skin.

"Is something on your mind, Luke?"

"No. I just stopped by to bring you dinner." And to tell her that she'd healed a deep and painful part of him. Although he would never forget what had happened to his sister, Maggie had helped him see Gwen as an angel rather than the victim of a violent crime.

But now that he was here, preparing to talk to Maggie, he couldn't form the words, fearing they would lead to another discussion—one he wasn't ready to confront.

Love. Marriage. Babies.

Luke was still afraid of making that kind of soul-searching commitment, especially with Maggie. He didn't trust her reckless spirit, the youth and the vigor that made her who she was.

She drove him crazy with worry. What if she tried to go after Paulus on her own? He knew damn well that the thought had crossed her mind.

"I want a promise from you," he said. "A solemn vow."

She searched his gaze. "What?"

"That you'll stay away from Paulus."

Her shoulders tensed. "We've already established the fact that I'm not getting involved in the sting operation." She looked him directly in the eye. "But if you want a vow, then you've got it. I'll stay away from Paulus."

"Okay." He backed off, but she was still meeting him eye to eye.

"It's your turn," she said. "To promise that you won't try to end the marriage dare before New Year's Eve."

He expelled the air in his lungs. The sheers that draped the sliding glass doors were open. Beyond the balcony, the moon lit the beach in a golden hue. He imagined watching her dance on the shore, her robe billowing, her hair catching the moonlight.

His mermaid. His muse.

"I promise," he said, before turning away from the wonder of the sea and the woman who seemed to be part of it. The woman he couldn't get off his mind.

On the morning of the coronation rehearsal, Maggie wore an elegant apricot-colored dress, spun from the finest silk and accented with a strand of pearls. She was, after all, the daughter of a former princess and the sister of the soon-to-be-crowned king. And today she knew she must look and behave the part.

Gazing at her reflection, she debated on how to style her hair. Should she wear it loose or work it into a French twist?

Maybe something in between, she thought as she pulled it back with a rare, jeweled barrette. Preparing for the long day ahead, she slipped on a pair of low-heeled pumps, then walked onto the balcony and let the ocean breeze caress her face.

And then she saw Luke, exercising the dog. They'd just completed their daily run and were headed toward the house. They made a striking pair—the powerful warrior with his copper skin and raven hair, and the loyal mastiff with his fawn-colored coat and dark, masked face.

Suddenly Luke stopped and glanced up. Did he sense she was there? Did he know she had been watching him?

Everything seemed so uncertain now. She'd admitted that she loved him, and he'd agreed to go on with the dare, yet they engaged in awkward glances and strained conversations.

Even with the distance between them, their eyes met, and she knew he would wait for her on the deck. Strained conversations or not, he wanted to talk, to warn her to be careful at the rehearsal.

She sighed and turned away. She wished he trusted her instincts. At times he made her feel like a child.

Maggie went downstairs and caught the aroma of coffee

brewing and bacon frying. Breakfast, she assumed, would be served shortly. She passed two of her brothers on her way outside. They sat in the living room, a newspaper divided between them, both men attired in dark suits. The entire Rosemere-Connelly family would be attending the coronation rehearsal today. And on the afternoon of the actual event, each would hold an esteemed seat in La Cattedrale Grande, the Altarian Grand Cathedral.

Maggie walked onto the redwood deck and caught sight of Luke.

"Hi," he said. "You look incredible."

"Thank you."

He looked incredible, too, but she doubted he would believe her if she told him. Sweat beaded his forehead, and his hair, tousled from the wind, shone with blue-black highlights.

Luke shifted his stance. "I wish you would agree to take Bruno with you today."

Maggie glanced at the mastiff. Bodyguard or not, it didn't seem appropriate to bring a dog to the cathedral. "I'll be fine. My family will be there."

"Don't go anywhere alone," he persisted. "Not even for a second."

"I won't."

"Not just at the cathedral, but at the palace, too."

"Please. Stop worrying. King Daniel and his queen have been living at the palace for nearly a year. My parents are staying there, not to mention Princess Catherine and Sheikh Kaj. And of course there's my sister Alexandra and her husband, Prince Phillip." She paused to finger her pearls. "Paulus isn't going to blow his cover with everyone around."

"I know. I just wanted to warn you to be careful anyway."

Would he worry at the coronation, too? she wondered.

Or would he feel differently because he would be attending that event? Maybe Gregor Paulus and his accomplices would be caught by then. She certainly hoped so.

"Have some faith in me, Luke. I won't do anything to get Paulus's attention. In fact, I probably won't even see him." She envisioned a long, formal day saturated with Altarian protocol, something most of the Connelly heirs and their spouses were still learning. "If anything, wish me luck. You know how I tend to forget my manners." And royal manners, in her opinion, were staid and tedious.

Luke grinned, and she envied his leisure day. Aside from the presence of a nonintrusive domestic staff, he and Bruno would have the beach house to themselves.

"Good luck," he said, still smiling.

And what a smile, she thought. All those straight white teeth flashing against bronzed skin. "How about going for a midnight stroll with me tonight? We can count the stars." And steal a passionate kiss beneath a bright, crescent moon.

"That sounds nice. I've missed you, baby."

A tingle warmed her spine. "Me, too."

He pulled a hand through his hair. "I better catch a shower before breakfast. I can't come to the table like this."

All rugged and gorgeous. She couldn't imagine why not. Watching him go, she wished she could stay home with him.

And make love until they both ached for more.

As expected, the coronation rehearsal had been long and exhausting, but awe-inspiring, too. Maggie looked forward to the upcoming ceremony, imagining her brother taking an oath to govern the people of Altaria. She could already see him, kneeling at the altar, strong and handsome in the commander-in-chief uniform that came with the responsibility of the throne.

But for now His Majesty had arranged for a small, private banquet at the palace for the Rosemeres and the Connellys.

Maggie sat at the end of the table, next to her sister, Tara, who had been reunited with her long-lost husband, Michael Paige, a man who had once been presumed dead. The Rosemeres and the Connellys had suffered through tragedies and prevailed in triumphs, and Maggie was proud to be a member of both prestigious families.

The conversation was warm and friendly, but by the time Maggie finished a bowl of chilled pumpkin soup, her tenderhearted mood turned to disorientation. Suddenly she felt ill.

Drawing a deep breath, she lifted her water, then took a small, careful sip. Had the spicy soup disagreed with her? Or had it been the stuffed grape leaves and the shrimp dumpling appetizers?

Somehow that didn't seem possible. Maggie was accustomed to rich, elaborate foods. Then what was wrong?

She frowned at her empty bowl. Maybe she was coming down with the flu.

Not now, she thought. And not here. The last thing she wanted to do was spoil the beauty of this intimate dinner.

But a wave of dizziness had set in. The room was blurring, the unicorn tapestries melting off the walls, horns and hooves bleeding into the carpet.

She turned to her sister. "I'm not feeling very well."

Tara reached for her arm. "Do you want me to walk you to the nearest powder room?"

"Please."

With Tara hovering like a mother hen, Maggie sat on a velvet sofa in the ladies' lounge and cursed her body for failing her. She rarely took ill. Although she'd had a headache yesterday, she'd attributed it to stress. "I think I caught a virus," she told her sister.

"Oh, my," Tara said before she turned and asked the powder-room attendant to bring Maggie a moist cloth.

The middle-aged woman returned with the cloth. As Maggie dampened her face, she looked up at Tara, feeling guilty for taking her sister away from the banquet. It wasn't often the entire family spent an evening together. "Go back to the table and finish your meal."

"I'm not leaving you here."

"Please. I'll be fine. I just need to rest."

The powder-room attendant turned to Tara. "Excuse me for interrupting, ma'am. But if Miss Connelly would like to go home, I can call for a palace chauffeur."

"What do you think, Maggie?" her sister asked. "Do you want to return to Dunemere?"

"Maybe. I don't know. Just let me sit here for a while."

Although it took some prodding, Maggie finally convinced Tara to finish her meal. After all, she wasn't completely alone. The powder-room attendant was there.

"I'm coming back to check on you," her sister warned. "And I'm bringing Mother and Alexandra."

Wonderful, Maggie thought. If she vomited, the women in her family would be in attendance. Oh, yes. This was truly a royal affair.

After Tara left, Maggie closed her eyes and willed the queasiness to settle.

"The nausea will pass," she heard the powder-room attendant say, as if her mind had just been read. "But you will experience dizziness, blurred vision and drowsiness. Eventually, you will sleep."

Stunned, Maggie opened her eyes. The dark-haired lady sat in a nearby chair and clasped her hands on her lap, her demeanor suddenly changed. Maggie's stomach rolled. Catching her breath, she met the other woman's gaze, realizing the brunette worked for Paulus. "My food was drugged."

"Yes. When your sister returns, you'll tell her that you want to go home, and you sent me to fetch a guard. And so your family doesn't worry, the guard will escort you to one of the palace limousines with instructions for the driver to take you to Dunemere."

"But that isn't where I'll be going? Is it?" Paulus wouldn't send her home to Luke. "Where's Lucas Starwind? What have you done with him?"

"He hasn't been harmed. Yet," the phony attendant said in a cold voice. "But if you don't cooperate, Mr. Starwind will be killed."

Dear God. *Luke*.

Confused and dizzy, Maggie struggled to think, to reason. Why was she being kidnapped? For ransom? Or was Paulus going to use her as a bargaining tool, demanding exemption?

She balled the damp cloth in her hand. Did it matter? Eventually her family would discover she was missing, and the king would do what he could to save her. But if she alerted her family now, Luke wouldn't stand a chance. The man she loved would be murdered.

"I'll cooperate," she said, her voice raw, her pulse pounding.

The other woman nodded, and when Maggie's mother and sisters came to check on her, she told them that she wanted to return to the beach house. Her mother tried to convince her to lie down in a guest room in the palace, but Maggie insisted on going to Dunemere. She would feel more comfortable in her own bed, she lied, and she'd already called ahead to tell Luke to expect her.

Luke, she thought. Her lover, her heart—the man they might kill.

Five minutes later Maggie went willingly with the Royal Guard, knowing the impostor was an accomplice in her kidnapping. And as she climbed into the car that was waiting to take her to an unknown destination, she prayed Luke was safe.

Luke stepped onto the boardwalk with Bruno by his side. He'd received an anonymous phone call instructing him to go to the pier. The caller had claimed that he had pertinent information regarding the Connelly case.

He stopped at the rail and faced the ocean as he had been instructed to do. His instincts told him that something was terribly wrong, and for that reason he'd brought the dog.

Death, he thought, clung to the air, like salt from the sea. He gave Bruno a command that told the dog to watch for suspicious strangers. If someone intended to plug Luke in the back, Bruno would alarm him first.

His senses keen and alert, he gazed out at the ocean, at the water that sloshed in dark, ominous waves. The 9mm he wore clipped to his belt had become an extension of his body, and on a night such as this he wouldn't hesitate to use it.

If someone was going to die, it sure as hell wasn't going to be him.

Hesitant footsteps sounded, and Bruno growled deep in his throat. The footsteps paused, and then a masculine voice came out of the night. "Call off the dog."

Not on your life, Luke thought. Giving Bruno the command to wait for further instruction, he turned to view his opponent.

The other man stood tall and thin, a long, hooded coat draping his lean form. Luke knew it was Gregor Paulus.

The edge of the pier they dominated was isolated, with

streaks and shadows dancing across the boardwalk from the wind.

Luke moved closer, and both men faced each other. The glow from the lampposts cast a buttery light, making Paulus appear gaunt.

"You have information for me?" Luke asked.

"Yes." Paulus's features distorted, and Luke suspected the breeze had carried Bruno's scent to his nostrils, irritating his allergies. "Maggie Connelly has been abducted, and she won't be returned until you uncover a document proving that Rowan Neville is the Kelly crime family's Altarian contact."

The impact of Paulus's statement slammed into Luke with the force of a Mack truck. But years of covert military operations and private investigations kept him steady.

"How will I uncover this document?"

"It will be provided for you within two days. And at that time you will shift the focus of your investigation, clearing my name and framing Rowan Neville."

"What happens to Maggie?"

"You will be contacted and given the location of where you can find her. But only after you interrogate the security chief and claim that he admitted to the wrongdoings, including Miss Connelly's kidnapping." Paulus squinted and sniffed. "You will tell the Connellys that Rowan Neville panicked, fearing that you didn't believe the lies he'd told you about his children being threatened."

Luke imagined lunging at the other man and ripping his heart out, then tossing the bloodied organ into the sea, feeding the sharks. "How did you take Maggie away from her family without their knowledge?"

The royal aide detailed the abduction, pride sounding in his nasal, allergy-irritated voice. "Of course, once the family returns to Dunemere to ask you how Miss Connelly is faring from her illness, you will have to tell them that you haven't seen her. This will cause a panic, no doubt. Which means you must play your part, Mr. Starwind. The heroic lover who will go to the ends of the earth to find his woman. And put her kidnappers behind bars.''

"Am I supposed to clear Rocky Palermo, too?'' Luke asked, knowing that Rocky held Maggie captive somewhere.

"Yes. Although it's a known fact that Mr. Palermo is associated with the Kellys, he wasn't part of this particular operation. The hit man who aided Neville is Edwin Tefteller, the one Rafe Connelly captured in Chicago last month.'' He paused to dab his nose with a handkerchief. "When all of this is over, I'll resign from the royal service, and both Mr. Palermo and I will disappear quietly. You'll never hear from either one of us again.''

Luke pictured Rocky's hard, brutal face. "If Maggie is harmed in any way, if that son of a bitch touches one hair on her head, I'll come after you and Palermo. And I'll torture both of you until you moan for mercy like the cowards you are.''

"There's no need to get testy.'' The other man stepped back as Bruno growled again. "As long as you and that beast,'' he added, including the dog in his summary, "are willing to cooperate, Miss Connelly won't be harmed. But if you make one false move, your lovely lady is dead.''

A shiver knifed Luke's spine. He knew that meant Rocky was waiting for word from Paulus on the outcome of this meeting. "I'll cooperate.''

"Very well.'' The royal aide had the gall to smile. "It's been a pleasure doing business with you, sir. But I must return to the palace. I intend to be there when the king learns that his sister is missing. I am sure that he, like the rest of the Rosemere-Connelly family, will be devastated.''

Gregor Paulus turned and walked away, but Luke knew he had to let him go. Maggie's life depended on it.

The building was dim, and the faint, scattered security lights that shone on the machinery made the hulking pieces look like monsters with ill-shaped heads and gnarled teeth.

Bound and gagged, Maggie sat on a cold concrete floor, frightened and confused. The drug made her head fuzzy, and her eyes wouldn't focus. She thought she knew where she had been taken, but she wasn't sure.

Refusing to sleep, she battled the drowsiness she'd been told to expect. How long would she be kept here? And when would Paulus make his demands?

She tried to swallow, but the gag limited the movement. Her mouth ached, and her throat felt parched. As her eyes watered, she thought about Luke. Was he being kept somewhere nearby? Had they drugged him, too? And how had they gotten past Bruno? Had they killed her dog?

Footsteps sounded, and she cringed. She saw her captor's hazy figure approach, so she closed her eyes, feigning sleep and praying that he would leave her alone. Even in her confusion, she knew who he was.

# Thirteen

Luke knew exactly what he had to do.

He had to find Maggie.

Tonight.

He couldn't leave her alone and frightened, just as he couldn't betray the Connellys and allow Paulus and his accomplices to go free.

Still standing on the pier, he checked his watch. How much time did he have before another man or woman joined Rocky Palermo? Before the security on Maggie tightened? An hour? Two if he was lucky?

Because Paulus had been vain enough to detail the kidnapping, Luke figured out how many players were involved. Besides Rocky Palermo, it was possible four others had pulled this off: the attendant in the ladies' lounge, the kitchen maid who'd drugged Maggie's food, the man who'd impersonated a palace guard and the phony limo driver who'd taken her to a preconceived location—the place where Rocky would be.

Luke suspected the guard and the limo driver were the masked computer hackers Rowan Neville had told him about. But he wasn't sure who the women were. He hadn't counted on females being part of Paulus's operation.

Bruno looked up at him, and he reached down to touch the dog. "I didn't keep Maggie safe," he said to the mastiff. Just as he hadn't kept Gwen safe.

As an image of his sister's kidnapping surfaced, Luke willed it away. He wouldn't let guilt distract him from this mission. Gwen was dead, but he wasn't going to lose Maggie. With Bruno's help, he would rescue her and bring her home.

Home. To his arms. His bed. His life.

Don't, he told himself. Don't fall apart. Don't slide into the despair of surviving without her, into the gut-wrenching fear that they will kill her just to spite you. He knew emotional agony would only trip him up, and he couldn't afford any mistakes.

He had to focus, not with his heart, but with his head, with the cognitive skills that made him an effective investigator, a civilian soldier.

But the only way to do that was to tap into his enemy's mind. To think like Paulus, to become him for an instant in time.

With the wind blowing and the sea crashing in black waves, Luke closed his eyes.

Gregor Paulus was a man who had chosen to hide in plain sight. He'd kidnapped Maggie from a heavily secured palace, thumbing his nose at the royal family in the process.

Where would a man like that take a captive?

Somewhere familiar. Somewhere that gave him a sense of power.

Luke opened his eyes, and suddenly he knew. The textile mill. Paulus and Cyrus Koresh, the now-deceased owner, had been comrades, and Paulus probably still had a key.

It made perfect sense. Particularly since the mill was closed for several weeks and wouldn't reopen until Koresh's brother flew in from France to sell a business he'd inherited but didn't want.

The textile mill produced a variety of goods, and that meant the building was filled with various types of machinery, including enormous looms and vats for dying yarn.

Maggie could be hidden anywhere in the factory, if she was truly there at all. Luke paused at an employee entrance. He didn't have time to disengage a sophisticated alarm system, but there was a good possibility that it wasn't activated.

Taking a chance, he broke into the building. Silence greeted him, and he welcomed the sound of nothingness. Drawing his gun, he sent the dog a few paces ahead. Bruno knew Maggie's scent.

They crept through the mill, taking to the shadows. The factory seemed ominous at night, dimly lit and foreboding. A huge, circular machine that knit yarn into fabric could have easily spun a web.

Bruno stopped, and Luke took heed. A bullet of adrenaline shot through his veins. Maggie was near. But so was Rocky.

In the next second he saw a figure cross their path. A man, broad and muscular, a gun in his hand.

Inhaling a steady breath, he watched Rocky pace. Back and forth. Agitated. Impatient. Waiting for reinforcements.

Dream on, you son of a bitch, Luke thought as he gave Bruno a command. Trained to kill, to protect its master at all costs, the mastiff lunged before Rocky knew what hit him.

Struck with fear, Palermo lost his weapon in the battle.

And as he lay on the ground with the snarling dog's jaw attached to his neck, Luke knelt beside him.

"If you so much as bat an eyelash, my friend here is going to rip out your throat," he warned in a low, vile whisper. "So if I were you, I wouldn't move a muscle."

With that said, Luke picked up the hit man's gun and went to Maggie.

And suddenly the emotion he'd been banking flooded his system. Bound and gagged, she sat on the floor in her silk dress and pearls, tears streaming down her face.

His Maggie. His muse. Dear God, what had they done to her?

He removed the gag, and she gulped a breath. "I thought you had been captured, too," she said. "I was so afraid. That woman said they would kill you. Oh, Luke, is it really you? Please tell me I'm not dreaming."

"It's me, baby. Everything's going to be okay." He untied her wrists, and went to work on her ankles. He had to move fast, but he wanted to stop and caress her, to hold her and never let go. "One of the other men might be on his way here," he told her. "I have to call the palace and inform the king."

He made the call on his cell phone, then used the gag and ropes on Palermo, wishing he could let the dog rip him to shreds instead. With Bruno's help, he forced the muscle-bound hit man into the back seat. The mastiff took control of the prisoner, snarling in Rocky's face.

Next, Luke scooped Maggie into his arms, and she put her head on his shoulder. She looked so pale, so tired and weak.

"They drugged me," she said.

"I know." He carried her out of the building, put her in the passenger's seat and drove directly to the hospital, where armed guards handpicked by the king would be waiting.

\* \* \*

Maggie slept in a hospital bed while Luke kept vigil in a nearby chair. Throughout the evening, concerned family members had filtered in and out of the private room after presenting proper identification to one of the Royal Guard stationed outside Maggie's door. She would suffer no ill effects from her ordeal, at least not physically. But Luke worried about her emotional state.

He'd been given clearance to stay the night, but he'd refused the blanket the nurse had offered him. He didn't want to sleep. He wanted to be aware of Maggie, to see the rise and fall of each breath she took, to listen to the little sighs she made while she dreamed. Restless dreams, he noticed. Her subconscious mind was troubled.

The door creaked open, and Luke reached for his gun. Who would come into the room at four in the morning?

He saw the trusted guard and relaxed.

"Rafe Connelly is here. He wants to see you."

"Send him in," Luke responded.

Rafe looked exhausted. He'd stopped by a few times earlier, but now the shadows under his eyes had darkened. Luke supposed his own face was just as drawn. Adrenaline, fear and Lord only knew how many cups of vending-machine coffee weren't a healthy combination.

"How's she holding up?" Rafe asked about his youngest sister.

"Still sleeping. But that's good. The doctor said she needs the rest." Because the room was dim, illuminated by only a soft night-light, Luke squinted. But in spite of the hazy glow, he knew the circles under Rafe's eyes weren't an illusion. Nothing about this night had been conjured by sleight of hand, mirrors or magic. Every heart-pounding hour had been real.

"I came by to tell you that it's over." Rafe moved closer,

his footsteps deliberately light. "Paulus and his team are in prison. The Royal Guard caught every last one of them."

Luke released a heavy sigh, the burden of fear lifted. They couldn't go after Maggie now. She was truly safe. "Who were the women?"

"The powder-room attendant was a member of the Kelly crime family we didn't know about, but the kitchen maid was actually a true employee with the royal service staff. She was Paulus's secret lover. They'd gone to great lengths to conceal their relationship."

"And the phony guard and limo driver were the Altarian computer hackers who'd stolen the files?"

Rafe nodded. "The limo driver told us where the rest of the CDs are being stored. He seems to think the police will go easy on him because he didn't kill anyone." A small smile tugged at his lips. "For being a technical wizard, he isn't too bright."

Luke smiled, too. And then he watched Rafe walk toward Maggie and stand beside her bed.

"My sister went willingly with the kidnappers," Rafe said, his voice barely above a whisper. "She jeopardized her own life because she thought yours was in danger."

Luke's heart clenched. "I know."

"She loves you, Starwind."

Another clench. Another emotional pull that had his heart aching. "I know that, too." And he loved her, as well. He'd been in denial all this time, but he couldn't lie to himself any longer. Maggie had been living inside him since the moment he'd danced with her at Rafe's wedding reception.

The other man met his gaze, and for a moment they stared at each other. The look that passed between them said it all. The case was over. Maggie no longer required Luke's protection. What she needed from him went much deeper.

Rafe slipped quietly out of the room, and Luke knew he was headed to Dunemere to be with Charlotte, his new wife.

For the next two hours, Luke resumed his vigil in the straight-back chair, and when dawn broke, Maggie stirred.

"Luke?" She said his name softly, and he went to the side of her bed.

"I'm here, baby." He smoothed a strand of hair from her cheek. She looked sleepy, but not nearly as pale as she had been earlier.

She gazed at him with blue-green eyes. "Why am I still in the hospital?"

"The doctor wanted to keep you overnight for observation. I'm sure he'll release you later today." To ease her mind, he told her that Paulus and the others had been caught. "It's over. No one is going to hurt you ever again."

"You saved me," she whispered, giving him a look so tender, it made his knees go weak.

"Bruno helped. I couldn't have done it without him."

"Can I keep him, Luke? Will his trainer sell him to me?" She adjusted her position in bed. "I can't bear to give him back."

"I'll call his trainer today." And do whatever it took to make sure Maggie and Bruno remained together.

The mist of morning streamed into the room, and Luke and Maggie sat quietly for a short time. He still had fears, insecurities that he was too old to start a family with her. She was still in grad school. A lifetime still spanned between them. He hoped and prayed that loving her was enough.

"Christmas is just a few days away," she said.

"Yeah. It really snuck up on us, didn't it?"

She smiled. "We've been kind of busy." Thoughtful, she fingered a strand of hair. "Do you think we could go back to Chicago for Christmas? I'd like to see how your mother is doing, and I need to get away from here for a little while. Just a short break before the coronation.''

''Sure.'' He wanted to spend the holiday with her, snuggled in front of the tree he'd decorated. ''I think it's snowing back home.''

''Good.'' She smiled again, and he knew his heart would never be the same.

On Christmas Day, Luke's town house smelled like roast turkey, corn bread stuffing, cranberry sauce, mashed potatoes and pumpkin pie. Nell and Dana had cooked and brought the traditional meal, and now the holiday was winding down, with both women preparing to leave.

Maggie reached out to hug Luke's mother. This was the first time Dana had been to her son's home. Although she hadn't been taking her antidepressant long enough to benefit from its full effect, the medication appeared to be helping. She'd panicked a little on the long, congested drive, but once she and Nell had arrived, she was thrilled to spend the day in Chicago—a city she hadn't seen in twenty-seven years.

''Are you going to be okay on the way home?'' Maggie asked.

Dana exhaled a deep breath. ''I don't like all that rush-rush traffic, but I should be all right. And if I get too nervous, I can always take the tranquilizer the doctor gave me. He discouraged me from using them too often, but he thought I might feel better knowing they're available.''

''Luke and I are proud of you.''

''Thank you. It actually feels good to get out. And to see the two of you together,'' she added in a soft whisper.

Maggie squeezed Dana's hand. Luke had been open with his affection in front of his family, and Dana and Nell had noticed every tender kiss and warm gesture. But in spite of his loving behavior, he'd yet to say the words. He was still holding back, and Maggie didn't know why.

"We better get going," Nell put in. "It'd be best to get home before dark."

Another round of hugs was exchanged. Maggie waited at the door while Luke walked the women to their car and made them promise to call as soon as they arrived at the farm.

A light coat of snow blanketed the ground, and holiday lights twinkled as far as the eye could see. It felt good to be home, Maggie thought. But it worried her, too. The case was solved, and her life would resume in Chicago. But how long Luke would be a part of it, she couldn't say. He hadn't mentioned the marriage dare or what the outcome would be.

Luke came back and took Maggie's hand, then guided her to the sofa. The Cherokee tree, as she called it, glimmered with lights and Indian jewels. Strands of turquoise beads draped each branch, and leather-wrapped feathers made an earthly statement.

"I have another gift for you," he said.

"You do?" They'd already exchanged a bundle of presents with his family.

"Yeah. But I have a question first. How many children do you want?"

Caught off guard, she blinked. "I'm not sure. Two, maybe three." Her heart fluttered right along with her lashes. "Are you offering to give me a baby? Is that my gift?"

"Yes. No. Sort of." He couldn't seem to get the words right. "This is…I'm…" He paused, leaving the sentence dangling. "I figured you'd want to finish grad school before you had kids."

She decided not to comment on his assumption since she

wasn't quite sure where this conversation was leading. "I'm confused, Luke. What's going on?"

He reached into his jacket pocket and produced a ring-size box. "I've been carrying this around all day." Flipping open the top, he presented her with a marquise-cut diamond that blazed like a star.

A rapid pulse burst through her body. "Oh. Oh, my." It was beautiful. Dazzling. And completely unexpected.

"I'm asking you to marry me. And have my children. But I was hoping that you didn't want to wait too many years before we started having kids, because I'm not getting any younger. I'll be old and gray before you know it."

And that, she realized, was why he'd been holding back.

He glanced down at the ring, then back up at her. "I love you, Maggie, and I know you love me. And I apologize if this isn't a very romantic proposal. But I need to know that you're going into this with your eyes open. I'm nearly forty years old, and you're still in your early twenties."

"My eyes are open." And she was staring right at him, memorizing every rawboned feature in her mind. "We don't have to rush through our lives, worrying about our age difference. We'll live each day as if it's our last. We'll enjoy every moment, and we'll have babies when the time feels right." She slid a hand into his hair. "You're going to make an incredible father, whether our first child arrives next year or three years after that."

He leaned forward and brushed his lips across hers. "My beautiful, free-spirited Maggie. Do you know why the Gypsy gave me a muse? Because she could read my mind, and she knew that I'd fallen in love with you the first time we danced."

Her eyes watered, misting with tears.

"*A qua da nv do.* It means my heart. And that's what you are." He took the ring and slid it on her finger. "When

Paulus told me that they'd kidnapped you, I forced myself to stay strong. But deep down, I was afraid they'd kill you just to take you away from me.'' He paused, his voice rough with emotion. ''I couldn't have survived without you, Maggie. My heart would have died.''

''We're fine. We're both fine.'' She couldn't stop the tears from falling. ''And we're going to be together for the rest of our lives.''

''Promise?'' he asked.

She nodded and crossed her heart, then placed her hand over his. It thumped against her palm, strong and steady. With lights blinking on the tree and ice fogging the windows, she unbuttoned his shirt. She would never forget this glorious Christmas Day.

He scooped her up and carried her to his room. The four-poster bed was carved from a rich, masculine mahogany, and his sheets rivaled the color of grapes turning sweet and dark on the vine. Maggie tasted his lips, the potency of his kiss.

They took their time undressing each other, hands questing. She knew he loved her. Not because he'd told her, but because she could feel it in his touch.

He fanned her hair around the pillow, slid his palms over her skin, following the curve of her body, molding her, claiming her as his own.

''You healed me,'' he said. ''You won the dare.''

''Because you let it happen. A part of you wanted to be healed.''

He lowered his head and ran his tongue over her nipples, sending delicious little flutters low in her belly.

''You bewitched me, Maggie. You bewitch me now.''

The playful licks turned to a deep, hard suckling. Reaching for the bedpost, she moaned and arched, thrilling him.

She could feel his fire, the heat and the hunger, the scorching contact of mouth against breast.

Intent on giving pleasure, he moved lower. It was exquisite torture. Tender yet somehow edged with talons, with the promise of a hot, explosive climax.

He dipped his tongue into her navel, and her stomach jumped. But as he trailed that warm, wet mouth over her thigh, her entire body convulsed, anticipating more. So much more.

In one quick motion, he lifted her hips. "My beautiful Maggie. I can't get enough of you."

She slid her hands into his hair, and he kissed between her legs. Kissed until her breath sobbed and her soul quaked.

Chips of cedar burned in a clay pot, and the diamond on her finger flashed like lightning, a streak of white blazing in the wood-smoked room. She gripped the bedpost for support and let him push her over the edge.

And when her heartbeat stabilized and her breath returned in gasping pants, she saw adoration shining in his eyes.

"Luke." With sighs and strokes, she enticed him to join with her.

Anxious and aroused, he made a low, primal sound and covered her body with his. She held him close, soothing his desire, taming the urgency.

Maggie wanted this feeling to last.

He caressed her cheek; she pressed her forehead to his and cherished the man she would marry. And then they made love.

Slow and easy, yet brimming with passion.

They moved in unison, dancers lost in each other's eyes. Images of winter sweetness filled her mind, like honey swirling and spinning, then melting over snow-kissed skin. And it would always be this way, she thought as his heart took hers.

This feeling was hers to keep.

Always and forever.

Days later Luke and Maggie returned to Altaria, but this time they shared a suite at Dunemere. Bruno had spent Christmas with the royal family, being pampered at the palace, but now he was back at the private beach with Luke and Maggie.

After a vigorous run along the shore, Luke showered, shaved, dried his hair and then proceeded to attire himself in a black tuxedo.

Maggie stood at a full-length mirror, putting the finishing touches on her appearance. Her satin dress, the color of the moon and sprinkled with sequins that could have been stars, flowed to the floor like a December rain, reflecting glints of light. Her hair was swept away from her face and pinned into an elegant twist. Iridescent pearls rested at her neck and adorned her ears. A pair of gauntlet gloves and satin pumps completed the stunning ensemble.

Luke had to remind himself to breathe. He loved her beyond reason, this woman who had healed his heart.

Suddenly he had the urge to unzip her dress, slide his hands through her properly coiffed hair and pull her onto the canopied bed in a flurry of white satin and floral-scented skin. Love, he thought, moving toward her, was a powerful emotion.

And so, heaven help him, was lust.

Aware of the desire brewing in his loins, she met his eyes in the mirror. "Don't you dare, Lucas."

He grinned, knowing full well that he had to behave. "Can't a guy fantasize around here?"

She turned, running her gaze quite deliberately over him. "Maybe I'll indulge in a little fantasy myself. You look dashing, Mr. Starwind."

"Thank you, Miss Connelly."

"I have something for you." She went to the dresser and opened a jewelry box. Producing a small diamond earring, she held it up for his inspection.

Luke smiled. He knew his pierced ear fascinated her. He removed the tiny silver hoop he always wore and let her slip the diamond in place. The faceted stone winked against his dark skin.

"Perfect," she said, brushing his lips with a tempting kiss.

He tasted her lipstick and went after her tongue, doing his damnedest not to mar her exquisite image. A long, black limousine was already waiting to take them to the cathedral.

She kissed him back, refreshed her lipstick and promised to indulge his fantasies when they returned from the ball tonight.

He intended to hold her to that promise, knowing she wore a mouthwatering bustier, adjustable garters, thigh-high hose and a pair of sheer lace panties under her dress.

A few minutes later Luke escorted Maggie to the car. This afternoon the Royal Bishop, Altaria's religious head of state, would minister King Daniel's coronation.

When Luke and Maggie arrived, they followed the lavish procession and took their designated seats. A provision had been made for Luke to remain by Maggie's side during the ceremony. Although he wasn't part of the Rosemere-Connelly family yet, his engagement to Maggie was official, the ring on her finger a testimony of love and commitment.

Awed by his surroundings, Luke studied the opulent inlay and marble columns stationed between carved archways and colorful mosaics.

Clearly, the Grand Cathedral lived up to its name. The remarkable medieval structure, built of high-quality stone, had withstood the ravages of time. And because ancient architecture fascinated Luke, he knew many of the original stones contained masons' marks, signs and symbols denoting the early craftsmanship. The mark befitting the ceremony today was called the Sign of Honor, a symbol that transformed into a crest—a coat of arms incised on the stones.

King Daniel's sword, sheathed at his side, bore that very crest. Standing at the front of the cathedral, he wore the impressive armed forces uniform Altaria bestowed upon its commander-in-chief. A blue sash spanned his chest, and gold braiding trimmed a doubled-breasted jacket decorated with medals, ribbons and gilded buttons.

The ceremony began with the Royal Bishop addressing the people in attendance. As the bishop spoke, the young king faced his subjects.

"I present unto you King Daniel, your undisputed king. For all of you who come this day, he offers homage and service. Are you willing to do the same?"

In one clear voice of acceptance, the people responded, "God save King Daniel!" and a shiver raced up Luke's spine.

The king turned and knelt at the altar, waiting for the bishop. The holy man then administered the coronation oath.

"Sir, is Your Majesty willing to take the oath?"

"I am willing," the king said.

Luke listened while Maggie's oldest brother placed his hand upon the Bible and swore to govern the people of Altaria according to the country's laws and customs. He completed the oath by saying, "These things which I have promised, I will perform with honor. So help me God."

As the coronation robes were draped around King Daniel's broad shoulders and the crown centered upon his head, Luke held his breath and Maggie's eyes filled with tears. The Imperial Crown, encrusted with priceless jewels and enhanced by the kaleidoscopic light from a stained-glass window, shone like a beacon of authority.

The king bowed his head in prayer, and those assembled did the same, humbling themselves to the Creator above and beseeching His guidance for the rest of their days.

It was, Luke thought as he closed his eyes, a moment he would never forget.

The magnificent stone castle had impressed dukes, duchesses, lords, ladies and heads of state who'd been invited to lavish balls over the centuries, and this celebration was no exception.

The Emerald Ballroom housed an exquisite dining room and generous dance floor, where modern renovations blended with the mystique of medieval architecture.

Malachite floors swept the interior in polished splendor, offering swirling shades of green. Light spilled from crystal chandeliers, pouring over the grand hall like a fountain. Twisted columns shimmered with gilded inlay, and circular tables were set with fine linens, indigenous floral arrangements and bone china bearing the royal crest.

The Connelly family sat with the king and queen in the center of the dining room. King Daniel looked strong and handsome in his uniform, and Queen Erin, a former royal protocol instructor and the lovely woman Daniel had married, dazzled the eye in a stunning gold gown and diamond tiara.

Maggie's entire family was present, each adding their own special flair to the gathering. It was, she thought, the most glorious affair she had ever attended.

Queen Erin had selected the menu, choosing recipes from around the globe. The appetizers, prepared by a renowned chef, tempted the palate with a variety of international flavors. The crispy artichoke flowers hailed from Italy, and the crab and coconut dip boasted Caribbean roots.

Yes, Maggie thought, everything was perfect. While she enjoyed truffled quail eggs and caviar moons, Luke favored sweet-corn flans, an appetizer that probably reminded him of a Cherokee dish. Corn, she knew, was a staple in his heritage.

She turned to smile at him—her lover, her warrior, the man who had risked his life to save hers.

He returned her smile, letting her know how pleased he was with the choices they had made. Because Maggie wanted the opportunity to plan the wedding of her dreams, they'd decided to marry the following year. And in the meantime, they'd agreed to divide their time between Maggie's downtown loft and a country home Luke intended to buy, where the richness of the land would soothe his Cherokee soul.

While Maggie studied her fiancé, he leaned toward Mandy Connelly. The six-year-old sat beside him in a taffeta gown and jeweled barrettes, looking like a fairy-tale princess with white-blond hair and sparkling green eyes. Maggie knew Luke had bonded with her niece, and seeing them together warmed her heart.

"Will you save a dance for me?" he asked the child.

"Yes, thank you, sir," she responded, her royal manners intact. Mandy was a precocious girl who could wrap a man around her little finger and tie him in a loving bow. Clearly, Luke had been knotted nice and tight.

Mandy's father, Drew, touched her shoulder. He was the man she had practiced that perfect little bow on. "Should we make our announcement?" he asked her.

The child glanced at Kristina, her adoring stepmother. They exchanged a knowing smile, and Mandy took the helm. Tapping on her water glass, she got the attention of everyone at the table with a delicate crystal chime.

"My dad and Kristina are going to have a baby," she said, flashing a sister-in-waiting grin.

"Two babies," Drew put in as he nuzzled his wife and winked at his daughter. "Twins."

The Connelly family erupted in joy. The king proposed a toast and flutes were lifted in celebration. Luke clinked Maggie's glass, and they smiled at each other.

"Do you think that could happen to us?" he asked.

She knew he meant the arrival of two babies at once. "I don't know." She glanced at Drew, who shared a toast with his twin, Brett. Her brothers were lucky to have each other. "I hope so."

"Me, too," Luke said.

Touched, she brushed his cheek with a gentle kiss, then noticed her father watching them.

Grant Connelly, attired in a traditional tuxedo and diamond cuff links, sat next to his bejeweled wife, beaming with pride. All of his children had found love and happiness. No one in the family was immune, including Maggie's cousin, Princess Catherine, who dined with Sheikh Kaj at her side.

Nearly two hours later, the six-course meal ended in a decadent dessert, a cognac trifle garnished with sugared cranberries and mint leaves.

As Maggie dipped into the custard and cake, Luke sipped a cup of black coffee. "Can you imagine how they must feel," he said, referring to the king and queen. "Knowing their firstborn son will rule a nation someday?"

Maggie smiled, realizing Luke was still thinking about procreation. "It must be an incredible feeling," she agreed as the king reached for the queen's hand.

The royal couple danced the first waltz, the picture of

grace and elegance. Soon other couples joined them, and the ballroom came alive with music and regal splendor.

"Would you like to dance?" Luke asked.

Emotional and misty-eyed, Maggie nodded. Moments later, as they glided eloquently across the floor, the rest of the world disappeared. Suddenly they were the only two people on earth.

She gazed into his eyes. "It's just like before." They had fallen in love the first time they'd danced, and on this magical evening, they were falling in love all over again.

"You really are my muse," he whispered. "My heart. My inspiration."

Lost in each other, they stepped onto the balcony. Beyond the castle, stars lit up the night, and the scent of winter flowers bloomed in the air.

As Luke lowered his head to kiss her, Maggie closed her eyes, knowing a Cherokee angel named Lady Guinevere rode across the sky on a winged horse, granting dreams, wishes and marriage dares meant to come true.

\* \* \* \* \*

# THE ROYAL HOUSE OF NIROLI

### ...International affairs, seduction and passion guaranteed

## Volume 1 – July 2007
*The Future King's Pregnant Mistress* by Penny Jordan

## Volume 2 – August 2007
*Surgeon Prince, Ordinary Wife* by Melanie Milburne

## Volume 3 – September 2007
*Bought by the Billionaire Prince* by Carol Marinelli

## Volume 4 – October 2007
*The Tycoon's Princess Bride* by Natasha Oakley

### *8 volumes in all to collect!*